AN
AGE OF
WINTERS

OTHER TITLES BY GEMMA LIVIERO

AN AGE OF WINTERS

A NOVEL

GEMMA LIVIERO

LAKE UNION
PUBLISHING

Published by Lake Union Publishing, Seattle

www.apub.com

Amazon, the Amazon logo, and Lake Union Publishing are trademarks of Amazon.com, Inc., or its affiliates.

ISBN-13: 9781662520617 (paperback)
ISBN-13: 9781662520624 (digital)

Cover design by Faceout Studio, Molly von Borstel
Cover images: © David Wall / Getty; ©Nadia Chi, © 0leJohny / Shutterstock

Printed in the United States of America

What else is woman but a foe to friendship, an unescapable punishment, a necessary evil, a natural temptation, a desirable calamity, a domestic danger, a delectable detriment, an evil of nature, painted with fair colours!
—*Malleus Maleficarum*

PROLOGUE

Winter entered three months early, ahead of the discovery of Hermann Kropp's body below the river's silvern crown. The nine-year-old had been sent by his mother to meet the wood bearer when the church bell tolled three. When he was not back by evening, his parents, Irma and Peter Kropp, began knocking on doors to ask if anyone had seen their son. It was only by chance that Hermann was seen at all when one of the searchers caught his stocking on the same splintery mooring that had snagged the clothing of the boy. Had he not been found that night, the ice drifts would have merged and trapped his body until the great thaw of 1627.

The search by the villagers of Eisbach concluded at the edge of the river where lumps of ice bobbed and shifted closer to one another to prepare for an age of winters. This slow freeze that was streaked with gold from a dozen fire torches would have been a delightful spectacle if not for the ghastly secret that lay below the surface. With a ring of bruises around his scraggy neck, Hermann's body had been left to dangle with the current, the crown of his head bumped repeatedly by ice.

The river boy was not the first murder. There were two other infantile bodies found prior in the weeks that fed into winter, with wounds that were inconsistent.

The smallest victim, only eight months old, was found by the graveyard fence face down in the dirt, the cause of death a ragged gash across his throat. The second was discovered in the forest lying on a bed of sticks. Freya Pappenheimer said she had only turned away for a second when the victim, her four-year-old daughter, had disappeared. No one had seen little Lottie leave when Freya had questioned them. Apart from a narrow cut across her windpipe, the child's body had been unmarked, with no signs of a struggle, her legs straight and her dress arranged in a modest, nurtured way, hands resting together on her abdomen. The strangely peaceful scene suggested the murderer had spent some time with the victim and may have even had some regret. The baby, however, was strewn like rubbish into his deathbed, as a final insult.

The priest of the parish, the Reverend Felix Stern, had visited the grieving families, which he found burdensome. His sermons became imbued with a sense of hopelessness, heightened further by the child murders, his ailing health, and the bleak sunless days that were enduring throughout the autumn. Stern was unlikable and ill tempered, mostly from the constant growling pain within his bowel that made him walk cupping his belly, his tall body permanently bent forward at the hips. He had been empathetic during his youth, but by degrees—village life, ungrateful, small-minded, mostly illiterate parishioners, and his health—it had become difficult to sound genuine when offering words of sympathy. He was brusque and dispassionate and these days could only offer prayers rather than words of consolation.

Stern's interview with Hermann's parents had produced no new information or suspects.

"Was the boy usually home on time?" asked Stern.

"Oh yes," said Irma Kropp, her voice breaking. "He was a good boy. He took care of his younger brother."

Peter Kropp had stood by devoid of emotion, with eyes of stone, Stern had thought on his way home.

The graveyard baby's mother, Ursula Döhler, had not bothered to name the results of her last two birthings. In a previous interview, she appeared emaciated and hollow-eyed, with a child of around three sucking noisily on her drooping breast, which she seemed not to notice. She had unmoored herself during the conversation and drifted away, her answers then directed to the closed shutters that Stern thought resembled the state of her mind.

Frustrated with Ursula's vague responses, he focused his attention on the murdered baby's older siblings: sad, grubby-faced, scrawny things that fidgeted constantly and were made to stand to attention for the priest's visit.

"Do you miss your baby brother?"

Stern could be intimidating sometimes and the boy of around five turned and ran away.

"A whipping you'll get from me!" Oma Jutta said from the corner of the room, where she'd been examining the proceedings gloweringly with lips pinched and eyelids scrunched. Though she was more forthcoming with information, revealing that her daughter-in-law was useless and rarely watched the children.

"It was no wonder the boy was taken," Jutta continued. From the chaos he glimpsed through the door, Stern had silently agreed. It was inevitable something would happen to at least one if not more of them.

"Do your job and find the killer, Herr Reverend, but don't come back here," the older woman stated in a hostile tone. "There's nothing you can do for us unless you bring a big, fat pig to feed this unruly brood. My own son up and left us for a whore, our means gone, too, with the worthless arse."

Stern had found the woman obnoxious but knew that grief affected people in different ways and decided not to report her for effrontery, an offence that few in his position would ignore. Despite his surly attitude towards many of the villagers, he was otherwise fair minded. He knew that speculation oftentimes hindered the process of finding a perpetrator, and his knowledge of law was occasionally at odds with his own sermons. His past fatalistic preaching about a supernatural evil that lived amongst them insidiously was likely to arouse suspicion against one another. Instead, his sermons from that point concentrated more on the murders themselves that deserved the punishment of hell in the hope of driving the perpetrator to confess. Expecting a wave of finger-pointing, Stern also warned that accusing others without evidence was not the way forward.

The prince-bishop of Würzburg, Philipp Adolf von Ehrenberg, believed otherwise—Reverend Stern's approach was too soft. After a private meeting at the fortress where Ehrenberg resided, Stern was ordered to instruct parishioners that all suspicious activity by their neighbours, friends, and family must be reported, no matter how trivial. On the following Sunday morning, Stern moved sluggishly towards the church with a sense of doom.

"One cannot walk past the home of another without inspection," Stern said, pointing at the congregation that morning. "There is malfeasance occurring within this community, and we must protect the children. Do not be afraid to speak out about your neighbour, if there be differences that weren't there before. A crime such as this may also be worked in tandem. Evil does not always act alone."

The Reverend Stern did not like the words he used. He'd had several glasses of ale prior, and even those did not dull the thought that he had issued an open invitation for spying and personal retribution. He could see it in the gazes of the people in front of him, many of whom were less virtuous than they made themselves out to be. For people, he had discovered, were truly heinous and vindictive at times, and if it wasn't for his work that gave him a place at God's table, he would gladly avoid them. His stomach pains were more intense lately. He was also tired of burying children.

Before the sermon was over there were whisperings in the church, a shifting that caused silk and coarse linen to rustle throughout the pews. The villagers looked at one another from under hats, bonnets, wimples, scarves, and pious black veils to view their godly neighbours, from the poor to the more affluent who rarely mixed company other than on Sundays. Before some had even left the church, suspicions were muttered and alliances formed, and in the weeks following fourteen people were questioned. Two of them were imprisoned, one being Freya

Pappenheimer, and another, a drunkard known to roam the riverside and forest at night.

Just prior to these arrests, Lance Pappenheimer, Freya's husband, had requested an audience with the priest to name his own wife in the death of their daughter, Lottie.

"She'd not lain with me for weeks, and I told her it was against God's will. Then come some months later, I found a small bottle she'd been hiding, a liquid she admitted taking so she'd not fall pregnant again."

"Where did she get this . . . liquid?" said Stern, who thought the reasoning shallow and Lance spineless in the way he spoke only to his hands.

"I don't know. I found an empty bottle in the cupboard, and she couldn't help herself; she had to be true and admitted her sin. She had always been God-fearing."

Reverend Stern remembered how sick the woman had been for months after the delivery, how she had cried out during the birth for nearly a day. He did not know how women had such fortitude.

"Then if she is so true, as you describe, why would she kill your daughter? It seems to contradict the pious wife you portray."

"Women keep their intentions secret, Reverend. They are not always what they appear."

Stern could not rule out such testimony, since the killing did indeed seem very personal. He was obliged to mention this to the prince-bishop, who ordered Freya's immediate imprisonment. Ehrenberg had been eager for a suspect, and a breath of evidence was all he needed.

The following week after her arrest, Lance Pappenheimer had brought a letter from his wife that he felt was proof she had become godless. Since he could not read words, Lance had been made aware of the contents having asked another member of the clergy to translate verbally. Frau Pappenheimer's ability to read and write was something that had always grated against Lance's sense of superiority.

My dear husband, could you please find compassion in your kind heart and bring me some food. I have known you to be true and caring. I am not given bread with any regularity and the water supplied is putrid. I say again that I took the potion out of fear that I may not survive another pregnancy. It was selfish and I see that now for we are in the hands of our Lord as it should be. I'm sorry with all my heart, and if you withdraw your accusation, I promise that I will be a better wife.

Reverend Stern shook his head. "I fail to see, Herr Pappenheimer, where your wife is guilty of murdering her own child or any other."

"She admitted to a potion," he said, sounding surprised that the accusation was even questioned. "It is against God's will to dabble in magic and prevent a conception. You have said so yourself in church."

As time would show, the villagers took passages from scripture, laws, and the church's list of sins and used them to justify an accusation, oftentimes with only a vague association to a particular crime. And usually when it benefited the accuser in some way. Taking a potion did not make Lance's wife a murderer, but he was right—it was indeed against the pope's canon to distribute items or incantations associated with the dark arts.

"Did she say where she purchased the potion?"

"She had learned earlier about it from her now-dead mother, she told me. Her mother knew someone who made such things to alter nature. I didn't think to ask who sold her the liquid, but I remember that some months back Freya went on a trip to buy some wool and was gone a whole day."

Stern decided he would investigate this as a separate crime but would not yet dismiss a link with the murders. Where there was such practice, there were likely others worse. But Stern never got the opportunity. Freya, starving and learning that her spouse had no such desire to withdraw his accusation, had scratched a cross into her chest, then hanged herself in prison with her skirt that she had torn into strips, plaited, and tied to the bars in the door. She left a note:

I am no murderer, and I say this as someone loyal to God and the church: I am damned nonetheless. I cannot live with this accusation but more so I cannot live without our daughter. I wish my husband the best. Be it so that my husband now unencumbered will find a better wife than I who might give him plenty more healthy children. In God's merciful hands, Freya.

Since that time Lance had not been seen. Stern had gone to his house to counsel him but found the place abandoned. Stern was satisfied that Freya was not guilty and that the murderer was still amongst them.

On a day when his pain had subsided a little, Stern took a walk once more to inspect the site where Lottie Pappenheimer had been found. There was something he had missed, he was certain, perhaps about the location.

He heard a thud, or rather felt it through the ground. At first he thought it to be a branch that had fallen, but several more of the same sounds followed. Stern stopped walking and listened to detect if the noise was animal or human. After a short pause, murmurings were issued that he could not distinguish. At that moment the light in the forest dimmed, and an icy wind blew his thin woollen robe against his body.

Stern considered walking on, as he did not care to encounter others he might have to converse with, small talk that made him irritable. Then came moans from the same direction that resembled someone or something injured. He fought briefly with his conscience, then turned towards the sounds, stepping lightly on fallen snow to avoid disturbing whatever creature was beyond his line of sight. Between the barren trees, he caught movement in a small clearing on a carpet of snow. He paused and squinted, unable to distinguish exactly what he was witnessing. He recoiled behind a tree, hurriedly retrieving his eyeglasses from his coat pocket and placing them firmly on the bridge of his large hooked nose.

He breathed rapidly, feeling a sense that something terrible was taking place. He turned to peer once more through clumps of spindly birch before releasing an audible gasp that drew the attention of the subject he had spied.

Stern hobbled home and went straight to his room, locking the door behind him, forgoing his evening meal, and gulping down the ale from his pitcher to calm his nerves. He would have promptly written in his diary everything he witnessed, or even sought an audience with the prince-bishop that night to reveal an awful truth, but his pains grew suddenly worse. He could do nought but lie in agony, hope the ailment was gone by dawn, and relive the eyes of hell he had stared straight into.

LETTERS

Letter of referral to be presented to the prince-bishop of Würzburg

12th November 1625

Herr Reverend Zacharias Engel arrives with much exper-
tise. At thirty-eight years of age, his quick mind and his
dedication are two of the qualities you will find when he
deals with the calamity that has befallen your bishopric.
Of Germanic lineage, Reverend Engel is specialised in
such areas and has studied the law, with particular focus
on the dark arts and despicable crimes. He has consulted
with the most knowledgeable clergy, read the books on
demonology, and has a complete understanding of law
and administration, and, therefore, is deemed the best
intermediate investigative replacement for the Reverend
Felix Stern. He will work to ensure that the canon laws are
applied, and we ask that he has the support of your office
bearers at his disposal. I have complete faith in our repre-
sentative to eradicate the evil that has befallen Eisbach.
    Respectfully,
    Bishop Apollo Dietrich

Letter to the Vatican: Bishop Dietrich

1st December 1625

Your Grace, Bishop Apollo Dietrich,

I have completed three-quarters of my journey to the bishopric of Würzburg. In the last two days, the weather has forestalled me, the snow so thick, the wind howling. I have stopped at an inn until the worst has passed and will recommence as soon as the weather lifts. I have decided to leave my cart and travel the remaining paths on horse alone. I have taken as many personal items as possible and asked the innkeeper to store the rest until I come back to collect them at a time when the weather is my ally. But it will not be soon, with winter so deeply entrenched. The innkeeper and other locals have suggested it will be months before it clears, though some speculate longer, that the season is colder than normal, the storms greater, and prior, throughout summer, the flooding of the rivers at times challenging. Only on horseback and by sled can deliveries be made to much of the bishopric, but some have failed to make it there at all. The innkeeper can no longer rely on deliveries by river but makes the arduous journey himself to collect his stock by sled. He is even thinking of closing and moving southward until this ends. "If it ends," he told me.

Many of the villages across the territories of Franconia are haphazard in practices. In my humble opinion, I find the inhabitants brash and rancorous, and I discern an unsurprising lack of devoutness, unlike the holy cities that bustle with fervour and piety. But this is not a complaint. It is a simple observation of the potential magnitude of the challenge I face in the bishopric to which I am headed.

I have read again the reports by the Reverend Stern sent from the prince-bishop. I fear there is little of substance that can help me save the souls of the villagers and find the cause of so much apostasy. It is apparent that Stern had been too lenient with the suspects and his questioning careless. I am concerned that the perpetrator or perpetrators may have succeeded with further infantile murders.

Thank you again for tasking me with this challenge and for the copy of the letter of recommendation which you had previously sent to the prince-bishop of Würzburg. Since his notification of the Reverend Stern's affliction, or "delirium" as he referred to it, I am keen to continue Stern's work, though with a more thorough, disciplined hand. Your advice that he has lost the favour of parishioners tells me that the task will indeed be challenging. I thank you for the opportunity of a more senior role within the papal enclave after my work here is complete. Thank you also for your recommendation and my prior secondment to Paris, which is most timely on matters of witch hunting and maleficence. I will be guided by your words and God's will.

Sincerely,
The Reverend Zacharias Engel

CHAPTER ONE

Sleet tapped at the large window demanding entry. In woollen socks, I padded along the dim hallway towards the arc of light. I pressed my hands against the cold glass expecting to see the usual bleak view of untidily thatched rooves, heavy with snow, and the regular shapeless villagers about their business. But the scene that day beheld a dark stain on a white tablecloth made from snow and sky. A tall, dark horse stood on the crest of a hillock carrying a rider in a long black coat and wide-brimmed hat. The image at first was flat and still before a small turn of the man's head brought life to the world I beheld. I followed the gaze of the stranger to the city and tower in the distance, and to the prison where people entered and were rarely seen again. I shivered and drew tighter my shawl as the rider continued on towards our village.

Hooves sliced through the snow rhythmically, as if in dance, tail up, head leant forward like that of the man, whose face was hidden. Other horses in stalls on the snowy paddocks knickered when the rider passed. The man gently reined in his beast at the bottom of the hill closest to the brook and spoke with Herta Jacobs, the blacksmith's daughter, who had also seen him and stepped outside to investigate. They conversed for seconds, and I watched her point upward in my direction. I drew back from the window afraid that I had been caught spying, caught idle. I knew then who it was. The Reverend Zacharias Engel. I had heard his name mentioned several times by others. This dark stranger would be my new master. He was coming to live in the house where I was working, and I felt excitement in my chest and fear in my belly.

I set about what I must do. To be truthful, I had become idle in recent weeks without a master. I had not been so fastidious with the cleaning and my own attire. Now, I slipped into boots and rushed into the barn at the back of the property where the houseboy, Walter, was on his back drawing pictures in the air with his finger. The priest, Reverend Stern, who had been my master, left for reasons of poor health, and I'd been requested to pack up some of his belongings and cart them to the castle. In the weeks since he was gone, I was required to keep house using a stipend afforded by the treasury in anticipation of his replacement. It had not been as much without Stern, but Walter and I did not take much to feed and keep.

Walter was grateful for the work, as was I. He'd come from nothing, a baby, a foundling, left in a ditch roughly fourteen years ago. We were kindred, close like siblings, both without a past, both unknowing the exact date of our births.

I instructed Walter to fetch a basket of wood and to swiftly warm the room that Zacharias Engel would occupy after he had taken care of the reverend's horse. I wondered if it was this cold where Engel had come from. I could not imagine anywhere colder than Eisbach, where the brooks and river were frozen, where the icy wind burned through skin and bore chill into bone.

Herta's father remarked often that there had been a shift in the weather patterns in recent years. "A new age of chicanery," he'd said, "as if God was playing with us to see how we'd fare." He had quoted that from Stern, though he had added also that winters would continue to worsen. I was used to expressions of doom and did not see the weather events as significant since it had been irregular in design as far back as I could remember, but there was no denying that winter was arriving earlier each year, leaving later, and ruining harvests. Sin was deemed the cause, preached in sermons across the territories, since there seemed no other reason to explain the diabolical events that had beset our village.

I was not sure about sins, since their definitions were vague, and the number committed grew each year. I had lost count of what was a sin and what wasn't, and what was punishable and what wasn't. By the virtue of ignorance, I felt certain I had committed very many of them and feared that somehow not only God would know my thoughts but the powers on the ground would learn of them, too.

For several weeks we'd had no Sunday service, and people were eager for the newcomer's arrival, for guidance. Zacharias Engel was replacing Stern, but the timing of his arrival we suspected had much to do with a prisoner talked about in whispers. Formerly a respected judge, Leon von Kleist had been accused of killing his wife and baby twins and poisoning his daughter, now in the care of a convent and apparently too unwell to speak. It was said that Kleist was in league with the Devil and might be responsible for the heinous crimes against the other young victims. It had also been suggested by town gossips that those crimes had something to do with Stern's illness, that he'd been cursed as he came close to solving the murders.

But Reverend Stern had a weak disposition as well as a delicate stomach. He was always hard to please and frail. *Is there no quail? Again?* he had said, coughing into his handkerchief, unable to hide his disdain at the slime he examined in the cloth and perhaps at the sight of me also.

One morning, I could not rouse the Reverend Stern from his room and called for Bertram the blacksmith to break open the lock of his door. Inside, we found the priest foaming at the mouth and babbling nonsensically, some of it obscene. Herr Frederik Förner, the commissioner at the castle, came with his men to collect him for examination and questioned villagers in an attempt to learn the cause. Herta, who was a source of gossip, said they had asked her father if he had seen anything strange, and when her father replied that wages for work were lower, that business was drying up, and the prince-bishop was slow to pay for services, they ignored his concerns and left. Herta's father gave nothing they could take away except that he was more so a nuisance with his complaints.

The weather and the murders weren't the only strange happenings. On the day that Stern had gone to bed and lost his senses, another girl, Cilla Graf, only five years, was reported as missing. It seemed that children were mostly the target of the misfortune. It was not all that uncommon for children to drown in the summers and freeze in the winters. But everyone believed deep down that something other than those two events had likely occurred.

Cilla's scarf was found in the church but no other sign of her. She had wandered off, people were saying. She had become confused, it was suggested. Though that would have been out of character. Since the first three murders, her parents had kept a close eye on her, and she on them. "She was mistrustful of everyone," her mother had told people. "She would not have left the path between the cluster of houses and the church." Cilla's father, Harald, had traversed the villages one after the other in a search that proved futile. Others hinted that Stern's loss of mind and the missing girl were somehow linked to Leon von Kleist. Though the killings of his children and wife were enough to condemn him anyway.

In the weeks following Stern's removal, several people were taken into custody: one was Kleist, one was a woman accused of adultery by her husband, and another woman was said to have cursed her neighbour's baby out of jealousy. The baby, who had gone to bed full of vigour, was cold and blue by morning and for no apparent cause. Without proof of the last two accusations, the two women were released. Though it would soon come to pass that proof wasn't necessary.

"Kat!" Walter called me as I was removing the last smudge from the window in the parlour. "He is coming!"

I had let Walter stay in the house while it was just the two of us. I checked the damask-covered chairs for stains where we would sometimes sit to eat, bent down to wipe a streak of mud from the floorboards, then ran to the glass in the hall to tidy my cap. I tucked in stray strands of chestnut hair and wiped the crumbs from my eyes, "the colour of mouldy bread," my husband had commented. Walter and I stood behind the door as if we were conspiring to ambush. Zacharias Engel's knock was sharp and clear, but seemingly patient since there was only the one. I would come to know his tolerant trait, the way he used time to learn the truth, the way he would give enough rope with which to hang oneself.

It felt like my insides were hammering against my chest as I opened the door, and then my breathing stopped at the sight of him up close. Engel brushed the ice dust from his coat and stepped across the threshold to the centre of the entry, bringing with him a sudden rush of sleet and a gust of cold that swirled about our ankles. I saw a difference immediately between the previous dweller, not only in age but from the way the newcomer carried his upper body in the shape of a cross, with his chin directly forward, not halfway down his chest like Stern's. He was measured, his movements from one to the next seamless, which gave a strange illusion of stillness even when he walked. And I had not seen a priest so young in appearance. It was rumoured he was close to forty, but I could not find a wrinkle past twenty-five.

He stood there looking over our heads to the hallway beyond, as if to find others, before returning to examine Walter, then me. I looked down self-consciously to stare instead at his stockinged legs, exposed without his holy robe. Realising my curiosity had rested unwittingly on the mound between his legs, I felt heat rise upward from my neck and forced myself to look towards Walter, who was the first to speak, "Good morning, sir," since I was unable to find my voice.

"Welcome, sir," I said, forcing myself to briefly look into his eyes that were the colour of the sky. Not the colourless sky above our rooves that day, but the one in the church's stained-glass windows behind Jesus on the cross. He wore his soft, black curls in a tail down his back.

Though handsome, the priest was also fierce looking, eyes surrounded by thick lashes under heavy, dark brows.

"My horse has had a long journey," he said to no one in particular as he pinched the tips of his gloves then slid them from his hands. "She'll need a rest for a day or two."

Without delay, Walter squeezed past him on the tips of his toes to exit the house and lead our new master's horse to the stalls inside the barn. Zacharias Engel nodded his head at me and tapped the side of his thigh to prompt me like one would a pet hound.

He entered the hall, surveying the humble furnishings before pausing to contemplate the painting on the wall of the Virgin Mary. Continuing his tour, he made no showing of his feelings about his new accommodation as he ducked slightly through the door openings. When he was satisfied that he had examined enough, his gaze rested once more on me and stayed there, his expression quizzical, as if I were a peculiarity or an object that might require repair.

From the stores at the castle where I filled my basket with rabbit, parsnips, cabbage, salt, and sage, I had learned that people were wary of the newcomer. Reverend Stern had made little impact here, quietly tucked away in his room with ale when he wasn't slurring his words at the pulpit or falling asleep in the parlour, dangling his arm dangerously close to the fire. I had heard that Zacharias Engel was the youngest to have graduated from university in law and theology and had risen from nothing, a commoner from pious parents, but one that showed great promise from an early age. The nods and curiosity in the castle storeroom showed both awe and wariness about his impending arrival. I was good at picking up feelings. I had mastered the art of observation while myself remaining unobserved and uninteresting.

"Leave it!" Zacharias said when I went to pick up his soft leather bag. "You won't be able to lift it. It's full of books . . . What is your name?"

"Katarin Jaspers," I said feebly, feeling foolish that I had not introduced myself at the door. "I am your maidservant, sir."

"You are younger than I would have expected, Katarin," he said, "to have such an important role."

I wanted to say the same about him. Just nineteen winters old, I was a widow, something that made me seem older, but not yet wise. Not then.

"But experienced, sir. I have been doing this work since I was eight."

He peered down his long, straight nose and seemingly straight into my soul. Mere seconds of such scrutiny and I could no longer hold his gaze.

"Are you not cold in here?" he said.

"I'm sorry, sir," I muttered to my leather boots, worn at the toes. The fire in the sitting room had turned to embers only. "Walter will kindle a fire in your room."

"Of course," he said.

"You must be tired, sir, from your long journey." I did not know from whence he came but I presumed, since there was mention of his studies in Rome, it was far away.

"You can show me now where I will be sleeping," he said as he picked up his bag.

I led him up the stairs and could hear Walter introducing Zacharias's horse to the other one in the stable. I wished the boy to hurry with the wood.

The master's room was sparse with a single bed and a cross on the wall. Zacharias noticed it was crooked and straightened it. His eyes wandered around his surroundings, but the newcomer gave nothing away. He walked to his window that offered a slightly elevated view of the village, the brook close by, and the city in the distance, before moving to the hearth to examine the ash I had not cleaned out since Stern had left.

"I will be up at eight," he said in the same earthy timbre of distant thunder, "and I would like to take my refreshment then in my room."

Walter responded to my silent plea, arriving with armfuls of wood, his nose streaked with black where he'd scratched it with charcoal fingers.

"You don't wish for supper, Herr Reverend? We have some cold pigeon and onions that were readied earlier."

"Not this evening. It is good for the heart and soul to fast. To be hungry is what drives a person harder, to work harder, to be thankful, don't you agree?"

I nodded but I did not agree. In the times when I was hungry, the last thing I felt like was working or showing gratitude. Still, the words stayed with me while I skinned the rabbit and chopped it into squares ready for tomorrow's breakfast stew. To silence my growling stomach, and still with bloodied hands, I tore a piece of freshly baked bread and lashed it with lard.

"He is tall," said Walter, watching me gnawing at the crust of bread while he licked his lips and leaned across the table on his elbows. I handed him the rest, which vanished quickly behind his small square teeth.

"You need to wash," I said. "You are covered in grime."

He dipped a cloth in a pot of water warming on the stove to wipe his face and hands. We could hear Zacharias stepping around his room, a scrape of a chair, a clearing of his throat. Walter stopped what he was doing to listen, afraid our master might come down to the kitchen and catch him loitering.

"Hurry up," I said and tilted my head in the direction of the back door.

Walter had become used to spending much of the time inside and, having the place to ourselves, staying up late by the fire in the parlour, playing games. The house with two floors was larger than most, though its construction did not stop the floors from groaning, or block the northern drafts, or prevent the windows from shaking in heavy winds. Though what it did have were fireplaces in almost every room but mine. It was the privilege of sharing space with the clergy. Most houses were small, the animals and owners lumped together, but we had a separate barn that housed Walter also.

Zacharias stayed in his room for the remainder of the day. I woke just as light stretched its arms into morning and stepped out from my room behind the kitchen. Outside, several crows cawed and circled the sky. On the floor above, Reverend Engel shuffled and paced. I put a cauldron atop the heat. Walter had already lit the fires, and the house was warm, bless him. Truth be known, he was probably freezing, which would have woken him early to seek warmth inside the house again. I returned to my room with a pan of water to wash my face and armpits, climbed into my shift, which I had rinsed and placed beside the kitchen fire the previous evening, and drew my mustard-coloured kirtle over my head to girth with ties at my waist.

I carried a tray with a bowl of stew, a piece of bread, and warmed mead up to my new master's room. It is what I would do for Stern, who would be cross if I took too long, though nearer the end he had lost his appetite and sometimes I would retrieve a full tray.

Zacharias Engel called me in at the sound of my knock and barely glanced my way when I entered. He appeared to be writing down notes from a book he had on his desk but shielding the words with his free hand. He stopped, closed the book, and looked at me.

"Do you read, Katarin?"

"I can neither read nor write, but I can sign my own name."

He nodded as if he expected this and handed me a shirt that required washing. I attended to the task immediately with boiled water and lye in the wooden tub near the door to the kitchen. I was eager to please him. Below the front collar was a rust-brown smudge that I suspected was blood from shaving, for Engel's face was as smooth and white as a baby's. After I laid the shirt on the drying rack and returned to collect his empty tray of food, there was no answer from my knock this time. Inside, his table was clear of papers, and another shirt hung on a hook. From his window I saw him on foot heading towards the city. He had slipped from the house unheard and unseen, again differing from the previous inhabitant, who clanked and banged his way from room to room.

"Kat!" Walter called from downstairs. "Come and see!"

Walter ran like the devil from the house, his feet slapping the path of slush and spraying me as I caught up. Several times I nearly tripped on the hem of my skirt.

"Hurry!" he called over his shoulder. "Before they take it away."

"What is it? What are you talking about?" I called to the back of him as we turned into a neighbouring farm.

Walter stopped suddenly and breathed out several cloudy breaths.

"There!"

Above us, crows complained of our arrival and flew a short distance away. On the ground was a goat lying dead with its eyes open, tongue blue and hanging out the side of its mouth. Herr Brühn, the dead goat's owner, had seen us from his window and stepped out into the paddock, his large legs leaving deep cavities in the snow behind him.

"What is this then?"

I'd seen dead animals plenty, but there was something ominous about the way it lay there watching us. Walter stood by the animal, unable to break his gaze, frowning and pouting. He took death hard. I noticed that the hem of his trouser was beginning to look tatty and would need fixing, the collar of his shirt beneath his jacket browned and in need of washing. I'd grown lazy.

Brühn examined the animal and looked suspiciously at Walter. I never liked the farmer. He was not affable towards us, almost hostile at times, his eyes nestled so deeply in folds of wrinkles that I could not tell you the colour.

"Did you do this?" he asked Walter, his tone suggesting he'd already made up his mind.

"No!" I answered for him. "He did not."

"He can speak for himself. Did you do this, boy?"

Walter shook his head. I could tell he didn't trust himself to speak. Walter wouldn't hurt a soul, and I told Brühn this also. The farmer seemed only mildly satisfied and shook his head.

"Well, someone did. I will have to go see the city officials. Someone must pay for my goat."

It was a veiled threat, since we were the closest "someone" and therefore on the top of his list of suspects and enemies, of which I believed were many. I held Walter's trembling hand. I knew he had taken blows from previous employers, from Stern, from adults who could do with him what they wanted, and only when Brühn walked away did the trembling stop.

"I hope he didn't feel anything," Walter said.

"Brühn?" I said jokingly.

"No," he said seriously, before his large brown eyes found the smile on my face. He elbowed me gently and smiled, too.

I felt an overwhelming desire to keep him under my wing always.

We walked home, and Walter's face was sombre, watching his feet as he trudged. I reached for his hand again to grip it firmly.

"What do you think killed him?" I asked. It had appeared as if the animal died of fright.

He raised his head and shrugged, then squinted while he thought deeply about the question.

"Looks like he caught a disease," he said. "But I suppose they'll blame it on Leon von Kleist like everything else."

I pinched his arm for his scepticism, then put my arm around him affectionately. He was only half a head smaller than me, with bony, narrow shoulders.

Kleist was in the prison and already a leading suspect in all the murders, which I'd learned from the gossip in the castle storeroom. No one so far had given explanation for motivation.

"What are they going to do with him?" asked Walter, of the prisoner.

I had wondered about this also.

"You two are glued at the hip!" said Herta, catching us unawares at the back door. She sounded light, but I detected envy. Her hair was plaited with a shiny red ribbon, a present from her father for her birthday. I wished it were mine.

Herta and I had become friends of sorts though she was not quite fifteen, and I believed it was really Walter she was always hoping to see, a sentiment not reciprocated.

However, that day she had other things on her mind. Her main task was to find out something about the new resident, Zacharias Engel. *What is he like? Why was he chosen? Can I see his possessions in his room? Does he frighten you?* It was not my nature to gossip, only listen to gossip and store it for my own use.

"He's not been here a day!" I said, exasperated. I was clearly irritated by the questions; however, this did not deter her. She had followed me into the kitchen.

"It seems a waste that he be a man of the cloth," she said, falsely coy, then smiling when she caught my eye. Truth be told, I did not like such talk about my master, but though it was defamatory to speak in ways that were not godly, I inwardly agreed.

"I've heard he's come to burn someone," continued Herta, sounding eager for such event.

"Who told you that?"

"My father spoke to one of the prince-bishop's men. They're planning to burn the murderer if they prove his crime. Is it true?"

"You'd best ask someone else. I'm not going to spy for you, Herta."

She pursed her lips to express her disappointment before noticing that Walter had crept away while her back was turned. She uttered an impatient goodbye and left. When I peered out the window, she was talking to Walter in the doorway of the barn. She said something to make his face redden and his foot to rub the ground back and forth impatiently. I liked Herta, but there was always a feeling of menace about her, that she would eventually cause trouble.

CHAPTER TWO

All week my master had been back and forth spending much time at the castle in the city. Everywhere I went the villagers would make comment about him. He was a curiosity, a distraction from the tedium. Accompanied by Commissioner Förner, one of the prince-bishop's inner circle, Zacharias's first task was to call on the people of Eisbach. After that, his activities were haphazard, as he went between the city and the village at any time of day or night. Sometimes, he would eat in his room and sometimes in the dining hall. He was so quiet that I would be surprised to find him in places I wasn't expecting. I had to be careful about my snooping, about my conversations with myself, about being idle.

One day, when I'd seen Zacharias disappear into the snowy distance on foot—he preferred long walks, he told me—I searched around his room, hoping to find something of note. On a shelf, he kept a small bottle of sweet-smelling oil that he wore in his hair and a comb made from ivory. On his desk were books, paper, quill, and ink. In one of his leather-bound books, on pages of vellum, I discovered strange drawings of demons and women on broomsticks, and another depiction of people, lots of them, burning in fire, and of a naked woman standing in front of a demon as if she might give herself to him, like Eve tempting Adam. I closed it quickly and tried to shake the images from my head. There was a painting at the church that showed people burning in hellfire. After the first time I examined it, I could not look at it again.

Sitting in the pews, out of the corner of my eye, I could see the bright red and yellow colours of hell, the details of which—the gory punishments that awaited sinners—would haunt me as I tried to sleep.

It was past supper when the reverend returned one evening, his hair loose, his face flushed. In the hall, I gasped when he appeared behind me like a shadow.

"I didn't mean to frighten you," he said.

"Forgive me, sir," I said. "I didn't hear you enter."

Zacharias Engel went directly upstairs without another word as I hurried away to the kitchen to discover Walter had vanished, all but a few breadcrumbs on the table to show he was there. He'd been whipped before for lesser offences than being caught inside the house. I slipped out to the barn with a large plate of food for Walter before Master entered the kitchen a short time later, his hair tied once more neatly behind him.

Zacharias hadn't given me any instructions, unlike Felix Stern, who made lists of the food he wanted. I had prepared salted pigeon soup, herbed rabbit, and pickled cabbage.

"This food looks decent," he said in his deep voice that slipped across my skin like warm oil. I'd not had a compliment before, albeit formal and awkward, and I turned to busy myself with his beverage so he could not see my pleasure. I heard the squeak of the chair and discovered that he had seated himself at the cook's table.

"Would you not prefer the dining hall?" I asked, unsure whether to place the glass of mead in front of him.

"I did not know you had been married," he said, ignoring my question.

I felt my face redden, for I had fair skin that made it so.

"I did not think it important, sir." I wondered who had gossiped about me. There were too many to guess.

"You are too young to lose a husband, Frau Jaspers, but it has no doubt added to your understanding about life and given you the experiences to run a household."

It was not a question, so I wasn't sure if I should respond. I would rather not have had the marriage experience at all.

Herr Jaspers was over three times my age and partially blind. He was found with a cracked skull against the hearth, a fall deemed the apparent cause. I would be lying if I said I missed him. It was a release. I'd not given him an heir, and by law he left me with nothing. Fortunately, because he was someone of note, I was recommended to Reverend Stern and had been in his employ a year.

"Please sit," Zacharias said, gesturing to one of the wooden chairs at the table. "I would like to ask you some questions."

I hesitated and then noticed he was still watching me intently. It was not my place to sit with the master of the house. I rubbed my hands down the front of my skirt and looked to where I might place myself, how close. He eliminated the agonising choice when he indicated where to sit, nearest him.

"Have you yet eaten?" he said, cutting his food into pieces.

"No, sir."

He pushed his plate towards me. "Eat some if you want."

I hesitated, unsure if he was sincere.

"Please," he said again, gesturing towards the plate. The partaking of food with my master was an activity that seemed most inappropriate, and I awkwardly extracted some flesh with my fingers.

He ate like he walked, with stillness and quiet. I was used to Walter, who ate noisily, who flopped his elbows on the table, who scratched his head often on account of his lice, which I would pick out with my fingernails.

"Tell me, where were you before you were married?"

"I worked in the castle from the time I was a child," I said, after swallowing several times to dislodge the morsel of rabbit from the back of my throat.

At the age of thirteen I was old enough to be sold off. My husband had paid a generous indulgence to the church for his sins, of which there were many, and I was offered as a token of goodwill as part of the bargain also.

"Where were you born?"

"I don't know, sir."

I felt ashamed that I didn't know. A monk once told me that my parents had given me up because they couldn't afford me. He told me I'd been given opportunities that other children would love to have. I don't know if that was true about my parents. I have no memories of my time before the castle. I had often dreamed of being an illegitimate child of someone highborn. As well, the monk said that it was abandonment disguised in a blessing, saving me from a lifetime of begging. I don't know if that was true either.

"How do you find this village, Frau Jaspers?" he said.

It was a question that was too broad for me to find the right response. I looked from one of my hands to the other while I thought up an answer he might want to hear.

"I find it well," I said, raising my eyes to see that he had set down his utensil and folded his hands in the lap of his gown that now concealed his legs.

"Did you know Leon von Kleist, and are you aware of the crime he has been accused of?"

"Not all that well. But yes, sir, I'm aware he is accused."

He raised his eyebrows.

"Gossip, no doubt. There should be a law against it."

"Yes, sir." I was sure there was, something I was certain he knew also. And in a village this small, it was hard not to notice things, hard to keep secrets.

"Did you ever see sign that he might be capable of such murders?"

Kleist sometimes came to the village, where his wife once lived, and he had always been polite. I'd not heard any bad word come from the man nor any about him, nor had I seen him unkind.

"No, sir. He was a quiet family man. He didn't much engage in small conversation."

Zacharias Engel paused. I could see him thinking, storing my words.

"Have you noticed any strange happenings in town?"

"Aside from the murders?"

There had not been another one since Kleist's arrest.

"Yes," he said, his stare making me uncomfortable, as if I were guilty of crimes also. "Aside from the murders."

Since the cold and both before and after the murders, I had seen many happenings, and most things I found strange. Such as the way people were quick to complain about the smallest thing, about the way Reverend Stern used to argue with himself late at night, the time when Maude Meyer stole coins from the butcher's stall, that Walter would talk to animals, how Frau Heinz would make a strange sign in the air whenever her husband left for work, how Herta Jacobs would lift her skirts down by the brook in the hope she would ensnare a man to wed, how Brühn was caught by Walter taking women's underclothes off a fence where they were put out to dry. But I didn't tell him these things, nor did I report them to authorities. Neither did I mention the goat that lay dead in Herr Brühn's paddock.

"Strange?" I queried.

"People talking about things you don't understand or things that confuse you?"

It is dangerous to say what one truly thinks. That was what my husband used to say, and he would say much about a lot and especially when he was drinking. I'd learned to hide my thoughts and feign my ignorance.

"Did you not see the dead goat?" he asked.

I felt caught, and heat once more prickled my neck and cheeks. Of course Brühn would have mentioned Walter and me when he reported the death to city officials.

"Yes, I did, sir. I . . ."

"You what?" he said, now stabbing gently at something on the plate while he waited for my answer.

"I'd forgotten about that."

Truth was, Zacharias muddled my thoughts.

"You can speak plainly with me with what you see, what your thoughts are."

On the one hand he seemed formidable, and on that same hand he sounded trustworthy. But it be the other hand I was unsure of. The hand that usually holds the secrets that people don't show about themselves.

"I have heard that you could be arresting people, sir," I said. "That you are not only replacing the Reverend Stern but that you are here for other tasks."

There was rumour that the prince-bishop and his lawmen were clamping down on sin, though I was still not sure which one. Whether it was the murders or something else.

Zacharias's blue eyes shone a shade of green under the flame of the candle.

"People shouldn't gossip," he said. "I can assure you that I work in the interest of the people. That if there is maleficence here, I will find it . . . But you are correct. I am here to interrogate the suspects."

He was intriguing, not least by the way he stretched out his words for effect, gave away so little, and stared too long. The way, right then, he stayed silent long enough to gain more information.

"I have heard"—from Herta, though I didn't say her name—"that there are many people being charged with crimes across the territories, not just here."

I presumed she had learned that from her father. She told me that people had been seen across the country entertaining strange practices, such as devil worship, and there were whispers it may have spread here. Though I could not bring myself to say this. It sounded both absurd and dangerous to speak of such.

Zacharias pressed his lips together and widened them into a smile.

"It is my job to inform people what sins to look for, since it is the uninformed who allow evil to spread. The Devil chooses the weakest

willed and those with impure thoughts. I am here to help people recognise sin."

The phrase "impure thoughts" brought up some of my own, and I
spoke quickly to erase them. Eisbach did not have such men that looked
like the Reverend Engel.

"I feel that many sins would be too obvious to miss, sir, such as the
murder of children. That it isn't a case of going looking for them. In the
course of time, people can't help but reveal their true selves and their
sins, unable to bear such burden alone."

He stared at me curiously so that I turned to my lap, wondering
if I'd said the wrong thing, made myself look more stupid than I was.

"Thank you for joining me," he said, standing up and leaving half
his meal. "You have been very helpful."

I couldn't see how and became worried that I had said too much,
had been too forthright.

Zacharias paused at the doorway. "Frau Jaspers, you will likely hear
things while I am in this house. You may be privy to some information
on the people I have to investigate. I suggest in your own interests you
say nothing about what you learn, as market talk shows only indolence
and malice."

The sinister warning beneath the gentleness of his tone made me
shiver, and for a minute after, I could do nothing but stare at the door
he had gone through.

When I told Walter later about the discussion that our master was
searching for sin, he suggested the reverend start searching in Herr
Brühn's drawers. I stifled a laugh and cuffed the boy affectionately on
the back of the head.

EXCERPT

(FEATURING THE REVEREND ZACHARIAS ENGEL)

THE WITCH HUNTS—A HISTORY, BY HERR FREDERIK FÖRNER, PUBLISHED 1633

(Introduction: While this history of the witch hunts is not exact in so far as every minor word or description being recorded, what I can attest to are those conversations and events that I personally witnessed or experienced. With the use of my notes taken throughout that time, I am furnished with details with which to offer a truthful account wherein this place and period sits . . .)

I cannot speak for those persons who have their own version to tell, but I can say the character and legend of the Reverend Engel, sent from Rome to cure the village of diabolism, has grown more with speculation than facts.

I first encountered the Reverend Zacharias Engel at the castle door to escort him to meet with Prince-Bishop Philipp Adolf von Ehrenberg. My first thoughts were that he was well favoured in appearance and with a penetrable gaze that seemed to enter my very soul, and that such trait would be beneficial to interrogation. He was tall and youthful looking, his stride long and confident, dark haired and well groomed. He wore boots of soft leather, a robe of fine silk, a collar of the whitest lace, and a cloak that was made from a silky dark Eastern sable, clasped at his throat by onyx and silver.

We made small talk as I showed him through the castle rooms, where he would be requested to dine from time to time. It was important that delegates of Rome be treated especially well.

I asked what his first impressions were of the village of Eisbach. He replied that he found most inhabitants locked behind their doors due to poor weather. Before commencing his journey, he had pictured an idyllic rural setting, the villagers full of good health having been raised in the comforts of pastures and fresh air, and a community united. He said he had found none of those for obvious reasons, which I at first assumed he meant was due to poor weather.

"I have seen mostly pale, obscured faces with black seeds for eyes peering out from doorways, fearful of a future that seems bleak and filled with hunger and disease," he had added, which I thought might be a slight on the quality of Ehrenberg's rule. I, too, had commented to others that I found the village full of immoral dolts and drunkards who appeared to despise the attendance of delegates from the city.

His residence, Engel said, had pleasantly surprised him, and the staff, a young widow, Katarin Jaspers, and a houseboy, Walter, were attending well to his needs.

"I was not expecting something so grand," he commented about the clergy house. "It is better than others I have encountered in the region."

It seemed to me another insult, his expectations of building standards in the territories were that he assumed them to be inferior. These early comments allowed me quickly to take his measure. I began to see he was above himself, my instinct telling of potential issues in the future. The house he was staying in was certainly one of higher standards.

I entered the hall of Ehrenberg. He was bent over his desk with quill in hand and in no hurry to pay us attention. Our ruler was small in stature, with dark hair, a coifed moustache, and a short, pointed beard. With his constantly roaming eyes, he displayed an air of either wariness or disinterest depending on the company. Engel presented a copy of the personal letter of introduction, but Ehrenberg gave it a cursory glance only and cast the paper to reside with others in the pile on his desk that he found equally as tedious. He had already received the advice about Engel. Anything further was excessive and time wasting.

"What news from Rome?" the prince-bishop asked as Zacharias seated himself on the opposite side of the ruler's table. On a tray between them were several goblets, a pitcher of wine, and a tankard of beer. There were also cakes made with fruit and honey, several boiled quail eggs, dried figs, and roasted almonds.

"It will be no surprise that Bishop Dietrich is most concerned about the events happening in Eisbach," said Engel. "But that is not the only village to be examined. There are strange occurrences elsewhere."

"Yes," said the prince-bishop, nodding, already aware. "And what is being done about them?"

"The Holy Roman emperor is sending representatives to other towns and villages to report back also."

"Please, Your Reverence"—Ehrenberg waved across the contents of the table—"join me. Help yourself."

Zacharias eyed the food and drink momentarily, but his mind, from the look of his frown, was clearly elsewhere.

"And the city?" Ehrenberg asked. "How is Rome?"

"It is a wonderful, complex city, I might tell you, that does not have this weather."

I took this also as another criticism rather than an observation.

"It is perfect wine weather," Philipp Adolf von Ehrenberg countered, "would you not say?" He extended his hand towards the jug of wine.

"No, thank you, Your Excellency."

I could tell from his pause and stare that Ehrenberg was offended by the refusal.

"Then take some with you. It will cure your temper and keep the fleas from your bed. And how do you find your lodgings?"

"Quite adequate, Sire."

"It is probably more modest than what you are used to."

"It is but a small sacrifice," said Engel, sounding both humble and insincere.

"That residence, and position, I understand, is only temporary while we destroy the evil that has invaded the village, and until such time another priest is installed to replace you. Is that correct, Reverend?"

"Yes, Sire."

"Your task of course is to examine what has forsaken the village in recent times. You must ensure the piety of the inhabitants and report in writing the details of any interviews. You must also come immediately here when summoned."

Engel opened his mouth to respond, then stopped. He forced a small nod.

"You will lead the interrogation. However, I have officials, who will assist you during any interrogation. Herr Förner is my commissioner who oversees the methods used to glean information and will note all that transpires, and I have several more lawmen at your disposal to assist as you see fit."

"Thank you, Your Excellency. I feel I am best equipped to work alone. Nevertheless, if the commissioner is attending and taking notes, then my reporting would seem unnecessary."

I could tell instantly from the prince-bishop's silence that followed, His Excellency was not impressed by the foreigner.

"I'm sure you are most experienced in these matters," he said. "But such times call for more extensive measures in the interests of the bishopric. Our commissioner and his men are well practised in our customs here, and I am sure they will not interfere with your spiritual objectives for those accused. Unless of course it is required."

Engel's nod, I felt, was feigned appreciation.

"Here is a list of people to interview," said Ehrenberg, passing him a document. "No doubt you have Stern's notes about the earlier infantile murders."

"I was sorry to hear about his poor health," said Engel.

"It is a pity, but it was at least an opportunity for new blood here," Ehrenberg said, leaning forward, and adding in a lower, more serious tone: "The commissioner will give you the details of your first accused, Leon von Kleist. This was a task not meant for someone stuck in their ways and addled, like the Reverend Stern. There is the Devil at work here, who may have even reached the priest, and I want you to find the people he had working for him."

"I assume, Your Excellency, that this man imprisoned is yet to be found guilty."

"Undoubtedly, he is guilty of the murder of his wife and children," said Ehrenburg, stunned by Engel's suggestion, "but he has not yet confessed to diabolism, something that I am certain he is also guilty of and a subject in which you are very skilled. Are you not? I expect you will be more persuasive."

The prince-bishop wanted an execution sanctioned by someone other than himself. But I did not yet know how vast his aims were.

After other perfunctory conversations on matters of administration and an invitation to a banquet in coming days, the prince-bishop instructed me to accompany Zacharias Engel back to the village and acquaint him with the area. Engel instructed Walter, his houseboy, who looked in fear at the sight of both of us, to guide him to people of interest since I did not know everyone personally. I read out the villagers' names from the list, and the boy led us to various abodes.

After several hours, at the conclusion of our interviews, the priest released the boy, found hunched and shivering and seated in the snow, his head between his knees to thwart the daggers of wind. His small legs ran to flee the cold but I daresay from us as well.

The villagers we had called upon had found Engel an immensely handsome curiosity. In some I saw awe, in others I saw fear. A priest chosen by the papal authorities with a strong network of allies.

Taking refreshment at the Eisbach Inn, we briefly discussed the interviews. He said so far they had given him little else but examples of odd and seemingly innocuous behaviour: an accusation, a sighting of a goat, dead animals, people babbling to themselves, and people arguing. Others had been chosen to give character assessments of the man accused of signing a pact with the Devil, Leon von Kleist, none of whom spoke ill of him. Still, I noted the names of those who reacted suspiciously to questions. Next, I led Engel to the river's edge where the boy, Hermann Kropp, was found, and to the graveyard also. Since it was growing late in the day, it was decided that he would investigate the forest, the scene of another murder, at another time.

I returned to the castle with a certain apprehension. I couldn't say exactly why, only that I felt we were on the precipice of change, but whether that meant the inhabitants of Eisbach were about to fall from a great height or find a bridge to something better, I could not yet say.

CHAPTER THREE

Cilla Graf was still missing. I had known her from the market square. She, along with the other little ones, had followed me around like puppies. Cilla would stand back from the crowd, observing when the girls would play with my hair. She was cannier and more cautious than others, and she would eye all the people she didn't know well distrustfully. It was strange to many that she would leave the main track voluntarily. And then there was another death. A ferryman, a father, a husband, a son, all the same, who walked out in the night, sat in the snow, and died sitting with his back to a tree, legs out in front of him, his lucky, or not-so-lucky, stone clutched in his hand. People were desperate; they did desperate things. The ferryman, like other boatmen, had lost his only trade on the river owing to the freeze, and a man who had no means to look after his family felt shame.

"There is a new midwife helping Maria Unger," said Walter, entering the parlour, where I was wiping fine ash from the front of the hearth. "Someone went to get help from Maria, and a stranger answered the door."

I turned my head sharply towards him like a dog with a sudden scent of hare.

The last time I had seen Maria was a few days before Zacharias arrived. Maria was well liked and fair minded. People went to her with all sorts of private matters. I had never heard her gossip about anyone or say a bad word, and she had carried some of my secrets also. She had cured my menstrual cramps and treated me during my miscarriages that caused me long periods of fever. Herr Jaspers had stopped her coming eventually. He said it was unnatural the way women lean on one another for support.

"They say the girl is young and very beautiful, though I haven't seen her."

"Why does Maria need help?" I asked.

"They say she is sleeping. That she will not wake up."

I walked to the window. Her house was not visible from ours, but I looked to the bend of the river before it disappeared and curled towards the city of Würzburg, expecting this mysterious assistant to emerge from her house, which sat alone and surrounded by trees. *My house is an island to many,* Maria would jest. *What is an island?* I had asked. She had laughed that I knew so little of the world.

Fear gripped me suddenly, and I clutched the back of my arms as if I might be faced with a sight unbearable.

"What is wrong?" asked Walter, who had seen me tense.

"Nothing," I said, then wickedly flicked him with my dusting linen. "I must go to see Maria," I said, removing my apron. I had half an hour before I would commence my kitchen tasks, to spice the mutton and potatoes and let them stew.

In retaliation, Walter flicked me back on my forearm, and I squealed at the sting of it. At the same time, Zacharias entered through the front door, a dark shape that blocked what feeble light the day had offered. He had appeared soundlessly, without warning. When I turned to Walter, the boy had vanished behind me, the sound of the back-door latch clinking into place.

"Frau Jaspers," said Zacharias, "I need you to accompany me to visit Inge Rutger, Kleist's servant."

"I don't—"

"I think it would be better that you, a woman, were there to comfort or encourage her to speak. From what I have learned she is prone to hysteria and may cut the interview short with a bout of it, as she has done under heavy questioning before with the commissioner. Another woman might calm her."

Inge was not as social as some of the maidservants living on the larger estates across the river. I didn't know her all that well, though I saw her sometimes at the market and was familiar with the house and property she cared for. The Kleist family always attended sermons at the church in Eisbach but never stayed to mingle afterwards.

"You can recommence your house duties later," he said.

I put a scarf around my head and walked alongside the reverend. People stared and some bowed before him as if he were more senior than he was. Zacharias appeared unaffected by this adulation. He returned a nod occasionally, though I could tell his mind was somewhere ahead of us. Flecks of snow littered the shoulders of his cloak, and I had the urge to brush them away as I did for Walter.

We crossed the bridge, just before the pathway to Maria Unger's house, to reach the fields on the other side. I could spy her house with its missing shingles and a door that had a wide gap at the bottom. I had been there in the past to know the house let in too much cold, the lock on the door broken, the walls damp. *My house will fall down around me, and the plague might stain these walls, but I will still not leave,* Maria once said. She took payments in coin but mostly in food. Zacharias followed my gaze.

"I visited the midwife, Maria Unger, recently."

"I heard she was sick," I said.

"She is indeed. I must ask that you not call on her. She is unable to speak, and until we understand what it is that ails her, she must not be disturbed. But she has her niece looking after her and appears to be in good hands."

He did not observe the house for as long as I did, attempting to see a new face through the window. Maria had never mentioned she had any family, and I wanted to tell him this but bit my bottom lip instead.

"You wear such a frown, Katarin," Zacharias said as we reached the fields on the other side of the river. "Don't worry about this interview. You are merely there as support. That is all I expect of you."

I was not worried about the interview. I was consumed instead by the fact he had once more addressed me by my first name and puzzled by the sudden familiarity. I looked sideways to check his mood, but he walked with distance in his eyes that swept the view of the river south where several people were ice-skating, metal blades twinkling. We crossed the vast fields of the Kleist estate and arrived at the large house, much larger than the one I worked in. It sat with its back to a forest that stretched across hills gently rising and falling for as far as the eye could see. Where once I could see farming animals in the fields, there were none.

Inge flinched when she answered the door to Zacharias and frowned when she saw me there, too. Her shoulders curled forward defeatedly so that her neck had to work harder to hold up her head. Her hair was dishevelled, the skin on her face red, her lips cracked from the cold. I felt pity immediately, for there were rumours she had to leave the bishopric to find work elsewhere. No one would give her charity, her association with Kleist a "taint." She gestured to a settle where she thought we should sit.

"I have brought Frau Jaspers. I hope you don't mind."

Inge shook her head and sent me a nervous look, a silent plea for understanding. She sat like me with both hands in her lap, gripping her own fingers for support.

"I need to ask several things . . . Firstly, about the doll."

We watched her fidget, eyes darting between us, then at the stairs that led up to the bedchambers, presumably where she had seen the object in question.

"What about the doll?" she asked finally when nothing else was forthcoming.

"Where did you find it?"

"Under Master's bed."

"You found it after the murders?"

"Yes, and days after the arrest."

"Why did it take so long to find it?"

"I can't say, sir. It just appeared."

"Could you describe the doll for me," he said.

Inge swallowed back her nerves.

"It was straw and sticks, with no face, and no adornment."

Zacharias reached into his coat pocket and drew out the doll that had been given to him by the commissioner as evidence. Inge drew back in fear.

"Were you aware that this object is similar to the one found on Lottie Pappenheimer, something her parents had stated she didn't own?"

When he put the doll on the floor between us, Inge closed her eyes and lowered her head. I moved to sit beside Inge to hold her hand reassuringly. I could feel her body trembling, not that I blamed her. I could barely look at the ugliness of it.

"Is this what you eventually saw?"

To be fair to Master's questioning, it did seem a strange thing to miss.

"In truth, Your Reverence," she said, her eyes still averted, "I had not performed any cleaning after the family fell sick and before Leon's arrest. It had been chaos in the house, the grief distracting me from my tasks. I took myself away for a time."

I wondered about the nature of the relationship with her employer, the fact she referred to her master's first name.

"During what time?"

"The night of the dance, I left."

"Why?"

"I was afraid."

She grew restless by Zacharias's silence and turned to me for some kind of comfort. I gave a small nod of my head and squeezed her hand, though I did not like the questions any more than she.

"He was not himself. I did not sleep after the twins died. I tried to keep Ruth away from Frau von Kleist, who had grown ill, but Leon would yell and curse at me and tell me to leave them alone. My mistress was too sick to say anything at all. She just watched the goings-on. But I could tell she was afraid."

"Afraid of her husband or afraid of dying?"

Inge was surprised at the question. I could see that she was considering it. She could find no answer.

"So, the doll could have been there all along, or someone could have put it there later."

I was curious about this line of questioning. To me, the facts were simple: the doll was found. I had been raised to see much of life as black or white. What you see is the truth. What you hear may not be.

"Was your master good to you before that?" said Zacharias.

"Yes, which made it hard to tell the officials the truth."

"To whom did you speak?"

"Commissioner Förner."

"You told him that your master acted strangely. Can you describe this again?"

"Leon stopped looking at me in the eye, sometimes forgetting I was there," Inge said, frowning at the floor. She was genuinely, I believe, trying to remember. "He babbled things in his sleep. He would go missing in the night."

"Did you manage to understand anything he was saying? Can you repeat any of it?"

She shook her head. "It was in a language I'd not heard used. I told the commissioner. It made no sense."

"Was this behaviour before or after the deaths of his sons?"

"Before and during, and after."

"And do you know what else he is accused of?"

"He went to the forest and danced as part of some kind of ritual."

"Ritual?"

"It is what people are calling it."

Gossip grew larger with more definitions.

"Is there anything else you can tell me?" asked Zacharias. "Anything odd that you have noticed."

"No . . . Yes. After he was gone. The prince-bishop's men came here and made a map of the area. They took most of the animals and let go of the workers except for me. They also went through his desk and took all his papers."

"What men were these?"

"The commissioner and the men who worked under him."

"What sort of papers?"

"I don't know, sir."

She was illiterate. Zacharias nodded as if he had read my mind.

A loud thud against the window made Inge and me jump. Zacharias stood up and we followed him outside. A small bird lay motionless beneath the sill. I went to pick it up to see if it was alive.

"Don't," said Zacharias. "It will right itself."

I saw the bird's legs move; then it jumped to its feet, spread its wings, and flew away. It was an omen, I remember thinking. This bird far from its flock had come to tell us something. Come to warn us. To warn me. I shook the feeling away.

"It was nothing," Zacharias chided, as if I were a child. "Just a bird."

We parted with Inge, who was quick to shut the door. I stood there looking over the estate. There were large, empty pens that I remembered had held vast numbers of stock. Zacharias peered inside the barn, where a few chickens ran flustered and squawking, but no pigs or geese. Gone also were Kleist's large black stallion, with its white feathered feet, and his wife's golden mare.

As we crossed the river, the midwife's place glowed yellow in the distance. I was certain I saw the face of the girl who Walter had talked about watching us from between the partially opened shutters. Minding my feet as we stepped off the bridge, she was gone by the time I looked again. Zacharias had stopped to ponder southward, a breeze sweeping the hair back from his brow.

"It must be beautiful here in the summer," he said.

I followed his gaze. During a break in the clouds, a stream of light cloaked the scene in a hazy iced blue, but I didn't see any beauty. This place held many secrets, and now it held death. I was lost for a moment in a memory so that when I turned to my master, he had already left along a different path.

"Sir, that is the wrong way!"

"You must show me where in the forest the children were found," he said, without looking back.

I could not will my legs to walk.

"It is quite far. I cannot, sir."

He stopped to consider me, raising one dark eyebrow inquisitively. "Why not?"

I was grateful that thunder sounded close.

"Because we should be home. The storms here will carry us away."

He pressed his lips together.

"We will be quick. Come!" he said, reaching out to take my hand. His hands were calloused and strong like those of farmers swinging scythes.

Another clap of thunder and I imagined it was God telling me to turn back. But we walked on, and my breathing grew shorter and my heart beat faster.

"I would like you to show me the forest where the witching sup-posedly took place."

"The witching, sir?" This was news to me.

"It is a word we use to describe the actions of those possessed by the Devil."

He wanted me to show him where Lottie Pappenheimer was found.

"I'm sorry, sir. I do not know the exact location."

"But you know the pathways through the forest, surely?"

He was watching me intently, checking for signs of something. Deceit perhaps.

"I do, Master."

"Do you have any idea where this ritual might have been performed?"

"There is a clearing in there, sir, where a number of trees have been felled, though I can say nought about a ritual," my voice breaking half-way through the sentence.

Ahead, trees looped their limbs to form an arbour, a gateway to the forest. As we approached, several crows flew out through this darkened entrance. I pulled my hand away and crouched down, my arms above my head protectively.

"Don't be frightened," he said.

I raised my head to see that he was once again studying me. Lightning flashed across his face, and his cloak sailed behind him in the wind. He held out his hand and I took it tentatively, then we weaved through barren pine and birch before the thunder shook the earth and snow beneath our feet.

"How much farther?"

"Far. The forest is deep, Reverend. I am not sure we will make it in time. We should go back and try another day, a different way."

He examined the sky through the trees, the air around us grey, the bear-shaped cloud above us about to open its jaws to release its rage.

"You are right," he said, letting go of my hand. "We should be getting back."

We headed down the hill as a gust of wind whipped my skirt above my knees, and closer to the village we ran to beat the rain.

"Thank you, Frau Jaspers," he said quickly, then dashed up the stairs to his room. "I might need you again for such delicate matters."

I stood a moment to watch his shadow move back and forth through the gap at the bottom of his door.

"Where were you?" asked Walter, who sat just inside the back door, a single candle in the centre of the cook's table, a flank of meat not quite thawed. I told him all that had occurred, for there had been few secrets between us.

"He is a strange man," said Walter voluntarily. "But I do not fear him."

And yet I did. Or was it that I feared myself around him, what I might do, what I might reveal? What I might feel.

⎯⎯◆⎯⎯

It was late when the storm woke me up. It pushed against the house, and the windows and doors fought back. I heard the whinnying of a horse in the barn. In amongst this I heard another sound: the front door clip shut. I put my shawl around my frigid body and crept to the room at the front of the house.

Rain blew sideways against the parlour window, whipping the glass with long, watery tails, the noise of which drowned out many others. The sky lit up the village briefly, and I could see Master stepping through the thick snow, his long legs carving in and out like a sharp knife through lard. I waited there watching for an hour, wondering if perhaps he was forced to report to the prince-bishop in the middle of the night. I thought of my hand in his. I thought of his skin, the rough and smooth of it, the fingernails bitten halfway down to the quick.

Sometime past midnight, when the storm had passed, I fell asleep on the chair by the window. Several hours before the cock in the barn crowed raucously into the void, I saw Zacharias returning and scurried back to my room to burrow into the cold sheets of my feathered bed.

I had a topsy-turvy night for the rest of it, dozing occasionally. While I was preparing the breakfast in the morning my thoughts were with him, with his words, his hands, on our interactions the previous day, on our closeness. I was fearful of him yet bedazzled by him also. My mind was so cluttered I didn't hear Walter enter.

"Didn't you hear me?" he said, presumably louder than before, dragging me out from under Zacharias Engel's imagined gaze.

"No, what?"

"Herr von Kleist is going to burn."

EXCERPT

THE WITCH HUNTS—FÖRNER

Engel arrived at the castle as requested, and we entered the circular, tall vessel of red brick pointing upward to the heavens and capped with a "witch's hat" that Engel had ironically remarked upon. A small, high window, that no being other than one of supernatural form could reach, gave the only light to the dark, damp space inside. To the side of the cylinder was the rest of the prison, a rectangular vestibule of numerous cells, but which hid the size of it below the ground.

Engel and I entered the structure and proceeded down the stairs to the cell that held the accused, Leon von Kleist. I had already interviewed the prisoner and gleaned from his manner that he was guilty of some if not all accusations. I found him extremely disagreeable, however, the prisoner's temperament was understandable, not only due to the calamitous accusations against him, which the man had fought aggressively, but also from the conditions applied at the prison: a dark and damp dungeon like most, with rooms that were ill-equipped for human habitation lest the human be a criminal. Kleist's chamber pot had not been changed in days, and the stench from it along with festering carbuncles on his ankles, caused by heavy iron restraints, was overpowering.

My instructions were to ensure that Engel gain a confession by any method possible and take a detailed record of the examination. Such techniques of torture were necessary, some already applied, but once advice came through of Engel's appointment, Ehrenberg had instructed us to wait. I believe this was for two reasons: one was a test of Engel's skills, and the second, which I am more convinced about with hindsight, was that the prince-bishop did not, initially anyway, want blood on his own hands. A conviction sanctioned by a delegate of Rome would only fortify the powers he had already and the penalties he would shortly enact for such crime of witchcraft.

Engel did not appear to despair at the sight of Kleist's conditions, nor did he seem distracted by pity. He was there to serve justice and free the community from danger, he told me, a vague response to an earlier query about his own methods. The conditions of the prison were secondary, the crime the man had been accused of primary importance. The task, however, was made more difficult because of the witness accounts in the prisoner's favour; one in particular was from a respectable member of the merchant class, who described Kleist as honourable and a loyal servant of God who continued his church attendance throughout the period of speculation.

Leon von Kleist had long, thinning grey hair, his complexion pitted and pale. He had a slight curvature of the spine that was noticeable when he stood. This impairment had preceded his imprisonment. His clothes were layered in grime that concealed the fabric, which had once been of quality. He had been imprisoned for several weeks, and without family the officials had seized a portion of his funds to pay someone to bring him food. Though it was minimal from the look of him. His collarbones and ribs protruded through his damp garment.

When Engel commented to me quietly about the force used against the prisoner, evidenced by a bloodied circular pattern on the back of his head, I did not admit to its cause being that of an iron baton. Nor did I confess to being party to this early treatment, of which I was. Several of Kleist's fingertips were jagged and crusted with dried blood from the pinching device used for the purpose of extracting information that so far had not drawn a confession.

Kleist's eyes followed the priest around the prison cell as he walked to examine the channels of water at the edges of the room, which had leaked through the walls and dampened the earth beneath our feet. The guard, once retreated, stood with one ear to the window of the door should any discipline be required. I sat on a bench furthest away from the prisoner. Engel moved to the interviewing chair closer to the accused, but not so close that he could reach the prisoner, shackled to the wall.

It was the prince-bishop's hope that Engel could bring about a full confession of a crime. I had seen an image of the prisoner at his home that I had visited prior: a small portrait of Kleist, a Bible open on his lap, his wife, three small children, and a dog. The piety of the picture was in stark contrast to the heinous murders he had been accused of. The priest's purpose was to fill in the gaps between the family in the drawing and the man who sat hunched before him.

The facts were that his wife died in high fever from apparent poisoning and his three children poisoned the same, two of those dying within days, the other close to death. But pertinent to the case was how Kleist was able to remain healthy throughout such plague, and whether maleficence was the cause. After the deaths of his two youngest children, he had displayed strange behaviour. He had been seen wandering in the fields where his family was buried and cursing at God during that period. Inge Rutger, his maidservant, had sworn on top of the Holy Bible about his strange actions, with full knowledge that her honour was at stake if she did not tell it truthfully.

"What is your full name, age, and occupation?" Engel asked the prisoner after introducing himself and announcing his intent.

The prisoner sighed deeply, as if he found the question tiresome.

"My name is Leon von Kleist. Forty-one years. Judge. Landowner."

"Judge?"

Zacharias seemed surprised, by the sound of it, as if learning this for the first time. I was certain I had included it in my notes on the case I had shared the previous day.

"Are you not a merchant and owner of farming lands?"

"I was that also," said Kleist.

"Do you know the charges against you and by whom?"

"I know all the nonsense and the nonsensical," Kleist said huskily.

"The first charge is that of murder of your family," continued Engel. "There is evidence they were given a concoction that made their tongues colour blue, that you had cursed them with fever, then finished them off with poison."

"It seems I am already finished then!" he scoffed without looking at the interrogator, then coughed harshly. "Your work is done!" he rasped. "You are free to leave."

Engel recognised, as I had, that madness and melancholy had befallen the former gentleman.

"I would like to hear your views on what happened, what you remember . . . in your own words."

Kleist became more attentive.

"Why? Who are you?" he said, as though he had just woken and was seeing his interrogator for the first time. "What do you plan to do with me?"

The priest reminded him who he was and his purpose, and Kleist sat up a little straighter. He had then looked at Engel directly through rheumy eyes. He was not an old man but could be mistaken for one. He began to cry. Large, dry sobs, his throat restricted, the sound hoarse and unpleasant. I assumed it was the guilt that was tearing at his conscience, that perhaps the Devil had freed him momentarily. But I could not rule out that such behaviour might also be a ruse.

"If there is something you wish to confess, the weight of it will be lifted from your soul," said the priest. "I can free you, Herr von Kleist. I can pull you away from the Devil's grasp."

Kleist tried to stand up and move forward, but a sharp jolt at his ankle reminded him of where he was.

"Get out of here! Get out!"

"What madness has taken you, sir?" Engel said, unmoving from his chair.

"It is you who are mad . . . Priest!" He said forcefully the last word, leaving spittle on his lips.

"Herr von Kleist, I wish you to tell me of the events that led you here. I am trying to help you. I am your only chance of redemption."

"I have nothing to be sorry for. I have paid for that which God has found me guilty. He took my twin boys, then my wife, then gave the sickness to my daughter, then left me with loss. If I am guilty of something, I have been punished tenfold."

Kleist's daughter had been taken to a convent far away to convalesce. Amongst the papers I had handed Engel was advice from the abbess that the girl was too far gone in the mind to give her testimony. Her already small body was wasting away, unable to take food. No treatment so far, they had reported, had proved successful.

"I have read your statement," Engel told him. "It was said that your wife's fever was too late to cure, that her tongue had turned blue."

"Then you will know that on my wife's final night, my daughter, my sweet little Ruth, came down with that same wretched affliction, and I begged God and that useless healer that not everyone be taken from me. Everyone I love."

He closed his eyes, frown lines deepening with memories.

"Who is this healer?"

"Frau Unger, a boil on society. She provides herbal mixtures that do nothing but fill people with false hope. I had asked for Ehrenberg's physician but was advised that he was otherwise engaged, most likely dining with that scoundrel."

"Scoundrel?"

"Ehrenberg. A traitor to God himself."

"Why, sir, do you say this?"

"Because he wants my land, he wants my goods."

I stood up to intervene, to silence such talk with a strike to the prisoner's head, but Engel was not interested in pursuing such enquiry and quickly moved to another question. I returned to my seat. As commissioner, I knew that loyalty was the main ingredient in keeping my position. However, I knew also what he said was true. Ehrenberg had already sequestered the former judge's vast estate.

"And it did not affect you, this fever?"

"I was not taken, one would think, by the grace of God. But God did not offer me his grace. He left me here on this forsaken earth instead to face crimes I did not commit."

His look was pleading, as if that would somehow tug at the interrogator's heart, but Engel's expression was hard and unyielding. I did have pity for the prisoner of course. No man should finish his days as he had done, but the murders committed had removed any chance of mercy, according to the law. Where once as a younger man I held the naive belief that a measure of goodness was in everyone, such thought had been dashed with the type of work I had been hired for: that of weeding out the worst of humankind.

At the sound of the scratching of my quill, Kleist called out to me.

"What are you writing in there, in that notebook, in your dark corner where your face is near disguised?" he said. "That I am damned?"

"He is simply recording our interview," explained Engel, diverting the attention back to himself.

"Good. Then I hope at some point in time people will be reading and judging you all for your perverse misuse of justice . . . you, in particular," he said to the priest, "a man of theology no doubt, a man trusted to make the right decisions." Kleist made another scoffing sound, but Engel remained composed, so oddly still that it seemed time might continue on without him.

"At your house, Inge Rutger witnessed you dancing with your daughter as her mother lay dying."

"My wife, Sigrid, and I watched our beautiful sons die one after the other on the rug in front of the hearth, their tiny bodies heaving from whatever ailment sent to spirit them away. Those boys that my wife had carried, that she had chosen to feed from her own body, the birth nearly taking her life. Then the day I was somehow cursed, my wife took ill before their tiny hearts stopped beating. She had kept her own illness from me, and I had been too distracted by the sickness of the boys to notice. The dance that I performed, and willingly, was for Sigrid, who asked that our daughter, Ruth, not weep, that she should see her daughter and I dance one more time, to be joyful . . . Then I watched Sigrid be placed into the mire with the others . . .

"My healthy daughter not more than eleven years, the image of her mother, turned quickly ill after my wife's death . . . That silly maid knows nothing!"

"Inge?"

"Inge was an idiot who stole from me regularly. I feigned ignorance of her moral failing for she was the daughter of my loyal horseman, now deceased. But what does she gain from this? A moment of prestige. A chance for people to look at her. She, who was my wife's friend and companion, who my daughter treated like a sister. She, who now makes such falsities against me."

"You do not deny that you danced as your wife lay dying? Was she not telling the truth?"

The prisoner's eyes were wide, his face puffed with rage, teeth together like an animal wild.

"I deny that there was any evil intent in doing so," he spat. "What she saw was concluded by interpretation only."

"It is not the only thing you have been charged with."

From his coat pocket, the priest pulled out the small faceless doll made with sticks for limbs and straw for hair that I had passed him earlier. A similar doll had been found with Lottie Pappenheimer.

"This was found at the house, under your bed," said Engel.

The accused examined it from a distance, struggling to focus on it at first.

"I know nothing about such an object, no doubt something else alluding to wickedness to besmirch my name."

This was evidence that had come to light more recently. Inge had made no mention of the doll initially, and it was curious that it had not been found earlier.

"I have heard everything said about me. I was seen dancing with the Devil on the Sabbath, I was seen copulating with an elderly widow," he said and laughed, hard and brittle. "I am surrounded by imbeciles."

"You are saying that these people lie?"

"I am saying that these people are malicious. That two of the witness testimonies are from people I did not judge favourably in civil disputes."

"Will you renounce the Devil," said Engel, "and ask for forgiveness for your sins?"

"How dare you ask that which I need no forgiveness," shouted Kleist, standing. "I can tell that you believe none of what I am saying. You have made up your mind. You are a cold, cold man, Priest, that I can tell. You have not an ounce of pity. You, too, are fooled by frauds. Get out! If you do not wish to help me, get out!"

Engel waited several moments for the man to calm.

"You must speak the whole truth if I am to help you," said the priest.

"You are deaf and blind to the truth," said the prisoner. "There is nothing more for me to say."

Kleist sat back down, his chin on his chest, and moments later a rhythmic hissing sounded through his lips.

Kleist had an answer for everything, but still the evidence weighed heavily against him. It was likely just a coincidence that the people he had dealt with unfavourably were also witnesses against him. Both from godly homes, I had searched hard to find deception in their expressions and words and found none.

Inge's statement was already included to substantiate the allegations and was the most damning. I wondered whether she understood the consequences of her testimony that would bring about her eventual eviction from the Kleist property. Though I told him he would find no new evidence, Engel had been too curious not to hear directly from Inge also; of this I would later learn.

I stood up and went to the prisoner to shake him awake. He was even more agitated, swiping at the air. I was forced to slap him hard across the face. The reverend at this point turned away and saw no reason to question him further that day, suggesting the prisoner was too exhausted to talk. I was disappointed that he'd not worked harder to extract a confession.

"I will come back again tomorrow," he said.

There was no time. My instructions had been clear from His Excellency. I pulled Engel aside to speak with him out of earshot of Kleist.

"Your work is done here," I told him.

"But I have not been given enough time."

"It is orders, Your Reverence, that we cannot go against. A confession will be forthcoming by the end of the day, and I would ask that once it comes, as I know it will"—I had hoped to God the man wouldn't die in the process—"then it must be sanctioned by you, a member from the holy city. An instance of diabolism must be treated differently."

"I do not yet see diabolism from this man."

"Then you have not been paying attention."

He locked pale eyes onto mine, and though battle hardened and unaffected by various forms of depravity that I had witnessed in my forty-three years, there was a feeling that I might be dealing with someone who had experienced even more than me, whose calm and arrogant manner told me that he was not used to orders from positions like mine.

The prince-bishop had been very curious about the newcomer and could talk of nothing else when I convened to present a report. I could tell he was undecided as to whether to fear, envy, or favour him. With such interest, I will admit that a small amount of envy of my own had crept in, the fact that this man had taken such interrogation tasks away from me, much of my role reduced to notetaking.

"One thing I can assert," I told Engel outside the cell, after I had called for the prince-bishop's special lawmen to come and perform their tasks of persuasion, "is that at no time was the castle physician requested by Kleist to attend to his family. He is lying about that. He is guilty of murder, I am certain of it, and it would be strange that his maid would risk her livelihood for a lie. She is obviously honest and faithful to God."

Engel said he did not doubt the latter. There was scarce work for girls like Inge, especially in such weather that affected incomes and trades. The servant admitted that she had enjoyed working for him and his family, and they had treated her well. That his later actions, though frightening, were out of character.

"So do you sanction what we are about to do, and will you bear witness?" I asked the reverend.

Engel hesitated.

"Innocent lives were stolen by this man," I reminded him. "Small children."

Engel looked back at the prisoner, then nodded just the once.

We were both there to witness Ehrenberg's lawmen first hang Leon von Kleist by his arms behind him, and with weights tied around his ankles, before burning his feet and the hair from his head in patches. By the time they were pinching out the rest of his fingernails with pliers, the priest had closed his eyes, his lips moving in what I presumed was prayer.

It took only two hours before the prisoner confessed to the murders of his family, to diabolism and ritual magic, to having made a pact with the Devil. He nodded at the end when I asked whether his conscience was now clear.

Engel showed no emotion, neither elation nor relief, at the conclusion. He was impossible to read.

CHAPTER FOUR

A swarm of starlings flew over the marketplace in Eisbach, where a crowd had gathered to watch the execution. The birds swooped and dipped and spun around in patterns, gliding across the ceiling of white, while murmurs of the assembly grew in fervour like angry bees. Ludwig, the stonemason, spun around to whisper to his wife that the scene above was an omen, that these birds had not flown to escape the winter but had stayed to ensure the outcome. People in the village searched for signs everywhere for everything.

It hadn't always been that way. When the weather was good, people had been too busy to notice signs, but the changing of the weather made them go looking for them. The show of birds was the only incident that distracted the crowd otherwise fixed to the dais in front of them. Expressions were eager, almost hungry for the event, and men and women weaved through the spectators handing out nuts tied in hessian and thimble skins of honey, courtesy of the castle stores.

There had been public executions before of murderers and thieves, and those who preached against God. They were hanged, these criminals, while the accused were jeered, and the proceedings were cheered. It brought people in from the fields, but this one brought people in from other villages and towns close by. Tethered horses lined the slippery track into the village. Not even the snowfall that was potentially turning savage was deterring villagers from across the bishopric and city dwellers. After a notice was posted in the market square the previous week, word of the execution had spread as fast as a northern gale. There were incentives to attend. Refreshments during the event, free jugs of ale afterwards, compliments of Ehrenberg, and many workers at the castle were given several hours' leave. This was a way for the prince-bishop to make a point but sweetened with gifts and festivity. Though many had cynically commented that these treats had been paid for anyway with their taxes to the church.

Eisbach had caught the attention of Rome, and it appeared pointed that Kleist's execution was to be performed where the child murders had taken place. From his attendance at church, he was known to all, and this would serve as a warning that no one, even those of standing, was exempt from punishment.

I had witnessed public hangings of criminals accused of murder or treason in the past, but I had never seen such desire for an execution. I had experienced enough of death to know that I did not wish to witness another, but my master had mentioned that he would see me in the square, when I brought him his morning meal, and it seemed disrespectful to not attend. Or worse a declaration of guilt. *Only the holy need come,* he had said at the last sermon.

I did not know yet if I could speak plainly to the reverend. Since our trip to see Inge the week earlier, he'd hardly been at his house, spending most of his time at the tower, questioning people, and then at the castle listening to small civil matters that the prince-bishop had called him in to witness. When he did request food or a quiet word about a task, his voice would burn a hole in my lower belly that I ought not feel. Even amongst sin and death I was thinking about a man who was promised to God. He was guarded, distant, mysterious, and untouchable. He was nearly always in my dreams.

Someone called the crowd to silence, and several of Ehrenberg's men entered the marketplace followed by the prince-bishop in a cloak of soft red velvet, on a horse with a shimmering black rug, trimmed with tassels of gold. As he eyed the crowd, everyone clapped. Our holy leader was not unattractive, thick dark hair with glints of red, smiling at everyone, but he was spoiled, and I had heard that he would throw things, breaking porcelain and glass when he was angry.

Sigi, Herta's brother, caught sight of me in the crowd and leered. His light hair lifted in the breeze, exposing his overlarge, reddened ears that jutted out from the sides of his head like they had been placed there as an afterthought. He smirked at me and I pretended not to see him. He and the pack of wild dogs he ran with were always hungry for trouble.

My master entered the square behind the prince-bishop's procession. Zacharias was dressed in black as usual in long boots, his robe, and his fancy cloak, his hat pushed back a little so that his features were clearer. Beside me two girls had noticed him also.

"He would be a fine one as a husband," said one.

"Hush," said the other, though she said it with laughter in her voice. "You'll find yourself on the stage next time."

I wished for the earth to cave in beneath their feet.

"It is true," said a woman nearby. "He'll be coming for you both with your trulls' mouths."

The girls stopped talking and meekly lowered their chins.

Zacharias Engel did not eye the crowd but stood facing the track that led from the city. In the distance I could see the prisoner being escorted to the square, and a ruckus was developing as others saw him coming. A girl with a shawl that concealed most of her face stood high on her toes to see above the people in front of her. I could glimpse the tip of her nose, and dark-rose lips, a profile I did not recognise. She wasn't looking to where the prisoner was to enter but to my master who now stood alone on one side of the podium. He had been facing the track, but as if he knew, as if he felt the eyes of this stranger upon him, Zacharias turned and seemed to pick her out of the crowd, holding her gaze for several seconds.

The wind picked up in gusts suddenly and broke the spell. It blew the girl's covering backward from her head, revealing her silken hair, a pale shade of straw. As she reached up behind her for the edge of her shawl she glanced my way, and I had enough time to capture her brown eyes that were threaded with gold. I had not seen her in the village before, but I suspected it was the face I had glimpsed through Maria's window. My curiosity was extinguished as the jeers of the crowd grew in intensity from a low rumble to tumultuous applause as Leon von Kleist, hunched and ragged, reached the public square.

Kleist was barely dressed, his face and hands purple from cold or bruising, it was hard to tell. His long light-grey hair, which was normally secured tidily at the nape of his neck, was completely gone. His scalp was black and matted with dried blood. His bulbous purple feet made it clearly painful to walk so that the guards had to drag him upright by his scraggy arms to reach the pyre. Everyone except Zacharias, Inge Rutger, and me found that comical.

Inge wept at the sight of Kleist. Her name had been constantly mentioned in the castle stores, some feeling pity, some spurning her for not coming forward sooner when she first witnessed odd behaviour. It was said she had been asked to leave the bishopric. With her eyes swollen from sleeplessness and tears, I was certain the rumour was true. She looked both terrified and sad, and I made my way through the crowd of hard men and soft women to reach her. Just at that moment, she stepped nearer the prisoner and I saw her call to him, her words drowned out by the noise of the crowd.

There had been a rumour that Kleist had been bedding with Inge, though I didn't give much credence to it. People were quick to think up new crimes, to safely throw stones at those who weren't strong-willed enough to fight back or weren't there to defend their name. That was the worst in humans, the way they banded together in common malice.

Kleist neither heard Inge call nor looked up. It was as if he had no mind at all for whatever was happening around him. Two lawmen lifted him onto a small makeshift platform of roughly hewn logs and tied him to a centre post. I'd witnessed hangings before, but the sight of the pyre of wood made my legs go weak. Inge Rutger turned and left the group, sobbing. I thought best not to follow, to draw any more

An Age of Winters

attention. Admittedly, I did not want the stain of Kleist's crime to attach itself to me in any way.

Under a shelter of fabric, the prince-bishop sat on a chair on a stage, ten or so yards from the pyre, where speeches were made and travelling artists had performed their theatre. The square was for joyous occasions once, though few entertainers had come through in recent years. Artists had become beggars, their skills unwanted, and there was no spare coin to give them.

Our holy leader, Ehrenberg, spoke: "Of the charges, this man will burn by fire."

The crowd was silent, waiting for more words to follow.

"Make no mistake, good people of Eisbach and the bishopric of Würzburg, there is diabolism about us in forms we may not recognise, and we cannot let it slither its way into our lives. Fire is the way to cleanse the decrepit and dirt from this man's soul." He flung his arm out towards the crowd in a theatrical fashion.

"I'd say it will remove more than dirt," said a man gruffly behind me.

I experienced a moment of panic. I felt a weight press hard against my chest and a trickle of sweat where my collar met my neck despite the cold. I must have sensed then that this day was only the beginning of the end of life as we had known it.

I had known Kleist's family and had spoken with his wife once or twice. I had mentioned that they weren't outwardly social, but they weren't distant either. I had heard that Kleist was often seen talking to himself, whimpering and calling out. If I were to guess, I would describe that as grief. I understood grief well enough. I miscarried several babies, and one birthed dead. My husband had shrugged, said that it was common, that his first wife was barren. Several nights later, he lay on top of me again while my body still bled, while misery gnawed at my heart, the grief making me cold sometimes and hot at others.

Kleist seemed not to understand what was going on around him. He opened his mouth, I thought to speak; then I saw that his tongue was black and swollen. He had been punished enough. I recoiled from

65

him then and felt conspicuous for it, too, for belonging to the crowd that worshipped death.

Two men flanked the prince-bishop, one his spokesman, whom I did not know, and the other the commissioner, a commanding, stoutly built man with a thick moustache, one eye askew, and a face full of scars.

"What charges will be applied?" Ehrenberg asked his spokesman.

"There are several charges, Your Excellency," he said thinly, stepping forward. "The first is the charge of—"

"Speak up!" shouted someone in the crowd, and others squawked like geese in agreeance.

The commissioner snatched the paper from the other man's hand.

"The first charge is that of witchcraft ritual magic," bellowed Förner, quietening the throng instantly, "to cause havoc across our communities."

There were gasps and mutters from the crowd. I put my hand over my mouth and briefly held my breath. *Witchcraft?* It sounded absurd to hear it aloud. Talk of it in hushed whispers in the common areas had not yet made such a crime so real.

Zacharias Engel folded his hands in front of him and watched the commissioner without expression. The *witching* that Master had mentioned earlier, and so casually, was finally spoken publicly.

"The second charge is that of murder of his wife and his two infant sons and the bewitching of his daughter, who has been left feeble..."

"Silent!" the commissioner yelled to the audience, whose grumblings threatened to drown out his words. "The last is that he has made a pact with the Devil to conspire in the deaths of others."

I couldn't think how they knew this, who the people were who had witnessed the evil. The last charge was so broad it could encompass the deaths of all children, and the first suggested, broadly again, that he'd had something to do with the weather. I surveyed the crowd. Though many were jeering, there was also fear in some, in their wide-eyed, rigid stares, of things they didn't understand.

"These crimes," continued the commissioner, "require the penalty of death, for such crimes are heresy according to our laws and should be shown no mercy, otherwise God's wrath will be upon us all!"

If cold and disease were the measure of our sins, such wrath was already here.

"Heretic!" someone shouted, and a chorus from the crowd echoed the word. Kleist, who had been still, raised his head slightly, his eyes drifting towards the person who shouted before the effort was too much and he lowered his head once more. I wondered if Jesus pinned to the cross would have had the same bewildered look.

The prince-bishop eyed the people below him, seemingly satisfied by the response judging by the small upward creases at the corners of his mouth. He stood to speak.

"It is only with death that we might lift the curse from this bishopric," said Ehrenberg, "that our people will be spared from starvation from storms, from poor crops, and from disease that we have endured."

He hadn't endured anything. He had a personal physician living with him in the castle to treat his ailments. His treasury was full after years of hoarding. His larder, until recently, fully stocked—for him, his office bearers, and other clergy—from the toil of others across the territories.

Working at the clergy house for the Reverend Engel, I was fortunate enough to have access to the storeroom, too. I could not complain.

I made a sign of the cross when light shot out from the sky and to the ground of a distant hill. The prince-bishop then sat down as the sky grumbled beyond the village. People shifted their feet aware of the sign, restless as the sky hurled its fury. These people barely had enough food to last a winter. Some had resorted to selling items from their houses. This execution was the excuse they needed to end their dire circumstances and God would now favour them, or so they had thought.

A woman spoke from within the crowd, and people close by turned to look at her. I craned my neck to see that it was Zilla Lucke who was pushing roughly through the bodies and dragging her half-witted adult son behind her. Jon was built the same as his mother, and Frau Lucke was by no means a delicate woman. Many people cursed at her, and she cursed back at them. Jon hung his head and made little eye contact with anyone. Zilla saw me and pushed someone out of the way to speak to me. She had come directly from toil, her skirt muddied and her hair as unruly as coarse twine.

I had always liked Zilla. She had been forced to raise Jon and mind the pig farm on her own. When he was a small boy, a roofing accident had left Jon with a mind of a child for the remainder of his life. Zilla's husband never forgave himself, for he was the one who had ordered Jon to perform the fateful task. Boris Lucke fought in wars that he did not believe were his to fight and died in battle far from home with a heart tormented by guilt. Originally of noble birth, Zilla stored away her silks to help Herr Lucke when times had needed it, and when money dried up after her husband's death. She was never afraid to speak her mind, to get her hands dirty, to muck out stables, to birth piglets.

"Katarin, you must get out of here," she rasped, gripping my arm. "This is no place for you."

I'd had much to do with Zilla in the past. She had favoured me since I was one of the few to show an interest in what she had to say. When I worked as a child in the castle, where she and Jon would deliver freshly slaughtered pigs, I would meet her at the doorway of the stores to receive the carcasses.

You are too small to be carrying such a heavy weight, she said once. *I should speak to your betters.*

I don't have any betters, I replied, unsure of what she meant, and she had laughed. *As you say.*

"I can't go," I said to Zilla. "My master wants me here."

"I can't stay and witness this barbarity." She shook her head and made her way back into the crowd to leave, Jon following close behind. I was touched that she had thought of me, had in moments taken me under her wing. When I turned back to the stage, the commissioner was watching us. I did not like that we were seen. Seconds later, he was distracted by the arrival of the executioner carrying a torch. Master bent his head to speak to the accused with what I assumed were words of absolution. Though Kleist had been imprisoned before Zacharias's arrival, it was clear now that the decisions about the execution were connected to the latecomer. He would be remembered as the one who changed the execution from hanging to fire.

Not since our first discussion had he returned to the kitchen to sit and speak with me, but sometimes when I passed the doorway to the sitting room, he would call me in with queries that seemed harmless enough. Where first I'd been reluctant, stories ran off my tongue, told in part out of fear but more to impress him. I had told him about the drunk men down by the river, and the fight between two wives over a piece of gristly meat at the market, the pulling and twisting of hair. I had commented on those people who gossiped about anyone who kept to themselves, and those who were unruly. Standing in the crowd, I wondered then about the motive behind the questioning and watched him view Kleist with detachment. Zacharias stood still, not a tremor about him. He appeared not to notice the cold, unlike many who blew on their woollen-less fingers.

There was some difficulty lighting the fire. The crowd moved forward, thirsty for death, before they were ushered back by guards. Kleist was aware now of impending death, his expression all at once changing as he looked fearfully at the doings of the man who held the torch. He clenched his jaw and eyed the crowd. He hated everyone. Next, he turned to Zacharias Engel. It seemed he hated him the most.

The fire took to wood as thunder rumbled once again and ice crystals peppered the condemned man's head. There were murmurs, not joyous this time. The fire whooshed upward, caught his rags for clothes that fused with his skin, then spread like crawling ants towards his head. Kleist screamed words as he burned, but I could make no sense of them. Smoke from burnt flesh spread above the crowd and dusted us with ash.

I squeezed and released the folds of my skirt several times to stop my tremors.

Some people shielded their eyes. Children cried out for their mothers. A woman spewed green into the snow. I remembered the mysterious girl with pale-yellow hair and found her nowhere to be seen. Some cheered, *"Our children are now safe!"* but time would show they weren't.

The prince-bishop mounted his horse to commence his return, flanked by two now holding a cover above his head and a trail of his retinue behind him. After nodding to the prince-bishop as he passed, Zacharias mouthed something to himself. A moment later he turned from the scene of charring bones and melting flesh and walked in the direction of our house, a lonely figure disappearing behind a sudden wall of snow.

I wondered if he was joyous that he had destroyed his first sinner.

CHAPTER FIVE

Serenity cloaked Eisbach in the days that followed the "spectacle," as the execution was named, and leading up to Christmas celebrations. A state of numbness and exhaustion for some, relieved that the evil had been cured, and there were no new arrests, and no need to fear a knock on the door. The blizzard that had kept everyone inside had ceased, and there was a pensive, hopeful joy as people hung crowns of twigs, twine, and ribbons on their front door and called out greetings to one another.

In the village square, the spectacle was whispered about in the initial days afterwards, but talk of it was quickly dismissed in the public forum. At any mention of the details, villagers found excuses to be elsewhere, afraid that revisiting the event might provoke an evil or, worse, an accusation.

Zacharias became less intense during this period. I can't say that he was buoyed by the spectacle, but he walked the lanes with his hands behind his back, leisurely, fists no longer clenched at his sides. He had not grown particularly warm towards the two of us. On the contrary, he was still very formal when he entered a room. He viewed us sometimes suspiciously, perhaps still looking for sins, eyes roaming curiously, too, as though we were specimens in jars that I had seen in Maria Unger's house. Walter seemed less fearful, and the rash that sometimes irritated the skin of his cheeks and neck and the crease of his elbows had disappeared.

Unlike Stern, Zacharias spent little time at home. He would visit the castle for meetings and offer spiritual guidance to those who sought it privately. He would take long walks in the afternoons, sometimes along the frozen river, sometimes gone for hours. He observed things, studied them. People jumped to attention when he arrived at the square, whereas they would have cringed or laughed or scoffed at Stern. There was more respect for Zacharias, who had presence, who had the ears of the emperor and prince-bishop. Even the height of him, above most men, commanded esteem. When he walked through a crowd, I imagined him as Moses parting the Red Sea. He was an oddity but a welcome one, someone even revered since he was seen as our protector, someone who sought to save our souls. Though there was terror there, too. He could raise the fires if he wanted, choose who he thought should die.

<hr />

On the day before Christmas, icicles hung on trees like shiny ornaments and small children ran about in the snow independently of their mothers. Some ventured further to the river to ice-skate, the imminent danger of losing them thought to be gone. The prince-bishop had sent every house a pouch of wheat or two potatoes to celebrate, and for those who had given witness accounts of strange events, a bird too tough for His Holiness, dripping, or pigs' trotters were also part of the hamper. I didn't much care for such incentive, but I liked the fact that children's bellies would be full during this holy week, that village grudges against the more affluent would be temporarily withheld.

In our household, we did not have to worry about empty bellies. I was aware of my privilege and oftentimes in the past would sneak apples or dried figs from the castle stores to the children in the square, small hands clenching tightly to my skirt so as not to be forgotten. When I would run out of fruit, they would run away. But these times had been getting rarer. Even the castle storeroom was only half-full on any day, with Raine, the cook, keeping close account of who took what and how much.

I wondered about Kleist's animals, whether the meat we were taking was from them. I had heard that his house was being prepared for a wealthy merchant who had purchased a lease from the castle at a great price. I wondered who the merchant had paid it to and where Leon's daughter, Ruth, would live if she survived.

After Master had left to prepare the church for Mass, Walter and I finished our chores quickly so that we could play in the snow.

"I dare you," I said to him when he picked up a handful of snow. He hurled it at my shoulder with a strong arm for such a lean boy. I chased him as far as the old castle ruins at the edge of the village, where we would sometimes go to dance, and skip, and prance, pretending we were highborn, and Walter would bow his head to kiss my hand and I would curtsy like we were duke and duchess. Here, we could be whoever we wanted to be, unshackled to our fates. Sometimes Walter would stand on the stone wall and sing the most beautiful melodies, and I would imagine servants, fine silks, and social gatherings for people who had come just to see me, an orphan returned as the rightful heir.

Out of breath, we lay down in the snow on our backs surrounded by cragged, broken walls and knew our clothes would need drying near the fire as soon as we were home. It didn't matter so much that day. Master had requested new cloth for us after he had observed the state of our garments not long after his arrival. Walter had been squeezing into clothes too small for him, and my clothes were worn through in places. With the new linen, I had sewn a new shirt and breeches for Walter and a new dress for me in time for Christmas Eve. It was not like those of merchants' wives in the city, but it was fresh, light blue, the bodice fitted and the hem clean and long enough to hide my old boots.

As I lay there on my soft white bed staring at the sky, tiny pieces of heaven fell gently on my face. I experienced a moment of deep joy. I turned to Walter, who met my gaze, and suspected he felt the same.

"I'm going to marry you when I'm older," he said, in a most serious tone.

"Are you, now?" I said, humouring him.

"Yes," he said. "I'm going to look after you. I'm going to have my own farm."

"And how will you pay for this farm? With river stones? No, boy, you are meant for someone better. Marry a merchant's daughter and take a dowry."

Though that was unlikely, too.

"You're too young for me anyway," I said.

He sat up suddenly and looked away.

I felt such love for Walter, but he was just a boy with big ideas beyond his station. He was a handsome youth with an old soul, and he would become a fine man and husband, I was certain of it. I knew why Herta wanted her hands on him, which I had to prevent at all costs. Herta would break his spirit and mould him into a different man. She could be cruel and flippant and seductive within an hour. And she was far from chaste.

Besides, my heart was for another. Big dreams beyond my station also, beyond all sensibility. I was in love with an idea, a mystery. *Zacharias,* I would whisper to the walls at night. By morning, my reality would remind me to be more pragmatic than fanciful. He was, after all, a man of God.

With Walter's back turned, I grabbed a handful of snow to let fly my revenge.

"You . . . !" he said, shouting at me as I jumped up and fled. He followed me until I ran out of icy breaths, a stitch in my side forcing me to stop.

"Truce?" I said when he caught up.

"Truce."

We walked back and he was silent, hurt still, for I had always spoken plainly. In my youth, I had worn my heart on my sleeve, which did me no good. When my husband had chosen me for his wife, I told him that I felt no love for him. On our wedding night he slapped me hard across the face as punishment, then forced himself on me from behind before I had reached the bed. I learned to shut my mouth, to close my thoughts, but it did not stop me entirely.

I had spent my years with adults from all different social standings, which helped extend my comprehension of life and its intricacies. I had a memory for things. In the castle I had picked up much about the world through conversations, and I remember a castle woman in a satin dress reading to me from books about seas that flowed to the edge of the earth, never spilling a drop beyond it. I did not fully believe what the monk had told me about my past and have thought often of what this woman was to me, whom I have not seen since I left the castle employ.

I reached for his hand, which then sat limp in my own. When he wouldn't look at me, I shook his arm without response. I shook it again, and this time he smiled shyly from under his mop of brown hair, flattened from the damp. He was sweet and tenderhearted. I threw an arm around his shoulder and kissed his head that always smelled of horse.

"I'm not worthy of someone as sweet as you, Walter. I am not the perfect person you imagine me to be."

He didn't say anything, but I saw that his frown had disappeared.

"I think you are perfect," he said awkwardly.

A sudden cramp in my belly paused my steps.

"What is wrong?"

"It's nothing," I said, continuing: "After you're finished in the stalls, come to the kitchen so I can comb the knots from your hair."

We parted on good terms, he to the barn and me to the kitchen to prepare dinner and dry and plait my hair.

That evening, as a celebration of the birth of our Lord, Zacharias treated Walter and me to a cake made of honey, raisins, and nuts baked in the castle's kitchen. I caught Walter's surprise, his jaw open wide enough in which to cram an orange. We had been invited to eat with Zacharias in the dining hall, and I cooked a goose stuffed with pork fat, apple conserve, and rye. The conversation at our dinner was about the weather, about Master's time in Rome and descriptions of other places I'd not heard of where the sun shone all year round, and about houses built into cliffs above seas that swallowed ships. He was lucid with some wine, and it was a rare glimpse into a man who was normally staid, guarded, and groomed for God's work. He asked us no questions that evening, gave a rare smile on occasion, then stood to leave.

"I am returning to the church to finish writing tonight's sermon," he said, it seemed, with some regret. "Enjoy the rest of your dinner."

And we did. With wine as well, we gorged ourselves on the cake and laughed at things we ought not find funny. We laughed at Herr Goosem's whining, the basket weaver's bug eyes, the woodman's bad breath, and even Zilla Lucke's temper, though we meant no harm to any of them. We were full of life and brazen, and the release to say anything that night was the first time I felt truly free.

I sat third seat back in the pews for midnight Mass, wedged between Walter and old Herr Pohl. He was nearing eighty years, something of a rarity in this bishopric. On the other side there was a section reserved for more notable people, those with land, those like Leon von Kleist. The prince-bishop rarely attended any village masses. He had his own churches and a private chapel, where clergy who lived in the city heard his thoughts, gave him absolution, as one would.

Walter nudged me when we saw several women who had rushed to the pews closest to the front. I felt a rise of jealousy when Zacharias smiled at their arrival. I conceded that although the women in the church had taken a little more care about their appearance, I was grateful there was something lighter about the congregation. They were polite, not bad tempered that day, and there were a lot more than usual in attendance so that some were forced to stand at the rear of the church. During Stern's tenure, many gave the excuse of sickness or disaster not to attend.

The gilded sconces that surrounded us were reflected in the darkly polished wood. Zacharias stood, head bowed slightly and still like a statue, on the pulpit surrounded by stained glass that the castle had installed there as a gift, the vibrant-coloured lights of which surrounded Zacharias's head like a halo. His skin glistened like porcelain under candle lights that hung above us. I sighed. He cleared his throat into his fist as the hum of whispered conversation faded to silence across the pews.

"Devout subjects of Würzburg, parishioners of Eisbach," he said, his arms outstretched. "I want to say thank you. With the aid of members of the bishopric, we have fought the Devil and won."

People murmured. They had never been thanked before. Some sat up a little straighter, perched on the edge of their narrow wooden benches, hanging on to his every word.

"But . . . ," he said, looking around at the faces, his eyes brushing over mine and back again so quickly one might have missed it, "one must not fall back to ways that are too comfortable. We must not be conceited, for that is what the Devil wants and when we least expect him. One must always look out for one another and establish a common goal, a unity, so that he does not try and separate us. The village has undergone hardships, loss of life, forces of nature, but we must not allow happenings to break our spirit and our oath to God. It is your spirit I trust in, your spirit that I will never forget."

There was talk at the market square that he was here only temporarily, that he was destined for greater things. Such talk bothered me. It meant that we could end up again with someone like Stern. But this thought did not dampen my elation, and not even that of the village sceptic Arnold Pohl next to me. He leaned forward, both hands on his walking stick, one ear cocked to catch all of the reverend's words as if these were the last that he would ever hear. It was "the Zacharias Engel wonder." Everybody, it seemed, wanted a piece of him, some besotted, some fearful, depending on how many sins they might have committed, but mostly grateful he had found the source of their troubles.

Though not everyone liked him. Zilla Lucke still didn't come to church, along with a handful of others.

"He is dangerous," she had said in a low voice, looking suspiciously over my shoulder into the house when she came to sell us twine and pieces of cloth. We always paid her well. She had one swine left, and I wondered what would become of her large farming lands. "Satan comes in all forms, finds clever disguises. Anyone who thinks Kleist was guilty of murder is a fool and that Zacharias Engel is an angel come to save us is a bigger fool."

It seemed the town, and especially the church, was stuffed full of fools. I did not take much notice of Zilla. As much as I liked her and believed her to be kind, she had grown more irrational in recent years. Death and misfortune had visited her too many times. Her crops were gone, her last sow had not been able to produce, and earlier this year her boar had caught a disease and died. I had no idea how she and Jon would survive the season. The money she made from cloth-making and sewing repairs was meagre, as most could ill afford such luxuries as new linen. But she wasn't the only one who suffered. Too many farms did not yield the previous year because of heavy rain, frost, and snow, and a plague had taken many lives the year before that. The village was slipping further into destitution, and everyone clung to the hope that the reverend had found the cause.

Zacharias preached further that day about hope, about trusting in God, about belief. His words and voice had a calming effect on the congregation. He managed to avoid scrutiny, something Stern was subjected to daily. In hindsight, Stern, though odious to live with, sometimes attacked dogma and leadership, and more often spoke truth. But truth is not always what the people want.

Behind me, I heard the church door creak open, then the soft footsteps of someone heading towards the front of the pews. Receiving frowns of aggravation from those who had to accommodate, the girl with the straw-coloured hair squeezed in beside people in the aisle across from me. Once seated, as if she had sensed me watching, her shining golden-brown eyes abruptly found mine, and I turned my attention back to Zacharias, annoyed that I'd been caught gaping. My master did not appear to notice her arrival, but there was a minor pause in his words before he continued.

Zacharias said that blackened days were still upon us with the weather, to wait it out. The burning had not eliminated death altogether. There was still age and sickness that had put another two in the ground. God would watch over his flock, but evil would always be amongst us, waiting. We had to be vigilant, and he was here to make sure our souls were protected. Frau Lucke would say later, when I quoted what he'd said, that he was "covering his arse" in case the bishopric had more bad luck with storms and weather and death. But we the parishioners were strangely comforted.

"We must pray for the innocent who were unjustly taken from this world. And we must pray for the safe return of Cilla Graf. She must not leave our prayers until she is found."

Harald and Kristine Graf sat with their heads bowed in prayer, a baby nestled between them.

"This Christmas, let Jesus wash us of our sins. Let him cleanse us of spite, of envy. Let any past sin be our sin, jointly, so that together we are stronger. Let us pray for absolution and resist further temptation. Let us endure these times, for God will reward the faithful."

He paused before his eyes wandered across the congregation and stopped on me briefly. A draft travelled under my seat and lifted the light wool of my skirt, as if he had sent that himself.

"We cannot always see what is right in front of us. Temptation is there in disguise."

I sneaked a look at the people along my seat ogling the priest and wondered if Zacharias was aware of his effect. They were as still as apples in a bowl, sinners trapped together, and somewhere in the middle of our collective core was the rot of disease. For a fleeting moment, I felt a sense of impending disaster before returning my focus once more on God's favoured child and pushing such thought purposefully to the back of my mind. Reverend Engel was here to make the spiritual sickness in our village go away. He was here to make my life more bearable, to relieve me of past indiscretions, to relieve others. We were in his hands, at his mercy, and I had to believe that he would summon good fortune to the village, and we would once again prosper.

When the mass was over, Master walked down the aisle, his long holy robe trailing on the floor behind him. People wanted to touch him and leaned closer into the aisle. He held out his hand, the hand that wore a red ruby ring for the service, one I'd not seen before, and people bowed. He was adored. He was our saviour. Or so we thought then.

The mysterious girl was quick to leave and disappeared into the crowd that funnelled through the large oak doors. By the time I was outside, she had vanished into softly falling snow. Built on a rise, the church sat a distance from the villagers' homes. A stretch of land separated it from the rest of the structures. I could not fathom where the girl could have got to so quickly and looked about me in the crowd again to try to find her.

"Did you see that girl?" I asked Walter.

"What girl?"

"The girl who came late," I said.

"That is the midwife," he said. "I told you about her."

Zacharias, a head above the crowd that surrounded him, waved me over.

"You go on home," I told Walter. He commenced to follow some parishioners whose torches would light the way.

Herta hesitated, as if she might stop to chatter; then, seeing Walter leave, I was instantly forgotten. Meanwhile, Zacharias was contending with invitations for dinner and requests for blessings. I thought the stragglers would never leave.

"You wanted to speak to me, Master," I said when the crowd had finally dispersed.

"Please wipe over the pews and sweep the floors while I pack up my books and papers and put away the items of offertory."

"Yes, sir," I said. I liked the task and the smell of oiled wood. The church was never more impressive than when it was empty, with its coloured glass and engraved oak panels along the sides. Only the painting of hell marred its perfection.

When we were finished working, I lit a torch, while he removed his cloak to shield the both of us on the walk home. It was as if this had always been my life, and I could see more purpose as we tramped back to the house. I wanted to cook for him, clean his shirts. I wanted to serve him for life. Even the scent of him, of fragrant oil on skin, was intoxicating this close. I would change for him. I would be better.

Once home, and despite the lateness, Zacharias called Walter into the house, and we ate the Christmas leavings together in the kitchen.

"You are good with animals, Walter."

"Walter is good with a tune also," I told Master.

"Truly?" Zacharias said with curiosity.

Walter turned red.

"Well go on then, boy!" commanded Master, who had a touch of mischief in the creases of his eyes. "Stand up and sing!"

Zacharias thought to make a fool of him in jest, but as Walter began to sing, it left the reverend spellbound. He leaned forward, elbows on his knees and the tips of his fingers together. Walter's tune had a melody that spoke to the soul, and the words about lands and kings brought a tear to my eye. Maybe it was the wine, or the warmth, or all of us there, but nothing had quite so touched me as it did in that moment.

When Walter had finished the song, Zacharias stared at the boy soberly. I thought for a moment he meant to be critical, but then he stood up and clapped, and Walter was red in the face with embarrassment. The priest had dropped his staid defence, and I had seen curiosity and awe. Just for a moment, he was someone free and light, not mysterious and sombre.

"You are wasted in the barn, Walter. You should be a performing artist with your skill."

I looked proudly at Walter, as if he were my prodigy, as if he were my own blood.

"Finish up the rest of the food!" said Zacharias. "I'll just have bread and cheese in the morning."

He was gone from the room, but he gave a backward paternal glance at each of us. The day had been a wonder, a moment in time that was not like any other.

Walter and I ate heartily and steadily like the horses at the trough and played games into the waking hours. If I could have one wish it would be to have that feeling right then, of comfort, of family that endures, captured and frozen in time.

But no moment stands still.

CHAPTER SIX

One night, in the early days of the new year, and after Walter had left for bed, I stoked the fire in the kitchen so that the warm air would drift into my bedchamber behind it. Master was out late, perhaps caught once more in the city, and I had grown bored of keeping his dinner warm, wondering if he should return at all. Inside my room I removed my clothes and sponged my body and underarms and between my legs with the same lemon-scented water I had left for Zacharias. Fleck, my mouser, climbed onto the bed to wash himself, too. I stood a moment to look at the shape of my body in a piece of glass I kept under my bed and unashamedly approved of what I saw. If I'd had means, a noble family name that brought with it a title, and with my full hips and bosom, I would have been in demand as a wife.

A shuffle in the doorway forced me to turn to learn the cause. With the house to myself, I'd not thought to close the door, and it took me seconds longer than it should have done for my hands to cover the parts of the body that men should not see.

"I'm terribly sorry," said Master, averting his gaze and pausing a moment before he walked away.

I dressed quickly, embarrassed, not just about my nakedness but more so that I'd been caught admiring myself.

The reverend raised his head as I entered the parlour, his pointer finger pressed up against some text in one of his books so as not to lose his place. I stood just inside the room, afraid to venture too close to him, not sure what I should say. I did not need to admit my sin of vanity and pride; it was clear enough by the heat I felt in my face.

"My apologies again, Frau Jaspers, for what just happened," he said. "The door was open. I had no idea."

I nodded and returned to the kitchen to warm his food. I set down his eating utensils at the dining table, glancing towards the door behind which he was seated, afraid to face him, but also thinking, remembering, that he didn't move away immediately. I felt a moment of exhilaration that put warmth inside my chest.

"Can you stop with the service a moment," he said, once more surprising me by his sudden appearance in the kitchen. "Please sit. I would like a word."

I lifted the heavy pan away from the fire, then placed myself at the cook's table and sat on my hands to keep them steady.

"If I can be so forward," he said, sitting down opposite, "I couldn't help noticing that you are damaged on your back."

"They are old scars, sir."

"They are long and vicious scars, by the looks of them. Who did this to you?" he said, his regard of me intense.

I hesitated, afraid of revealing a truth that might be perceived as a complaint.

"This is not a court, Frau Jaspers."

I opened my mouth but could not find a reasonable explanation for the scars, for there were none and many at the same time.

"Was it your husband? Did he beat you?"

"Yes, he did, sir."

"I am a confidant and a friend right now, do you understand?" he said softly. "You can speak freely. I will not judge. You will not find any recourse from anything you reveal. I shall not write this down."

He looked ethereal sitting behind a candle, his face glowing, his palms not flat on the table like in sermon but open. He was inviting me to trust him, yet by opening my heart I would be breaking a rule I had set long ago, which was never to trust anyone fully. To always keep the deepest pieces of my heart for myself. Once those pieces were given it was hard to steal them back.

"He used a scalding pan, or poker, sir. Sometimes it was a whip, but usually an iron 'cause it was heavier, if I did or said something wrong."

"What activity could possibly have earned such treatment?" he said, frowning and tilting his head.

"I did not manage to get a stain out of his shirt. One time I knocked over a waste bucket. Another time I had brought animals in from the cold and not removed them before he arrived home."

He nodded for me to continue, and I grew braver.

"Another time I would not lie with him when I felt nauseous with child, and again later after the birth; I said I did not want to lie with him so soon."

"Where is the baby?"

"Babies, sir. With the angels."

"So young and yet so uncared for," he said, not looking at me then but at the flame of the candle. "I will pray for you."

He left for the dining hall, yet it was like he was still there, his presence so large everywhere he went. I went to sleep with those large heavy-lidded blue eyes watching, and the memory of the words he spoke.

One day, a messenger came to the door asking for Master to proceed urgently to the square. He did not say what it was, only that he was to meet one of the villagers in the market. I returned to my laundry task, washing his bedding that was so clean it barely appeared slept in.

Herta came to the back door. Though she seemed a little timid that day, I assumed she was still up to no good. I could tell she had come here to tell me something, or find out something.

"I know more about the new girl."

"What girl?"

"The midwife. She is Maria's niece."

"I know that already."

She shrugged.

"Have they found out the cause of her illness yet?" I asked.

"The girl?" she asked curiously. She was not as quick-witted as some.

"No! Maria Unger. Have you heard anything further?"

"She won't last much longer because she is not eating. Her food is made liquid and fed through a glass cylinder."

"How do you know this?"

"From Margaretha Katz. That's her name."

"You've spoken to her?"

"Papa has. I was there listening. She has asked him to make a lock for her door. She also gave him a treatment for his boils."

"Is she not a midwife?"

"She is much more than a midwife; she is a healer of general ills, like Maria was," said Herta, picking at her nails nearest the window to spy Walter through the slats of the barn wall. "She makes potions."

I gave Herta a fierce look. Calling them potions could spell the end of them both.

"You mean she makes herbal medicines."

"Some say she makes magic potions, that she is homeless, that she travels from town to town. Some recognised her as working for a wealthy man in Bamberg who was put in prison for his practise of the dark arts. They say as well that the man was married, and the pair were committing acts of sin. Together."

"Who says this, Herta?" I asked, shaking my head with disbelief. The more Herta spoke of someone or something the less likely it were true.

"There is no need to be like that. I heard it for certain. Everyone is talking about her."

"Everyone?"

"Did you see her at church? She is very beautiful."

"Herta, I'm very busy today. While there is an ounce of steady weather, I have to finish the washing and run some errands for the reverend."

"Someone else who travels across the territories for trade recognised her," she continued, disregarding what I said. "He told my papa she was banished from another town in the west."

This awakened some interest, and my instinct told me there might be an element of truth in it. It would help to explain her sudden arrival. I put the woven basket of heavy washing down to listen.

"They say that the wife told the husband, a nobleman, he had to be rid of his concubine, that there was a large fight between the husband and Margaretha, and she was then forced to leave in the dead of night because so many were angry about it. The wife's father threatened to have her thrown in prison, so the nobleman had no choice other than to send his whore away."

"Herta, stop that talk! Why was she in the house with a nobleman?"

"They say that she is very clever. She knows Latin. She can read and write."

Herta had been known to exaggerate. I could tell her, say, that Master was upset with my cooking, and she would likely tell others that Master has a temper like hellfire and takes to me with his horse whip. Even so, for every rumour, I had learned there is a skeleton of truth.

"More news, too," she said, sounding pleased. "Arnold Pohl has been accused of sorcery."

"By whom?" I said, stopping what I was doing.

"Herr Goosem."

"Herr Goosem is a dolt. And a half-blind and deaf one at that. What is he saying?"

Goosem was his neighbour.

I picked up the basket and carried the sheets to the drying bench in front of the fire. Herta followed me in.

"He said that Arnold Pohl killed his goat for satanic rituals," she continued. "There has been another found dead. Pohl has been seen wandering through the town babbling."

"He is old and lonely," I said.

Herta shrugged to say she did not care either way. All the same, she should care, I thought. She might be next.

CHAPTER SEVEN

Walter had not yet swept the snow from the path to the barn nor cleared it from the back door. When I called out, he didn't respond. Peeking into the stall, I saw him sitting on the floor beside Master's horse lying on her side.

"Did you not hear me call?" I scolded him. "Why did you not respond?"

"Master's horse is very sick. She will not eat or drink, and she will not stand up. She can't tell me what's wrong."

"Why didn't you come to me sooner?"

"Master will be angry if he finds out."

"He will not beat you, if that's what you think. Come into the warmth and I will let Reverend Engel know."

"I can't leave her . . . She doesn't want me to."

I shook my head. I liked my cat, Fleck, but Walter had an unnatural attachment to all animals. Once when I had left a trap out for vermin, I caught him closing it up.

I had learned that attachments were temporary, that animals came and went quickly. I had a dog once, which I had grown very fond of, but my husband kicked him out in a snowstorm, and I never found him after. Walter had spent so much time sleeping in stables and barns with animals that it was inevitable he would find friendship there. They were more predictable than the humans he had lived with.

I delivered the news about the horse to Zacharias when he emerged from his room. It took him a moment to respond, his mind on other things. He was clearly eager to be somewhere else, dressed and carrying a bundle of papers. Several days had passed since he had seen my naked form, and I assumed by now he had forgotten the incident.

"What is wrong with her?" he said.

"I'm not sure, sir. Despite Walter's gentle care of her, she can no longer stand."

"You must see if the blacksmith can help. He may know something about these conditions."

"Yes, sir."

He nodded to the boy, then left immediately. I could see that Walter's hand still trembled, frightened that he might be to blame. People could turn. Of that much we both knew. What had happened to the boy was worse than what happened to me at times at the hands of people who owned us.

I rushed down to Herta, who told me that her father was busy in the next village and would not be home that night nor the next.

"He's not the time to nurse another horse," said Herta. "You should try Frau Katz. She might know what to give it."

Walter hastened to fetch the midwife.

"Do not enter the house, Walter!" I called after him, with a feeling of dread about what lay within her walls.

I waited by the window to watch for Walter's return, and out of a cloud that rose from the track Margaretha emerged with him. She was a little taller than him and smaller than me. I drew back from the window as she came closer, and the pair walked straight to the stalls inside the barn.

A short time later, Walter came to collect me.

"What is she doing?" I asked.

"She has been examining the feed and the mare's excrement. She wants to meet you and says to bring a cloth and a bowl."

With the items I followed Walter into the barn. Inside, Margaretha was kneeling beside the horse. I could see only the back of her head and her slender hands gently stroking the horse's flank, the mare nickering in response.

Margaretha stood up to face me.

My past glimpses of her had not fully shown how beautiful she was, skin unblemished and a light shade of gold.

"Good day," she said in a soft, gravelled tone. "My name is Margaretha. And you are Katarin."

"Yes," I said.

"I have heard much about you," she said. *By whom,* I wondered with some trepidation. Was Maria now lucid enough to speak? Had Herta told one of her many lies? I assumed it was most likely Zacharias. It was on the tip of my tongue to tell her that I'd heard things about her, too.

"The bowl and cloth, please."

I passed them to her.

"What is wrong with her?" I asked.

"Something has made her feverous. The weather, something she has eaten, or from another animal. It is hard to tell where it came from just yet."

"Can you help her?"

"I will do what I can."

We stood a moment, the three of us uncomfortable without words.

"Will you leave me, please," she said, bending down once more to attend to the horse. "What I do may distress you."

Walter hesitated.

"Are your methods proven?" I asked.

She stood up to face me again.

"You do not trust me."

"I don't know you."

"I practise the same as Tante Maria did."

91

I remembered that Maria gave medicine to Zilla's pigs to stop their worms.

"Very well," I said.

I put my arm around Walter to lead him outside, and to spy through the slats of the barn. I squeezed him tighter when his teeth started to chatter.

Margaretha pressed her hands down firmly on the horse's abdomen. The horse whinnied once, then grew still. Margaretha took a bottle from her bag and tipped the contents into the side of the horse's mouth. She spoke to the horse as Walter did, murmuring in her ear, the words unclear. She then made a cut in the mare's belly, a small one, and placed a bowl underneath to catch the drips of blood.

Walter gasped, and I put my hand over his mouth to stop him from crying out. He had not witnessed bloodletting before. It was not uncommon. I'd heard of the practice being used many times when I lived at the castle, and once when my husband got a fever, Maria had performed this on him also.

Margaretha then put drops from another bottle into the blood and studied it a moment.

Next, she dabbed a cloth to the wound before taking a needle and thread and sewing it up.

When she stood up, we both scurried into the kitchen.

She entered moments later.

"The mare needs this once a day," she said, handing Walter a small blue bottle and to me the bowl wiped of blood. "She has a bad stomach and needs better hay. It may be wise to destroy what you have in the stalls and sweep the floor of any remnants that might be contaminated by mould or rat faeces . . . As far as administering the medicine, I don't need to tell you what to do. You have already seen."

Walter looked down at the floor guiltily, while I held her gaze.

"Only four drops on her tongue," she said. "A better diet and the drops and she will likely recover in a week, maybe two."

"Thank you," I said, and she made no motion to move.

"I do not do this for free."

I grabbed a fistful of coins from a jar hidden in the kitchen and returned to count three small silvers into her outstretched hand. She examined them closely.

"It is not enough," she said.

I placed another two, which was more than we had paid Maria Unger for any service.

She nodded and stowed them away in her skirt pocket.

"She is beautiful, no?" I asked Walter when she had left.

He shrugged indifferently, his mind still with the mare and other concerns.

"What if she dies?" he said. "It will be my fault."

I grabbed his shoulders gently to look directly in his eyes.

"Master Engel is not like others," I said to reassure him. "He will understand. Horses die all the time. People die. It is sometimes unavoidable."

Zacharias arrived home from his engagements looking harried while Walter went to source new horse feed. I told him about his horse's treatment, and he did not flinch about the cost but gave me more coins for the jar. He left then in a hurry.

"They have found something in the forest!" Walter said upon his return, pulling my arm to follow him. "I just passed Herr Reverend heading to the square with Margaretha."

We ran from the house all the way, and I was out of breath and feeling nauseous by the time we reached the crowd of people gathered, too dense for us to see what it was that held their interest.

"What have they found?" I asked a villager making his way back from the front of the group.

"A child! A dead one."

I felt light-headed.

"Have they found her?" shouted Kristine Graf, Cilla's mother, who had just entered the square. Still in her nightgown, she burrowed through the bodies. "Let me through!"

A moment later, Kristine shrieked at whatever she saw and fainted, and several people carried her out. Harald Graf arrived just afterwards, his face crimson with excitement, nudging people out of the way to learn of the victim.

"It's not her!" he shouted gruffly, pushing back through the crowd. "Not our Cilla."

He went to his wife and lifted her tenderly away from helpers.

"It is a boy not three years old they think," said one of the villagers.

"He didn't come from here," said another man pushing his way out from the swarm. "It's hideous, whatever it is. A creature covered in red markings."

I swallowed back bile. I did not want to see what had been described and promptly departed.

Master returned home sometime later, his face paler than snow. I followed him upstairs to his room.

"Are you all right, sir?" I said from the doorway.

"There has been another child found in the forest," he said, hands on his hips and talking to the window. "He had been buried in a shallow grave. The hunters' dogs found him."

He turned to me suddenly.

"Come in, sit down," he said. "No one in the crowd recognised him, but I feel that Maria Unger would have known, since she has helped deliver most of the babies in this village. Do you know of anyone with a male child who has gone missing in the past?"

"No, sir," I said, perched on a chair, "and if Maria knew about him, she never said a word about it to me."

He thought deeply a moment.

"I feel that someone must know something."

I nodded in agreement.

"I would like you to come with me in the morning to see the body that is currently at the church. Perhaps you will recognise him. It is possible he was not born with the markings, an affliction that came later. No one at the village spoke up for the boy. Regardless, it is clear that the child has been murdered."

I felt my chest tighten.

"Murdered, sir?"

"It is possible the child was strangled senseless first before his neck was cut. It would have been a painful way to die. He was not buried deeply. The falls of snow protected him for a while until the hunters dug him out."

"Perhaps there is someone else . . ."

I did not want to see the child.

"I trust you more than anyone," he said in earnest.

—◆—

The next morning before the village came to life, I walked with Zacharias to the church. We were alone in there, and at the same time we weren't. There was a body on the altar with a holy cloth covering it. Around the dead child several candles had been lit. The picture of Mary and doves and crosses decorated the glass window above him, and off to the side, where I refused to look, was the long painting of hell. Zacharias walked ahead to the table while I remained frozen by fear partway down the aisle.

"Come!" he said, impatiently.

I took a deep breath and moved towards the body. I could feel the hellish gawp from those in the painting beside me.

He pulled back the cover and I saw the boy. He had a bluish hue to his face, his hands clenched tightly, thick straight hair that had grown long and unkempt prior to his murder. His neck was purple and swollen, with a deep score that stretched from one side to the other. The most obvious difference that Zacharias had alluded to was his markings. A wide red-brown smear extended from his forehead—on a head that was deformedly large—across his left eye and down to the base of his neck, disappearing under the collar of his filthy shirt. It was hideous to look at, yet I could not look away. I felt suddenly ill and put the back of my hand to my mouth.

Zacharias reached his arm behind me as if to catch me, for I did not think my legs would hold me much longer, overcome by the horror of it. I had lost my tongue and wished to be gone from the church and the "creature," as the people had begun calling it in the square. I pulled away from Zacharias's hold to run down the aisle. I pushed open the front door, then ran several yards further to retch in the snow.

Zacharias followed and placed his large hand on the centre of my back.

"I will take you home again."

I was unsteady on my feet, his arm then wrapped around me for support.

"I'm sorry I put you through that. Have you ever seen this boy before?"

"No. I never saw him and such marks of the Devil."

"A mark of the Devil, or maybe just a defect," he countered.

His response surprised me. I imagined a man of his experience would have offered the first.

"The mother who had this child would be tainted, sir, whether she has done any wrong or not. It is enough to condemn her whoever she may be."

"That is true, Frau Jaspers. Nevertheless, the child is nothing more than an unfortunate consequence of our times. Sick children are born daily. I will request that the castle physician examine the boy. He has been well preserved in the snow. It is abhorrent that he died by such violence."

I did not see the point. I already knew that no one would claim such an abomination.

"He was not buried deeply, the ground possibly too hard. It is difficult to know how long ago he was placed there, and it is a miracle that wild animals didn't find him first."

I did not see this as a miracle, such a creature found. Even the animals, I thought, had avoided him.

"Could moving the child curse the village?" I asked with a burst of courage. "Do you not think it should have been left there?"

"It is a child, Katarin," he chided. "It is just a shell of a child. And if by some misfortune this small boy was used by the Devil, his soul at least is freed and no worse can come to him in this sacred house and the soil of the Eisbach church he'll be buried in. He will stay in here till then."

I did not think it wise to bury the child in the graveyard, though I had no authority to speak on church matters. I was fearful that even burying it would not be the end of it. That it would somehow reappear again. Hunters were superstitious, and it was doubtful they would return to that area of forest.

Back at the clergy house I prepared Master a pack of bread, cheese, and ham while Walter connected the cart to Stern's old horse. It was not until Master left for the castle to discuss the marked boy and other cases that I wondered for what purpose he took the cart, which would come back empty.

CHAPTER EIGHT

The stench of thick woodsmoke in the kitchen forced me outside at midday. I stood a moment in the cold to breathe in fresh, still air and listen to the mournful calls of a calf for its mother outside a byre. The hills that sat ahead of the forests seemed shrouded in purple from some trick of the light, and wisps of fine mist hovered low over rooves. In the barn, Walter had already left to find more wood to burn. Master's horse was standing now but with legs that were still unsure. I did not want to admit aloud that Margaretha may have saved her life. It did not mean the midwife was trustworthy. I had my doubts.

I could not stop to rest. There were tasks to be done. After the gift of food from the castle had been consumed, the villagers were back to searching for ways to feed their families. On the way to the market, I saw Ursula Döhler, the mother of the murdered baby, crouched down on the ground, her basket on its side and empty. She had her arms over her head while several children were busy collecting the contents from her fallen basket. When I approached, they scattered into the crowd nearby, plunder in their arms.

"Are you feeling unwell, Ursula?"

She raised her head, her eyes half-closed as if she had been sleeping. Her dress was covered in stains and her hair was pinned untidily at the back of her head. She did not respond at first.

"Where is Oma Jutta?" I asked, unused to seeing Ursula with this task.

"She has sent me to buy things. She says she is poorly today."

She then jumped up, realising her basket was empty.

"Everything is taken!" she wept. "Those little terrors! Jutta will beat me. She rarely lets me go on my own. She will never trust me again."

I put my arm around her and took her to rest on a stone fence nearby. I could feel that she was just a bag of bones. She wiped the snot from her nose with the back of her hand, leaving further streaks of grime across her face. She had not been the same since her baby died. I noticed that her belly was rounded and larger than it had been the last time I was this close to her.

"I don't know what will happen. Jutta is always angry. She beats the children, and now I am sick with another. I am sick all the time."

"Ursula, is it the baby that is making you unwell?"

She nodded. "If Maria was here, she would give me medicine but without Jutta knowing. She calls it Devil's poison."

She stood up suddenly.

"I need to get home," she said, "but I have nothing to bring."

I drew two coins from the pocket at the front of my kirtle and handed these to her.

"Buy what you came for and then go home to rest," I told her.

"I can never rest with the children," she said, taking the money quickly before slinking away.

At the market people sold their wares, shoes their children had outgrown, strips of leather, tools, and pans; as well, fare such as roasted nuts, boiled raspberry preserve, nettle roots, and onion pies made with thin pastry. There were no hunters with their kills that day, their offerings growing more infrequent. In servitude I did not receive a wage as such other than a few coins thrown my way. But I did have some money hidden. When my husband would send me to market, I would purchase a slightly smaller portion of meat and use thickeners to make the stews last longer and keep whatever was left. Only once did Herr Jaspers notice the food was bland, and I complained about the leanness of the vendor's meat that day. Fortunately, he'd been drinking and did not make further grumble, which he was prone to do, to examine everything I did and find fault.

That day, I bought chestnuts for the children who had been sent out by their parents to beg. Another boy nearby with a sweet but muddied face, with months of grit under his fingernails, sat on the cold ground and shovelled a whole piece of pie into his mouth.

"Is that food you should be taking home?" I asked, hands on hips, knowing there were plenty of mouths to feed in his household.

He didn't answer, lowering his eyes sheepishly. I tilted my head to view the sky and saw it darken momentarily, a large cloud just above us, and when I looked once more ahead, the boy had disappeared into the small crowd. I did not need to purchase anything, for the larder was currently full, but I purchased a spoon, anything from people who were desperate for coin. As I pocketed the item and moved to leave, I saw a figure on the first hill near the village. I recognised the child with the pie and suspected he was prolonging the time before his lashing that he would no doubt receive once home. My curiosity got the better of me and I began to follow. Moments later, another figure appeared on the track ahead of me.

The girl pulled back her scarf to rearrange it around her head, strands of flaxen hair escaping to catch the wind. I followed their trail in the snow, the heeled shoes of Margaretha and the tiny imprints of the child. We were both, it seemed, following the boy, and I hoped my crunching steps were masked by the sounds of her own, for I was curious to learn her intent. I lost sight of the boy beyond the next hill towards the forest. One time she turned her head to the side as if she had heard me, before entering the forest where I suspected he had gone also.

I stopped to catch my breath, the bottom of my skirt and boots soaked through. In front of me was the entry to the forest, a fearful place that kept the secrets of the dead, where wolves would catch their meagre winter prey. But curiosity about the child and Margaretha was greater than any fear that day.

Twenty yards deep in the forest I caught a final glimpse of Margaretha, who had removed her dark-green headscarf. All trace of her then vanished between the barren trees, and I could not find the trails of either. I stopped to listen for sounds while ice crusts formed on my lashes and my fingers became numb. The cold had clawed its way inside my clothes. That I might die, another tragedy of Eisbach, another unexplained death, seemed good-enough reason to leave until I heard a faint cry, unable to discern if it was human or animal.

A heavy drop of rain hit my face, and a dark cloud swirled above the trees. Several more drops fell quickly after that as my feet disappeared in a mist that snaked its way through the forest.

"Boy!" I called through clenched teeth to stop the air from burning my throat. "Margaretha!"

The cry of a rook circling above me was my only response. Travellers often spoke of bodies in the snow, of people who had rested too long, and long enough to freeze, eyes plucked and flesh in ribbons from hungry birds. *Not today,* I warned my feathered foe.

The wail of a child closer by and a memory of Zacharias fuelled my courage to persevere. I made pace, venturing deeper, when behind me came the sound of running steps to stop me dead. As I turned towards it, sharp teeth and fur filling my thoughts, a smaller bird burst out from the misty forest floor. I jumped back with fright, heart thumping against my chest, before tripping and landing heavily on a fallen branch. Where my sleeve was torn, I felt my arm was sticky with blood and a scent for the predator I pictured.

The rain grew heavier, weighing me down, and I sat a moment wondering what madness it was to come here. Then a miracle came moments later. Not far from where I had fallen, a patch of fog cleared to reveal the boy curled sideways on the ground. I crawled towards him and laid my ear against his chest to hear his feeble heartbeat.

I picked him up, placed his head on my shoulder, and listened for sounds to lead me out of the forest, the rain making this task near impossible. Twice I changed direction and despaired until the tolling of a church bell in the distance gave me guidance.

My legs felt like those of a newborn foal, wobbling unsurely from the exhaustion and the weight of the boy and the heavy rain. The world around me began to dim and I collapsed with the child in my arms. It was blessed relief to lie down. I closed my eyes.

"Kat! Katarin! Get up!" someone was calling to me. I lifted my head to find no one there but a deer that stood only yards away. The sound of a hammer on iron told me I was close to the edge of the forest and startled the deer to run. I stood on jellied legs, raising the child to place his head once more on my shoulder. He coughed, his small body shuddering, and I wrapped my arms tightly around him. He grew heavier with each step as we reached the open sky. Now at least I could sight the houses beyond the hill.

Nearing the village a small crowd rushed towards me, the mother also reaching for her boy.

I don't remember anything else that day. I slipped gratefully into darkness.

⟨⟩

Herta told me the rest when I had recovered from a brief illness days later. She said that Zacharias Engel seemed to have materialised out of nowhere and stepped forward to scoop me up in his arms. He had carried me home, Herta following, and taken me to the spare room beside his. Herta had removed my damp clothes down to my shift while Master went for blankets and to order Walter to put wood in the fireplace. Herta said I spoke things that made no sense, that I had a fever.

"You spoke of cats," she said. I hoped that was all.

"Fleck? Where is he?" I sat up to see him perched and watching from the bottom of the upstairs guest-room bed, a room with a window that I'd never had before. Even at my husband's house I had slept in the dimmest corner where he would frequent when drunk.

"And of Margaretha," Herta said.

"What about her?"

"You spoke her name, and she came to see you and put drops on your tongue."

"What drops?"

"Medicine for the chill you caught. Then you shouted for her to leave."

Even feverish I was suspicious.

"I don't blame you," said Herta beside me on the bed, and Fleck had moved to curl up on my lap. "She watched Zacharias carry you."

"Margaretha?" I asked. "What do you mean?"

"In the village when Reverend Engel was carrying you. She looked as if she would eat you up for supper. Green-eyed she was."

Herta loved the drama.

"She was there in the village when I returned?" I asked.

"Yes. Why?"

I shook my head. "It doesn't matter."

"You are quite the talk of the village. Zacharias has gone to check on the child's welfare. Apparently, the boy is well, and the family received a parcel of food from your kitchen."

My head still hurt. I was not sure why I had collapsed, if it had only been the cold. All I knew was the fear I felt in the forest was very real. Many had been avoiding the forests, even for wood, since the creature had been discovered.

Walter entered the room with a steaming bowl of broth, and Herta's attention was suddenly diverted.

"You should stack the hearths," I told him.

"I've already done it," said Walter.

"What about supper?"

"I have taken care of that, too."

I stared in disbelief.

"Don't look like that," he said. "I've been watching you long enough to know what to do."

I took several mouthfuls of broth before my eyelids began to close. Fleck followed Herta and Walter when they left, and I drifted off to sleep. Sometime late in the night, I woke to a candle burning low at my bedside, the room warm with glowing embers, and Zacharias seated beside me on the bed.

"How are you feeling?" he asked.

I pushed myself up to sit against the wall, my hair free and long around my shoulders.

"Much better," I said.

I felt my cheeks burning at the vision of him carrying me through the village and modestly drew up the bedding to cover my thin garment.

"The mother of the boy is very grateful," he said.

"Is the boy recovered?"

"Yes, he is as fit and as strong as a bull, his mother says. Loud apparently, the little rogue causing havoc once more. He told his mother he went looking for burrows to find a rabbit for dinner but got lost. How did you come to be in the forest? I thought you were too afraid."

"I overcame my fear when I saw him wander off from the market." I neglected to mention Margaretha's appearance. I was still unsure if that part was real. "Then I heard the boy crying and I followed the sound."

"If not for you the child would have died. It was perhaps the fate of the other child missing, Cilla. Wandering too far from home and buried now under a fall of snow. But it grieves me that the murders of the other children remain unsolved."

"Are they not all linked to Leon von Kleist in some way?" I asked, remembering the words spoken by Frederik Förner at the execution. "Many believe he was the cause of all the deaths."

"The man confessed to being in league with the Devil, the death of his family, and of ritual magic. That was all the commissioner required."

"But the doll . . ."

"I admit the doll, sometimes associated with ritual magic, is odd and appears to link Leon with Lottie's murder. However, my instinct tells me that he had nothing to do with placing it there in his house. Still, I believe the object is connected to the other murders in some way. Something tells me that the killer or killers of those three children still walk free. But you must not speak of it. People are already becoming fearful again after the boy with strange markings was found."

Some of the broth I had consumed earlier rose to leave a sour taste in my mouth.

"I should be helping Walter," I said.

"No, you must not get up," he said, his hand still next to mine. "Herta has volunteered to work in the kitchen this evening."

"What of this boy?" I asked tentatively. "Did you learn anything about him?"

"I have visited other villages and no one has reported him as missing. He will now be buried . . . Instinct tells me this murder was perpetrated in isolation, unrelated to any other."

He raised one eyebrow questioningly, as if I had something to say about it. I swallowed, ran my tongue over cracked lips.

"Sir, Margaretha Katz was in the forest at the same time," I said quickly.

"The midwife?"

I nodded.

He stared at me a moment, and I wished I could read his thoughts, for his eyes gave nothing away, not even curiosity.

"You could be mistaken. She was already at the village when you arrived."

Could I have imagined her? She weighed heavily on my mind.

"I will question her about this," said Zacharias, "but ask that you do not mention it to anyone. The fires of enthusiasm for accusations are already well lit without adding more kindling. Anyone accused must remain innocent until proven otherwise and done through proper legal means, not from marketplace gossip . . . You must sleep now and get better."

I placed my head on the pillow and watched him leave. He turned as his hand reached the door latch, as if there was something else he wanted to say. Then he was gone.

In the early hours of the morning, while it was still dark, Fleck's scratching outside the spare room door woke me. I rose, removed the sheets to wash, and stepped quietly past Master's silent room. Downstairs, I let the cat out the back door, then lit the candles, prepared ingredients for Master's breakfast, and placed the pot on the grate for boil. I ironed my old kirtle near the fire, and returned to my own bedroom to wash and dress, and plait and pin my hair.

Back in the kitchen, I was comforted by the noises of morning that I'd not put my mind to before: the flutter of a bird nesting on a joist, the scraping sounds of houses being dug out from thick layers of snow, and the murmurs of Walter in the barn speaking to the animals. I had an image of Zacharias carrying me in his arms, and I smiled to myself.

"You look smug," said Walter, opening the back door as Fleck rushed inside to beat him. He held up a dead mouse by its tail, looking accusingly at Fleck.

"You are a good boy," I said to my furry companion, who squinted with satisfaction and licked his paw.

Walter threw the mouse across the yard for the crows, and Margaretha entered my thoughts again to cloud the good ones.

"I knew you were lost in the forest."

"How?" I said, amused.

"The animals told me."

He was an odd little boy with a huge imagination.

"Walter, don't talk like that anymore."

"Like what?" he said, puzzled.

I shook my head. "Doesn't matter."

"So how was cooking with Herta?" I asked.

"Awful! She does not stop talking about herself. But she told me something, Kat, that you should know."

"What?"

"There are many people who talk about you and me here in the house as if we are privileged. They say I am strange."

"Ignore them!" I said. "They are jealous that we are with Reverend Engel . . . They can't see how hard we work. And they don't want to see because it suits them to be angry at someone."

Walter appeared glum as he watched me knead the dough again, then shape it, sprinkle it with flour, and place it on the metal grate above the fire.

"If Herta or anyone says it again, Walter, remind them we have no family, no one to take us in should things turn sour. We are not free like them. And who knows what tomorrow will bring?"

I dusted his face with my floury hands to distract him from his melancholy.

Later, when my chores were done, I stepped outside. The sound of hushed voices led me to the side of the barn, where I found Walter and Jon. Jon's dog sat faithfully at her owner's feet while he scratched the animal behind the ears. Jon was backward and forgetful, but he would not hurt a fly. And though his mother was quarrelsome, she would do anything to protect her son.

"What did Jon want?" I asked Walter when he'd gone.

"He said that the prince-bishop's men took him to the church to speak with Reverend Engel," Walter said anxiously.

"What about?" I could not think why anyone would want to ask Jon anything.

"They asked about his mother."

"Zilla? Why?"

"They asked about Jon's stomach aches, but he can't remember much else about it."

I shrugged in a careless manner, attempting to put Walter at ease.

"It is probably nothing to be concerned about," I said, sensing otherwise. These men were not the kind for casual conversation; there was usually motive.

EXCERPT

THE WITCH HUNTS—FÖRNER

I was instructed to collect Jon Lucke, son of Zilla Lucke, from the market-place, where he often came to sit, and bring him to the church in Eisbach. What was thought to be an easy enough task, by two lawmen and myself, turned into physically restraining the resisting boy and packing a cloth into his mouth. By the time we reached the church of St. Augustine, where from Engel would conduct an interview, he was in a state of hysteria.

The two sisters, Maude and Claudine Meyer, and their mother, Ingrid, neighbours of Jon and Zilla Lucke, had prior come to the city to make direct claims that Zilla's son had been given a concoction of ale, blood, and poisonous plants, and they were convinced that it was a witch's brew. According to their statements, Jon Lucke had appeared frightened of his mother at times, and terrified of attending church. Zilla had told her son that the place of worship was really the house of the Devil. He was often found by his neighbours curled up in a ball on the floor and covering his ears with his hands as if he was drowning out commands from something or someone.

The person accused of giving him the concoction was his mother, Frau Lucke, a widow, whose husband, warrior and nobleman, had served and died six years earlier fighting for the Catholic League against Protestantism in Bohemia. Zilla had not been seen at church since the news of her spouse's death reached her a year after his demise, and many parishioners described her demeanour as "surly and rude." Zilla had not employed anyone aside from her son to tend the homestead that had fallen into disrepair over many years. Zilla's age and the changes in weather had worked against her, her joints and other ailments past the point of repairing themselves.

Maude, the older of the two sisters, said that she had witnessed Zilla running naked into the forest one night and sighted a goat by her side. Maude had followed Frau Lucke and seen her dancing erotically with beasts around a fire.

Ingrid said that Maude in particular had taken Jon under her wing, and she was especially concerned about the man-child's welfare. She had not spoken much to Jon herself at any time, learning all the information from her daughters. According to the girls, Zilla Lucke had poisoned her son to keep him from speaking with them and revealing anything further about her practices. In her statement, Maude advised that Jon had told her that his mother had conversed with a goat and he had heard the goat speak.

Consulting with the prince-bishop and myself in the days following the statement, Engel agreed that if proven to be true, such behaviour was appalling and went against God and the law, and that it was important to obtain further evidence from Jon. During my brief enquiries prior to the interview, I had learned that Zilla had also been seen arguing with a woman at the market the day before the woman suffered a miscarriage, and several people had witnessed this event. Other witnesses advised that the former pig farmer behaved erratically, sometimes spitting at people who stood in her way. The damning statements by the Meyer women were only brought to my attention first in this instance, as they had been unable to locate the priest at the time. I would learn in time that he had a pattern of disappearing for long periods, his whereabouts unknown.

Engel sat alongside Jon in one of the church pews. Jon's shoulders were slumped, and although he was now sitting straighter and not curled sideways on the seat, he still held his hands over his ears. He had been crying uncontrollably since being dragged there. The lawmen sat at the rear of the church in the shadows while I sat at the end of a bench behind Engel to record the interview. Facing my direction, Jon was aware of me, too, though he tried hard not to look my way. He had experienced both my iron will and fist and wanted none more. Engel went behind the altar and returned with a cup of holy wine, an odd if not unorthodox thing to do. After much coaxing and followed by sips of wine, Jon grew calmer.

Jon, according to church records, was twenty-five years old except had a cognitive age of roughly eight years or younger owing to damage to his head from a fall while mending a roof as a boy. He had no skill of pen, and his vocabulary was limited. He had fair hair, a round face, hazel eyes that always held an unformulated question, and a freckled complexion. He wore a shirt in fabric coarsely spun but which was stitched with an even hand. Jon's feet were bare and the hem of his trousers edged in filth, consistent with travel along the thick reeds and slush beside the river and the sty he tended. He acknowledged that it was his mother who instructed his dress. Without her, he did not remember his shoes and other items vital to his keeping.

Due to a failed farm and a lack of income it had prior generated, Frau Lucke now sold pieces of linen and stitched the clothes of several farmers and widowers for a fee. She owned one old sow, which was no longer fit for breeding. Frau Lucke was known to hunt rabbits at night-time and break their necks with her hands, an occupation that she had done for many years.

"She often used unholy language and outbursts of anger," said one female witness, of which such characteristics, as instructed by the prince-bishop, were to be included as evidence. The prince-bishop had reminded Engel that historical information about any of those accused factored as clues to behaviours; as such, these were used to determine the weak wills of those more likely tempted by supernatural forces. Frau Lucke had been accused of behaviours deemed as witchcraft by several villagers.

Of low intellect, Jon would have had limited understanding of the purpose of Engel's questioning and any consequence thereof.

"I'm a godly boy," he had whimpered firstly. I could tell that Jon's declaration was rehearsed, in the event that an interrogation should take place. It was clear from what the Meyers had revealed that the boy did not believe the same godly description applied to his mother.

The Meyers were of lesser means than the Luckes, owing to the fact they lost their crops to frost and farming animals to disease long before the rest of the village. They believed now that these events were a result of sorcery, which pointed firmly at Frau Lucke.

Engel appeared to proceed with the interview cautiously, without any sense of urgency, first telling the boy in a soothing voice about his sick horse, distracting him from what had just passed.

"Jon, I did not see you and your mother in church. Are you both well?" prompted Engel finally.

I could see why he chose a question that Jon would likely find innocuous.

"Yes."

"That is good to hear. Do you and your mother like coming to church? It is beautiful in here, is it not?"

Jon looked around and fixated on a dove in the stained-glass window.

"Jon?"

The boy turned his attention back to his lap.

"Mama said that it does not do well for us. That God can visit us in the house instead if he wants to. God stopped visiting the church, she said, when it killed Boris."

"Your father?"

Jon nodded.

"Is that something you agree with?"

He appeared confused, as if he had forgotten his answer just given. He scratched at the back of his hand, and Engel sought to distract him with another question.

"Do you have a friend whom you trust, whom you tell things to?"

"Maude."

Jon liked her, as was clear from the way he stopped scratching, his interest aroused.

"Do you have many visitors at your home?"

He shook his head.

"Mama does not like visitors, so Maude comes when Mama isn't there."

"Where does your mother go when she leaves home?"

"Sometimes into town. She tells me it is an errand, but Maude said—"

"Try to tell me in your words where you think your mother goes."

His eyes combed back and forth across the floor before he answered.

"To deliver clothes, to purchase the grain, to see if there are scraps of meat left at the market that she can buy cheaply."

"Is this what she tells you or something you've seen?"

"Sometimes she takes me with her and sometimes she doesn't."

"Jon, do you know Cilla Graf?"

"Yes."

"Can you remember the last time you saw her?"

He shook his head.

"Did you ever see your mother with the girl?"

"She's pretty."

"Did you ever see your mother with her?"

He shook his head again, and Zacharias paused his questioning a moment while the boy took time to stare curiously at the statue of Jesus.

"I want you to tell me what you told Maude."

"Is she here?" Jon asked.

"No, she isn't . . . Tell me, Jon, as if it is the first time you've ever told anyone. Tell me what has occurred that has given rise to your recent thoughts about your mother."

He seemed very alert at this point, expecting the young girl, Maude, to walk in, and I noticed that his demeanour had improved at the thought of such contact.

"Has your mother done anything to cause you concern?"

It appeared he was thinking hard, before he fixed on a point above the priest's shoulder.

"I came home at dusk. Mama had asked me to go to the forest to dig in the ground and find some roots of nightshade. It was hard. It took me a long time to find them because of the snow."

"Did she tell you what they were for?"

"I was poorly, my stomach was sore, my heart ached."

"What did she do with the roots?"

"She ground them and added some blood."

"Blood from where?"

"She said it had to be fresh blood."

"What kind of fresh blood?"

He looked confusedly from side to side.

"It's all right, Jon. Only good things come from truth. God will protect you. You are safe here."

"From rabbits, she told me. For my strength."

"And did you drink this?"

"I drank it, and it made me feel sick for a while, and in the morning I felt better. But during the night, I heard things. I heard Mama talking to someone, and when I went to check it was a goat she was whispering to, and the goat said something back."

He choked back a sob.

"Where did the goat come from?"

"I don't know."

A number of people in the village owned such beasts, and none had been reported as missing. Jon emitted a strange whining sound then scratched his head.

"Hush now, boy," said Engel. "Did you hear the conversation?"

He frowned and thought for several moments before he stopped thinking at all, and he was once more distracted by other things in the room. He turned to look at the picture of hell and began to rock himself and hum.

"Did you hear what the animal said to your mother?"

He indicated he had not, which did not align with Maude's version. He continued humming.

"Stop that!" said Zacharias, a little firmer, putting his hand on the boy's leg to steady him.

"You told Maude something different, did you not?"

"I need some water."

"Did you not?" Zacharias repeated, frustration in his tone.

"I can't remember."

Jon looked towards the back of the church fearfully.

"Did the goat instruct your mother to harm you and the villagers?"

He closed his eyes and muttered to himself.

"Is this true?"

"I think so," he said and whimpered. "I have not seen it again. It did not come back."

"Were you lying about the goat, Jon?"

"No!" he said, suddenly still.

Engel pulled his hand away. I took from this transaction that the boy it seemed had been trying to protect his mother, walking back his words. Ultimately, his conscience told him otherwise.

The priest put his hand on the crown of the boy's head and asked God to watch over him, to protect him from evil.

"I have to go home to Mama," Jon said. "She needs my help with the fire. Her hands don't work as well, she said."

Engel nodded and blinked quickly, and something akin to regret flashed across his face. I could see the priest pondering the small boy trapped inside the body of a man, where he would remain for the rest of his life, and I could not tell whether he was pleased with this confession or not.

All of a sudden, Jon raised his head to gape at the priest in a moment of lucidness, perhaps an understanding of what he had just done. Tears began to stream, for his words could not be unspoken. Jon took off like a startled deer to leave, and I put my foot out to stop him before he reached the church door.

"Not a word to your mother," I warned. Though it would be unlikely the boy would remember much of what was said. He looked fearfully my way before rushing to leave, the door to the church slamming back against the wall as he passed through. His Excellency's men left also.

Engel stood at the doorway to watch them go as I closed my notebook and moved to stand beside him.

"What will become of Jon now?" he said, still looking in the direction the boy had taken.

"It is not something you need to think about," I said. "It is Zilla Lucke you must focus on first."

He turned to study me, and I suspected he thought less of me than the day before and that I had likely worn some disdain of my own. The differences between us were widening.

"There are things I need to finish now," he said as he stepped away. "Have a good day, Commissioner."

He walked down the hill and paused halfway to view the village below as the wind whipped about his robe.

In the distance a bell tolled faintly, and the putrid smell from the skinners blew in on a breeze. I thought of his question about the boy, and something moved in my chest. I had lost people before, I had regret.

I clenched my fists to strengthen my resolve. My position did not allow for pity.

CHAPTER NINE

"Cilla Graf was found behind the church," said a messenger, teeth chattering from the cold, between the small gap of the open door. "She is with her parents now, and they have asked that Reverend Engel come."

I was loath to open it wider. Outside, the wind blew sideways, howling like an angry beast and ready to inflict damage on anything or anyone that stood in its path. By the afternoon another roof would be gone, and several shutters splintered, and a villager would freeze to death without enough turf or wood to burn. Our house shook from the force that had so far resisted all of nature's assaults.

Zacharias, upon hearing the girl's name from the landing, had rushed downstairs. He was not yet fully dressed, holding most of his clothes in one hand, his long mane tousled and free. He wore only his stockings and night shirt, which was open to expose the skin on his chest. My eyes were drawn to a scar on his breastbone.

"What news?" he asked the boy as he pulled the door open to allow him entry. I pushed with some force to shut the door behind him as the messenger was led into the parlour. "Katarin, bring him some warm milk."

I rushed to the kitchen, eager to return to hear what the boy had come to tell. By the time I arrived, Zacharias had fixed the last button of his robe in place.

"And it is wolves they say," said Zacharias, confirming an earlier part of their conversation. "Are they sure?"

The boy gulped from the cup I handed him, then wiped his mouth with the back of his sleeve.

"Her arms are mangled," he said, "and her throat and face."

"Are people certain it is the girl . . . Cilla Graf?"

"Yes, sir. The parents have identified her from clothing and hair."

"Wait here."

Master went upstairs, and the rattle of windows and doors filled the silence before he returned with a small coin to hand to the messenger.

"Thank you, boy," he said. "Let Frau and Herr Graf know I will be there shortly."

Zacharias watched from the window as the boy disappeared into nature's fray.

"It is a godforsaken place," he said, the meagre light through the window tracing the shape of his long legs and wide shoulders. "What was she like?"

He turned to view my response.

"I didn't know her all that well. But I saw her with other children in groups. They would always greet me at the market. I would bring them little gifts when I could."

His eyes lingered on my face for a moment, then dropped away and returned to the window.

"Fetch my cloak, Frau Jaspers, and my Bible from upstairs."

I ran first to get his cloak, then hastened upstairs for the Bible, which was beneath a pile of papers. They scattered apart in my search, and I noticed that he had drawn circles and squares and other strange shapes and symbols over several pages.

At the front door, Zacharias had already put on his boots and cloak. He pulled his hat down over his ears.

"May I come with you, sir? It's just that these have been my people for a long time."

"It is bad out there today. Safer for you here."

"I am used to it, sir."

He thought about it while he adjusted his sleeves.

"Very well. It might be good to have another person to watch the responses. Fetch your shawl . . . No, wait! Take Stern's coat!"

I took the woollen coat from the hook near the entry. As my hands slipped into the pockets, I felt a piece of folded paper. While Master walked a short way from the house to survey the sky, I furtively withdrew the paper to spy it held some words, before replacing the note as he called out to hurry.

We traversed the stretch of snow that separated our house from the rest. Master did not speak for the short journey, not that I would have heard much in the wind that battered our ears and blew ice dust in our eyes. It took every effort to keep up with him, retrieving each of my feet from the thick rug of snow. We wove around a cart that was half buried, as we approached the Graf house.

The house was full of villagers brave enough to face the weather to console the couple, who had another small child in a basket on the floor. An older woman lay watching from a cot in the corner. I could hear her deep rasps that mingled with the weeping of the mother. On the table was the small lump of Cilla under a loosely woven blanket. Throughout my life I'd seen maulings from wolves, sheep left half eaten, their insides almost completely gone. That bothered me, but not so much as animals that fell down dead sometimes for no reason. There had been a series of those recently, poultry dead, sheep, goats, even horses.

Frau Graf was too weak to stand up fully as she reached for Master's hand. He pulled the woman towards him and enfolded her in his arms. She howled with grief, and her husband stood up to touch the reverend on the shoulder, as if just the touch of him would end his pain. I knew how they felt. I felt it, too.

"May I see her?" he said as the woman tore herself away when her legs began to buckle. Herr Graf helped her back to her chair.

She nodded and wiped her face.

Master went over to the table to examine the girl. He pulled back the cover as I stepped beside him. Cilla's neck was deeply gashed, and her child's soft brown hair, dried now from the warm fires inside the house, framed the hideous mask of gore that had replaced her face. Her arms were mutilated, pieces missing.

I turned away quickly when I felt the remains of my breakfast shift within my stomach. Zacharias covered her and sat down. I remained standing and mildly nauseous closest to the door in case I were sick.

"Frau Graf," said Zacharias, bending forward and reaching out to hold both her hands. "When did you become concerned about her return?"

"A little over an hour after she left," answered Harald Graf, whose wife was struggling to find her voice. "She had gone to pray for her grandmother who is sick, and she only ever stayed on the path to the church. She was too fearful to have ventured elsewhere."

"And she would never go without her shawl," said Frau Graf tearfully. "The cold put an ache in her ears."

Frau was holding Cilla's shawl in her hand.

"Is that it there?" asked Master.

"Yes. We had found it in the church when we first went to look for her."

Zacharias stared at the blue cloth.

"A wolf may have taken her as she left the church," said Zacharias.

"I've never seen one on the track," said Harald Graf. "They're not like that. A bear maybe, yet we would have heard something, someone would have."

"It seems she was attacked at some point," said Zacharias. "Is there any other reason she would have left the track and gone to the woods alone?"

"There is no reason she would have gone alone," said Frau Graf. "No reason at all."

"There is more," said Herr Graf.

"No!" said his wife.

"We have to tell him."

The couple held each other's gaze and some invisible communication between them took place.

"Your Reverence," said Kristine Graf, bending down to a small chest on the floor. She retrieved a stick-and-straw doll and held it between two fingers, in such a way to suggest it was detestable. "They found it inside what remained of her clothing. It did not belong to her. I was going to burn it because I fear it in my house, even touching it, but my husband said we must show it to you."

Master took the item from her and examined it.

"Have you ever seen a doll like this before?" Master asked.

"No," she said, gesturing towards Cilla's grandmother, Oma Leisl, who held up a small cloth doll with embroidered features. "That was Cilla's, not this . . . Reverend Engel, I do not want this thing in my house."

"I will have Frau Jaspers burn it," he said, taking the item, then handing it to me. I tucked it into the coat pocket.

We did not stay for much longer. Master read them a passage from the Holy Bible and reassured them that a burial would be swift. We walked against the wind, and Master reached out to hold my hand, dragging me behind him. Visibility was so poor I could barely make out his dark shape in front of me.

At home, Walter had set the fires blazing. I once more raised a query about the doll.

"If I had to guess, sir, the dolls found at Kleist's house and with Cilla were made by the same person. And from description, Lottie's also."

"I agree," said Zacharias. "It does not seem like coincidence. They are most certainly linked, or some of them, or the murderer wants us to think so. Perhaps the murderer, or the Devil, is toying with us."

I was amazed by his ability to inquire beyond the obvious.

"If a demon," I broached, "is working through these people encouraging them to murder, then the doll might be his symbol."

"Yes, that is possible," he said. "A symbol or a ruse."

He was true to his word, and on the following day when the wind and snow had ceased, Cilla had her burial. The stonemason, who seemed to hold the busiest of trades in the bishopric in recent months, etched her name and short years into permanency.

Most of the villagers attended the service at the church, and we followed the coffin carried by her father and helpers.

Margaretha stood, eyes resting on the coffin for much of the time. Sigi and Herta were there with their father Bertram, the blacksmith, a large man with ruddy cheeks and an easy manner. Sigi caught my glance and smirked. A boy without a purpose is a boy who chases mischief.

Zilla was there, too, and had respectfully taken particular care of her attire. She wore a silk scarf around her head and had dressed Jon in a clean shirt and his Sunday jacket. Jon watched a hawk fly above us. I thought it would be easier to be Jon. To explore and accept the simple things in life unquestioningly. Zilla kept a respectable distance away from the crowd, knowing how many felt about her. She had not been blessed with the gift of conversation, her manner brusque and clumsy, often throwing insults and uncaring where they landed.

Frau Graf scattered some soil over the coffin and many of the women wept, their children pulled close to their hips. At the conclusion of the ceremony, everyone was solemn. Even Zilla. She approached the grieving woman and told her it was unfair that her daughter had been taken so young. Frau Graf extended her hand, and Zilla glanced at it suspiciously at first, then reached out also.

I wondered if I should mention to Zilla about Jon's interview, then thought better of it. It would not be the first time the boy had become confused, but nothing had come of it since. My interference may cause her to act, and not necessarily in Jon's best interest.

After that day, men came from the city under orders from the prince-bishop to patrol the village and surrounding areas at night, though it was not an easy task with weather extremes, raining heavily or snowing one day to the next. I had heard that these guards were often found at the inn by the end of the day. The conditions got to everyone.

"Not even the Devil would want to be outside these days," commented Bertram Jacobs after the church service. Herta's father rarely forwent an opportunity to comment.

Men from the village hunted for wolves at night and boar during the day whenever there was a clear-sky moment. After a successful hunt, a she-wolf was dragged through the marketplace leaving a bloody trail in the snow, her body dumped in the centre of the square to a cheering crowd.

Walter stood beside me, his face wet with tears.

"Don't be upset. It is probably the same animal that killed Cilla."

"It's not," Walter said.

"How do you know?"

"I just do."

In the castle stores I heard more gossip. Someone was burning that day. A man in the city who passed by another man's horse and commented on the state of its distended belly. While they conversed, the horse fell down dead.

CHAPTER TEN

Walter didn't respond to my calls through the doorway of the barn. That morning, I was met only by the soft clucking from the hens and the rattling wheels of a cart in the village. When I had exhausted my search elsewhere, the whinny of Master's horse drew me back to the barn.

"Shh!" I said, stroking the nose of the mare, almost fully recovered from her malady. I put my face on her neck and breathed in her earthy, sweet smell until a scuffing sound alerted me to Walter, whom I found curled up on the floor in the corner behind her.

"Walter!" I rushed to his side to see that his shirt had been torn. "What happened?"

His arms were protectively wrapped around his middle.

"Leave me," he said, surely humiliated to be found in this condition.

"Tell me what happened!"

He grimaced.

"Let me look at you," I said, touching his shoulder.

He sat up so I could lift up his shirt and examine where he'd been punched and kicked. When I ran my hand over his stomach, he flinched.

"It was Sigi, wasn't it?"

I didn't need an answer. It wasn't the first time. Sigi was a bully and a coward. He would only ever harass boys who were smaller or weaker with his band of thugs to support him.

I helped Walter to stand and took him into the sitting room, where it was warm. I washed the broken skin with watered vinegar and rubbed it with fat, then placed a bandage made from old sheets around his middle. I helped him into one of Stern's shirts, though large, which would suffice until I repaired the tears in his. He groaned a bit from the pain of lifting his arms, and once dressed he rested by the fire.

When there was a shuffle outside the front door, Walter sat up suddenly, his pain temporarily forgotten as Master strode indoors. His stern expression softened as he approached.

"What happened to you?" he asked.

"The horse kicked him by accident," I said.

His eyes roamed between Walter and me.

It was no use telling him the truth. Sigi's father was well liked. Sigi did not have the nature of his father, who could be gruff at times, though just and gentle also. People excused Sigi for many things on account of how much Bertram Jacobs did for them, and his son could appear contrite and charming when it suited him. He would deny any wrongdoing, blame someone else. It had happened before. If Master said anything to Herr Jacobs, it would come back on Walter again somehow. Some people got away with things and others didn't. It was just the way it was.

Zacharias nodded to go along with the lie. I was sure he knew differently.

"You may rest inside the house tonight if you wish, Walter. Frau Jaspers will take good care of you, I expect."

"Thank you, sir," he whispered.

When Zacharias left again that day, and Walter had fallen asleep, I stormed over to Herta's house. Sigi opened his front door and his eyes wandered over me, suggesting that he liked what he saw. He was built large and broad like his father, a small mouth like Herta. He might have been considered handsome to some, only that his nature made him repellent. I knew that Herta was afraid of him and that sometimes he took to her with fists.

"Ah, the ice maid!" said Sigi. "The heroine of the forest. Come in!"
I entered cautiously to find he was alone.

"You knew that Herta was out today. It is why you came."

A nefarious-looking smile told me I'd been tricked. He knew I would come, the message inked in Walter's bruises.

"If you touch Walter again—"

"You will what?"

"I will have you killed," I said in defiance, though the shake in my voice weakened my intent.

He threw back his head and laughed.

"You wanted to see me," he said smugly. "I know you did. I just gave you a good excuse . . . It's been a while."

He grabbed me around the waist, and I bit down hard on his shoulder.

He jumped back, touched the area I had bruised, then stepped forward to slap me hard across the face. I tasted blood where my teeth had been forced against my lip.

"You vicious little cat!"

It was wrong to come, I knew that then, but as I tried to leave, he grabbed my wrist.

"You liked me once," he said. "Only a short while ago. What's changed?"

"Nothing's changed. You're still a child who pretends he's a man."

His mood darkened further.

"You think you can make the decisions?" he said.

I searched the objects around the room that I might use if he attacked me again.

"I don't want you," I said. "I have made that clear."

"Not clear enough."

"Then I make it clear now."

He laughed, and I dreaded what might come.

"You think you are vied for. That you are the beauty of this village. But you are just a servant who owns nothing who was married off to an old man who bought you some prestige but for a moment. Now a widow, you will be an old maid with no old man to keep you. I am your only chance."

"I am content where I am."

"What has changed?" he asked again.

"Nothing."

"You and the priest?" he said, his head in the direction of the clergy house then sneering. "You are not beautiful. You are not like Margaretha, the most desired woman in the village and in the whole bishopric, I would imagine. It seems your reverend agrees. He has been to her place at night. I have seen him there often."

"You are lying!"

As he stepped forward, I took a step back.

"It is true! Other people know it, too. No one says anything. They are the untouchable golden couple."

Any fear turned to anger then.

"My master is spoken for by God."

"You are a fool if you believe he is chaste!"

"He goes there to pray for Maria Unger."

"That is what he says?" he scoffed. "He is lying to you."

"You sound jealous," I said. "Has Margaretha spurned you, too?"

The smirk on his face quickly disappeared.

"She has rejected you, hasn't she." I forced a laugh, and it was my turn to roll my eyes down the length of him. "Like me, she thinks you are a dolt. You probably showed her what you had to offer, and she laughed."

As he went to grab me, I picked up the fire poker and hit him across the side of the head. He yelped, and I started for the door as he came for me again.

"I know who you are," he shouted after me as I made it to the street. "I know your secrets and I will hold you to a promise!"

Herr Goosem poked his nose outside his window to spy. I rushed past him, my head covered, and my face hidden. When I arrived home,

I shut the door and slid to the ground, my back against the wood. I was tired of cruelty, and afraid that Sigi would say something to Herta, who would have more fodder to gossip with. The fact I was alone in the house with him meant he could make up any story. I thumped the floor with my fist, angry at myself for going there. Never again!

There was a commotion behind the house, and I followed the sound of Walter shouting. When I got there, I found him laughing beside Master's mare, who was leaping spiritedly in the snowy paddock, bucking playfully and swinging her head.

"She is better than ever," he said, the smile on his face broad. "Margarctha's an angel!"

I thought of Sigi's words. Had I missed something about my master and the midwife that may have been in front of me all this time?

"It looks like someone else is feeling better, too, but you should be resting as the master said," I scolded.

When Zacharias came back later that evening from a meeting with the prince-bishop, his mood was dark, and in the several days following he made no mention of Margarctha, as if he had forgotten all I had said, nor did he wish to converse or leave the house. When I brought him dinner one night, I found him seated on the edge of his bed and noticed the two letters that arrived the previous day had not been opened, as if there was some dread about what they contained. The ham and cheese I had brought him for his lunchtime meal uneaten.

"Is everything to your liking, sir?" I said, thinking that the problem, his silence, was me.

"Yes," he said, taking a cursory glance at the food. As I was about to leave and close the door behind me, he called me back in and gestured me to the chair in his room. He was pensive, and spoke as if it wasn't to me.

"I believe things are going to get worse here, Katarin."

That familiarity again made me warm and cold at the same time. Warm to hear my name, but cold in the serious tone he used.

"I believe the parents of the marked boy live in this very village, that they are covering up the murder. The prince-bishop is on the hunt for those responsible. He believes that evil has spread across the bishopric."

"The child may have come from anywhere," I told him. "There are many hunters and travellers who stay off the road and follow the forests. Perhaps it is a child who died in travel."

He tilted his head. "You have thought about this yourself."

I was not sure if this was a compliment or a veiled accusation, that I might somehow be concealing information.

"As for Cilla Graf . . . ," he said. "I must move fast on this. I can feel the tension in the village mounting, and the prince-bishop wants a head. Someone has to pay."

"Might not Kleist have been responsible for her murder? He was still free on the day that Cilla went missing."

"It seems too convenient to blame one man for all crimes," he said wearily. "From what I have seen here, there is no end to wickedness or blame thereof."

I could tell he was not only tired from the task of finding suspects but that there were also many people coming forward once more with their observations and petty grievances. People fought over small things, and with dwindling livelihoods, jealous neighbours seemed to divide the village further. The more a person had, the more likely they would be accused of something. Theft was becoming commonplace. In the city, people had been thrown in prison in recent days, children beaten by lawmen, men fighting over food, one bludgeoned to death. In Eisbach, two youths were sent to the prison in the city for stealing. I had told Walter that he must keep a closer eye on the animals, to place a lock on the barn.

"What happened to your face?" said Zacharias.

I touched my cheek that was tender and red.

"In the stores, I had reached for something high, and a sack of onions fell down on top of me."

"You should limit your trips to the city if you can," he said. "You and Walter should take better care of yourselves. These are turbulent times."

He stood up to examine my injury, his hands placed either side of my face. I can't remember how long we were like that. If it were seconds, it felt much longer while I held my breath. He broke away suddenly.

"I have to go out tonight, and I may not be back till the early hours."

After I retrieved his supper plate from his room, I climbed into bed fully clothed. When I heard the door unlatch, I rose to follow him. The night was brighter than normal, the moon forcing a pathway through cloud.

I followed him stealthily and hoped that I did not cross paths with Sigi, who was often out after dark. Zacharias began along the track that would take him to the city before veering off the route towards Maria's house. Crouching down behind a tree, I watched him knock once on the door before it was opened to let him in. Yellow light flickered from within the house of someone moving with a candle in hand.

I felt a fool wondering for how long these nightly trysts had been happening. He was a man of the cloth, a man revered by many. Not that I truly believed his holy orders to be an issue. If he were to break his vows surely it should be with me. There was an attraction between us, I was certain, a desire he felt obliged to withhold. Nonetheless, I wanted to believe it was something deeper. Since he had come into my life, I felt seen.

I could not bear to spy through the window, afraid of what I might find. Tears began to well just as the door opened again. He stepped outside carrying several bottles.

"Thank you, Frau Katz," he said formally. "I will pass on your good wishes."

I stayed hidden to watch him disappear into the darkness. I sighed with relief. Sigi, it seemed, had lied. But it did not stop all my fears.

Margaretha's presence unsettled me, and the conversation I'd had with
Zacharias about seeing her in the forest was as if it never occurred.

⇒

"What happened to you?" said Herta when she visited the next day,
studying my face, searching for clues.

I told her the same fictitious story I had told Zacharias.

"Does it hurt?"

I shook my head.

"My brother said you visited him."

She had possibly connected the two incidents. She knew her
brother.

"He's lying," I told her.

Herta smiled sceptically as she sat down slowly on a stool. She
rested her chin in the cup of one hand. At that moment she looked
sweet and innocent, her red hair ribbon tied prettily in a bow.

"What do you want, Herta?" I said, irritated by her presence. "I'm
very busy."

"Who said I wanted anything?"

"Walter's out, in case you're wondering."

As I rolled out some pastry, Herta reached over to pinch a piece. I
let her get away with it but when she tried to take some more, I slapped
the back of her hand.

"You have spoken with Margaretha?" she asked. It was a subject I
did not care to think about. All the same, she had raised my curiosity.

"Yes," I said, patting down the pastry into greased pans. "Why do
you ask about her?"

"Does she have lots of bottles of things? Does she have a book of
magic?"

"Herta! There is no such thing. Besides, I have not been to her
house . . . not while . . ."

I had to keep reminding myself that Maria Unger was still alive.

"I heard that some healers cross between this world and the other, the dark world," she said. "That they are ungodly in their methods."

"It's not true. Maria was a good and kind woman as you know who had a book of herbs and remedies to treat conditions. There was nothing magical about her."

I could not say with certainty what methods Margaretha used, if she dabbled in the black arts. I stirred the stewing meat in a pot, then turned to examine the sincerity of the visitor.

"Did she use human blood in there? There were rumours—"

"Herta, enough!" I said, crossing my arms with displeasure. "There is something on your mind, something else you want to ask me."

Herta leaned back on the wooden stool and gripped the sides of it, looking keenly out through the window to the barn.

"It is a secret," she said, her focus back on me. "I need your help with something, but you have to promise you won't mention it to anyone else."

Strange that she asked me to keep a secret since she was incapable of such action herself.

"Of course."

"It is about Ursula Döhler,"

"What about her?"

She looked around behind her.

"We are alone here," I said, exasperated, looking at the fading daylight outside, aware that there was still much to do.

"She is pregnant again. That turd she was wedded to left her that little gift before he ran off with the hangman's daughter!"

This wasn't news. Neither was the fact that her husband had left prior to the baby being murdered and tossed into the graveyard.

"What's that got to do with me?"

"I spoke to her. Papa took me with him when he was called to fix a broken window latch. Ursula's crone of a mother-in-law, Jutta, locks them all in when she goes out, so none escape, not even Ursula. She is rarely allowed out on her own, and she can't get away to see Margaretha. She wants me to do it. But Sigi might see me. I thought you—"

"No!"

"You pass by there to go to the castle stores."

I shook my head. "For what purpose?"

Herta leaned in to speak quietly. "For a potion."

"A potion?" I was genuinely confused and focused on the rash around her lips.

"It will stop her sickness. She is unwell all the time."

My hand instinctively went to my belly.

"I can't do that."

"Please just speak to Ursula about it. I promised her you would."

I knew the potion she was asking for. I had taken some myself in the past, something only spoken about amongst women.

"I can't if Ursula is locked in."

"Before daybreak on Fridays, she is allowed to pray once a week at the grave of her baby, but she will go to the ruins instead. She will meet you there."

"Why can't I just visit her at home?"

"Jutta listens to everything. Ursula is afraid of her. While Papa was there talking to Jutta, Ursula spoke to me."

"Why does she trust you so much?"

Herta shrugged. Ursula must have been desperate to take such a risk.

Although I did not wish to do this, it might give me the excuse to check on Maria.

"When I make a delivery for Papa tomorrow, I will indicate to her that you will meet her."

I reluctantly agreed to listen to Ursula's request, though it did not mean I would agree to helping her.

When I delivered Zacharias's meal to his room that night, I found him preoccupied with a book and blank paper beside it. He rolled an inked quill between his fingers, poised to write. The two unopened letters were gone. I set down his tray.

"Frau Jaspers," he said as I turned to leave. "I have a query about sermons, in particular the one I would perform next Sunday. What do you think people want to hear most?"

I thought the question strange. Very rarely did people in his position care for the opinions of servants.

"I think, sir, given that people are not coping as well with circumstances, you might make it lighter, a shred of hope like you did at Christmas. So much of Reverend Stern's sermons were about sin and hellfire. It does no good to talk of such things all the time. People want hope more than anything. They want a blue sky, they want a plentiful crop, a roasting fowl on Sundays. How it used to be."

"I cannot give them better weather unfortunately."

"It doesn't matter. Just the hope of it is good enough for now."

He looked down at the blank page, then up again.

"Frau Jaspers, you are a light in this house. I could not imagine how this place would be without your efficiency and wisdom."

I did not know quite how to respond. I had never had such compliment before. He had pulled me into an imaginary embrace. I was like wax, melting in his presence, unable to find enough solid form to respond. How easy it was to be moulded by this man.

Someone shouted in the street and distracted us from the conversation, a blessing perhaps stopping a response that might cause me embarrassment. Zacharias got up to look from the window.

"It was nothing," he said. "Too much wine."

"Oh," I said, suddenly remembering and retrieving the visiting card from the pocket of my kirtle. Walter had passed this to me earlier. "A man called for you this morning while I was out tending to other tasks."

"What man is this?" Master said, glancing at the stranger's card I handed him.

"Walter didn't know him. He was not from here."

Zacharias's expression darkened. I had learned in my short years that it is only those with a past that have such fear of outside visitors. Zacharias was an anomaly, a person with secrets I was certain, but a person unguarded with his thoughts at times also . . . And this contradiction was both alluring and confusing.

"Did he say what it was about?" Master asked.

"He had some urgent matter to discuss regarding a letter he sent you."

I saw the shadow slip away, and Zacharias's expression was one of knowing then.

"Walter suggested he call back tomorrow."

"If it is who I suspect, he is wasting his time."

CHAPTER ELEVEN

Late the following morning there was a sharp *tat tat-tat* on the front door. I glanced in the hallway glass and hardly recognised myself—dark circles around my eyes from a mind that rested only briefly during the night hours, much of it wishing for things I might never have.

The man on the other side of the door had a long, otherwise unremarkable face under a hat with plumes of blue and gold, and with shoulders that were small and narrower than his hips.

"Is this the residence of His Reverence Zacharias Engel?"

"Yes, it is."

"I must speak to him. I sent him a letter to ask if I may call on him and hinted at the reason, yet I've heard nothing back."

"The roads are treacherous. It is likely his reply has arrived in your absence."

"That may well be, but I'm here now and I must speak to him as a matter of urgency. My name is Doctor Sebastian Spengler. I am a man of science and philanthropy."

"Reverend Engel is not here. I do not know when to expect him."

"I have come a long way from Nuremberg. I am tired and cold, and stiff in the joints."

I could see that he was suffering to some degree, for he was unsteady on his feet and used a walking stick. Something was troubling him, and I thought surely a man in his condition who had taken the time to come this far should be offered some courtesy. He was by no means a pauper from the gold on his fingers, his cuffs of fine lace, and a thick pelt of satin-lined fur draped around his body.

"You may wait in the parlour if you wish," I said, wondering whether I had invited trouble into the home.

"Thank you . . ."

"Frau Jaspers, sir."

I prepared some warm mead and sprinkled it with cinnamon and cut a piece of bread fresh from the fire, then smeared it with dripping.

"Thank you, my dear," he said, and sipped noisily before emitting a sigh of appreciation.

I stayed to keep him company. He chattered about the weather, the state of the roads, how he almost had to turn back. I was relieved to hear the click of the front door latch alerting us to Zacharias's arrival, and I rose to meet him. He appeared flushed and angry. He bounded up the stairs carrying a small sack under his arm and without looking our way. As he went to close his bedroom door behind him he saw that I had followed.

"What is it?"

"I'm sorry to interrupt you, sir. The man who called yesterday is waiting downstairs, and he has come a long way to see you."

"Doctor Spengler?"

"Yes, sir."

Zacharias sighed.

"He is a quacksalver! I will see him off quickly."

"Yes, sir."

He shut his door, and I returned firstly to the parlour to inform Spengler that Master would be with him shortly and then to the kitchen. A minute later, I heard Zacharias approach the visitor. I stepped quietly into the dining hall and put my ear to the door that separated this room from the one where the interview was taking place.

"Good day, Herr Reverend," said Sebastian Spengler. "Thank you for agreeing to see me."

"I can assure you that it is not a good day. I do not have the time, Doctor Spengler, to listen to the theoretical views you alluded to. You know the church does not take kindly to your experiments that you wrote about in your letter. They are less than holy to say the least."

"Sir, I implore you to listen to what I have to say," he said. I detected that he was nervous from the way he stumbled over his words at times. "I would like the opportunity to explain what I have found. I am a pious man, indeed. I attend Sunday service whether ill or weather. I do not seek to upset the Holy Roman Church, nor the prince-bishop Ehrenberg. Any advice or finding is purely for the purpose of helping my fellow man. And my work, I believe, is worth examining."

I pictured my master's fierce blue gaze causing the man to struggle with coherence, the former I imagined not yet seated as a gesture to imply he was unprepared to engage with him for very long.

"Firstly, sir, I appreciate your housekeeper for providing refreshments. It has been a long journey. My conscience could not allow this matter to disappear from record."

"It is concerning Lenn von Kleist, is it not? The matter you wrote about in your letter is finished now. He has paid a penance for an evil caused."

"An evil that still exists after his death, sir," said Spengler, raising his voice and striking a blow against Zacharias's words.

"I pray for his soul," said the reverend.

"As do I, sir," said Spengler, defiantly. "As do I! I knew a man different from the one you knew. I have attended various events in this region over the years, and I had on occasion met him."

There was silence.

"Very well," said Master. "Take a seat once more. I will listen."

There was shuffling and chairs scraping, and when Spengler spoke again it was in a calmer, softer voice.

"Maria Unger, the midwife, I understand is gravely ill. I visited her house to be informed of this and was told that I must not enter."

"That is correct. We are unsure of the affliction. We do not want to risk others."

"I noticed that the girl staying there now appears quite well."

"She is experienced with ailments and very cautious."

"I stopped a passerby, who informed me of the unfortunate nature of the circumstance that the girl living at Maria's refused to answer. Apparently, this girl, her niece, is attending to Maria. I might say that I have not heard of any relatives before. Maria was an orphan when she came to me many years ago. I was the one who mentored her and taught her about the various healing properties of herbs, roots, and oils. She was an excellent student until she followed her heart north, only to have the scoundrel desert her eventually, although she found her place here in the village with a healer she was apprenticed to. We remained in contact over the years, so I can assure you that the girl who is looking after her is not a blood relation."

I could hear someone adjust themselves restlessly in a chair and assumed it was Zacharias since it came from his chair closest to the door. Spengler continued:

"Regardless of the girl, there is the matter that I came here to advise. I had learned from other sources that you oversaw the case of Leon von Kleist and others in the village accused of . . . sorcery. It must have been shortly before Maria Unger's circumstances changed, that is her ill health, she wrote to me. There were two issues that were, and I believe still are, of urgent importance. The first is that Maria sent me a sample of wheat from Kleist's stores. She had worked with me many years ago when I was studying the effects of spoiled and diseased grain on those who had ingested such. My findings, which Maria witnessed at the time on mice, showed that diseased and mouldy wheat affected the moods of those who had eaten meals produced from such. It causes fever and other changes in the body and mind. In some cases, they show signs of violence, but mostly it causes a malady that is often incurable. I believe that Leon had been affected but not to the extent that his family experienced. From these studies, such contamination is known to affect various animals also."

I thought of Master's horse.

Walter came into the room and I put my finger to my lips to hush him, then waved him forward to listen, too.

"So are you saying that he could have killed his children after eating this wheat, that his mood was changed—"

"No, that's not what I'm saying. Maria advised that the mother and children were badly affected, but Leon did not suffer as much. It is probable that his portion at the time did not have contamination; I cannot say for certain why he reacted differently. To back up my own findings, I forwarded copies of correspondence noting the same experiences by a French doctor who had found similar effects. It is rare, yet it does happen."

"This contamination does not exclude Kleist from the guilt of his crimes."

"Ah, but it does! There is one symptom here that is consistent with others investigated. The infected victims examined by me, as well as those by the other physician, all presented with a blue tongue."

There was silence from Zacharias.

"Maria stopped writing, which was unusual, and then I heard from a colleague in Würzburg that Herr von Kleist had been executed." Doctor Spengler sounded melancholy then. "I believe that he was wronged by the powers here."

"That is a strong accusation, Herr Doctor."

There was a long pause from Spengler.

"I am sorry," said Spengler. "I do not mean to accuse you personally. Only that the timing of this finding was unfortunate. The information was not on hand for Reverend Stern before he became ill, nor made known to you, of course, and neither to the prince-bishop to make a fully informed judgment."

"The man confessed."

"I know of the methods, Your Reverence, to gain a confession."

"There are things that you don't know. A doll left near the bodies of murdered children, the same kind that was left under Kleist's bed."

"A doll with a child or in the house of children means nothing."

I heard footsteps cross the floor. When Zacharias spoke it sounded more muffled, and I imagined him nearer the window, his back to the room.

"Doctor Spengler, I appreciate you coming all this way. Nevertheless, the matter is finished. There is nothing more I can do about it."

"I will go willingly, sir, though I leave this bishopric where evil still resides not from men like Leon von Kleist but from the inaction to find the real enemy, whatever it be."

"How so, sir?"

"Evil did not leave with Kleist, as you are well aware. And such calamity is happening elsewhere in Franconia. Execution is most desired by the emperor it seems. These accusations are spreading like a plague, and for what end? More death."

More silence.

I turned to Walter, whose mouth was open with dismay. He understood like me what we had just heard. That there was reason enough to suggest Kleist was innocent, even of the killings of his own children and wife.

"You have come a long way for little good, I'm afraid," said Zacharias.

"Perhaps I have, perhaps I haven't."

I wondered what to make of that. Had he left the door open? I was sure Master would close it firmly. He had to else he would suffer the ramifications both from the people and Ehrenberg.

"There is one other thing. The girl who is taking care of Maria, who has taken over her house. How well do you know her?"

"I know her well enough. She has been a great asset to the village and the people beyond it. She has cured a woman with chronic joint ache. She provides remedies for prisoners in pain, and free of charge. She has also delivered a healthy baby boy."

But the mother was now bedridden from the birth and not expected to live. Master failed to mention this.

"She has even cured my horse. Her work continues."

"Hmm," said Spengler. "I would, if I may, suggest you regularly look in on Maria. She was very dear to me. If you would do me that favour."

"Of course."

There were sounds of movement.

"I will have Frau Jaspers pack some refreshment for your long journey home. The weather is turning again. I suggest you leave promptly."

Walter and I crept like mice back into the kitchen. We arrived just as Zacharias swept in with his long cloak already donned and a wilder look in his eye than I had seen before.

"Kindly show Doctor Spengler out to his cart and offer him something from the kitchen for the journey," he said, throwing on his hat to depart hastily at the rear.

"Will you be back for supper?" I asked, but his mind was elsewhere, and he left without a response.

I filled a small cask of mead and tied some cheese and bread into a piece of linen before showing the older gentleman to the door. I escorted the doctor outside to where his horse and cart were tied. He appeared distracted in thought, after his unsuccessful conversation with Zacharias. I wished him a good journey.

"Thank you, Frau Jaspers," he said, his attention pleasantly turned, before searching for the piece of tin I'd long since removed from my finger. "What a lucky man is your husband to have married someone so fair of face and kind of nature."

"I am a widow, sir."

"Oh, ah. I'm sorry."

He lifted his hat and made to leave.

"Doctor Spengler . . ."

"Yes?" he said, turning back.

"The girl who has replaced Maria. Her name is Margaretha Katz. She's from Bamberg. From what I have heard, she worked для a wealthy man."

It seemed important he should know this. I believed firmly that she was not who she said she was.

"I am very curious about her, I must say," he said.

"There are more who would agree with you," I said presumptuously. "It appears that many in the village here have taken to her, and very quickly. Be that as it may, I am still very worried about Maria. She was a good friend of mine . . . Is a good friend."

"Do you know the state of her?"

"No, sir. I, too, would take comfort knowing she was in good hands."

I was too lowborn to specifically ask someone for a favour or instruct a person of high rank to perform a task on my behalf, but he grasped my meaning and shared my concern.

He nodded. "I will see what I can find out."

I closed the door and leaned against it, my breathing rising and falling rapidly from what I had overheard and my involvement in a conspiracy with Sebastian Spengler to find out the truth. I believed that everyone had underestimated Margaretha's cunning and that the reverend was being drawn inch by inch into her deceitful web.

CHAPTER TWELVE

Above me, clouds with their plump woolly bellies were motionless and the air outside so clear that I could see for miles as I stood by the window of the main bedchamber. To the west were snow-capped hills and the frozen river that snaked through the valley, dotted with different-coloured moving shapes that trudged along its side. To the east, the trees of the forest appeared like an army of men, tall and unyielding, and ready to trample all in their way. Beyond that was a sky that was tinted red in places. *Jesus bleeding from heaven,* Reverend Stern used to say. I shook the thought away. It marred what should have been beautiful. I straightened Master's bedcovers unnecessarily, since he was fastidious, and drank in the smells of leather, sweet exotic oils, and books.

He had arrived home late the night before and left for the city early that morning with the horse and cart. I had risen before the cock crowed to lay small rolls of dough to brown and crisp on the iron above the fire. I wrapped several of these in linen with a large hunk of cheese for the journey. Zacharias had leaned down from the cart and taken the package from me, his long hands brushing mine, his eyes lingering a moment on my face, and a small smile of gratitude offered before he raised his chin and contemplated the journey ahead of him. As I had seen proud wives do, I folded my hands and stood to watch him go. He had such an effect on me that when I had finally entered the house, I caught my reflection to see I was smiling unknowingly.

I returned to the kitchen to prepare the evening's meal and put more than a whisper of love into the task. I skinned a hare and chopped off its legs with a cleaver, then the rest in smaller pieces before throwing it into the boiling stock where the meat would fall off the bones to then melt on the tongue. Most of the bloody innards I brushed off the table into a bucket, and they made a slapping sound as they hit the tin. I would use these to make a stock. To the stew, I added carrots and leeks, and thickening made from dough soaked in chicken livers, rosemary, and the juice from the fowl I'd cooked days earlier. For Master's sweet-meat I made sugared melon on a bed of sweet pastry. The smells from the cauldrons had drawn Walter in, and he sat there at the end of the cook's table breathing in the fumes of the bubbling, salty meat and fruit boiled in sugar and fat.

"What are you making?"

When I told him, he said, "You didn't go to such trouble for the Reverend Stern."

"You didn't shine Stern's boots like you do for Reverend Engel."

He smiled only briefly before his expression turned sullen.

"What's the matter with you?" I asked.

"Jon was supposed to be here today. We were going sliding on the ice after I'd done my chores. He's spending much of his time with Maude Meyer."

"That little thief!" I said. "What does she want with Jon?"

I knew that Maude's mother had been unsuccessful with finding either daughter a husband.

Herta tapped on the back door and spied through the window. Walter groaned.

"You could take Herta instead."

"I have an urgent errand to run."

"Of course you do," I said, giving him a wry smile.

Walter squeezed past Herta in the doorway and grumbled a greeting.

"You haven't forgotten about Ursula tomorrow," she said with annoyance in her voice as she watched Walter leave. "Papa will be visiting on Saturday, and I will go with him and secretly pass on the medicine then, while Jutta is distracted."

I pinched my lips together to show that I was still none too pleased about it.

"Papa said that he saw the reverend travelling with Margaretha on a cart to the next village last week," she said, climbing up to sit on the worktable. "They were going to examine animals that have fallen down dead. Just like that! Several of them in pens."

I did not know which was worse, Master spending time with Margaretha or the phenomenon she just spoke of. I wondered if he would see her again today, maybe share my rolls with her, and suddenly the idea of food for him had lost some of its flavour.

"It is strange, no?" Herta said, swinging her legs. "The animals?"

"It is probably just a disease," I said, remembering Margaretha's words and the conversation I had overheard the previous day, "or they are fed up with always going hungry."

"Reverend Engel looked very fine today," she said, jumping straight to a different topic, seemingly satisfied with the reason I had given her. "I saw him leave. Although he looks fine every day, do you not think? It is not out of the question that a good-looking man like him, if it weren't for his robes and vow to God, should marry a pretty, healthy young widow like you who was already known to carry a child, albeit one that died, or even Margaretha, a beautiful spinster. Her hair . . . is it not beautiful the way it hangs like silk? I'd say it's healthy for men of the cloth; then they don't go strange in the head. I've heard that men in other countries, religious folk, can have lots of wives. It is a pity that you are not highborn and more likely a beggar's bastard."

Herta could be complimentary and sting at the same time. It was most certainly intentional. The small yellowish pustules around her mouth had spread, and her attempts to hide them with flour paste and clay had failed.

"I once heard of a Protestant priest who married his maidservant, and they have a dozen children now."

"Herta, you should not talk about Protestants so openly."

Most of the Catholic clergy equated Lutheranism with Satanism. The prince-bishop had exiled others in the past, those who tried to preach new paths of Christian thought. The Jews had been cast out also. I did not know where else they would go to find a home since a similar sentiment had spread across the territories.

"Anyway, you are lucky. Even if he doesn't marry you, he might bed you at least."

"Stop it, Herta!"

It wasn't that I hadn't thought about it. I had entertained thoughts of him, and I'm not sure I would have refused him if it came to it. But her prattle and the sound of her voice made me want to scratch off my ears.

"You have heard the news about Margaretha?"

I did not have to wait long for her to continue.

"It wasn't just the merchant, a very respectable man, who sent her away. It was the whole town who had chased her away. She had delivered two babies dead, one dead in her own house. She was bad, they said. Apparently, there was evidence that she caused the latter death with potions."

"The story keeps growing about Margaretha," I said. "It is likely she prescribes the same cures that Maria did."

"Some think that she practises sorcery."

I knew that some people, those that didn't benefit from it, saw it as such.

"Who told you about Margaretha?"

"At the market. Someone who knows someone who knows someone."

"I'm busy, Herta," I said, rolling my eyes, though she was reluctant to leave.

"What is it?" I asked.

She acted shy all of a sudden and covered her mouth.

"I need some ointment for my rashes."

"Let me see."

She uncovered her mouth and leaned forward to allow me to better study the blisters.

"How did you get these?"

She bit her top lip and lowered her eyes. It was the kissing disease that I'd seen on Sigi's face also and several servants in the castle. It was a sin to have relations outside of marriage, and Herta was unlucky to wear hers so visibly.

"It was a boy. A friend of Sigi's."

"Herta! You can't be taking such risks! What has your father said?"

"He's not here. He's not seen them yet. That's why I need to get help."

So, it was not all about Ursula. She was using Ursula, perhaps even convincing the pregnant woman to take the remedy so that I would go on her behalf and save her from a pounding should she be caught.

I shook my head and turned away.

"You should not be running with those wild boys."

"It's not my fault."

"Did he take you by force?"

She reddened then, and I took that as a no.

"I know that there are medicines for these things," she said coyly. "I will need something that will stop . . ."

"Stop what?"

"You know."

I did know of what she spoke, what she was trying to prevent—a prevention that was a sin and a punishable offence.

"It will cost you. She won't give you potions for free."

"But I don't have any money."

I thought about the money I had hidden. I could spare a coin.

"Very well. I will pay. But you owe me."

"Next time Papa gives me money for the market. I promise."

I nodded, though it was doubtful I would see any coin repaid. She jumped off the table to go find Walter.

At the supper table that evening, Master did not compliment the food.

"Is everything to your liking?"

"Yes, of course, Frau Jaspers," he said. "It's been an exhausting day of interviews and confessions. One neighbour has accused another of cursing animals out of jealousy and spite. It is hard to get to the truth of it."

Then realising he was speaking too candidly, he asked if he could be left alone. When I returned with the pastry, he had already gone to his room. I covered a pastry for the morning and took another to Walter in the barn. I fell asleep exhausted, too, that night, but was alerted by a creak of the boards on the stairs and a shuffling sound on the stone floor. Barefooted and with just my nightgown and shawl, my hair free and spilling over my shoulders, I crept into the parlour where the noise had stopped. It was dark, and the midnight light from the window only made the shadowy corners of the room appear more sinister.

"Sit down!" Master said from the darkness, and I jumped a little at the harsh break in the silence. His speech was slurred. "I should speak with you."

"Do you want the fire, sir?"

"No, Frau Jaspers," he said. "Sit, please."

I did so on the settle opposite, where my face was partially illuminated, where I could not hide my fear at the strangeness of the situation.

"It is not looking good for Zilla Lucke," he said from the darkness.

"How so?"

"Jon has accused her of sorcery, and now there is talk at the castle that the marked boy was hers and the Devil's."

"It is nonsense, sir, if I may say so."

I could now make out his shape in the chair.

"Jon loves his mother," I continued. "He would never intention-ally do anything to harm her. If he has said any words against her it is because someone else has put them there."

Zacharias was silent for near a minute. Thinking he had fallen asleep I wondered if I should go.

"If you had a secret that was burdening you to the point that you no longer wanted to be here, would you share it?" he said finally.

The suggestion frightened me, since I carried many secrets.

"Sir, most unburden themselves by confessing in a church."

"How very astute! That is indeed what has happened. The river boy's father has confessed to killing his son."

"Herr Kropp?"

"Yes."

Admittedly, I wasn't horrified by the action, more the announce-ment of it and the sharing of this information. I knew people did many things in times of trouble. I knew that many people were only virtuous in public.

"Did he say why?" I asked.

"The boy it seems was running wild. He would hit his mother, though she loved him no less for it. He would strike them and throw things, all the while his mother would only speak highly of him. He would scream in the night and keep his parents and younger brother awake and fearful. One night he hit his mother with a pan and with such force that she was unconscious for half the hour. Peter Kropp struggled to control him. He could not live with the boy who was not sound. He said for years it went on like this and then when he couldn't take it anymore, and while Irma and his second son were out, he put his hands around the boy's neck and held his head in a bucket of water until he grew still. He then placed him in the river hoping the current would take him far away and if he was found that it would be consid-ered misadventure. But the water was cold and slow, and Hermann became snagged close by."

Master poured himself another drink. I wondered then how often priests would listen to sins and have to carry them, all of them, like weighty baggage. I wondered if this place was beginning to vex him as it had done Stern.

"It is something he cannot tell his wife," he said softly, as if he was only talking to himself. "She couldn't live with him after that. He can barely live with himself. He is a haunted, broken man, not only from the loss of his son but for the reason he caused his death. Added to his suffering is this truth he keeps from his wife, who has been affected badly by the loss and continues to grieve."

"It appears selfish, such an act, to not give himself up, but then Irma Kropp would be left alone without someone to care for her and the younger boy," I added. "It sounds like Peter did this out of love to protect the rest of his family, and to spare Irma from the truth was better for them all. Perhaps Hermann is now at peace in a better place."

My eyes had adjusted to the darkness, and Zacharias's features had become clearer.

"You are right of course, Frau Jaspers. However, Peter Kropp has not found his peace with it."

I had seen a weakness in Zacharias, and it was the first of more that would slowly reveal themselves. But even now I wonder about that moment, whether he was simply attempting to gain my trust, to test my undying loyalty, for a situation that would come later, and using whatever means to do so. To draw out my own secrets. The God-fearing villagers trusted him with theirs, and he was releasing some to me.

"And you know what else I think . . . I think that Jutta killed the infant," he said bitterly. "That she, the unpleasant cow, could ill afford another mouth to feed."

I thought of Ursula, who was pregnant, and wondered if it were true, and whether this new infant once born would fare any better.

"And Lottie Pappenheimer?" I asked.

"The more I think about that girl, the more I think the doll was made in haste and especially for her as a gift in the afterlife. Perhaps it was one act of regret, or perhaps a mercy by the killer."

"Mercy, sir?"

"Yes, a mercy out of love. Despite what I believe, there is possibly no way of ever knowing the truth about it. The mother of Lottie hanging herself, the father abandoning the village and not heard of since . . . But Cilla Graf and the marked boy . . . Those killings are elusive and not the work of anyone currently under suspicion. I fear that good people will be accused of these and die for naught."

"The Devil lays traps for the weak," I said, trembling inside, reminding him of similar words he had spoken during a sermon.

He said nothing to this, and my mind began to trick me, the shape of him deformed, the back of his chair like the wings of a fallen angel. He moved then so his face was more in light, and it was Zacharias again, handsome though more weather-beaten than when he had first arrived.

"The murderer is still free," he said. "That is what we do know. He, or she, has assumed a personality that is trustworthy. Would you agree, Katarin?"

I opened my mouth to speak but nothing came out. He frightened me with his intensity, expecting me to give him answers that I could not.

"And then, to add to the misery, it seems that Kleist's daughter, Ruth, has finally succumbed to her illness. She has taken her father's secrets with her, which is just as well. There is no life for her out here . . . You must not speak of this, Katarin."

He stood up and commenced to walk forward, and I asked him if he wanted a candle to light the way since the stairs were in blackness. He waved away the suggestion. I wondered if he would remember telling me, since he drank the whole jug and more besides, and if he did remember, whether he would regret it.

Before dawn, I rose. With no sound from Zacharias upstairs, there was time to get to the old castle ruins and back again before he woke from his heavy liquid slumber.

I wrapped a woollen blanket around my head to cover my face and made my way towards Ursula, looking behind me to see there were no faces at the windows below until I reached beyond the incline where I couldn't be seen. Rain fell in large drips, making patting sounds on the ice along the embankment of the brook. The path was treacherous, but the route was unlikely to be trodden this early and away from the main thoroughfare. There was a clicking sound beyond the hill behind me, of someone dragging a cart in thick snow before it stopped, followed by cursing as the driver commenced shovelling to free a wheel.

A year ago, I would not have been afraid to be seen heading to the ruins on my own, though it was that the mood had changed. People did not veer too far from activities at home for fear anything vaguely considered out of the ordinary would be labelled as questionable.

Ursula was there waiting, waiflike and sickly, with stringy greying hair. Life and years had not been kind to her. She was unnaturally aged for someone so young, and clearly malnourished, with wrists like those of a child.

I had been to her house in the past, running errands for Reverend Stern. The house was chaotic, her husband, still living there then, sitting in the corner yelling out commands, the place fetid with animal urine, the mother-in-law Jutta sitting with her black bonnet of mourning, lines of disapproval permanently etched in the creases around her pursed lips. I had heard that she had money once, before her husband died, and she had lived well before this place, without children and animals and damp walls. She had been forced to move in with her son and daughter-in-law and their children.

Ursula looked terrified when she saw me, and for a moment I thought she would lose her courage and flee.

"Did Herta tell you?" she said under the grey predawn haze.

I could see she was missing several teeth I'd not noticed before, since she spoke often with her head down and through a tiny gap in her mouth.

"Yes, but I am not sure I can help you."

She stiffened, and I felt her anguish. I was her only hope. She had lost a baby, and some said she had lost her mind with him, that the killer may as well have thrown her into the graveyard dirt, too. I thought again of Master's suggestions that Jutta was the cause of it.

"Herta said you could."

"Herta says a lot of things. I do not know Margaretha well. I do not even know that she carries such cures."

"If she is a midwife and a healer, she will know how to help me. The sickness is much worse this time. I can't bear it. When Jutta goes to market, I hit my stomach hoping I will lose the baby."

I cringed from the thought of what she was doing to herself and from the apostasy that would see her hang should she admit this elsewhere. Her immense pain was smothering me. Every inch of me said to run from this woman.

"Why?" I hesitated to ask.

"Because my husband is gone. We barely have enough food each day for the family. Jutta hates me. She will despise the child like she does the others. They have no future. They have no father to make money, to carry us through the never-ending winter. Because each time I have a birth, a piece of me dies and goes to hell anyway, with the thoughts I have about it."

I was aghast that she would admit this.

"Do you not have any love for your children, for this child you carry?"

I reached to touch her arm, but she backed away suspiciously.

"I do. It is just the sickness makes me think strange things."

"Have you spoken to Jutta about this, about your sickness?"

"She knows," said Ursula with a touch of madness in her stare. "She sees everything, and still she does not care. Please help me, or I will dash my own head with a rock. I would rather spend an eternity in hell than this hell on earth."

Her words were appalling, yet I felt every one of them.

"How far along are you?"

"Over halfway through."

"It could be dangerous for you. I know what medicine you speak of. Sometimes it works, sometimes it doesn't, and sometimes there are worse consequences."

"It is not what I wish for. Not really. Believe me that I cannot care well for the other ones if I am so poorly," she said.

There was silence for a moment until the bell of the church tolled, and this seemed to ignite my decision.

"If I get this for you, you must not speak a word of where it came from."

"If you get this, I will remember you always," she said, pulling a small coin from her pocket and placing it in my hand. "For the healer."

I wondered how she had managed to steal this from Jutta.

"I will pass the items on to Herta and any instructions," I said.

She stood there watching me as I left to walk home. Only Herr Brühn saw me walking past and grumbled something I could not discern.

Once inside, Walter was waiting for me.

"Where have you been?" he asked accusingly, like my husband used to.

"Mind your business."

"Master was looking for you. He has left for the castle now."

"How long will he be gone?"

"He said all day. He has a meeting with the prince-bishop and then with other parishioners."

It was an opportunity at least to find out more.

There was a drizzle of rain and the air an early morning grey as I set out to call on Margaretha, carrying a basket as if I were heading to the castle stores. Animals had been let out while the weather was bearable.

The creaking of wheels and the scraping of sleds by traders along the ice echoed along the river, their lanterns flickering. The melodious clang of the church bell rang out seven times.

Margaretha lived in a house set back from the main road, under an archway of elms. In the warmer months, leaves of the trees disguised the house from the road. In the winter, however, the barren branches that connected one another formed more like a prayer circle around her house. Snow had been cleared recently from the front door, where several sets of footprints told of recent visitors—messengers, I deemed, most likely sent to fetch her. A faint glow within told me she had risen. My breathing became more rapid. The unknown about her, the possibility that she was something far from what she appeared in Master's barn, caused me to pause at the door and put my hand against the rough wood, breathe in the cold, and expel it again with force.

Maria Unger had arrived in the region as a young woman, the ramshackle house gifted to her from another healer who eventually died childless. And it seemed that Maria had done the same for Margaretha, but without speaking to the older woman, this was not known for certain. Now at least, I had the opportunity to find out for myself how Maria was faring.

After I knocked, I heard the scrape of a chair against stone and an object smash on the floor. A few moments later Margaretha opened the door a small way so that I could see only part of her pretty face.

"I have come on behalf of my friends."

She raised her eyebrows as a question.

"It is for treatments," I said. "There are reasons the women cannot come themselves."

Margaretha paused, briefly turned away, then opened the door wider to let me in.

Inside, it was dark, with only one candle burning and dying embers in the grate. In one corner was a curtained partition, which I assumed concealed Maria on her bed, and on the opposite side of the house was a low cot with thick bedding and a nightgown lying across it. On shelves along the back wall sat many coloured bottles and jars, and nearby was Maria's book of healing on the table positioned closest to the fire. There were no smells of cooking, just that of pine, plants, and vinegar, masking, to some degree, a decaying odour of dung that Maria had used to block the holes in the walls from drafts. In a mortar on the table lay some partially ground seeds, a task I had likely interrupted.

Only one thing marred the order: a cup in pieces on the floor, its contents splattered, and another cup, partially drunk, that sat upon the table. I looked towards the curtain expecting Maria to appear.

"I'm afraid you cannot see her." Margaretha narrowed her eyes. "If that is really why you came."

"She is very sick?"

"Very. She must not be disturbed. She becomes very agitated if she is woken, and I fear that any interruptions will send her into another fit."

"Does she speak yet?"

"No."

"Reverend Engel has seen her," I said. "I hope that brings her comfort."

"I believe it does," she said.

"Can I not see her just briefly?"

"No."

It was frustrating to be this close to my old friend yet unable to sight her.

"Is she growing worse?"

"There have been minor signs of improvement, but she struggles to stay awake. As to the cause, I cannot yet say. And there is still no way of knowing if it is transferrable."

"It does not appear to have affected you."

She paused and inspected me a moment, her eyes running down the length of my dress and back to my face, before nodding. I had the feeling she had made some decision about me there and then.

"Please, sit down." She gestured to a chair, and when seated I felt the warmth of someone else before me. "You are much better now, after the incident in the forest?"

"Yes, thank you for the medicine."

"Tell me, what is it that you need?" she said, changing the subject and seemingly eager to be done with me.

I proceeded to tell her about Ursula without giving away her name.

"I can help Ursula," said the midwife, brushing away my surprise that she knew the patient in question.

I nodded my gratitude.

"And what of your other friend?"

"She has blisters around her mouth, and she wants to be . . . cautious about other activities in the future."

"Is she married?"

"No."

Margaretha watched me closely. "I see."

She stood up and perused the bottles, took one from the shelf, and placed it on the table. Then from another bottle she poured droplets of liquid into a mortar with dried leaves and crushed them into a paste. I could not tell you what ingredients she used. Margaretha then scooped up the mixture and placed it in a clay jar and stoppered it with cork. She placed this in front of me also.

"The blue one is for Ursula. This will calm the sickness but take heed . . . if she takes more than a drop a day, it may be dangerous to her health and that of her baby's."

Next, she flicked through the pages of Maria's book of herbs before returning to the shelves to search for something else. She then added a liquid to a yellow bottle and placed it with the other two remedies on the table.

"The balm for your friend, she should wipe often on the sores," she said. "She must use the whole contents. From the yellow, just a drop on her tongue as needed prior to any intimacy. You must tell her to choose better partners or find a husband, and if she is very young perhaps to stay away from boys altogether."

When I reached for the bottles, she kept her hands on top of them.

I dug into my skirt and retrieved several coins to place on the table. She opened her mouth to say something, then shrugged and pushed the bottles forward. I suspected it was not enough.

"Thank you," I said, and placed them in the pockets of my kirtle. I stood to go and cast my eye once more over the curtain that hid Maria. I so desperately wanted to draw it open to see her for myself.

"When she is better everyone will know," Margaretha said, diverting my attention.

She closed the door after me. I had gained very little about her from the visit, but I reasoned that, as a woman, and like me, if it came to it, she would protect herself at all costs.

EXCERPT

The Witch Hunts—Förner

They flung back the door, lawmen in their black coats and hats that hung low over their faces, smelling of sweat and animal hide. An acrid rush of cold air entered with them from the river the house sat facing, their boots treading heavily across the threshold. I followed behind with a torch. Gasps sounded from inside the dark recesses of the room as the intruders crossed the floor of the small space to reach the woman on her bed. They kicked the dog that lay in their way and disturbed the son, Jon, beside her from his slumber. He sat up in confusion. There was a rustling of coats and coarse linen as the woman grappled with the men who pulled her from her bed while the chickens squawked and jumped out of their ratty pen across the room, feathers scattering.

Zilla Lucke sat up under the light of the torch that I held above her head. Her expression of disbelief turned to one of fear. The dog reared and growled, and his complaint was met with a baton to the head. He fled yelping to a corner of the room. The woman was dragged onto the floor, then stubbornly used her full weight in an attempt to thwart the two men attempting to lift her to stand. It was pointless to resist, to waste such useless minutes. Engel was there, too, watching from the doorway. As the men dragged her across the floor, she resisted, twisting her body. She was a strong and large-bodied woman of fifty-one years. Wrenched harshly by the arms, she was held tightly by the guards on either side of her before being pulled roughly forward onto her knees. As she was dragged, her toes then snagged on a protruding floorboard, losing one toenail in the process and leaving a streak of black blood, under the colour of night, towards the doorway. She grunted and blasphemed, and her nightgown then tore open to expose her breasts before she shrieked at the men.

A thud and a groan echoed off the night walls. She had been struck hard on the head and dropped like a sack of grain between the strong arms of the men, who then dragged her to the horses tethered outside. They slapped her awake to make her stand and tied her wrists to a rope that was fastened to a saddle. Zilla stumbled behind them as they headed to the distant tower of heretics, dissenters, and the faithless.

I heard a whimper from the corner of the room and walked over to light the area where Jon was curled up in a ball. When I touched his arm, he winced and shielded his face. Jon was brawny, as I'd experienced before, yet in this instance seemed unaware of his strength.

"Jon," said Engel, stepping near to comfort him. "It is Zacharias Engel. Don't be afraid."

Jon was shaking uncontrollably. The priest coaxed him to stand and return to sit on the side of the bed. Although he was not crying, he was clearly suffering from an inner turmoil and unable to make sense of what happened.

"Where is Mama?" He looked upward to Engel, who towered above him. The reverend's face was partly in shadow and must have appeared menacing to the boy, reminiscent of a dark angel I had seen painted on a frieze.

"Your mother has gone to the city, where I will speak to her," Engel said.

"When is she coming back?"

The boy had not understood the gravity of his mother's situation, of her sin.

"I will come and see you soon," said the reverend. "In the meantime, try and sleep. You are safe, Jon. Stay indoors for now."

Jon did not know what he meant by that, nor did he think to ask, his head too jumbled with incoherent thoughts. He lay down compliantly on the bed, and Engel stretched a blanket over him.

Engel and I left the boy and the house, mounting our horses under a lucent moon that had split apart a sweep of cloud, the frigid river air filling our lungs. We quickly caught up with the two lawmen, who had been slowed down by Zilla tied behind them as well as the beasts that kept slipping on the arduous icy path. A short time later, the priest dismounted to help Zilla up from a fall, then walked the remainder of the journey to assist her. I refused his suggestion to place her on his horse. Despite his charitable acts, she spat at him one time and called him unspeakable, ungodly demonic names. Such usage did not bode well for her defence against the accusation of witchcraft.

We crossed the bridge towards the castle, dismounted near the stables, then proceeded further by foot to the prison door. The gaoler opened the gate to the tower, and we commenced down the stairs to the dungeon. The lawmen dropped the woman, who was now little better than a cumbersome lump of clay, in the middle of a prison cell. She had lost consciousness again by then. They pulled free one of her arms, wrapped protectively around her body, and tethered her ankles with heavy chains to the wall. She was given neither blanket nor water. When Engel queried this, he received only grunts from the other men. Torch in one hand, he examined with the other the gash on the woman's forehead, an indent from much force given.

"It's there for all to see," said one of the men.

"What is?" asked Engel.

"The mark of the Devil," he said, pointing to where a blemish stretched oddly under one breast.

Engel, as did I, leaned forward to examine it, close enough to smell the stale odour of her breath. The men who assisted were promised bounty not only for the capture of criminals and delivery but evidence of the witch's mark, too.

The lawmen left Engel, the gaoler, and I with the woman, who made a slight rasping sound as she breathed unconscious. I urged Engel to wake her for questioning, but despite attempts she would not be roused, and he was averse to continue. The first light drew strips of pale grey across her face, and I knew the prince-bishop would be rising soon and seeking a report. Zilla moved slightly, her eyes squeezing tighter a moment, but she did not regain consciousness by the time we left.

We walked across the earthen floor, past the prison cubicles along a corridor that housed the worst criminals—in this case, heretics in the city, interviewed by me, convicted, and awaiting punishment. I had also sent Engel copies of interviews and accusations of people in Eisbach that needed investigating, which he still had not followed up. I felt that the work was overwhelming him, suspecting he was not up to the task.

Engel commented that Würzburg seemed devoid of the joy of life as he walked to brief the prince-bishop of the successful capture of Zilla Lucke.

Prior to Engel's arrival and his letter of introduction to the prince-bishop, an earlier and more detailed biography and recommendations had been sent from Bishop Dietrich. I had learned that Zacharias Engel's first commission had been in a peaceful farming land with quiet folk who were godly, his church always full of parishioners who spoke well of him. It had been orderly there, some public nuisance, an exorcism, a trial of heresy, with punishments of hanging and exile, but there was little other maleficence. Shortly after, Zacharias Engel's studies of the Malleus Maleficarum had taken him to France, where he visited the locality of Jehanne d'Arc's execution, and then on to other places where witch burnings had since taken place. He had walked past the smouldering pyres where four women had been reduced to cinders earlier, and the odour of death was said to have emboldened his purpose.

Such words had convinced Ehrenburg that Engel was the ideal person for the job initially, yet there was now something our ruler could not put his finger on, something that bothered him. The priest wore a veneer that protected his thoughts and secrets. Not that it was wrong to have secrets, even desires, that were not in line with scripture, which the clergy had turned a blind eye to on occasion, but Engel both confused and enamoured the both of us. He was charming without a sense of it, or so it seemed. There was something, however, that disappointed His Excellency: the coldhearted-ness he'd been expecting was lacking.

Ehrenberg met us eagerly to hear about the arrest.

"Your Reverence, would you like some refreshment? Förner?"

I poured two cups of wine and handed one to Engel.

"You were met with some resistance?" Ehrenberg said, directing the questions to Engel.

"Some, Your Excellency," he said.

"And the woman? How is she now?"

"Zilla Lucke lies in a coma," said Engel. "I have asked the guard to send me a message when she is able to speak."

Ehrenberg appeared perplexed.

"You will have to make her, Engel! Throw water on her face!"

The corners of Engel's mouth twitched with a sense of acquiescence or disdain; I could not tell which.

"Your Excellency, I wish to visit Felix Stern and check on his well-being," said Engel. "I would like to question him."

"He is unreachable, cared for at a convent in the south. It is too far for travel when there is still much work to do here, Reverend. I am in regular contact with the sisters and there has been no change . . . What is your concern? You have seen his notes on the child murders."

"Yes, Sire. However, I was wondering if he has made some improve-ment in the meantime. It would be worth exploring, to see if he knows any-thing of the marked boy."

"You will learn nothing new, I am certain."

"As you wish," said Engel, bowing his head.

The priest stood tall and darkly handsome, a fact that was not lost on Ehrenberg. He had heard only good things about him and how his support was growing. Such power held by someone other than Ehrenberg did not sit well with him.

"Everything you do must be checked by me," said the prince-bishop, his tone suddenly stern. He turned to me. "Will you report?"

"Of course, Your Excellency."

"Engel, you must not pursue any quest I deem unnecessary. There is Devil's work here, and you must put any vanity aside and find it!"

The prince-bishop dismissed the priest as courteously as he could, given his mood and through gritted teeth. The reverend did not flinch nor seem to care about anyone's mood. What I had noticed in my short time with him was that he was impervious to those who idolised him and those who feared him, and those, like Ehrenberg, who were threatened by his rising appeal. I had been with the prince-bishop for many years and long enough to recognise the signs of his distrust. I had learned his insecurities that he kept hidden behind his status, fiercely guarding his role and envious of anyone who might seize attention away from him.

"What do you make of him?" Ehrenberg asked.

"I believe the parishioners in Eisbach are very happy to have him there."

"I didn't ask what those idlers thought. What do you make of him?"

I knew the power I held, and I was aware of such privilege. My answer would determine whether Ehrenberg would continue trusting him or not, and my thoughts till then fit with the latter. However, I was curious, and with the work still required, there was no one else with the skills to replace him at such time.

"I think, Your Excellency, that he is completing the tasks asked of him and using his skills wisely. I believe—while he is certainly godly, for I have heard that his sermons have reinvigorated the villagers—he needs further guidance on our practices."

"Hmm," said Ehrenberg. "That will be on your head. Keep a close eye on him."

Such instruction would prove testing as time wore on. Accusations would reach a point where I would have to delegate some of my tasks, made more difficult by the fact that Engel would at times go missing, his servants knowing little of his whereabouts.

After my dismissal, I attempted to catch up with Engel, who was returning by foot to the village and unaware that I was behind him. At a juncture approaching the village, one track led upward to the clergy house and another along the river in the direction of Zilla's house. He hesitated a moment, and looked northward, towards the river and far beyond, to the crudely built dwellings and slippery pathways that lined the edge. I thought he might head that way to check on Jon Lucke, but instead he surprised me by entering the forest. I turned back pondering the reason, thinking it odd at first, then speculating that he had gone there to look for clues.

CHAPTER THIRTEEN

Near on a week had gone since I had passed on the remedies to Herta. I'd heard nothing about Ursula and presumed she had taken the medicine. Master had left during that time to attend a feast at the castle—a celebration of marriage of the prince-bishop's nephew and his new bride—and a storm had occurred that hindered his return. At the end of the third day, when the weather was fair enough for travel, a messenger came to advise that my master was further delayed.

With conditions fair enough for travel, and though several days early for my usual replenishment, I made an excuse to go to the castle storeroom with the cart. Once in the city I saw no evidence of festivities. The streets were quiet with residents shut away, their chimneys puffing out smoke from flaming turf and wood.

In the castle kitchen the servants were talking about something in hushed voices, and they stopped altogether when I entered.

"It's all right," said Raine, the cook, to the other women. "Katarin worked here as a girl. She is not one to gossip. Not like us." She laughed throatily, exposing the gaps where many of her teeth had once sat, and the girls in her employ tittered loyally.

Raine, I remembered, had been hard on children, including me. She would strike out with those calloused, knuckled hands of hers if I did anything wrong. Despite that, the memories weren't all bad. She would tell stories of war and of spirits and frighten the servants out of their wits before laughing at our terrors. She was, as well, a good source of castle information. I had once thought her formidable when I was a child. Now that I was grown, she appeared shrunken, with deep rucks across her forehead and arms that were badly scarred from kitchen scaldings.

"There was a child taken last night in the city," said Raine as she pounded a slab of meat.

"Taken to heaven," added one of the women.

"That's right, yet taken strangely. Nearing two years old, she was found dead in a crib to a wealthy couple on the east side. There were no marks. Only that she went to sleep and never woke up."

It was not the first time I'd heard such things. Maria had shared stories of babies in their cribs dying without a cause.

"The woman said she saw a cat jump up onto a sill. A black cat. A familiar."

I was relieved that Fleck was mostly grey with patches of white.

"In a cat's disguise, it could have taken the child to the forest as a gift for the Devil, who had then taken its beating heart and returned nothing but her shell . . . What are you smiling at, Katarin?"

I shook my head as I reached up to the shelf that housed potatoes.

"You don't believe it!" Raine scoffed.

"How would this cat carry a child of two to the forest and back? The familiar would have to be a sheep or a dog at least."

There was tittering again and the cook threw the girls a surly look, whose grins fell quickly away.

"Have you not been listening?" said Raine angrily to me. "There is black magic here and the Devil at work. It does not take much to understand that the Devil crawls into a soul, then changes into any shape it wants with a strength of many men."

My smile had faded away, too, by that point.

"Anyway, they should have kept their windows locked," Raine said.

If the Devil was so powerful, how come he didn't just unlock windows? I said to myself since I dared not speak those thoughts aloud.

"There's no meat today, and you can't take too much of anything," Raine said, looking into my basket. "You're too early. You're not due for more until next week. And we aren't as stocked as we normally are . . . Anyway, the mother of the dead child is being questioned."

"She deserves it," said one of the girls.

"Sometimes babies die," I said.

Raine viewed me with suspicion. "Then how do you explain the cat?"

There were many things I could have said but decided to leave it. I was curious to learn about the wedding, which had been my original intent. I had not seen any carriages and presumed that guests had left in better weather.

"How was the marriage banquet?" I assumed that would have been a topic ripe for gossip.

Raine paused her task to gawp.

"There were none to wed," she said. "Where did you hear that?"

Kitchen tasks were all of a sudden stilled.

"Someone in the village told me this," I lied, "though they were obviously playing games."

Raine turned her attention to the other girls to see their reactions.

"You always were an odd one," said Raine, pretending to be light-hearted, returning to her work, though the words were bitter also, like her. "Always fanciful and above yourself for a bastard."

It was obvious Raine was jealous of youth. She would waste out the rest of her years working long days for the mostly ungrateful aristocracy and sleeping in a musty room that was barely large enough to fit a cot. I took some guilty pleasure from the thought.

I left to place my basket in the cart and climbed up onto the seat, looking upward from the bridge to the castle I had just left. I could see the prison tower and wondered if Zacharias was there and why he should lie. And if he wasn't there, then where? I did not expect him to tell me everything he did, yet he had been so candid at times. It was as if he were two different people, and I was not sure which one was real and which one wasn't.

I travelled through the laneways to see if I might find him on a visit. I was shaken but also hopeful that he had confused events and mentioned the wrong one. I made haste to return before the markets in the village dispersed for the day. The wind had picked up and grey clouds threateningly inched our way.

Master had asked me to continue purchasing items at the market out of charity. But since I'd been cooking too much to impress, the larder was almost bare anyway. I purchased the last of the venison before the vendor began packing his booth away. As I examined a basket of lemons partially rotten and another of dried fish, I saw Maude and Claudine, the neighbours of Zilla, laughing and whispering to each other at one of the stalls, and carrying armfuls of purchased goods. I wondered how they came to have so much money. Maude looked about her always suspiciously, as if she had just done something wrong or was about to. Claudine sucked in her lips as if constantly worried, but it was the mother who caught my attention most. She carried a purse that appeared filled with coin.

I was about to approach them when there was an ear-piercing scream. The crowd drew back with gasps of horror, and I wriggled my way through to see what had happened.

Ursula stood like a statue, blood down her arms and the front her skirt to the hem of her threadbare tunic. On the ground, in front of her, was a bloody blob of flesh. I walked nearer, unsure what I might do. On closer inspection, in the bloody mass, I could see a head and legs. Ursula gazed at the crowd blankly, as if her spirit had left her.

Jutta pushed her way through the crowds and ran to pick up the foetus and throw it into her basket. People reeled back in horror, making the circle of spectators wider.

"What are you looking at?" Jutta said, snarling at the onlookers. "My daughter-in-law has just lost her baby."

Somehow, while Jutta was out, Ursula had escaped the house unde-tected, carrying her dead baby. Jutta yanked on the younger woman's arm, and Ursula's expression of fervour turned to one of docility.

I felt sick in the stomach and scurried away.

"Wait!" Herta called, gasping, out of breath from running to catch up with me. "What happened? Is it the potion?"

I did not feel like talking to Herta, whose sores were clearing but not completely.

"She has lost the baby," I called back to her, then stopped so she could reach me. I spoke a little quieter. "Do not say anything to any-one, do you understand? You should never have involved me. And stop calling it a potion!"

Herta looked regretful. For a fleeting moment I felt sorry for her with the infestation on her mouth, for which there was no permanent cure.

"It's not our fault anyway," I said, looking over my shoulder as we continued home. There was a wind that made a howling noise through the street, helping to muffle what we spoke of. "We only did it to pro-tect Ursula."

"It is Margaretha's fault," she said. "She is a witch. She has brought evil to this village, perhaps even killing those children herself."

"You are angry because the balm she gave you hasn't fully worked."

She looked away, and I thought she might cry. Even so, I refused to comfort her. She could be vengeful when things did not go her way.

"Be careful what you say to people," I said. "Margaretha was not here when the murders happened."

"How do you know that? She appeared out of nowhere. She could have been hiding here for months in secret."

Herta, it seemed, was on a mission of vengeance already. I didn't know how long Margaretha had been here, so there could be truth in Herta's words. After speaking with Sebastian Spengler, it seemed she was cunning, which made it plausible that she would have found a place to hide, even protected by someone here in the village.

"My brother is besotted with her. All the men are. People who are not sick find reasons to send for her. Even the priest looks at her for too long. Have you not noticed?"

I had not seen it, or maybe I'd hidden it from myself. Such words crept under my skin.

"Be that as it may, Herta, do not speak of this!"

"There is something else. Margaretha has been seen in the forest by some. I believe that is where she meets the Devil, that's where she takes instructions."

"Herta, you wanted her medicine, now you accuse her of sorcery. You should be careful. These things can come back on you." *And me,* I thought.

She looked frightened then. I hoped it was enough to keep her silent.

I could hear voices coming from the rear of the property when I returned, and someone crying, the sound leading me to the barn. Inside, I found Walter consoling Jon on the floor with his legs splayed, sobbing into his hands, his dog lying near watching him loyally, head resting on her paws.

"Did you hear?" said Walter, his hand on Jon's shoulder.

"Hear what?"

"Zilla has been arrested."

"For what charge?"

"Witchcraft and consorting with the Devil."

I was certain such crime wasn't true and wondered if they were planning to take Jon also.

"It was the reverend, the commissioner, and other men who took her."

Jon was miserable, crying like a small child and struggling to understand the reasons that prevented his mother from coming home. Only a handful would miss her. She was an outcast and many would see her disappearance as a blessing. Had Master decided her fate like he had decided Kleist's? I could not see him arresting someone unless he was certain of evil, yet I knew other things, too. I knew killers walked free and the innocent were imprisoned or hanged. That's what happened. That's what I had accepted about life. What most people accepted. I knew of the fate of children like Jon, whose life was now cursed.

"Jon, would you like something to eat?" I asked.

He stopped crying at the thought of food, and I brought back a wedge of bread. He took it from me greedily. He wore only a thin shirt, his trousers torn, and skin exposed. Zilla would have been upset to see him dressed this way and without his coat.

"Jon, would you like to wait here for Reverend Engel?"

He shook his head. "I have to go home and wait for Mama."

Walter looked sad.

"Make a fire to keep warm," I said, "and say your prayers. Reverend Engel will come and visit you when he can."

He seemed in a rush to go, his mangy dog on his heels.

CHAPTER FOURTEEN

I had heard Zacharias return late and brought his supper up to his room. I had knocked on the door and when no answer was forthcoming, I found him fully clothed lying flat on his stomach deep in sleep. He could not be roused until lunchtime the next day, when he was in a mood, cold as stone, his eyes raking the room in disapproval.

"There is something missing in this village and in the city," said Zacharias on a chair in the dining hall as I placed cold boiled eggs and sardines and a pot of warm milk with cinnamon in front of him. "The places I have been have had cohesiveness that knits communities together. There is something very wrong here."

"Herr Reverend Stern used to say that God creates bad weather to draw us together in prayer; however, fear and blame are tools of the Devil to drive us apart."

Zacharias picked up some salt from a saucer with his fingers and sprinkled the eggs.

"The Reverend Stern was a wise man," he said, then commenced to eat.

I wasn't so sure about that or whether God had a hand in the weather. What I thought mostly was that the village had been beset by bad luck and that many were cold and hungry and deservedly bitter about their circumstances. Lack of food and warmth could drive a person to think bad thoughts and act out some of them simply to survive.

"There is a letter here for you, sir."

He took the envelope and placed it beside him with barely a glance. "How was the celebration?" I asked.

"It did not go ahead," he said offhandedly, as if it had been completely forgotten or irrelevant to anything in his daily life. "The bride from France refused to travel in such weather, and by the looks of things that could be months before she has a mind to. Instead, I had some unfortunate business to attend to elsewhere."

I believed him, of course. There was no reason for him to lie, nor did it sound like one.

"The prince-bishop has suggested that I move to the city for the remainder of my commission and find a replacement for Eisbach."

"The parishioners would not want you to go," I said, unable to hide my disappointment.

"It is just talk at this stage," he said, then saw my hesitation to leave. "Is there something on your mind?"

"I have a question, sir, if I may," I said, with a burst of courage.

"Go ahead," he said, returning to eat with zest as if he had not eaten for days. He gestured for me to sit down, and I took a seat opposite at the long table.

"It seems clear that Herr von Kleist killed his children and his wife. Even so, how was it deemed witchcraft? And what made him confess, sir? By what means does that happen? If the Devil is as clever as he is, then I imagine he would protect those who aid him from capture."

He swallowed the last morsel of food from his plate and wiped his mouth.

"I am probably not making any sense—" I said.

"Frau Jaspers, you are a perceptive woman," he said. "There is no harm in asking questions. The church believes that sin derives from the Devil, and such crime as murder is indeed a sign that his evil exists through his earthly aids, those of his chosen ones. Those we deem witches. As for the reasons people confess . . ." He paused a moment thoughtfully. "The methods used are simply to drive the Devil out.

When the Devil temporarily releases its captive, a confession is a sinner's reward."

There were pieces missing from his answer, information I would shortly glean from elsewhere. Something in his tone suggested they were just words without feeling, as if he were reading text from a book.

"Are you all right, Frau Jaspers? You look wearied. Have you not slept well?"

"I am well enough, thank you."

"Good, because I will expect more help from you in coming days if you would be so kind. You should be aware of the work that I do."

"Oh, I won't mind, sir," I said rashly.

"Did the good Reverend Stern talk much about his work?" he asked.

"No, sir, he did not. He did not talk much about anything. He was only out visiting if it was absolutely necessary such as the interviewing of suspects and tasks requested by the prince-bishop, or at the church to deliver a sermon, otherwise he preferred to confine himself to his room. I suspect the work was too much for him at such an age."

Zacharias dabbed his mouth with a napkin, then nodded to himself as if he had answered a question internally.

"You may have heard that Zilla Lucke was arrested two nights ago."

"Yes, sir. Jon told us. He is very upset." As was Walter, who'd hardly slept since.

"I have been remiss as well as busy. I must go and check on the boy today. And I would like you to come with me. I imagine you know him and his neighbours quite well."

I did know Jon and Zilla well, but though I had conversed with the Meyers and heard their names mentioned on occasion, I otherwise had little contact. However, the journey meant some time with Zacharias alone, and I was curious as to the state of the Lucke farm, which had fallen on hard times and which sat furthermost of all the farms from the village square on the track leading north.

We took the cart and horse as far as we could before the track was untraversable by wheels, proceeding next along a narrower path on foot. The boots that Walter had polished for Master earlier were already soiled in a mire of pulped dung, mud, and ice. We followed the curve of the track as it wound around the river. Several boys far from home were skating on the ice where it was thickest, and where several men had carved holes to fish. The stench of old blood and urine poisoned the air at the bend of the river where the skinners stretched and fleshed the animal hides, their workboards smeared with fur and fat and innards.

The Meyer house, with mother, Ingrid, and daughters, Maude and Claudine, sat first on the pathway, and we could hear the bad-tempered squeals of a pig as it was chased out the door by Ingrid and into a small enclosure at the side of the house. Ingrid saw us as she wiped the hair from her eyes.

"Good day!" Zacharias called out, and she responded with a wave before scurrying back inside.

"That's Zilla's pig," I commented quietly. I had not been there for a while, but I recognised the beast. I knew as fact that the Meyers had no pig.

Master stopped to observe the house, then we commenced further along the path to Zilla's house. We were confused by the front door off its hinges, thrown to the ground with apparent force, and several slats of wood removed or broken.

I remembered that the place was overflowing with poultry once, several pigs, and land choked with grain. There were none there now.

Jon was nowhere inside nor in the field behind that fed into the forest, where the girls supposedly had witnessed Zilla's sorcery. I did not know all the accusations against Zilla at this point in time, but I would learn more by the time we returned home.

Inside Zilla's house there was squeaking and scratching coming from the corners where rats had climbed into a sack of woodchip. I remembered there had been more furniture and crockery here on my previous visits. Both Jon and his dog were missing. The ash in the fireplace was cold, the linen filthy, and the place littered with neglect. We stepped outside and I followed Master as he walked the perimeter until we were once more at the front.

The sounds of feminine laughter travelled over our heads. Zacharias looked in the direction of the river that was lined with clumps of grasses and thick, coarse bracken capped with snow.

"Come with me," he said as we followed a narrow pathway to the river. We stepped onto the shoreline where snow and sand had foamed like soft pillows. Maude and Claudine stood with their backs to us and were surprised when we arrived beside them, their laughter ceasing abruptly.

We turned our attention to the cause of their merriment. Jon stood at the edge of an ice hole the size of a cart wheel, his pick tossed to the side of it, where he dangled something by a rope so that it bobbed just above the surface. He wore only his trousers, the rest of his well-muscled form exposed. He would have made a fine match for someone had it not been for the injury to his head.

At first glance it appeared he was fishing.

"What is happening here?" asked Master.

"I don't know, Your Reverence," said Maude. "We found him here acting strangely."

Jon bent over to put his hand on something below the water's surface.

"What is it that amuses you so?" asked Zacharias more sternly this time.

Their faces reddened and they both lowered their heads.

"Jon," said Zacharias stepping nearer. "What are you doing?"

I heard a rustle of cloth and turned to see the girls leaving.

When the boy didn't respond, Master stepped onto the soft edges where the sludge came to the top of his boots before stepping onto the ice. He doffed his cloak and draped it around the boy. I stepped closer to see what had taken Jon's attention.

The dark shape in the hole was that of his dog on its side, legs out stiffly, one blue eye, an ear, and part of its snout exposed just above the waterline.

"Come, Jon!" said Master, taking his arm. "Let the dog go. Come into the house and I will make a fire. You will freeze over if you stand here a minute longer."

Jon agreed, nodding to himself and muttering. He released his hold on the rope looped around the neck of the dog, whose body then slipped below the surface and drifted away under the ice.

"The dog was tainted by my mother," he said.

Jon's teeth were chattering and his arms and torso burned red from the cold. Master drew him under part of his coat for warmth and led him back towards the house. Jon did not once raise his eyes to see who was leading him, and I wondered if it were possible that he was possessed. That the Devil had found an easy mark with a mind so easily corruptible.

Zacharias helped Jon climb into bed and wrapped a blanket around him. I collected scraps of dry wood to start the fire, then set them to blaze while Master retrieved some tools.

"Are you feeling poorly, Jon?" I asked.

He didn't answer as he watched Zacharias bang what was left of the door back into place. I searched for food, the cupboards bare, the preserves and dried meat that I'd seen on earlier visits gone. Fresh droppings showed that chickens had been here until recently. I took note of what Jon needed, as I was certain that Zacharias would ask me to send a basket of food. The two rolls I had carried with us for the return journey I gave to Jon, who devoured them like a dog with a meaty bone.

When the door was fixed I stood up to allow Zacharias to take my place beside Jon.

"Sir," I said. "There is no food."

"You must organise hampers to be sent here," he said, while still facing Jon. "What happened to your dog?"

"He was a good boy," Jon said, his tears leaving a wet stain on his pillow.

Jon stared at the light that trickled in through the window. What was clear today, what was so different about him, was that he had worsened in his mother's absence. Without Zilla's guidance he was slipping further away from the world as it was. Master gave up waiting and stood to examine the house. I wondered if he was searching for clues of witchcraft that would be used against the boy's mother.

"Mama was making nut bread," said Jon. "Will she still be doing that?"

There was something deeply unsettling about the question. The innocence of it, after what we had just witnessed.

"I am certain you will have your bread," said Master returning to his side.

The man-child brightened, and during a moment of clarity he looked about him suddenly.

"My dog has gone to sleep for a while," he said with regret. "But only for a while, Maude said."

"Will you come back to my house with me, Jon," Zacharias said, "while we can better set you up here?"

"No," he said and shook his head forcefully. "If she wakes up, she will be hungry."

Zacharias stared out the window towards the neighbouring property.

"Jon, those girls . . . What were they saying to you down by the river?" he asked.

"They said the dog was ill and that the only way she would be cured was to hold her in the water. She would be better after that, after a sleep."

The two girls were makers of mischief who cared little for Jon. I was certain of that already. I also thought the dog was probably better off where it was. She had looked half-starved, and judging by the empty cupboards, I imagined there was nothing more to feed her with.

"Jon, I believe that Maude is looking after your pig in the next paddock. Did you know it was taken there?"

He shook his head, seeming not to care about the information.

"Maude doesn't like me now," he said dolefully. "She did before . . ." He drifted away.

It was my turn to look through the side window. I saw a curtain pulled back and a face of one of the Meyers peering out. The testimonies that were taken from this family had been damning, with specific details that I would come to learn in full. Zilla Lucke had been accused of dancing naked at midnight with beasts on their hind legs, talking to goats, and poisoning her son. She was a large woman whose back was curved, not from copulating with demons in disguise of beasts as was whispered to be the cause but of years of work that should have been done by a husband and a son with a sound mind.

Zacharias moved to inspect the house. The crockery was clean and unused, a sign Jon had not taken any care of himself. A shirt, blackened, sat in a bucket of water near a well on the property, possibly the last item of clothing Zilla had soaked before she was taken. A loom lay broken, pieces of it partially burnt in the fireplace. On the floor were small pieces of mouldy bread that had been nibbled, and crumbs were scattered towards the corners by rodents making a hasty departure from their crime.

The place, though disorderly, showed no evidence of witches, no book of enchantments. Only in the corner did Zacharias discover some cloth with a red-brown stain.

"Has someone hurt themselves in this house?"

Jon yawned, his eyes closing.

"Mama used to cough up blood."

I knew that Zilla had been ill for some time, which she rarely spoke of.

"Jon, is there anything I can do for you?" said Zacharias. "Do you have any relatives who you can stay with for a while?"

"No, he doesn't," I answered for him.

Jon looked at me and then the reverend as if he had just noticed us for the first time and it triggered some memory, for he started to sob.

"I will send a basket of food, and we will find some help for you," said Zacharias, who then turned to me. "You must see Herr Fisch, the carpenter, and ask him to board up some of the holes and fix the door properly. It will be taken out of my own coin."

I thought we'd head straight home, but as we passed Ingrid's property once more, Master doubled back and knocked on her front door. There was whispering on the other side and hesitation before Ingrid answered with the two girls behind her.

"Good day, Frau Meyer."

"Good day, Herr Reverend Engel," said Ingrid. She had a strange nervous habit of moving her lips back and forth even when she wasn't talking, as if she was mouthing out her thoughts and preparing her words in advance.

"I wonder if I might come and speak with your daughter a moment."

"Of course," she said, opening the door a little wider. I followed Zacharias into the house. There were extra chairs for a house so small and where we were directed to sit.

"She has made accusations I believe to the commissioner, and I must ask several questions as part of my investigation."

"We have already made our statements and been questioned," said Maude.

"It is important," said Zacharias, who continued to engage with only Ingrid, "that I confirm the facts. As you know, there is a woman on trial, and a son without his mother."

"Yes, it's very sad," said Ingrid, who retrieved a handkerchief from inside her cuff and dabbed at her eyes that were dry. Her two daughters sat beside, staring at her curiously, Maude then turning to her sister, smiling a little before hiding her reaction and bowing to the hands in her lap. Master pretended not to notice, though I knew him well enough by then to know that he had.

"Maude, you said in your statement that you followed Zilla into the forest. Can you tell me exactly what you saw."

"It is hard to recall, Reverend Engel, without feeling quite ill." Her face was flushed, and Ingrid put an arm around her daughter.

"Then you must try," said Zacharias flatly.

"I followed her under a shining moon so I could see everything very clearly," she said, putting her hand to her chest. The other two women were so fixed on Maude, it seemed they were willing her forward. "It is quite horrific to remember, and I have been left with nightmares . . . She met with a goat . . ."

Claudine cleared her throat or throttled a laugh, I wasn't sure which, but one glance from Master and she looked terrified instead.

"Zilla was naked talking to the goat and dancing, and there were other creatures too hideous to make sense of," said Maude. "And then I saw that something, a child or an animal, lay on the ground covered with blood."

"You didn't say this before."

"I have tried to block out the horror, Reverend."

"Which was it?" he asked. "An animal or a child?"

"I couldn't see what it was."

"You said there was enough moon for you to see."

Claudine could no longer look at her sister, eyes fixed on her feet.

"It was terrifying," continued Maude, clutching her chest and shutting her eyes. "I had to leave straight away. The sight of blood."

"Are you sure it was blood? It was dark after all."

"Your Reverence, it is all . . . It is all too much for Maude to recall," said Ingrid, hand on her daughter's knee. "There were other things. Frau Lucke would leave the poor boy, Jon, alone in the house for hours. I would see her go to the forest at night. As Jon will no doubt tell you she fed him with a potion that nearly killed him. I have relayed everything to the commissioner already."

Zacharias concluded the meeting, and the Meyer women followed us outside.

"I wonder if you would look in on the boy," said Zacharias to Ingrid. "He has experienced trauma and will need some care without his mother."

"Yes, of course," she said. "But . . ."

"What is it?" Zacharias asked.

"There is something not quite right about him . . . killing the dog."

He did not raise the point that the daughters were laughing about it, that they were cruel. Both of them with sweet, round faces and doe-like gazes, though Maude was shiftier, eyes darting between her mother and the ground, the corners of her mouth twitching. It was clear that Ingrid was implicating Jon in some way by raising this. All the same, Master did not respond as she had wished.

"I believe the boy is experiencing grief, and as you are no doubt aware he is not fully able to care for himself."

"Yes, of course we will look in on him, feed him, whatever we have to spare. Although we have so little ourselves."

Zacharias made to leave, then paused.

"The pig in your yard . . . Is that not Jon's?"

Nervous looks were exchanged between the sisters, Claudine pinching the skin on the back of one hand.

"We found it wandering," said Ingrid. "We penned it away until we could return it. Jon was out at the time. He is out a lot and doesn't feed it."

I wondered also about the chickens the Luckes had once, which were now missing.

"That's very good of you, Frau Meyer," said Zacharias. "Now you must restore it to the boy."

He left and I followed, looking behind me as Ingrid took one more glance before shutting the door. I was unsure if I heard tittering behind us as we left or if it was the wind whistling through the weathercock on the roof. I didn't have a good feeling about the women. There had been much ill will within towns and villages across the bishopric, particularly on freehold estates like this one. There had been long-running disputes over borders, and about fishing and netting and traps in the forest. The quality of the fodder Zilla had grown was better than her neighbours'. Zilla was far more capable, exposing the Meyers for their lack of skill.

"I want to take another route through the forest." He saw my face again. "I promise that nothing will happen to you as long as I'm there. If rituals were taking place around fires, then there may be some evidence."

We walked around for an hour and found no skeletons of animals, no sign of fires, no evidence of a "witch's sabbat." In fact, there was no proof of anything but the continuance of a bleak winter. Whether the snow had covered all trace of nefarious activities was still something to be considered.

Once we were home, Walter came to greet us.

"Some lawmen brought you these."

Zacharias scanned the papers he was handed.

"I will be back in time for supper," he said and left again.

CHAPTER FIFTEEN

Something wrenched me from sleep and I sat up suddenly. I was disturbed by the wind for a second night in a row, but there was another reason, too—I had a sense that all in the house was not still. I crept into the kitchen, my feet on cold stone, feeling along the wall and stepping in places I knew held no obstacles. A burst of cold air pressed my nightgown to my body and brushed the hair from my face.

I pushed the back door ajar, peering outside and greeted by the low howl of the wind and stillness from within the barn. I shut the door firmly, assumed the gap beneath it as the cause of the breeze, and hurried to climb back under blankets. Only moments after my head had found its place on the pillow, my mouser leaped heavily onto the bed and cried.

"What is wrong with you?" I scolded.

When I tried to stroke Fleck, he hissed.

I struck a flint to light the candle on the side of my bed. Fleck jumped off the bed and ran out of the room. I supposed that sounds of mice had caused his restlessness. It was then I heard a sound like a swish and the squeak of a furniture leg bumped across the floor. I hoped it was Zacharias coming to find some food in the night or wishing to find the wine to sit in the dark like he had before.

I caught a waft of something putrid, like rotting fish, as I entered the kitchen. The back door shuddered from the wind before calming. Someone or something had let in a breeze.

Candlelight shadows danced up and down the wall, and I shivered with no fire to warm my bones. Fleck was perched underneath the narrow hall table, and I put my candle down to scoop him up in my arms. He hissed again and clung to my nightgown, his body tense, pushing against me with his hind legs and twisting his body to get back to the floor. I put him back down, then lost sight of him as he entered the parlour, where I found the embers in the hearth still glowing.

"Who's there?" I whispered to the dark corners. The room was silent in response, and I determined that the earlier noise had come from Master upstairs.

The air was colder than the stone on the floor, and I saw the cause. The window was partially open, the curtain faintly billowing. It seemed that Fleck during the night had pawed his way outside. Despite the light breeze through the gap, the pungent odour hung in the air.

The candle blew out suddenly.

Something felt very wrong. I sensed that I was not alone.

As I turned to flee, a figure rushed out of the darkness and careered into me with such force that I stumbled backward.

"Who are you?" I asked breathlessly, attempting to gain some composure as my assailant stepped back into the dark.

"What do you want?"

"I want my baby," said the woman.

My eyes adjusted to the dull light to see her features, long skirt, and bare feet. She stepped forward, her face taking on more of the colour of dying embers, a strange mask of orange and grey.

"Ursula?"

She put out her arm in my direction, opened her hand, and the contents smashed to the ground. I recognised the small blue bottle that had contained the medicine she took for her sickness.

I took a step forward and she stepped back.

"You are a demon in disguise," she said, hissing like Fleck. "You killed my baby."

The weight of such charges took me by surprise. Such accusation would have me killed.

"You sneaked into our house in the night and slit my baby son's throat while it lay in my belly. You bled him, then took the blood away for your own evil purpose. Maybe to drink."

"I know not the sort of enchantment you speak of. I would not harm your child." I stepped closer to show that I wasn't afraid. "Tell me what happened."

"I have seen you kill. I've seen you creep around at night and sleep with men. I know that you change shape sometimes. That you become a cat. It is how you got into my house."

"Ursula, you aren't well. I need to take you home," I said, inching further towards her with the plan to put my arm around her and lead her to a chair.

I stopped when I saw the glint of something she held in her other hand. This close, the feeble light revealed a face that was badly bruised and beaten, one eye swollen, her lips caked with scabs from where she had bled. Her hands were trembling. Maria told me once that she had been regularly beaten by her husband and Jutta, that the old woman had spat at the midwife when she visited the girl during one of her confinements. Oma Jutta and the son did not want any meddling healers, even after Maria had offered her services for free.

"It isn't true!" I protested. "Tell me, what did you see before you lost the baby?"

She stared at me vacantly and thrust the knife forward. I jumped back.

"I saw *you*."

"That is a lie!"

"I know it."

Her face was empty of emotion.

"Where were you when your baby died?" I asked.

"My mother-in-law witnessed the murder and could not stop the killer."

Trying to make sense of the senseless was impossible. I suspected that Jutta fed her head with nonsense simply to be cruel.

"Then Oma Jutta is a liar. It could be she who harmed your baby."

Ursula shook her head violently. She had suffered much at the hands of people who cared little, though I could not escape the fact that my hand was in this also.

"The Devil is speaking through you now!" she shouted.

She rushed at me again, and I pushed her so hard that she fell backward onto the hard stone, releasing a groan when she landed. She did not move, and for a moment I thought I'd hurt her badly. When I reached to help her up, she uttered a growl, then moved to a crouching position, ready to pounce.

"You are cold," I said. "I can build up the fire and you can warm yourself. Then we can talk."

"Do not try and distract me with your words, witch!" she said. "You will get your punishment. And soon. I will make certain of it."

I spoke more firmly. "If I am a witch, what is to stop me from casting a spell to send you to sleep or to send you far away? I could banish you from the village, I could send all your children away. If I were a witch, why haven't I done that already?"

I saw her expression change, her eyes darting to the corners of the room for some kind of instruction. Fleck walked near her feet, his tail brushing her skirt, and she drew back in terror. This set her off once again and she sprang forward at me like a cat, the knife nicking me along the jawline, pushing me backward onto the ground so she was on top of me.

I screamed.

The madness had made her strong and wild, and the tip of the knife had then reached my throat. Zacharias appeared from out of the darkness, his large hand gripping Ursula's wrist and twisting it unnaturally until such pain forced her to release the weapon. It dropped beside my head with a clatter. He grabbed a handful of her clothing on her back and tossed her aside so that she landed on her front, badly winded. As she lay face down on the floor, he pulled her wrists together behind her back and pinned her down with his knee.

"Get me a rope," he ordered.

I flung open the back door and ran to the barn, waking Walter. The chickens scattered, and the horses tapped the ground uneasily.

"What is going on?" he asked as I found a rope hanging on the wall.

"Stay here!" I ordered and rushed back inside.

Zacharias tied her wrists together, then helped her to stand. She was a sorry sight, bruised, her clothes and hair dishevelled.

"I want my children back," Ursula said weakly. "That is all I want."

"You stay here," Master said to me. "I will take her home."

"Not to prison?"

"No. I will have Jutta watch her for the remainder of the night, and tomorrow I will decide what to do with her."

He covered her with Stern's coat and walked her out of the house. I paced for an hour afterwards. The event had left me shaken, but by the time Zacharias had returned the trembling in my legs had ceased. He found me wrapped in a blanket in the sitting room stoking the fire.

"Your face, Katarin!" He fetched a damp cloth from the kitchen and commenced to wipe away the blood from my jaw. He was so close I could smell his skin, his lips only inches from mine.

"Are you hurt anywhere else?" he asked.

I shook my head, though truth be known my head and back were sore from falling heavily. He went to the kitchen to fetch us both some mead.

"The loss of her baby," I said, careful to reveal only a partial truth, "may have caused her to act this way."

"I do not think it was the root cause of her malady," he commented thoughtfully. "I believe she was doomed already the day her husband left her. The death of her baby then brought forward her downfall in a loveless house.

"I spoke to her for some time to understand the reasons for her actions tonight. She believed that you took her baby. Do you have any idea why she would say this?"

"No, sir," I said, swallowing back the truth. "Only that someone might well have put ideas in her head or she, in her addled mind, has come to these conclusions herself."

"I agree," he said. "I told her that you were a good person and that you do not leave your house at night, and she must stop the accusations. She seemed to accept what I was saying. Though I will check on her tomorrow. Jutta appeared put out when I arrived with Ursula and called her daughter-in-law vile names until I gave her warning. I helped the poor girl into bed, and she fell into an exhausted slumber immediately. The children slept through it all . . . Katarin, you should return to bed. Do not worry about my morning meal. I will help myself to whatever is in the kitchen. You must make sure the windows are latched in future."

I was sure I had.

I climbed into bed and Fleck jumped in after me and curled at my feet.

⟓

When I woke it was quiet in the house. I checked that Master's room was empty and his bed was made. I found Walter, who told me that Zacharias had left early with the cart.

On my way back from the market with milk, I saw Zacharias riding the cart with Ursula beside him, her hands once more tied behind her back. A crowd of children followed and jeered at her until Master growled at them and they scattered. He did not see me as he met the track that would take them to the city.

"What has happened?" I asked someone.

"Ursula has slit her mother-in-law's throat while she slept."

"She is possessed," said another. "She might be another for the fire."

I shivered and watched the cart disappear round a bend. Part of me felt pity for Ursula and another part of me felt fear that I might be implicated in this mess. I hoped that Herta would remain silent. For surely, I was part of the reason the tragedy had happened at all.

At Jutta's house the door was wide open. There was evidence of a struggle, smashed crockery, chairs on their sides. I believe that Jutta would have put up a fight. Small and stout, she had a determined nature, and I pictured her with her lined, grim little mouth pressed together, her eyes narrowed as she tried to scratch her way free. A pool of blood on the bed suggested she had fallen back initially, and after the knifing more blood spilled thickly onto the floor. From there, a smear from the doorway to the ground outside showed where her body had been dragged to the cart. There was no sign of the children.

"They were collected earlier and taken to the city, where they will work for merchants who need servants or apprentices," I was told by Herr Goosem, who often appeared suddenly after disturbances to offer his thoughts.

"Or to the skinners," said someone else nearby. "They always need fresh hands."

"They are too small to work," I said.

"Then to the monastery if they're lucky," he said in a tone that meant they likely weren't.

Jutta's murder ignited the prince-bishop to send out more men. There were knocks on the door. Murder alluded to evil, which alluded to magic. Magic, it seemed, was contagious according to people who gossiped in the square. If people accused others while pretending to be outraged by sorcery and witches, then they might divert enquiries away from themselves.

EXCERPT

THE WITCH HUNTS—FÖRNER

Attending the interrogation of Frau Lucke was Engel, myself, and another lawman to assist when instructed. The interview had been delayed by a week due to sudden urgent business that required my attendance with the prince-bishop at a neighbouring territory on the matter of Protestants encroaching. Prisoner Lucke had been unresponsive and feverish during the time we were away, and I was informed by the gaoler that, under Engel's instructions, the midwife of Eisbach had been to visit her with medicine, which the prince-bishop would have never allowed. However, it was fortunate that she did not die before her day of confession. I noticed also that she had been given another nightdress.

Frau Zilla Lucke stayed on the floor while Engel sat in the interview chair, and I took my usual position to observe and record.

"Could you state your name," said Engel.

Zilla had her back against the wall. She appeared not to be listening, her eyelids half-closed.

"You be sent by the Devil," she said. "But you'll find no devilry in me."

"Frau Lucke, I must ask you just to answer the questions," he said coolly.

"You know my name," she said.

Zilla had a rasp in her voice, possibly on account of a lung infection. Engel asked if she wanted water, and she shrugged as if there was no point to it, a jaded acknowledgment of the inevitability of her predicament.

"Zilla Lucke, are you aware of the accusations against you?"

"I'm aware there are woodworms that have crept out from every rotting board."

"What do you mean?"

"I mean that once your name is smeared, other accusations follow."

"Are you aware of your accusers?"

"You mean the three witches at the property or the ungodly clergymen who want my land in the name of the Lord?"

I nodded to the lawman to discipline the prisoner, but as he moved forward, Engel raised his hand. The lawman hesitated and turned to me for instruction. With the prisoner now silent, I indicated that he resume his position.

"Be careful, Frau Lucke," said Engel. "Such talk is heresy."

"And that is worse for me?" she said, an eyebrow raised, challenging.

Engel paused and held the gaze. Zilla became uncomfortable staring into those pale eyes. She frowned, rubbed at her ankles where the metal had worn away skin.

"The Meyer women claim that you danced naked in the forest with the Devil and demons in disguise as beasts. That you are part of a coven of witches who commune on a sabbat. They suggest you raised a second child and sacrificed him to Satan, and that magic has damaged the mind of the other."

There had been further talk that one of the Meyers had witnessed a killing, that it might be the small "creature" found by hunters.

"They've added some new ones." Zilla laughed high pitched before breaking into a cough.

"Frau Lucke, you do understand how grave a situation this is? If you have performed those practices you are accused of, you stand to be punished. That you will be executed, burned."

"Humph . . . And how is all this to be proven, Priest?"

"Witness accounts are the proof, Frau, as well as the mark under your breast."

She laughed with scorn.

"I would think that you would want to help yourself for the sake of your son," said Engel.

Her demeanour changed, and she sat more upright and alert.

"Where is he? He is not part of any of this!"

"Any of what?"

"Any of this farce!" she cried.

"There is nothing spoken against him," said Engel.

Her eyes widened and she took large gulps of air, followed by an anguished cry.

"They will get him!" she said. "They will get him, too!"

"Silence!" I shouted.

"Could you explain what you mean by that?" Engel asked abruptly, trying to regain control of the interview. I was not at first in agreeance of the question, thinking she was about to disparage the prince-bishop.

"Those witches, those actual witches, those cruel women," she spat. "They taunt my boy. That Maude, she is an evil thing. I caught her exposing her breasts, mocking and teasing him while her sister watched and laughed. They are lazy girls, their mother also. They want everything I have. They are not prepared to work for anything. I have told them to stay away from Jon, but they lured him into their web."

"Tell me what happened."

"Several weeks ago, Jon came and told me he was marrying one of them," she scoffed. "I called him a stupid boy, and he ran away crying like he always does when I tell him things he doesn't want to hear. He came back saying Maude Meyer had agreed. It is nothing more than wanting my land. My husband's land! Jon's land! Then I went and spoke to their vicious bitch of a mother who calls me a hag under her breath, knowing well I can hear her. I told her there is no way any daughter of hers will bed with my son, will live under my roof. I called her daughters whores because they are!"

There was rage in Zilla's eyes that were ringed in scaly red skin. She was a woman, I had learned sometime after her death, who had always fought battles to simply survive—battles against the land, against people who thought her odd.

"Your own son has spoken out against you—"

"Why wouldn't he? He has been promised things that won't be delivered. My poor, dumb fool doesn't know that." She whimpered a bit and repeated the words more softly: "Poor, dumb fool."

"And the forest? They were specific about the deeds you performed there."

"All lies! Yes, I had a lover once, and met him there years ago. It is no one's business but mine. Instead, why don't you go and ask Maude how much they owe on their mortgaged land that they can't pay back. Why don't you ask them why they want Jon. Ask Ingrid why she would allow one of her precious daughters to marry a half-wit. Ask yourself these same questions. It should be obvious to everyone, Reverend." Then to the back of the room: "Write that down in your notebook!"

She continued: "Many in the village know, though they are too fearful to say, that you sent an innocent man to his death."

The lawman could not contain himself and stepped forward to strike a blow to her neck with a rod. Zilla cried out and cowered on the floor.

Engel pushed the man away with a strength that surprised me.

"Stop, Reverend!" I demanded. "He is doing what was required. You must reprimand the prisoner if she speaks such again. You can't undermine the prince-bishop nor me."

The lawman hovered near.

"Get away!" Engel ordered, eyes locked on the other man. I saw such fury in his face that I'd not witnessed in a priest before.

"Reverend," I said, standing. "You must cease the interview if you cannot control the prisoner."

"I am doing what is asked of me," he said, turning to face me directly. "Let me complete the task." Then lowering his voice, "Let her speak freely if you want more evidence against her. If you harm her now, she may not be well enough to continue."

I was not usually one to back down in an argument. I wanted the chance to interview her myself, but the sense of his words made it difficult to further object. I instructed the lawman to wait outside. He stomped angrily from the cell.

Engel bent down to help Zilla sit up again. She viewed him curiously. I could tell she was wondering what sort of man he was, who stood up to officials that had the ear of the prince-bishop.

Engel returned to his seat and gave Zilla a moment to rub her neck and compose herself, her eyes darting towards the door.

"If you are referring to Leon von Kleist, you are mistaken," said Engel in a calm voice. "He admitted to his crime."

"Did he?"

Engel was unperturbed by the question.

"Frau Lucke, we must concentrate on you. I am willing to listen."

"You need to study this further, Herr Reverend. Look at the motives. Did you know that the prince-bishop tried to buy Kleist's land a year ago for a price half of what it was worth? He wants everything. He wants no man to freely own his land."

I gritted my teeth but chose not to convert much of what she said to written form at the time. I knew that the prince-bishop would be enraged, and I did not want to be on the receiving end.

"It does not change what you have been accused of," said Engel.

"Do you think my estate is not worth something? There are acres of farming land when the weather turns good. If it eventually turns good. My land will go to the prince-bishop if I die. His enforcers will take it from Jon, who will not be aware they are doing it. As is customary, it should go to Jon, but we both know, don't we, Reverend, that this will not happen."

Engel crossed his arms and said nothing. I remained uncomfortable with this talk. It was obvious to whom such evidence might work against and I fought back the urge to end the interview.

"It doesn't really matter whether you do or don't believe me," Zilla said, gently shaking her head. "My fate has been written and you can't change it anyway."

"Leon von Kleist is a separate matter," Engel spoke quietly. "Your land is a separate matter. Fight for yourself. Fight against the allegations. Fight for your son."

She moaned and lowered her chin to her chest, her shoulders shaking as she cried.

"I had a silver plate, my husband's name engraved," she said, when she was better composed. "If you search my house, you will not find it. Because those women, those witches, would have taken it by now. And the money that I hid there also, that I had put away for Jon for after I am gone, is most likely missing, too. It should all go to Jon, though I daresay he will not see a coin."

"I will make certain that he has money," said Engel.

She dropped her shoulders and sighed wearily.

"Is there anything else you want to tell me that will help your case? If you admit to sin, you will be free."

"Free? Death is not freedom. If you mean to hear a confession, it will never happen, Reverend. I have wronged no one. I have lived my life as any good person should. I did not attend church . . . It does not mean that I don't believe in heaven or God."

"I'm afraid I can't help you anymore, Frau Lucke," said Engel, moving to leave.

"Will you do something for me, Reverend?" she said.

Engel stopped to listen. "Go on."

"Will you look after my boy?" she said, blinded now with tears. "He has no one when I'm gone. There is nothing for him, nothing in his future. His land will be taken, mark my words, for Jon will not fight it. He will not know how. And then where will he go? If you could find him work, someone who will supervise him. He works well that way with someone telling him what to do. He's a good, honest boy, a trustworthy boy with a heart that is easily led."

"I will pray for you, Frau Lucke."

He nodded to Zilla, then did the same to me and left.

Engel had not stayed to watch the confession being extracted by the lawman waiting outside and another I had sent for. It was the first time that I inwardly questioned such methods. The words that Zilla had spoken, that I had not written down in my report, were etched into my mind. The idea that she was perhaps right was etched there also.

CHAPTER SIXTEEN

Zacharias had been solemn during the sermon, as if his heart was not in his words. Afterwards, he did not stay to mingle with the parishioners, instead making haste into his small office at the rear of the church. When, after several hours he did not come home, I returned to the church to learn the cause of his mood with the excuse of cleaning.

I trudged back up the hill through the deep snowfall, the remains of a blizzard that had raged during the night. People had been out early to sweep the streets, dig out their houses, and repair broken rooves. I saw no candle flickering from inside the church as I approached. The clouds that hung around the village like heavy curtains made indoors feel like night, thence I could not see how he was working in the dark. I pushed open the large, engraved door with its iron ring handle that rattled with the motion, and in those seconds before I was fully exposed, I saw Zacharias drop Margaretha's hand as he turned to look at me. They were standing very close facing one another.

"Come in, Katarin!" said Zacharias. He leaned close to Margaretha, and I saw his lips move yet heard no sound. She turned and headed down the aisle towards me, her hair lying thickly over the front of one shoulder. With her chin raised she had a look of someone older, someone knowing. I felt the force of her, a woman with confidence, a woman unrattled. Women knew women. We knew that our power was sometimes silence, sometimes distance, that we were careful, that we were shrewd. And if we were to reveal such secrets, we might become weaker, easy prey.

I felt miserable. This man I had dreamed about might be in love with Margaretha. I hated her in that moment. I hated the village. I hoped he was just a fantasy in both our heads, that his marriage to God was sound, and that if he couldn't be mine, then he couldn't be hers either.

"You have brought items for cleaning, except there is no need. Margaretha was kind enough to attend to the task today." He stepped close to me so that I could clearly see a face unmarred by guilt, someone trustworthy. "I was just leaving."

We commenced the short walk home together.

"What else brought you to the church? Did you mean to pray? Forgive me if I distracted you from that."

"Sir, there is a rumour that Zilla will be put to death. There is talk of it in the marketplace. Is it true?"

He slowed his step and looked southward to the castle in the distance.

"The world has become unruly," he said despondently. "It has never been worse. Killing innocent people is not God's work."

They were words of truth. I had not seen so much dissent, so much chaos, so much disease of the mind that spread like a plague itself. And yet I did not know what to make of his feelings, whether those innocent people he referred to were those executed or the victims of murder. He did not directly answer my question about Zilla, though without a denial I presumed it to be true.

I felt melancholy—Margaretha bombarding my thoughts for the remainder of the walk—and we did not speak again until we reached the clergy house. What was clear in the clutter of my own mind was that since Margaretha had come, things had gotten worse, not better. I was determined to prove somehow that she was the cause of some if not all of those.

⇒⊳⇐

Master had asked me to take Zilla some fresh bread and milk. Upon entering the castle fortress through the stone archway, I stated my purpose. The guards recognised me from before and directed me to cross the courtyard. Access to the prison cells was through a tall, hatted cylinder that sat against the sky forbiddingly. I thought of the people who died in there, souls funnelled up to heaven or down through the earth to the fires of hell. The guards there roughly pushed aside the linen I had over the items in the basket, and I knocked on the wooden door to which I'd been directed. Keys jangled behind thick planks of oak that creaked inward, opened by the keeper of the door, and I was ushered into a dimly lit entrance.

From there one of two guards led me along a stone corridor, so narrow in parts that my shoulder brushed the stone. I was then led down a set of stairs, worn and polished from years of heavy tread, until there was so much earth above me, the idea of it caused my breathing to become shallow. The torches on the walls flickered as we passed, and I focused on the man's back.

We passed cells with bars on the top of the doors so high and dark that I could not see the sources of the moans and cries. A stench of rotting rushes and waste made me hold my breath for periods at a time to stop myself from retching. The guard, impervious to the odour, stomped onward and I gingerly followed. When someone with a male voice called out a girl's name and rushed at the door, we paused while the guard banged the bars loudly with his baton to send the prisoner backward. I knew that Ursula was behind one of these doors. These people dwelled in the dark while their fates were decided by those with the fortune of birthright. I would sooner be dead than here, should it come to it.

"Hurry up!" the guard said when he noticed I was not directly behind him. I moved up close as we arrived at the last door, where he jabbed his key into a lock. He pushed open the door with one hand, a torch in the other. It felt as if we had reached the bottom of the earth here. The air was thick and rancid.

Under the circle of light from the torch, Zilla sat with her head in her hands, her bare feet blackened from the dirt in the cell. She raised her face tiredly, eyes fluttering open. When she recognised me, her face brightened. She jumped up towards me, forgetting her ankle irons, and was jolted abruptly backward. Prisoners accused of apostasy, heresy, or murder had the further insult of being tethered. I could see her better then, and the sight was gruesome. Not as gruesome as Kleist but enough for me to guiltily recoil.

The tips of her fingers were caked in dry blood where interrogators had used steel pinchers to tear away the nails. Her hair was missing in places, replaced with scabs, and she had a bloodied nose.

"Katarin!" she rasped, close to bursting into tears. I felt something move in my chest.

"Herr Reverend Engel," I said, turning to the guard, "has allowed me some moments with her alone."

The guard looked me up and down while he decided whether the subject was worth fighting about. He shrugged and walked to stand with the torch just outside the open door, leaving us half in shadow.

"Reverend Engel asked me to bring you food," I said softly.

At the mention of Master's name, she reeled back.

"Then it is probably poisoned," she said, squinting at the basket. "He means to be rid of me one way or another."

"No, Zilla. I prepared it. There is nothing bad in there."

I put the basket down close to her. She peered inside then felt around, before pulling pieces from the fleshy loaf and cramming them into her mouth. So consuming was her hunger she momentarily forgot I was there. She picked up the pitcher of milk and gulped it down, two thin white trails escaping at the sides of her mouth.

I heard the guard jangle the keys impatiently, as a warning to conduct my task with haste. When Zilla had finished eating, she sat back to lean against the wall.

"I'm praying for you, Zilla."

She groaned in response.

I wanted to tell her that she shouldn't be here but for the guard who might report this. I did not have any words of consolation either since there were none. I could do nothing that might change the course of her fate.

"Has your priest told you anything, what is happening? What they are planning to do with me? I suppose they have said I will be killed."

"There have been rumours."

"Witchcraft, they made me say," she said and grunted her disapproval, "but then the next day I told them it was not true. They will come for me again and make me say things. I will make it hard."

"I'm sorry, Zilla."

"Do you know how my Jon is?" she asked.

I swallowed back my thoughts, and she saw or sensed this.

"What is it?"

"Master and I went to see him and . . ."

I wasn't sure what else to tell her.

"And what? How is my boy?"

I heard her voice break. I could not bear to tell her what we had seen.

"He is being cared for."

"Has he asked for me?"

"Yes. He is missing you."

She gulped back a sob.

"My boy, my poor boy, what have they done?"

"Oh, Zilla," was all I could summon in that moment, but the sympathy in my voice must have reached her deeply. She dropped to the ground, her face sideways in the dirt, her hand gently stroking the earth as if it were the head of her son.

I crouched beside her and put my hand on her shoulder.

"All will be well, Zilla," I said. "Reverend Engel and I will check on him again."

"What has Jon said about me?" she said, with more of the old Zilla, spirited and incensed. Though I was worried that she was speaking too loudly. "His mind has been poisoned. People have been putting ideas in it, untruths. I know they have. Maude, next door, that little whore! She does not want my boy; she just pretends she does. She has bewitched him. It is her that should be here in my place. Jon believes everything she tells him, and he parrots that liar, her sister, and their mother. They want my animals. They want my land."

"That's enough!" said the guard. "Out!"

Zilla reached one arm out beseechingly.

"I'm innocent. You know that, don't you?"

I wanted to nod and tell her that I believed her, but the guard was watching me closely now.

"I will come back, Zilla, with more food." Then wondered if I could, if it was a hollow promise.

I followed the guard with my basket, eager to get away. I crossed the bridge from the fortress and wound through the city, then out along the track to where Margaretha's house sat. There was a light in the window, and I stood there curiously to catch a glimpse of her. I had to find another excuse to visit Maria's house, to draw back the curtain and see her for myself. I believed there was much we hadn't been told. Nights earlier, I had dreamed of Maria as if she had been trying to reach out and tell me something. She had come to my room with her long dark-brown hair and her beaky nose, white as a ghost. She had burned my arm with her touch, leaving a large welt. I had woken in a sweat, checked that my arm wasn't marked, then shivered moments later from the cold.

Herta was in the kitchen when I got home from the gaol. She stepped away from the pantry with much the same look as that of a deer facing a hunter with a bow.

"Herta," I said. "You cannot just let yourself in."

"But I had nowhere to go!" she said. "You were gone for a long time. Where have you been? Were you in the city?"

"It is none of your business."

I saw the bruise on her cheek. The mouth sores were cleared, for now.

"What happened?" Though I knew the answer.

She shook her head.

"Did you hear about Zilla?" she asked.

"Yes."

"It is said that she has confessed to copulation with the Devil."

"Who told you this?"

"My father heard it, up at the castle. I didn't like her anyway. She frightened me."

"Hush with that talk," I said. "She is different, that is all."

All of a sudden, she burst into tears.

"What is wrong, Herta?"

"I feel responsible for Ursula. I should not have listened to her. I'm still aggrieved that she killed Jutta, that she put a knife to you."

Herta had a heart after all.

"It wasn't your fault," I said, attempting to console her. "You were trying to be a friend."

I put some snow in a piece of linen and handed it to her to place against her cheek. She did not need to tell me who was responsible.

"I know what you are thinking about Sigi, but he is not always like that," said Herta.

"You are making excuses for him." All I saw was someone cruel, who I'd seen torture cats, who I'd seen with others throw stones at Jon as he walked past. Who beat up those who were smaller than him like Walter. He did not have my pity.

"Where is your father?"

"He is away selling his services in the villages along the river. He said he had to go further this time, that there is no work. None in the city either—there is too much competition for blacksmiths. He has taken our cart to sell horseshoes, nails, and blades for skates and sleds. He will not be back for another week or more."

She did not wear a shawl, suggesting she had been in too much of a rush to get away from her brother.

"Sigi is meant to be filling the smaller orders, yet he has done nothing but drink our market money at the inn. That is why we fought."

From the look of it, the fight was a one-sided beating.

"I know about the pair of you," she said, glancing at me cautiously from under her brows as I squeezed out a wet shirt in a bucket near the door.

"What?" I said, moving past her to hang the item near the fire.

"He told me things about you. It was another reason we fought."

"Your brother is a liar," I told her. "You know that already."

"I wasn't so sure this time. He said some things, and I started to see some truth in it."

For a moment I felt no pity for the bruise on her cheek.

"He has tried a number of times to bed me, Herta. You should know your brother better."

She twisted her mouth and shrugged her shoulders.

"He told me a secret," she said.

I felt sick.

"What was that?"

"You know."

I felt anger then and turned away so she could not see my face.

"He has lain with you, and you should not be so ashamed. I have lain with others also."

Most of the village knew that about Herta, but I did not say so.

"I said that he might as well make an honest woman of you. He laughed and said he had thought about it, and knows that Papa would agree. "

I gritted my teeth and wished Herta's mouth closed. She was a stupid, foolish girl who was left too much to her own devices.

"Herta, please leave," I said sharply.

"There is no need to speak to me like that. I'm trying to help you."

"Go and find Walter in the barn," I said, knowing he was somewhere other than where I was sending her.

"I thought you didn't approve of me seeing him."

"Not today!" I said.

"Well, I won't see him then," she pouted. "You should be grateful that someone like my brother is interested in a servant girl. You are a good cook, you clean houses well, and you would make a loyal sister-in-law."

Herta was lazy, desperate to have another woman in the house so that she could share the workload, but more importantly Sigi would find distraction and leave her alone.

"With all our money gone, I'm wondering if you have some milk and food you can spare. Papa doesn't care about us since Mama died. He is always in the workshop or travelling."

I could hardly blame him. But he was too soft on both of them. They got away with too much.

I filled a small bottle with milk and cut some bread.

"Here," I said, passing them to Herta.

"Is there anything else?" she brazenly asked, disappointed with the small amount given.

"I will send Walter over with some apples."

Walter came home after she had gone, his expression downcast.

"You have heard more about Zilla," I said, recognising the reason for his mood.

He nodded.

"If they kill her," he said, "it is murder."

"God works strangely sometimes, Walter," I said. "In time, you will have to get over this. It is dangerous to question his decisions."

"Except it isn't God making the decisions, is it? It is people."

"Hush," I said. "It is heresy to make such comment."

"Just imagine if we all made comment. If we all stood up and said how stupid people are. They are looking for evil in all the wrong places."

I was astounded by his passion, yet I knew deep down he was right. Jealousy was the worst condition of all. It made people angry, violent, spiteful. It made us both a target.

He left then. I worried he would say too much his thoughts aloud and to the wrong people.

With a taper I went around the house lighting the fires and then the candles in the parlour and in the kitchen where I was preparing Master's supper.

Zacharias returned and came directly to the kitchen. His eyes looked very dark in the dimness, his slightly jutting canine teeth visible through parted lips as if he were to speak.

"Are you all right, sir?" I said as he passed me his cloak, which I then laid carefully near the kitchen fire to dry.

"I will take my meal here," he said. "There is something I need to explain."

"Of course, sir."

"I know it will be difficult to lose a friend like Zilla," he said, seating himself. With a towel I lifted his plate of mutton with turnips and herb sauce and placed it in front of him.

Tears welled and I blinked them away as I sat at the opposite end with a small plate of my own. Of late, my feelings were becoming harder to control, my attachment growing for the man I decided I could no longer live without.

"What you saw in the church was not what you think."

"I had not thought anything, Reverend," I lied, "nor is it my place to."

I had some idea what a hare felt like to be cornered, as if he had read my mind. For it was not only Zilla I was sad about. He was frightened perhaps that I might speak of what I saw to others. For the first time I had some power, yet I did not wish to use it. I was still in love with him. Yes, I could finally say it. I loved him and would believe anything. If he had said the world was spinning, I would have believed it, too.

When Master had finished his meal, he came to stand close. He picked up my hand and wrapped it in both of his.

"You are very dear to me, Frau Jaspers. I hope you know that."

I stared up at him and my heart beat so loudly I was sure he would hear it. He turned suddenly and I followed his gaze. Walter was standing in the doorway watching us with a strange look. Master released my hand, smiled at the boy, then walked away.

The next day when he had barely finished his breakfast, a messenger arrived to ask him to come to the city without delay. He climbed onto his mare that Walter had saddled near the barn, and Zacharias clicked his tongue for her to walk.

I believed him of course about Margaretha in the church. I had to for my sanity. He had become my obsession. And even if there was something between them, something more, I had more to offer him. I knew that. That it wasn't a sin. That we would run away. That God knew what people had to do to survive.

CHAPTER SEVENTEEN

Since my visit to Zilla, I had further difficulty sleeping. I had dreamed of imprisonment, of rats that nibbled my toes, of my clothes torn from me by guards. I dreamed of my fingers bleeding from scratching at the stone walls of my prison cell. The knock on the door the next morning pulled me ungratefully out of sleep, and brought with it trepidation. Visitors did not often mean good news.

I had slept through breakfast, but it did not matter since Zacharias wasn't home. I presumed that Walter had already left on an errand when there was no response from my call to the barn. I had not the stomach to answer the door that morning, to receive any more distressing news. I felt ill and dizzy. It was getting harder to get out of bed surrounded by so much gloom. I scoffed at myself and shook my head. I put on my kirtle, pinched my cheeks for colour, and hurried to the entrance.

Sebastian Spengler stood there once again in his finery. He smiled broadly at me with a glint in his eye to suggest not only was he pleased to see me but that there was news for me also.

"I'm afraid that Reverend Engel isn't here."

"It isn't only him that I seek. I came to speak to you."

"Doctor Spengler, please come in," I said in a commanding voice that sounded like the house was mine. He followed me into the sitting room.

"Would you like something to drink? Some warm mead after another long journey?"

"Oh yes, please! What a lovely, comely woman you are, Frau Jaspers. How lucky the man is who lives here."

He swept the length of me with his gaze, and I was quick to leave for the kitchen. I fixed the top button of my shift and loosened the tie of my kirtle to show less of my figure. His presence was both offensive and intriguing, and though I liked the wandering eye of certain men, his was not the eye I sought.

Once I had set down the tray in front of him, I sat opposite, my hands demurely in my lap.

"You are looking so well, my dear," he said. "Such colour to your cheeks."

"Thank you," I said, looking down shyly as if I were pleased.

"I have some news," he said more seriously with a frown, "and it is very important that Herr Reverend Engel learns of this."

I leaned forward.

"Firstly, did anything happen after I advised the good priest the last time I was here? Did he follow up on the contaminated wheat?"

"I can't tell you that, Herr Doctor. I am just a maidservant after all. I am not aware of everything that happens."

"Of course, my dear," he said, then sighed. "But it must be a consideration. It is a very grave injustice to kill someone who is wholly innocent. I implore that you speak with him about it. Did he tell all that we talked about last time?"

I was not in a position to speak to anyone, so I didn't answer.

"What is it that you have come to tell him that you would like to tell me also?" I said, encouraging him to hurry up since the suspense was so overwhelming and I was in danger of grabbing his shoulders and shaking the words from his mouth.

"Well, on my return journey to Nuremberg I went much out of my way to the city of Bamberg where Margaretha supposedly came from. There was a break in the weather, fortunately . . . I stopped at an inn in the city and enquired about a girl of her description. The keeper did not know her, but his wife felt sure she knew who I was talking about.

I was directed to a merchant's house, a rather fine house. And I might add he was a rather fine-looking young gentleman. I found him at home and he invited me in, though the reception was initially frigid. When I mentioned Margaretha's new location he looked grim. He seemed in great pain just at the mention of her. Knowing she was not far away was enough for him to shudder. The description I gave him was similar to the girl who had led him to grief, only she had used a different name. Even the fact that she knew which herbs to pick for remedies. It was too coincidental. Then he proceeded to tell me some of the events that had happened. He was keen to tell me some facts. I might add that his house had the latest of everything, that he had fine servants, gilded chandeliers, and beautiful rugs from the East." He paused while he was remembering.

I despaired he would not remember anything else, all the while my appearance was that of waiting patiently as expected of someone in servitude.

"Several years ago, Margaretha, as she is called now, was a ward of his wife. The wife's only sister had not married well and died, leaving Margaretha an orphan, which suggests does it not that she is not a relation of Maria's? The merchant's wife happily took on the responsibility of taking care of her niece. I want to say at this point, the merchant felt very ashamed talking about the situation but agreed with me that it should be spoken about so that other men did not experience the heartache he had endured." Spengler paused for effect. "The poor young man was duped, seduced. I was entrusted with his story since I am a man of science, who searches for reasons to understand rather than for personal gain or information with which to gossip. He appreciated this fact, and I will not reveal his name to protect him."

I had decided that Sebastian Spengler was an old self-inflated bore who liked the sound of his own voice.

"His wife was pregnant, late in the pregnancy. Margaretha had been there already for a year. It was the gentleman's wife's first pregnancy. They had been married for some years without success of having an heir and were desperate for a child. So, as you can imagine, news of his wife's pregnancy had brought the couple great pleasure. Margaretha was said to be overjoyed for them. The wife, a delicate little thing, I noticed from a portrait, doted on her niece, kept her close. Margaretha at first was considered a blessing. She had helped the man when he developed a cough and had helped cure his wife of the ailment of burning cheeks, which makes one look as if they have spent too much time in the sun. There is no doubt that the young girl was an excellent healer. In fact, the gentleman said in her favour that they'd no need of a physician.

"One night, since he was sleeping in another room owing to his wife's confinement, Margaretha came to him crying. She said that she missed her dead mother and brothers who had all died young and confided that she wished she'd had the life of her aunt and the love of a man like him. He did not know that she was a clever actress, a manipulator, a woman who could bring someone so pious, so adoring of his true love, to his knees."

I shuddered inwardly as I thought of Margaretha in Zacharias's arms.

"He was bewitched, he said. He could not think of anyone, not his wife who was suffering from cramps and swollen ankles, who in her final weeks of pregnancy felt poorly and was bedridden. While she suffered, he admitted that he went to Margaretha's bedchamber and found her disrobed. He rushed to hold her, and she clung to him, and they first made love on her bed in the room beneath his wife's private rooms. Oh, I'm so sorry . . . this is too explicit."

I must have blushed from his description.

"I will spare you further sordid details, for there were other instances that he recounted that have haunted me since. But that was not the end of her cunning. Margaretha prepared a special herbal concoction for the wife, and within days she was feeling better. She moved around the house until one day when Margaretha and the gentleman were caught together. The wife gasped at finding them, then collapsed on the floor, blood foaming at her mouth. The man was distraught. He instructed the girl to fetch the physician, but Margaretha remained shamelessly in a state of undress and the poor man had to go himself. By the time the physician arrived, his wife was dead."

"Was it her heart?"

"That is what the physician said. However, the gentleman is convinced that Margaretha wanted him to herself and that there was only one way of achieving this. He did not say anything to her immediately afterwards, nor to anyone else at first. Although rumours still spread, most likely from people who had seen them walking together and arguing in public. In the weeks following, he did not want to be alone with her, nor would he acknowledge her. She begged him to speak to her. One time in the town square she had followed him, crying and shouting and causing a scene. Not long after, he built up the courage to finally accuse her. She told him not to believe that she was capable of harm, told him that she loved him and loved her aunt just as dearly. He locked her in her room and then called the guard, for he was certain she was a witch and she had made a potion to kill his wife, as well as a love potion to draw him away. The girl has the face of an angel, while her heart lies black, make no mistake."

"Surely if the physician has verified the cause, the merchant should accept it?" I said. "I have seen people die before of strange causes."

"You are too kind. You look for the best in people. But I believe the merchant. For the final act proves a lot more. When the guard came, they did not find her in her locked room. She had vanished. He had no idea how she even got out of the room. Her belongings were taken, her clothes. There was no second key kept elsewhere."

"Could it be a different girl?" I said. "Are you certain they are the same?"

"It could be, but it is more than a little coincidental, do you not think, that they have a similar description?"

I did think. What was clear was that she was a lure who had a dazzling effect on men.

"I'm sorry, I can tell that you are distressed by this."

"Yes," I said, for there was nothing truer. I imagined that Zacharias would become her next victim.

"I would have preferred to speak to Reverend Engel directly," he said. "I trust you will pass this on as I have told you."

I did not think Zacharias would have listened past the first sentence, knowing how he felt about the doctor.

"Of course," I said.

"On the way here, I considered speaking directly with the commissioner. However, there is a process, and since I am an outsider who cannot give up the wronged man's name, the testimony will not have much clout without him and other witnesses. It is just hearsay, I can imagine the powers declaring. Also, my dear, I am a Protestant . . . No, don't be concerned. We share the same God. But as you can imagine the prince-bishop here will dismiss my testimony on that fact alone. It is even dangerous for me to be here.

"We would need the merchant, who does not want his name known, to come forward. There is no warrant for her arrest, so there is nothing the reverend can do on the legal side. Nevertheless, it is important he is aware and that he watches her with the eyes of a hawk. He should interview her the moment she does anything out of the ordinary. For I am certain she will reveal her true nature eventually with a misdeed, and let us hope it is not against someone who is close to you or another child."

He stood up.

"I must go. I have business that I need to attend to. I have let go much during my investigation and have another long journey ahead."

I was disappointed. I would have preferred that Zacharias hear this directly.

"Do you think I could visit Maria?" said Spengler. "She was a dear friend."

"She is suffering from an extreme form of lethargy that has rendered her speechless," I said. "Because of the potential for contagion, Reverend Engel has been her only visitor."

"Oh, pity! It saddens me that she is so unwell when she was once so bright and eager. I hope you will take care of yourself, Frau Jaspers, and be mindful of this girl's actions. If you know any man who might be in Margaretha's sights, you must warn him."

I nodded.

"I will write to Reverend Engel when I return so that he has a record of my account that I have given you today, and will request from him some information on Maria's condition."

At the door I helped him with his coat. His face was very flushed, tufts of white hair poked out from his ears. I estimated he was well past middle years.

"You are a very kind woman, Frau Jaspers. I appreciate the time. And if ever you run out of work here, this is my address in Nuremberg. I will make sure to find you employment."

I took the card he retrieved from his pocket.

"Oh, I couldn't," I said, when he passed me a silver coin as well.

"Charity should never go unrewarded."

He had a grin on his face that made him look like a jester, but his heart was as large as his purse. That much I could tell.

"That is kind of you, sir."

When he was gone, I leaned against the door and stared at the ceiling. I had to learn more about Margaretha. I had to find out something that would convince me she was as bad as Sebastian Spengler said. I hoped that Master's soul was not already corrupted.

Walter had returned with two pails of water.

"There's a new baby coming at the house of Herr Fisch."

"How do you know?"

"I just passed Margaretha, who is on her way there."

It was then I decided on a plan.

I walked through the village and along the river track that would lead me to the city. When I reached the turn in the track that led to Maria's house, I stopped a moment to make certain I wasn't seen. The tracks were well used in the morning, and I tied my bootlaces at one point as someone walked close.

"Do you need any help, Frau?" a man asked.

"No, thank you," I said, and he rushed on past, obviously late for his destination.

As soon as he was some way ahead, I hurried towards the house surrounded by trees with long, barren branches that spread out in a circle, like arms reaching out to hold one another. I was certain I would find something inside Maria Unger's house revealing Margaretha's true intent, and my chance to check on Maria's condition.

When I arrived, I found that the front door had been fit with a lock. Through the gap in the shutters, I spied a chair by the grate and the shelf filled with Maria's bottles. I pulled at one of the shutters with the tips of my fingers. It stuck momentarily before another quick jerk and it opened with a sprinkling of snow from the casing. I took another look behind me to further ensure I wasn't seen, then lifted myself up onto the sill to climb inside.

The house appeared abandoned, a pot uncleaned, a partially ground root in a mortar, and Margaretha's bed unmade. On the shelf at the rear of the house I examined some of the coloured bottles and stoppered jars containing potions, herbs, bark, rhubarb, rose petals, various roots of nightshade, and even specimens of mice, birds, and insects suspended in murky substances. There were new ones, too, that I hadn't seen before. I opened the lid of one and could smell blood and bone, the same smell from the skinners by the river. I replaced everything I had examined, adjusting the jars and bottles so that they did not appear moved.

There was no sound from the screened corner. I had no idea what I expected to find as I stepped towards it, but fear suddenly gripped me, and my chest rose and fell rapidly. I drew the curtain slowly open.

There was no great horror, even so I put my free hand over my mouth to prevent a gasp. Maria Unger appeared to be peacefully sleeping, her arms above the blanket and down by her sides. I noticed there were more white strands in her hair. She was two decades older than me, yet she looked even older with her sagging jowls, her mouth open slightly, her lips shrivelled. I sat on the edge of her bed and watched her breathing. Her eyelids fluttered.

"Maria," I said softly.

There was no reply.

"I know you are in there, Maria," I said a little louder.

Without warning, her eyes shot open, and I drew back from the bed in fright. There was fear in those glassy, dark eyes. Her mouth began to tremor, then twist as if she was trying to speak. She mumbled sounds forced out between her parted lips. Maria was trying to tell me something, and I leaned down to listen.

"What are you doing here?" said Margaretha, and I startled and moved away.

"I'm sorry," I said. "I just wanted to see Maria."

Margaretha looked from me to Maria, who was still trying to form words, mewling like a baby, her illness stealing her tongue.

"She is being well cared for," said Margaretha coldly. "I am seeing to that!"

She moved to the ill woman's side and began to stroke her hair back from her forehead.

"She needs rest," Margaretha said in a gentle voice. The sounds from Maria ceased, as she became captivated by the eyes of the younger midwife. "Visitors upset her, clearly."

"She has no rash to suggest contagion," I said. "It is not like the plague that many have speculated. Do you hold much hope for her recovery?"

"Come!" commanded Margaretha in her soft, deep voice that did not match her small frame. I followed her to the door.

"She has been getting steadily better, but it is still grim, her life right now," said Margaretha quietly, so that only I could hear. "I have seen conditions like this before, and full recovery is rare."

I did not know whether to believe her.

"You should not have entered here. I could report you."

"It won't happen again," I pleaded.

"Hmm . . ."

"I promise."

"Very well. I will not say anything this time."

I turned back to Maria, whose eyes were now closed. Margaretha opened the door, keen to see me leave.

"How is the woman you attended?" I said at the entrance.

"The mother is well so far, except we are unsure about the health of the baby. She arrived quickly. Too quickly. She is very small."

She commenced to close the door behind me.

"I wanted to see you also," I said. "I never thanked you for calling out to me in the forest the day the boy went missing."

"What do you mean?" she said, frowning.

"When I had fallen in the forest holding the child, you encouraged me to keep walking. You called my name."

"I know the event you speak of, but I made no such call. I followed the boy, then lost him as I went deeper into the forest. By the time I returned to the village to advise his mother of his whereabouts, you were there with him in the square."

She wore a puzzled expression, then shrugged dismissively, once more gesturing with her hand for me to go.

"There is one other thing . . . ," I said. "I wonder if you might call on Herta one day soon. I believe that Sigi, her brother, is dangerous. She came to our house with bruises and admitted as much."

She thought for a moment, then nodded.

"Goodbye, Katarin."

Once the door was closed behind me, I took a deep breath. The timing of births was unpredictable. I'd taken a risk at being caught here and lost. Even so, there was more that was troubling me. I was certain someone had called me in the forest. Was she lying, or had it all been in my mind?

I commenced the walk home, taking a backward glance. Margaretha was at the window watching me, and I turned away fearing that too long a stare and she might turn me to stone.

Walter met me tearfully on the track to tell me that a notice had been posted in the square advising that Zilla's execution would be the day after next.

CHAPTER EIGHTEEN

On the day of Zilla's execution, the sun had smiled briefly through the clouds for the first time in months. Some said that it was a sign of where Zilla was heading, where she was welcome. These whispers continued as the crowd grew larger. The change of feelings towards Zilla seemed unusual. People weren't there to bay for blood like they had previously.

Zacharias had not returned to the village for several days, since receiving a summons from the castle. He had not been home to compel me to go this time. Nevertheless, I chose to be there. The prince-bishop was due to oversee the event again, and most people wanted to be there for a glimpse of him as well.

"Have you seen Sigi?" one of Sigi's brutes asked me rudely, his large face pushed into mine so that I could smell his ale-laced breath. "Herta isn't here either."

"How would I know?" I said. "They have probably gone with their father."

There was no sign of the Meyer women either. Walter scrambled through the crowd to get a better view beside me. He had not witnessed the last execution, though this time he wanted to be here. I put my arm through his, but he drew it away. He had not been himself, and I knew this day was painful for him. He liked Zilla, but more than that, Jon was his friend.

"I can't see Jon here," I said. "Do you know where he might be?"

He shook his head.

I pulled his arm to drag him nearer the front.

The procession ceased near the centre of the square. The prince-bishop, the commissioner, and the lawmen took their positions on the stage, while Zacharias stood beside it and perused the crowd that was pushed back yards from the proceedings. Margaretha was amongst the crowd, and I was pleased to note that Zacharias appeared not to notice her. A number of castle workers had followed at the rear to watch the next spectacle.

The prince-bishop welcomed everyone as if it were a day of celebration. Zilla was yet to arrive, and all eyes darted between Ehrenberg and the road that she would travel through to reach the square.

The crowd was deathly silent this time as she hobbled with iron around both her ankles and wrists. She was not so damaged as Kleist but in discernibly worse shape than when I had visited her. Her feet were black, fingers crusted with blood, and hair torn from her head in places. Her shift was stained and soiled from the cell floor. Her arms, like dead weights, could not be raised when the executioner directed her to lift them. He had to do so himself to tie them to the top of the pillar above the crudely made platform and pyre around it.

"Let's hope she was not slow to confess," said someone close by. "They string them up here by their arms tied behind their backs, put fire under their feet."

I knew this was more than just rumour. I had heard recently of tortures in other territories, some being hanged until they were almost dead, revived with cold water, and their bones broken.

Zacharias stood still like a statue, hands clasped in front of him, tightly I noticed, so that the whites of his knuckles were obvious. The commissioner made to walk to the front of the stage to announce the crime, but I saw the prince-bishop shake his head and gesture with his hand towards Zacharias.

Master did not take the stage but faced the crowd from where he stood. The sound of chatter died down as people were eager to hear him speak. That this charismatic member of the clergy other than His

Excellency himself could command such respect did not go unnoticed by the ruler, who I saw eyeing him curiously. I was indeed privileged, or with hindsight perhaps cursed, to live in the same house as the person revered even more so, I felt, than the prince-bishop. People's eyes weren't on our ruler, who rarely came to our village except for important business such as executions. He had been supplanted by someone more palatable, someone accessible.

"It pains me, before God," said Zacharias, "that we have to send this soul early to be judged for that which is a heinous crime."

I noticed that the executioner had new rings of silver. He was making money from death, as were the innkeepers in the cities and villages, and the lawmen for the finding of witches.

"What is the crime?" someone called. I looked around and could not see the face behind the voice.

"It is the crime of witchcraft," said Zacharias.

There were gasps and grumbles from the crowd. It should not have been a surprise. The word "witchcraft" had been used too often recently, a word that silenced people and any criticism. Zilla appearing languid, her head hanging low as if it were too heavy for her to carry.

"Is there anything you wish to say?" the reverend asked her.

She raised her head to face him, wretched and defeated.

I saw the prince-bishop whisper in the ear of the commissioner next to him. I saw the other man pause, then consider Zacharias with a frown. Master had changed the plan. He had given Zilla a platform to speak, which seemed fair to all except the prince-bishop, who, having measured the effect Zacharias had on the villagers, appeared reluctant to object.

"There is . . . ," she said, her voice crackling before she broke into a cough that lasted several seconds. She tried again. "There is an evil here. It has been masked as something else. But there is an evil in the bishopric. There are people who you might trust, but beware—"

"Mama," came a cry from the crowd. People parted to let through Jon, who began to run towards his mother. Several guards rushed at him and prevented him from reaching her. He fought with ferocity, pushing his way until he was only inches from the execution platform. He began to bawl.

"Bring my boy here, please . . . ," she begged of Zacharias. I saw him close his eyes and grimace in an expression of what seemed to be regret. It was a minor fissure in his stoic façade before he composed himself for the crowd, who unlikely could not read his face like I could.

Zacharias waved the boy forward and the guards released him.

"No!" said Ehrenberg, overruling him, but Jon had already scrambled up onto the platform to throw his arms around his mother tied to the pole and sob into her bosom.

"Be brave, my boy," said Zilla. "We will meet again in a better place."

The people were silent. There was no jeering for her to burn. She had suffered, she had been mocked for being different, but the people did not mock her this time.

Crows flew above her, aware that death was close.

Ehrenberg raised his hand, and the guards rushed onto the platform that held the pyre to pull Jon roughly away. His wails were so woeful, so heartfelt, I experienced a pain in my chest such that I had never felt before. I felt his pain as if it were my own.

"Take care of my boy!" called Zilla to the crowd.

Jon scrunched his face, turning red, and then he howled. He broke free of the guards once more to throw himself on the ground. When several guards came for him again, he attempted to resist, briefly shaking them free, with a strength that was herculean. His shirt was torn from him in the fray; then a blow to the back of the head subdued him. The guards dropped Jon's limp body at the edge of the crowd. Several men rushed to help him stand while a woman wrapped her shawl around his bare shoulders.

"Enough!" barked Ehrenberg. "Get him out of here! Set the fire!"

Jon was dragged away through the parting crowd and Walter followed, as did Margaretha. I turned back to see that Zacharias's face had paled and he looked to the sky.

The fire started with a *whooshing* sound, and a sudden wind whipped it into a frenzy. Zilla caught Master's gaze and mouthed something to him, though I could not read what she said. The flames inched along the pile of sticks, then tongues of fire licked at the roughly made platform above it.

"This is not the end of me!" Zilla cried out as she watched the fire slithering towards her like molten snakes. It took her skirt first as the clouds closed over the weak sun once again.

I covered my ears to smother her screams of agony, watching her shrivel to black before my eyes. The smell again made me feel nauseous. The dismayed crowd dispersed before this next spectacle was complete. Ehrenberg became enraged, throwing down a cup he held as he stood to watch them go. There were no parcels of food this time, no free mead. There was no cause to celebrate, the people had decided. We had lost a friend, a mother.

The prince-bishop left with his retinue, and Zacharias stayed where he was watching the fire reduce Zilla to ash. I stayed also. My nerves were still raw from the wails of Jon and the smoky remnants of burning flesh and bone that stuck to my clothes and hair, a coating that I would once more wear for days.

Zilla's death was a reminder of what happened to those unguarded. I had to be careful. I had to look over my shoulder. I had to protect myself.

CHAPTER NINETEEN

In the days following, Zacharias did not talk. He had a messenger nail a note on the church door cancelling the next sermon. He did not come into the kitchen to ask me questions. He barely ate, and he was gone most nights. Some said that they saw him near the edge of the river, sitting on its frozen banks, sometimes looking towards the dark of the forest as if waiting for someone. Others saw him on horseback in a neighbouring village. I had no idea where he was sleeping or who he was with.

By day, I would look out the windows hoping to catch a glimpse. At night I would close my eyes to imagine Zacharias at my side, his hand over mine on the cook's table. I despaired that he might never return, and if these memories, like my childhood ones, would vanish over time. Walter, too, was moody and withdrawn.

Then one day Zacharias arrived back at dawn. There were still signs of late nights, dark smudges beneath his eyes, but he seemed buoyed by something, I could not say. He laid his cloak near the kitchen fire to dry.

"There have been more accusations in the city," he said to me as he perched on a stool in the kitchen. "They are burning witches everywhere."

He told me the story of a woman of wealth and charity who had recently been accused and confessed of the crime of aiding a Protestant, of taking him as her lover. She was a widow with vast lands and several young children.

"Will you interview her?"

"No, Ehrenberg is using his own officials for that," he said, his expression darkening. "She will be interrogated and burned there. He has set me other tasks here and in neighbouring villages. Accusations are many."

"It seems it does not take much now to receive a conviction," I said.

"Evidence in some cases is no longer a necessity once someone formerly renounces another," he said. "It is madness!"

I had no time to be startled by his frankness. Walter ran feverishly into the kitchen, where Master caught him in his arms.

"Herta and Sigi!" he said, out of breath and tearful. "There is a crowd outside the house. Margaretha found them."

Zacharias kept his arm around Walter, who remained in an agitated state, scratching at the crook of his elbows where his rashes had returned.

"What has happened to them?" Master asked.

"She had gone to check on them," he said. "They are both dead."

"Calm, boy!" said Zacharias. "Come sit near the stove. Katarin, get Walter something warm to drink. He is shivering."

My hands shook as I heated some milk and listened to Walker speak. He told Master what he had learned from others who spoke to Margaretha. "They have sent for a city official to examine and asked for you, too, Reverend . . .

"I had gone to see Herta last week, but there was no answer," continued Walter. "Herr Goosem said that he thought he saw them leave with bags."

"Goosem is not only meddlesome, he is half-blind and an unreliable witness," said Zacharias.

Goosem had so far made a number of false accusations against people.

When I handed the milk to Walter, his hands trembled and he would not take the cup. I placed it beside him, assuming he was still in a state of stupefaction from what he had witnessed.

"Katarin, my cloak!"

I met Zacharias at the door. He took the cloak and swung it around his shoulders, and I watched him disappear into the snow that swirled around his feet before shutting out the weather and returning to Walter.

"What do you think happened?" I asked Walter back in the kitchen.

"I am not sure," he said. "Only that it is a crime. That is what someone said . . . I did not hate her, you must know. I did not wish anything bad to happen to her."

"I know."

I held him for a moment, and he was limp and unresponsive against me, arms down by his sides.

"What made you go there?" I asked. "I thought they were the last people you would want to see."

He shrugged, and it was clear I would get little more out of him.

"Stay here and watch the pot of stew," I told him, then I followed Master's tracks in the snow.

A crowd had gathered outside Bertram Jacobs's house. Bodies suspended on linen were being carried outside, first Sigi, then Herta. They were laid on a waiting cart while Margaretha spoke some words in Zacharias's ear and placed something in his hand before they parted company.

"Carry them to the church," instructed Zacharias to the person who owned the cart.

Sigi's head had been caved in, smashed with a heavy object. Herta had blood around her mouth but was unmarked elsewhere. People made signs of the cross. I began to cry, and someone touched my arm to ask if I was well.

Many of us followed the cart for a short way, and, once at the church, villagers placed the pair on the floor in front of the altar. Zacharias told the crowd who had come to gape to leave. I turned to go.

"Not you, Frau Jaspers!" he said.

Once people were gone, I was left with Zacharias, who knelt down to examine the bodies.

Gemma Liviero

I glanced at them both, then averted my eyes from the hollowed wound in Sigi's head.

"It appears that Herta has killed her brother, then killed herself. Did you have any idea she planned to do this?" he said, standing up.

I shook my head.

"This was in Herta's hand," he said, pulling a small red bottle from his pocket.

There were many such bottles at Maria Unger's.

"Is there any reason Herta would have one?"

"You will have to ask Margaretha."

He stared at me, expecting more.

"She was your friend," he said.

"Friend" was too strong a word, but given there was no other relationship I could think of, I nodded. Herta was difficult to like, and I imagined difficult to love also.

"Is there anything you would like to tell me? Anything else that might have led to this?"

"Yes, she spoke a lot. She loathed her brother, who took to her with fists sometimes."

"Hmm," he said. "She had clearly drunk from this bottle she was holding. I agree with Margaretha's assumption. I believe that she had hit him and then realising he was dead, perhaps in a panic, she killed herself. She had saved herself the humiliation of an execution."

My temples throbbed.

"How long have you known about the abuse?" Zacharias asked me.

"She often had bruises and scratches on her arms, which she tried to conceal with clothes and clay."

"You should have told me much earlier if you had known for some time."

"I did not think anything would have been done, sir. This sort of thing happens." My voice broke as tears fell.

"I apologise for sounding too harsh. I understand that you did go to Margaretha. I can't find fault in that."

240

He inspected the faces of the dead once again, then covered them with cloth.

"The house seemed in order," he said. "It did not look like there was a fight. It did not look like Sigi had been taken by surprise. The door was locked, however the key was not in the door and nowhere to be found. Margaretha had knocked a number of times over several days and assumed they were out until she grew suspicious. Since Bertram Jacobs had not yet returned from his journey, she had to find someone to break open the lock . . . You must tell me everything you know about Herta. Every detail. Do not spare me and do not fear me either."

I bit my bottom lip and blinked several times. I sat down on one of the pews, and he perched on the one across from me and crossed his arms expectantly.

"Herta knew that Margaretha had potions. She had come to me and asked for a potion for Ursula, who was very ill with the baby she carried. Maria Unger told me once that the medicine was very strong and there were risks of losing the baby. Ursula, when I spoke to her, was aware of this."

"Are you saying that Ursula had thoughts of murdering her own baby?"

"I am not certain, Reverend. But I know that she didn't much care for being sick with any of them. And she was not coping well with the ones she had."

"So Herta went and got the medicine from Margaretha?"

"No," I said. "I went for medicine for both Ursula and Herta. Herta did not want to be seen by Sigi. He may have found out about the remedies she sought."

"More than one?"

"Herta needed something for a rash, a kissing rash, and something to stop conception. Margaretha supplied both."

I expected him to be surprised, yet his expression didn't change.

"Why did you agree?" he asked.

241

"I . . . I could not refuse, for Ursula's sake, since she was so sick with the pregnancy I feared for her life. She had threatened to harm herself if I didn't help her."

He sighed.

"Who else makes potions or supplies poisons? Are you aware of anyone?"

"No, sir. Only Margaretha."

"So you think that Margaretha gave Herta the poison she drank as well?"

"I don't know, sir. I don't know where else she could have acquired it. It is possible the potion was not meant to kill, maybe just calm."

"You should return home," he said. "I wish to stay in the church and prepare a mass for the two young lives deceased."

When I remained still, he raised his eyebrows quizzically.

"Is there something else?"

"I am not sure that Margaretha uses the medicine wisely, sir."

"What are you saying?"

"I believe she makes potions that may not just be for cures."

"One would have to accuse her of witchcraft. Is that what you are doing?"

"I would be no better than the hateful if that were so."

"Yet you said as much," he said thinly.

"Some people in the village are saying that you are seen at her house often," I said rashly, fearful that I was losing his trust. "I thought you should know. I tell them to mind their own business."

"People know nothing of the tasks I perform, the prayers I offer for Maria, the medicines I acquire for prisoners. They should not talk. If someone wants to accuse me of something, they can do so. My conscience is clear."

He seemed to be challenging me. I became frightened that I'd gone too far. I had to be careful, for I did not want to upset him. It was strange that one can fear someone and love them just as much. I had said so much already, I could not have left without telling him the worst of it.

I told him then of Sebastian Spengler and everything he had revealed, including the reason of faith he did not go to the commissioner directly, and Zacharias listened intently. I told him that the doctor would send him a letter to confirm everything.

"I know that Margaretha goes to the forest to catch animals."

"Many go to the forest to catch animals."

I believed that I would save Zacharias from Margaretha's grasp once and for all. She was dangerous, I suspected that much.

"I know that she puts blood in jars with other mixtures."

"How do you know this?"

"I saw them." I did not say that I broke into her house.

"I've seen the bottles you speak of. They are likely just medicines to cure."

"But it was only after Ursula had the medicine that she lost the baby."

He put his hand to his chin and studied the floor.

"Very well," he said. "Once I finish with Ursula's case, and the others I am told are urgent, I will speak with her. It does appear she has some questions to answer, given what you have just told me. If there is evidence of magic in her house, be sure I will find it. In the meantime, you cannot speak of it."

"Of course." I felt relieved that I had released what I had been carrying, not because of a belief it was a sin against God but that I could no longer keep such things from Zacharias. I had to be rid of Margaretha's influence. I had to expose her. I had to make him see.

"It has been a difficult week," he said. "There are many broken hearts, and there are things I must give thought to and people to visit. I will not take any supper. I will fast and pray for our departed friends."

"I know Herta is with the angels, sir," I said, blinking away my tears.

I did not say the same about Sigi.

He touched my face with the palm of his hand, giving me some kind of absolution or maybe letting me know he trusted me implicitly, that I was to trust him also.

"Go home," he said. "I will await the official who will confirm the cause of death."

I did not wait up for Zacharias. I slept well and heavily for the first time in months.

EXCERPT

THE WITCH HUNTS—FÖRNER

One of the lawmen had taken a statement from the niece of the midwife in Eisbach in my absence. I had been tasked that day to inspect a disturbance in another village, which amounted to nothing more than a dispute about the border between properties and a warning to one of the men of a flogging should he make a complaint again and waste my time. The statement read that Margaretha Katz had voluntarily come to tell of some accusations against her. The lawman conducting the interview saw fit to detain her, await my return, and send a message to Engel also, who arrived only minutes before I did.

Margaretha sat on a chair, unrestrained in the ground floor, tower cell, and staring up at the high window that let in a sliver of light and gave a thimble-size view of the sky. Her face was suffused with whiteness, and her hair was a pale shade of the sun at the crown of her head. The effect caused me pause, for she was without doubt a beauty, and I observed her profile briefly, before seating myself once more in the shadows. She turned towards me with a hint of a smile that gave nothing of her nature or thoughts.

"Why have I been held back from leaving? I have already given my statement to a lawman. I was told that there were whispers about potions that might harm people, and I have responded to say otherwise and explain the herbs that I use. I know what talk can lead to."

Engel clasped his hands together in his lap.

"You have not been charged with anything, but there are some questions that need to be answered."

"Then ask away, for I have nothing to hide."

"There is a doctor from Nuremberg who knows your aunt. He was the one to raise some concerns. Did Frau Unger ever mention him?"

"No, sir. Up until recently I'd had little correspondence with my aunt."

"This man from Nuremberg claims to know of you."

"I daresay many know of me."

She held his gaze.

"Where did you reside before you came here?"

"I worked in Bamberg most recently, but I was born in Cologne."

"What made you come to Eisbach?" said Engel.

"To work with my aunt. With no other family left I wrote to her, and it was upon her suggestion that I came here."

"Maria Unger had told people she had no living relatives."

Margaretha's lips tightened.

"My mother and Tante Maria had a disagreement years ago. She had assumed we were gone for good before I wrote to her."

"What state was Frau Unger in when you found her?"

"She was poorly. I knocked on the door and she didn't answer. I found her collapsed on the floor."

"Was she able to tell you the cause?"

"She was unable to speak."

"How long have you been a healer?"

"For two years now, sir. I worked with someone who used herbs to cure, and I have since spent many hours studying my aunt's books."

"And before that?"

"I worked as a servant in a house until the old man died."

"You sound educated. Where did you learn to read and write?"

"My father taught me. My mother taught me herbs. She and Maria had learned from my grandmother."

Engel studied her a moment.

"I have heard different things."

She showed no emotion. Her hands were unusually relaxed in her lap for someone under questioning.

"What have I been accused of?" Margaretha asked. "What else has been said about me?"

"It is said that you are guilty of adultery with your master in Bamberg. That you may have poisoned the man's wife and that she died with child."

Margaretha put her hand on her chest and scoffed with disbelief, a small frown appearing between her eyebrows.

"I have never worked for any such man. Who is this person who accuses me of these? Is it this stranger who has appeared out of nowhere?"

"It is someone who has met this man but who does not wish to be named."

"I would think that the husband in Bamberg wants to put the fault of his infidelity onto someone else. Servants, peasants, and healers are easiest to blame. It is not me he refers to, and since there is no one who dares show their face, then I cannot answer the accusation, sir. This is just a story."

"Do you have anyone to vouch for you?"

"My aunt has kept the letter that I sent her to advise of my coming."

"Do you have any family or someone who can corroborate the relationship and what you have told us?"

"I have a reference from an employer, sir. As for my family, they are all deceased . . . except of course Tante Maria."

Margaretha sat poised and outwardly guileless. There was no stumbling over words or periods of delirium.

"Will I find that when we search your house?"

She looked alarmed suddenly.

"Why my house?"

"We are searching for evidence of sorcery."

"Sorcery!" She stood up then. "That is ludicrous!"

"Silence!" I yelled, and Engel raised his hand.

"I am no witch, sir!" she said only to Engel.

"If you are no witch, we will not find anything that incriminates you."

She tilted her chin upward, which I read to be defiance.

"You must not go near my aunt!" she said.

"Is she still considered contagious?"

"There is much we don't know about her condition, and she worsens when people visit."

"How do you mean?"

"I can see in her eyes that she is agitated, and her skin becomes warm and clammy. It is best for her if she remains calm."

"I did not notice this."

"You have not been there lately. She is more aware."

"I agree," said Engel. "I have not seen her much lately with little time to spare. Is she so aware of things as you say to feel such fear anyway?"

"I believe she has a healthy, active mind trapped in a broken body."

"Then she is clearly not contagious. You appear well and unharmed after weeks in her company."

She sighed as if she found the questions frustratingly dull.

"She has shown improvement lately. I have been massaging her legs, and she has been moving her hands. I believe she understands everything. As to the cause of sickness, I cannot yet say."

"Has she said anything?"

"A word or so. But nothing that I can make sense of. I did make an earlier request for the physician to examine her, but he did not come. My description of her symptoms may have kept him away or perhaps he was aware that I have little means with which to pay."

Although sounding critical, I could not disagree with the reasons she put forward.

"I should like to verify this."

"Of course."

"What were you doing at the blacksmith's house?" continued Engel.

"Frau Jaspers, your servant, asked that I call on Herta. She hinted at family trouble. I had tried several times to visit until finally suspecting something was wrong, I asked for help to break the lock."

"And what did you find?"

"Herta and Sigi Jacobs were both dead."

Margaretha appeared grave at this point, closing her eyes as if remembering the grisly scene.

"What else did you see?"

"Sigi's head badly damaged and Herta with blood coming from her mouth."

"Did you see the weapon used on Sigi?"

"Yes, I believe it was a linen iron. There was one beside him covered with blood."

"And Herta?"

"She was holding a bottle in her hands."

"Had you seen the bottle before?"

She bit her lip then, some of her confidence slipping.

"I will say that I have a number of those bottles, which I distribute with herbs for ailments, mainly for women, for cramps, for headaches, and ointments for wounds. There are also herbs for sleeping and herbs for tempers. I believe, sir, that if you examined any home, you would find a similar such bottle given with only good effect."

"Do you have any love potions?"

"Love potions? I do not dabble in any magic, Your Reverence."

"The bottle is the type that Frau Unger has in her house. Could the bottle have come from there?"

"Yes. It is possible. And it is a bottle that normally contains herbs for tempers."

"Normally?"

"I believe the bottle that Herta had for tempers contained something else, something more deadly. I have no other explanation. The remains of the contents should be examined."

"It doesn't matter what substance is in there. It matters that whatever was in there killed Herta. That someone gave her some poison, with or without knowing the reasons she would be using it. You are the likely suspect in this case."

"I was the one who found her," she said more firmly. "If I had killed her, do you not think that I would remove all evidence of my craft?"

There were murmurs from two guards that stood outside. Zacharias studied her a moment before nodding.

"Is it true you hunt rabbits in the forest?"

"Of course, as do others. But there are few there now. Food is scarce. The hunters assigned from the castle have taken most of the village's food source from the forests now that their agrarian lands are covered with ice."

"What do you do with the carcasses of rabbits?"

She smiled. "It is a strange question, no? Is that what you ask of all the hunters? I think you will find the same answer from everyone."

"Answer the question!" I barked. She flinched and glanced my way before Engel prompted her for more.

"Aside from food, do you use any part of the animal for your treatments?"

"Sometimes I use the blood to mix with herbs. It is good medicine for women who suffer from dizzy spells. I do not call them potions, sir, as that implies something ungodly. What I provide are mixtures that have proven successful, that I've heard are used by the castle physician."

"Do you ever use a doll in ritual magic?"

"No, sir," she said.

"Have you ever used a potion, a mixture, to cause a miscarriage?"

"Never, sir! I do not dabble in magic, I do not dabble in death. I am being honest with you."

"Are you certain?"

"Am I being accused of such?"

"Did you do anything to Ursula Döhler that may have made her miscarry?"

"I gave her something that calmed the pregnancy sickness, a mixture of herbs commonly used for women."

"You saw her directly then."

She paused and appeared to be thinking carefully about her next words.

"No," she said. "I was asked to provide this for her."

"By whom?"

"Katarin Jaspers. Though she was asking on behalf of Ursula, who was unwell. Katarin's intentions, I'm sure, were honourable."

Engel stared at her a moment and she at him. She did not lower her gaze this time.

"However, I must tell you something now, Herr Reverend, that I believe is important . . . The other day Katarin broke into my house, and I found her beside Maria."

"She was a good friend of Maria's," Engel reminded her. "She has been very worried."

"Regardless, there was a bottle of powder found to be missing after she left."

"What is the powder used for?"

"It is a poison."

"I thought that you only dealt with herbs."

"I do. But there is poison also for mice and rats only, which people ask for, too, something you will find used often in the castle kitchen. My house occasionally has vermin, as I expect do others, sir. Even yours."

There was a short period of silence before Engel spoke.

"Are you saying that Katarin took these? Are you formally accusing her?"

Beside where I had recorded Katarin's name I drew a question mark.

"No, sir, only that I noticed the bottle missing after that."

Engel looked pensively off to the side to gather his thoughts, then turned to look at me. He appeared to hesitate before requesting the next task.

"I must ask you to take off your clothes so we can search for marks."

"What sort of marks?"

"A witch's mark," said Engel.

She broke into a smile, which she attempted to hide with her hand.

"You find that amusing."

"I find that ridiculous."

"Then you should not fear the search."

"In front of all the men here?" she said over the top of his shoulder.

"Yes. It is the commissioner's role to examine you."

Engel stood up and walked to face the wall, and I hailed a lawman to watch.

She slipped off her kirtle and laid it neatly across the chair. She did the same with her chemise beneath and stood there naked, her arms wrapped around her body. She closed her eyes and made no expression.

I walked around her, examining her skin that was smooth, her small waist and breasts. She recoiled from the touch. She was in good health, not undernourished as many in the village were.

"Lift up your arms," I said roughly.

On one side of her ribs there was a deep graze.

"What happened here?" I asked.

"I slipped on the ice and fell against a fence."

I studied her eyes to search for signs of deception but found none. Either she was very clever or very honest. One cannot always tell. I nodded to the lawmen to end the examination.

"You may put on your clothes," I said.

Engel gave her time to dress before turning to find she was once more seated.

"Her body is clear of marks," I informed him.

"You will stay here until I have finished my investigations," Engel said to Margaretha. "Your house will be searched. Other people will be interviewed."

"You must not take my medicines. The villagers are in need of cures."

Engel bowed his head as she drew her door key from her pocket, then we left the room and I called upon another lawman to accompany us to Eisbach.

"Do not go near Maria Unger until I have inspected her area first," Engel instructed us once inside the small, dilapidated cabin.

Engel watched us lift lids from jars and bottles and smell the contents. I noted that there were several circles on a shelf where bottles had once sat.

"This one smells strange," said the lawman of a bottle he encountered.

Engel put his nose to the unstoppered bottle, then tipped some on his tongue while we looked on aghast, expecting some effect that did not come.

Engel nodded, indicating it was harmless.

We then searched through her possessions, which were scant, and opened seams in her mattress revealing nothing but straw. I did, however, find two letters caught between pages of her book of herbs and remedies.

"What is it that you have?" Engel asked.

"It is the employer's reference that she spoke of and a letter from Margaretha to Maria," I said.

Engel reached out to take them from me.

"It is strange that a person such as Frau Unger, who knew her letters, kept very little correspondence," I said.

Engel shrugged. "I cannot offer the reason, Commissioner, but perhaps in such a position as hers, subject to scrutiny at times, she was careful, knowing how much can be misconstrued."

He was alluding, of course, to the potential for false allegations.

"I will write to the employer and forward you his reply," he said.

The other official I had brought with us moved towards the curtain.

"Be careful," Engel said.

"Open it!" I instructed, ignoring him.

Maria Unger lay there staring, her face frozen into a scowl, a fetid smell of human waste lingering. The lawman took a step backward, the back of his hand placed against his nose and mouth.

"Be careful," warned Engel again. "You must not touch her!"

I pushed the other man back in frustration and continued the investigation myself. I lifted the mattress and felt underneath it as I had done for Margaretha's. Maria followed me with her sunken eyes, her mouth open and drooling. It could well have been my imagination, but I saw terror in her stare. I rummaged lightly through the linen on the bed, then drew closed the curtain.

Once we had finished the search, uncovering nothing pertaining to sorcery, I accompanied Engel to visit those villagers whom Margaretha had tended. None mentioned a love potion or any other kind, though that was hardly surprising as they would be fools to admit to sorcery. There was only a case where the mother became ill during the birth and died shortly afterwards, but such complaint was not uncommon. Frau Fisch complained about her ill baby, while admitting also that her previous two children died at birth under Maria Unger's care.

"I find nothing here that requires further enquiry," said Engel as we returned on horseback to the city.

"I agree about her work here, but I disagree that we have exhausted the process. We have not interrogated her to the full extent."

Engel shook his head.

"Since there is no formal complaint of sorcery, and since the decision was mine to hold her here, under our current laws she can be released."

"I believe she could be lying," I said.

"She has come here voluntarily. It is not what witches do," he said cynically.

"It could be a ploy."

"She has no mark," he argued.

"How do we know that Margaretha Katz did not curse her aunt with magic?"

"I have seen how Frau Katz takes care of her," said Engel. "How hard a task that is. Would she not rid of her completely if she were so inclined and save herself the work?"

"You are aware that witness statements can be anonymous and are evidence enough in most cases to make an accusation. That is the new decree."

"I remind you, Commissioner, that she has come here willingly. And until someone makes a statement, she is free to go. Is that not the law?"

"There is someone out there who is obviously suspicious, the person who revealed the adultery," I countered. "I can be that witness if I believe I have seen enough to concern me."

Engel turned to stare at me, though I did not intend on carrying out the threat.

"That information was relayed to someone, a messenger only, who relayed it to me," said Engel. "We have to be careful, Commissioner, that we do not so crave blood as to believe every charlatan from outside the bishopric who might hold a personal grievance against us here. We do not know this person who said much about her nor whether they are talking about the same woman since a name was not supplied. As for the medicines missing, we should in fact be looking for a thief."

"What is Margaretha to you?"

"How dare you speak to me that way," said Engel in a sinister tone that I'd not heard him use before, reining his horse to block my path and force my horse to halt. "It is not your place to question me but to finish the interrogation as I see fit. Besides, you may relay to the prince-bishop that the supposed messenger of this information against the midwife is a Protestant. He will likely dismiss the account entirely."

"You know this to be fact? How?"

"Because he called on me and I sent him on his way. He is a man jilted by Margaretha, I suspected immediately. Yet he would never admit to such a thing. This is the revenge of a heretic."

I was not fully convinced, but I decided that I would go along with it for the time being while another plan was forming.

"Very well," I said. "However, this healer must be watched."

"You have my word, Commissioner, that I will not cease in the search for maleficence. It suits everyone's interest to be rid of it."

We rode on.

CHAPTER TWENTY

"She has denied the accusations," Zacharias revealed to me late that night. I could not understand why he was wilfully blind. That he could not see that her innocence was a disguise. I was certain she was capable of anything. "Margaretha told me that she gave you medicine for sickness for Ursula and that it may be a coincidence she lost the baby. I can find no motive as to why she might cause her harm."

"She is lying! Can't you see that?" Margaretha had somehow put it back on me.

He seemed aggrieved by my outburst, and his expression turned dark. I was angry that a man such as he could be so deceived. I felt certain she wasn't who she said she was, and I was more determined to prove it to him.

"Frau Jaspers, I have never seen you like this before."

"I believe what you said, sir. That there is evil here, that it wears a mask. It is easy to fool good people."

"I must remind you that I am a man of law," he said. "The decision I made has left my conscience clear. Margaretha noticed that some of her bottles were missing. She believes they were stolen. It is possible that someone was trying to incriminate her. Was it you, Katarin? Did you take any of her cures?"

I felt his words were a veiled threat to keep my anger in check, to remind me of my position. My legs grew weak with fear.

"She had caught me in the house. I had to make sure that Maria was being cared for. I have been worried about my old friend. But I did not take anything."

He stared at me, his eyes narrowed.

"Frau Jaspers," he said calmly. "With only one physician at our disposal, who rarely has time to visit the villages, for few can afford his fees, Margaretha provides a service to these people that they need. She is both a midwife and a healer. Many have given statements to say that she has not only cured them but that she is caring. Now, unfortunately, people will gossip about these interviews we conducted today. When they learn the reason, they will look her way for things that don't exist. They will distance themselves, which could lead to her ruin."

I did not care. With so much evidence, Margaretha had somehow walked free. I wanted to tell him, unashamedly, that I believed she was a witch, and the reason I suspected this to be true was the effect she had on him. He had dismissed the claim by Sebastian Spengler, someone with noble blood no less. I wondered if I had gone straight to city officials if it would have resulted differently. If so, it was too late now.

Zacharias told me he had presented all the evidence to the commissioner, and she had come out of the questioning even more pure than when she went in. But I knew she wasn't pure. It takes one guilty of sins to recognise sins in others. I also knew there was another side to Herr Reverend—he carried secrets of his own. I have always been good at studying people, at seeing things that others miss. Even so, I admit that he confused me. He was masterful in his aloofness; people revered him for it, and this distance formed part of his charm. I knew that even if I spoke of things, of Margaretha and my suspicions, it would likely be me that would be burned.

And then of course there was my heart. No one had ever affected me the way he had. I wanted to believe that we had a future—in what capacity I could not say—away from this dark place that held too many memories I wanted buried.

"If she is a witch, I will know it soon enough," he said.

He had softened suddenly; perhaps he had seen my fear and took pity. He tilted his head slightly, his face with its brilliant blue gems that seemed to caress my face as they roamed. I wanted more than his eyes. I wanted all of him.

"I am sorry, sir. I am truly sorry. I am concerned about you, that is all. I am concerned that the Devil is still amongst us, playing with our hearts."

He put his hands on my shoulders and held them firmly.

"I know," he said gently. "You have to be patient. I will rid this town of evil, you will see."

Just the touch of him settled my nerves, and I felt my breathing slow, my confusion disappear.

"Do you trust me?"

"Yes, fully," I said. I wanted to tell him that I would follow him to the edge of the world if only he would ask. He was my hope at the chance of a normal life, of being truly loved. I could not bear the thought of being apart from him.

⬥

Bertram the blacksmith returned from his travels to the news of his children as a shattered man. In the week since, he had let the business go and found solace in the ale jugs at the inn.

One day when I was coming back from the city, there was a commotion on the once sandy shore of the river, now a bed of slushy blackened ice. The blacksmith had fallen down drunk and knocked himself out. A group of men placed him on a sailcloth and carried him home, his nose and cheeks red and burned from the cold, his bare fingers purple with cuts that had not closed properly.

This incident wasn't the first one. He had collapsed at various locations, one time splayed out on the prince-bishop's dais with his pants around his ankles. Another time he had cursed God in a public place, which drew the ire of some. People gave only a certain time for grief, for everyone had been struck hard by circumstances and a lengthy period of strange behaviour would eventually be considered offensive. Offensive people could be disappeared with the crime of heresy. He was broken. I pitied him, yet I was also curious about how someone could grieve over two ungrateful children like Herta and Sigi. To be such a terrible burden to a parent but to still be loved by one as well. That love so binding, such as I had never known.

Another time Bertram turned up at our house banging on the door, drunk. Master told me to stay back as the blacksmith fell through the opening and onto the floor. Zacharias tried to lift him up and help him inside, but he pushed the reverend away and dragged himself up to stand. He was not wearing any shoes, his feet blistered.

"Evil is here, Priest," he said, words rolling over each drunkenly. "I know it. There is something wrong about both of them dying."

"Come and sit down," said Master gently, but the blacksmith was too deafened by the sounds of his own sorrows to hear the words of comfort from others.

"There is something wrong in this village, in the city. The two of them . . . It's not . . ."

Bertram shook his head.

"Come," said Zacharias again. "Rest here out of the cold. I will fetch you a warm drink."

Without warning, he stepped close to my master in a threatening manner so that their faces were a breath apart.

"It's got worse since you came, not better."

He was always a man who was direct and had somehow gotten away with it.

"I will pray for you, Bertram. I will pray for Herta and Sigi."

Bertram backed away.

"I don't need your prayers, Reverend," he said, head rolling on his chest a moment. "I'm done with praying."

He became more lucid when he recognised me near.

"You knew her," he said. "You knew them. What happened?"

I knew not what to say, but Master had already stepped in front of me to take the situation in hand.

"Bertram, I will walk you home." Zacharias grabbed his cloak from the hook and put it around the other man's shoulders. They left, and I did not hear Master return until the early hours.

CHAPTER
TWENTY-ONE

Spring did not begin with hope. We were snowed in for two nights, and the lawmen were unable to travel to the villages along the river. Plague-like symptoms then spread across the bishopric and interrogations were suspended for several weeks. Zacharias had been forced to remain in the city during this time.

When the weather had calmed to a degree, and accusations and arrests recommenced, Zacharias brushed through the door and stamped his feet on the stone to shake off the snow, the size of him filling up the rooms once more. I took his coat and hat, and he walked into the parlour to sit by the fire.

"I fear for you, sir," I said after he had explained the number of deaths from disease.

"Fear more for Frau Katz, who is out treating the sick as we speak. She is helping save many lives."

"Will you be going to interrogate the new prisoners, sir?" I asked.

"New prisoners?"

"The ones taken from the village."

He sighed and brushed some snow from his sleeve. "I have barely finished the ones already imprisoned. The prison cells are full. There are two scheduled burnings to happen in the city as well as . . ."

He looked at me with sudden intensity as if startled to find me there. "You must tell me first if you think anything suspicious. Will you do that, Katarin? Will you tell me of any events that are happening in the village when I am away? Such as the visits from lawmen, who they go to see?"

His voice had a hard edge, and the questions sounded more like a command than an appeal to my sense of duty. I told him that I had seen lawmen come into the village, haul several people from their homes, and take them on a cart in the direction of the city. He listened to the events, brows drawn together with concern.

By the next Sunday, the snowfall had eased, and snow was brushed from the tracks and shovelled out of doorways in time for Mass. A strange light through coloured glass gave Master a red glow when he preached from the pulpit that day. The picture of hell had seemed brighter, too, which I continued to avoid. Zacharias was still lavished with adulation by many, but some now in the church were less trustful, looking furtively over their shoulder, searching for someone to blame or fearing accusation.

Zacharias's sermon was about liars, about trust, and about Satan who was a wolf in sheep's clothing; who walked amongst us, tapped people on the shoulder, then negotiated a deal. He told the people to not be fooled by the wolf, to not be the sheep who accepted things blindly. That to accuse someone wrongly would embolden the wolf. I surveyed the congregation and recognised the faces of the sheep that Master was talking about. Margaretha was there, her face drawn up to him, patches of red light spilling onto her also. Zacharias then spoke of people who falsely accused others, who would be judged by God.

People left the sermon solemn and confused. To be the accuser now came with risks. Zacharias departed for the city straight after the church service and, to my relief, separately from Margaretha.

The following week and beyond there were no accusations. People greeted each other cordially again, and the sideways looks had gone, but this period didn't last.

One night, while Zacharias was out travelling to another village and not expected home till midday next, the commissioner, Herr Förner, and his lawmen came to our door.

"I'm sorry, sirs, Herr Reverend Engel is not home," I announced.

"It is you, Katarin Jaspers, that we must bring to the castle," said Commissioner Förner.

"I have done nothing, Herr Commissioner!" I said, suspecting that Ursula had told them of things that weren't true, and maybe the things that were.

I felt sick, imagining myself tethered in a dungeon cell, then dragged to the square for people to mock.

"His Excellency, the prince-bishop, requests an audience with you," said the commissioner, who nodded to his lawmen in their drab, dark, shapeless garb and tall hats to lead me by my arms to the cart outside. They did not say why they had taken me nor were they obliged to, these men who rounded people up, who decided who would be executed, while Ehrenberg's hands stayed clean.

"We must hurry!" said the commissioner, climbing onto the cart.

I did not have my shawl, and I sat in the back of the cart with my arms around myself as thunder sounded in the distance. We bounced over ruts and ridges, then across the bridge that wound up the hill to the castle. Someone came to lead the horse away as the first drops of rain fell, and the other two men led me through the empty kitchen and up a set of stairs to a big hall where to my relief a fire was burning to warm my bones. I was instructed to wait there. I examined the tapestries of Jesus, Mary, and war that hung around the walls. I knew this room that I had once had the task of cleaning.

One of the men came back to lead me to the hall of Ehrenberg. The room had high arched windows painted gold around the casings. There were cushions on a lounge near the window and a writing table covered in papers. Another large hearth was well stacked with wood, and mounted on the stone wall above it were several swords bejewelled with shining gemstones.

Ehrenberg stood by the window in his tufted dark-blue tunic that came down to his thigh. He had turned by the time I was seated.

Ehrenberg raised his eyes in greeting as he approached, and I bowed before him. He gestured to the chair in front of the desk while the commissioner took his seat nearby with a quill and notebook.

"Would you like refreshment?" the prince-bishop asked.

"No, Your Excellency," I said, my thoughts turning to poison.

He leaned against the front of the desk, crossing his arms. I looked briefly down at my hands and pinched my lips together nervously.

"I understand you once served in the castle for my predecessor."

"Yes, Sire."

"That you were rewarded for your loyalty by way of marriage to a merchant of notable esteem."

"Yes, Sire." It was not my place to describe in truth the brute of a man I was traded to.

"You are the housekeeper now for His Reverence?"

"Yes, Your Excellency."

"Does he treat you well?"

Lightning speared the hills outside the window and lit up the room so well I saw shards of bright silver in Ehrenberg's dark eyes.

"Very well, Your Excellency."

He waved his hand. "Just 'Sire' will do so we can get through this swiftly."

I bowed my head humbly, and thunder rumbled overhead.

"Could you tell us what he spoke about in his recent sermon?"

I looked to Ehrenberg at first confused. It was not a question I was expecting. I tried to remember.

"I am not sure, Sire." Though suspicion crept in as to what he was referring to.

"Surely, you are a God-fearing woman who would listen to every holy word spoken?" he asked, one side of his mouth rising up nearer his nose in an expression of disbelief.

"Last sermon was about the weather, and we prayed for spring to come, for new life, and an end to sickness," I said, attempting to throw him off the scent. "And there was an announcement of another pregnancy."

He did indeed speak of those things, and with the number of deaths climbing, the village had some good news.

"I believe it was a sermon prior to that, where he mentioned something about a wolf," said the prince-bishop.

And liars—I did indeed remember.

"He spoke about the accuser who could be just as guilty as the accused," I said, choosing my words carefully.

I stole a glance at Herr Förner, who wore a frown to indicate alarm.

"Did he suggest that people no longer hold suspicion?" said Ehrenberg.

It was possible that Master had been betrayed by someone from the village.

"It was a sermon about . . . caution."

Ehrenberg nodded.

"Where does Zacharias Engel go when he is not at home?"

"Here, to see you, to the city, to visit the people."

Ehrenberg made a hissing sound as he sucked in his lips and raised his eyebrows, then glanced at the man with the thick moustache, aware of something I was not.

"Have you noticed anything suspicious about his activities?" asked Ehrenberg.

"No, Sire."

"You know the accused, Ursula Döhler, is that correct?"

"Yes, Sire, though not on close terms."

"She has said that the Devil lives in your house."

I felt my throat constrict.

"She isn't talking about you, is she, Katarin?"

"No, Sire."

I wondered if I were tainted, my name now recorded in their notebooks.

"She is not sound," I was quick to add.

"Is she talking about someone else there?"

"No, Sire."

"Frau Döhler said she bought medicine from you for her sickness."

"I do not supply medicines, Sire."

Herr Förner raised his eyes and viewed me sceptically.

"But yes, I did approach the midwife on Frau Döhler's behalf, without knowing the extent of her malady."

"Do you believe Frau Katz was aware of the potency of the remedy prescribed?"

I wanted to tell them that I did not trust her. But for my loyalty to Zacharias, and his belief in me, it took every ounce of strength to hold my tongue.

"I have learned only good things, Your . . . Sire."

There was silence for a moment while the prince-bishop took my measure and the commissioner stalled his quill. I thought then I might break and spill out all the words I was holding.

"Hmm," said Ehrenberg, who stood, walked around behind his desk to take his seat.

I could have said something about Margaretha, I could have finished her that day but for Zacharias. I had to trust Master and to show him that he could trust me.

"I heard you brought food to Frau Lucke at the prison."

"Yes, Sire. She had brought me food sometimes when she would deliver pork to the castle kitchens. I did not mind doing that small favour as requested by Reverend Engel."

"Oh, yes, Frau Lucke was different when her husband was alive. Did she try and tell you anything, make any particular requests at that time?"

"Only to check on her boy, which I have not yet done on account of my work and the weather and the plague that shut everyone in for a time. But we've had hampers of food delivered in the meanwhile." I did not tell them that Walter had visited him earlier on, and that Jon had pushed him away, no longer spoke, and refused to leave the house.

Ehrenberg leaned back in his chair and regarded me at length, no doubt noticing that my hands were shaking.

"If you notice or hear of anything that is concerning about the priest, you must report it to the commissioner."

"Yes, Sire."

"And you must not, and I repeat, must not," he said, pointing his finger at me, "repeat this to Herr Reverend Engel."

"No, Sire."

A guard came to collect me. He escorted me back through the kitchen, opened the door to let me out, then shut it again behind me, leaving me in the rain and dark. I had a long walk home ahead of me. By luck, halfway there, a man with a cart stopped to take me the rest of the way.

The next day at the square, I found a crowd had gathered to view a sign pinned to the public podium.

"What does it say?" I asked someone.

"It is a new decree. That anyone with any information on another person who might be engaging with sorcery will remain anonymous and have no repercussions upon them. Signed by the prince-bishop himself."

With that note, the prince-bishop had undone Zacharias's sermon. He would not be happy. Ehrenberg had released his beasts to search for prey. Several new lawmen trawled the streets examining people's faces for evidence of sorcery after that. A suspicious look and people were stopped. At the markets, they sometimes pulled people out of a crowd for no apparent reason and took them away for questioning.

Not even the very young could escape an accusation. One day a child was pulled from his mother's arms and led away.

"Not my child! What has he done to deserve this?"

They didn't answer her. They didn't have to.

They threw the crying child of ten years into the back of their cart. I learned that the boy had told someone he had seen visions of the castle on fire and of a war that would last many years, and this had been reported. The following day his mother was also taken.

The accusations did not stop there. These men would come every few days, and everyone waited for a knock on the door. I would awaken each morning with an expectation of another rumour, another imprisonment, another person named as an enemy of God. People in the square wore their distrust in their stares, in their scowls, and watched for people who looked at them sideways. I had heard in the stores that a horse had fallen dead when the daughter of a gravedigger walked past the animal. She was found to have a mark on her back. When her mother declared that she was marked also, to protect her daughter, they put them both in prison.

"The girl who named her was a love rival," said Walter, who was with me when we heard. "She was jealous."

There were worse things to come. Another outbreak of plague, and people were ordered to stay indoors, another fear that the bishopric was being punished. At least it kept the lawmen away. But only briefly.

One day, the messenger boy, who delivered hampers to Jon, came to tell us that something had happened.

"What is it?" I asked.

"I am not sure," he said.

"What do you mean?"

The boy stared nervously at his feet. "Jon will not answer the door."

It was obvious the boy was too frightened to speak of what he saw. When Zacharias returned that day, we made haste to Jon's.

All the windows had been boarded shut inside, and the one large room that formed the house was near empty of furniture, some of it splintered near the hearth, that much I could glimpse through some cracks in the walls. Zacharias told me to wait outside, and I moved to peer through the partially opened door. He walked to the middle of the room, then stopped and hung his head and didn't move. I couldn't see what he saw, so I entered, too, and paused mid step. I covered my mouth not just from the horror of it but from the stench of death and waste matter in buckets unemptied.

Jon was hanging shirtless from the roof, his face purple and bloated, his bare, rake-thin body exposing his malnourishment. I held some suspicion as to whether he'd eaten all the foods delivered; if they had not been stolen. Food at that time was more valuable than silver.

It seemed he had been hanging for some days. In the chaos of our times, Zacharias had not been often to visit.

"Dear God! Help me, Frau Jaspers!"

Zacharias climbed up on a chair and cut him down with a sharp blade he had in his pocket.

He laid him down on the floor and kneeled before him. He stared, touched Jon's arm with tenderness, then closed the dead boy's hazel eyes and pondered him a moment. Jon's expression was the most peaceful I had ever seen it.

"This boy and his short life," said Zacharias sadly. "For what purpose?"

I wasn't sure if it was a question directed to me, but I felt I should say something.

"Perhaps it was truly witchcraft that drove him to do this."

His laugh in response had an edge of cruelty to it. Sadness had given way to anger.

"You are so naive, Frau Jaspers. The only witches are those three women who stole the Lucke's animals . . . Fetch that sheet!"

It would be considered apostacy what he had just said since it went against the holy and lawful principles endorsed by the prince-bishop. Was he saying that the people condemned to death were not meant to be killed? That Ehrenberg had wrongly ordered their demise? Many I suspected thought the same, but saying one's thoughts was willing one's *own* execution. If the prince-bishop learned of the words my master spoke, the consequence, I feared, would be dire. Not even the clergy were safe. There was a monk in one of the other towns we learned of recently who protested the sentence for an old man who did not attend church service. The monk was burned several days later.

I pulled the grimy bedsheet from Jon's cot and shook off the tiny mites. Master placed his hands on either side of Jon's face and studied him a while. Then he lifted the body that had stiffened with death and laid the boy down on the cloth, folding it gently over him as if not to disturb his sleep. He left Jon's side and walked outside. He stood a moment, his expression grim, then continued purposefully towards the Meyer property. I followed him warily. There was an air of unpredictability about him. Like when my husband went silent. It was always this lull before he struck me, as if my surprise was part of the enjoyment.

"You said you would look after him," he said to the Meyer women who had come to meet him outside. "I trusted that you would." Although he sounded calm, I recognised a menacing edge. Maude did, too, her hands trembling.

"We have done as much as we could," said Ingrid, intervening. "We have been checking on him."

"I would say seldom by the state of him and his house," he said through gritted teeth. "I would say that you and your daughters' callous disregard of decency is the cause of his death."

Claudine, the frailer of the two sisters, began to cry.

"Sir, you have no basis to accuse us of anything," said Ingrid. "We were good neighbours."

"Zilla said you were jealous of her goods, of her animals and land. It is the reason you twisted Jon's word, turned him against his mother."

I was astounded by this admission. That he would say this aloud. These words were unlike any he had spoken. They undermined the decisions by the prince-bishop, his officials, everyone.

"Why, they are false words, sir!" said Ingrid, her voice quivering. "Zilla was possessed, and my daughter witnessed her devilish practice. And it was you, Herr Reverend, who put her to death."

"A death that resulted from false accusations."

"The prince-bishop sanctioned the punishment," said Ingrid shakily, "and Zilla was dealt with according to the law. Are you saying that our holy leader is a liar?"

"You caused this," he said, ignoring the statement. "You wanted his land, but you didn't get it, did you? Ehrenberg has taken it all. Yet still you stole everything else from the house after Zilla was imprisoned. You stole his animals. You stole things right from under Jon's nose. A boy unable to take care of himself. He trusted you."

"Jon was tainted. We suspected he was changing into some other creature at night and entering our house to spy. We had grown afraid of him."

"You are a liar!" he said.

I had never heard Zacharias speak so. He then grabbed Ingrid by the arm and dragged her into her house, the girls running after their mother crying.

"Where is the furniture? Where is the fabric she made? Where are her jars of conserve, her dried meats?" He picked up a jar that I presumed was the very same of which he spoke and smashed it to the ground. Claudine shook and blubbered through tears. Maude stood dumbstruck and trembling. "It is right here, not in Jon's larder but in yours."

He picked up each jar and smashed them one by one to the stone on the floor. Bits of glass flew up and scratched Claudine's face, and she reached up to feel a spot of blood. Maude screamed as more glass hit the floor, and my pleas for him to stop did not reach his ears. When all the jars were shattered, he searched further until he found the silver dish with the Lucke name. He shook his head and sent the women a look with daggers from across the room before continuing to comb through their belongings. Zilla's silk wedding dress with pearl buttons was pulled out from a trunk. He then strode to the rear of the property. The pig had been slaughtered; hunks of meat rubbed in salt hung in a separate room at the back of the house.

I saw anger as a weakness in someone's character. Often enacted from drink, selfishness, and petty power. This rage, which threatened to burst through his skin, was twice as terrifying. Not just from what I witnessed but from how much of it I could tell he was holding back.

"Jon gave us the meat," wailed Ingrid, following him, her voice breaking, tears flowing. Her daughters had run out to the front of the property, and I could hear them bawling.

"Liar!" shouted Zacharias in her face. "It is probably you who is doing the killing! You three who are the thieves! Who are bleeding animals, who are selling your bodies to the Devil in the dark of night."

"How dare you!" said Ingrid weakly.

"The prince-bishop will have your hands chopped off for that. Since you took what belonged to him."

I saw terror across her face and thought of Master's talk of a wolf in disguise of a sheep. There were plenty amongst us, that was certain.

"I will report you!" said Ingrid.

"Please do!" he continued, louder still. "Speak to His Excellency. I'm sure he would like to know that the fat pig that should have gone to him went into your poisonous mouths instead."

He returned to collect Jon, threw the body over his shoulder, and stomped alongside the river back towards the village. I followed him, glancing at the girls as we passed, who were huddled together fearfully inside their doorway. I had trouble keeping up with him, losing my footing at times. He did not notice but continued ploughing a trail through the snow.

He cursed at the heavens, and I wondered if he had been masking such fury all along. That he was less godly than he appeared. The thought, though one of terror, thrilled me. He had made a mockery of the witch hunts. It gave me hope that he might leave and take me with him.

"Go home!" he said dismissively when we reached the village, then said more under his breath that I would not remember again till later. He took the path to the church.

When he was not back by dark, I tried to find him. Jon's body lay near the church's altar but there was no sign of Zacharias. I paced for hours that night awaiting his return. In the barn, I found Walter, eyes closed, in his bed of hay. He did not respond when I tried to wake him. I believe now that he had been feigning sleep.

By morning, when Walter came in to light the fires, Zacharias had not returned. It would not have been unusual, but from his temper anything seemed possible. I wondered if he was capable of worse.

"Did Master say anything to you about leaving, about visiting someone outside the village?" I asked him.

Walter shook his head and avoided looking at me.

It seemed that joy had left our house.

I followed him back out to the barn, where he had commenced brushing the horse.

"Walter, is everything all right?"

He nodded, though did not turn my way.

"Do you want to play a game in the snow?" I said, hoping that this would make him happy.

He shook his head.

I stepped forward and took his arm, though he still would not look at me.

"Walter! What is wrong?"

"I don't know."

I sighed and dropped my shoulders. People grew more guarded with age. The boy I knew had changed.

I went back into the house and cleaned to keep busy. I prepared a special meal of venison stew and baked small cakes with the last of the honey and raisins. But Master didn't come back, and Walter wasn't hungry.

Two more days passed and there was still no sign of Zacharias. People knocked on my door to ask where he was.

I gave an excuse that he was called away on urgent business, but I knew if he was not back by Sunday service, this answer would not suffice. And then I worried that something had happened to him. I searched the river's edge and spied a badger collecting bracken for its nest. I watched it for a while until my bones grew cold and then trudged through the village square, hoping to spy him there. The mood was solemn, as if people could sense worse changes coming. I felt so alone without Zacharias and reluctantly found myself at Margaretha's door.

"What do you want?" she asked, sounding surly when she answered my knock.

"I am looking for Reverend Engel. Do you know where he is?"

"Why would I know?" she said and shut the door.

She had corrupted him in some way, I felt sure of it. I suspected that she knew I was the cause of her recent imprisonment. She would burn eventually. I was convinced of that, too.

At the clergy house, I found Walter sitting in the kitchen. He'd let the fire die out, and it was cold inside. I scolded him, but he did not seem to care. He looked up at me, and I could tell he'd not slept for days. I wanted to take him in my arms and wish his cares away.

"I know what you did," he said, words that sank my heart.

I was startled by the sound of the front door slamming shut. Master had returned.

CHAPTER
TWENTY-TWO

Some days after Jon was buried, Zacharias's movements again became erratic. Food was uneaten, his room rarely slept in. He would thud up the stairs, pace the floor, and disappear again. When he was home, he asked that he not be disturbed.

"I have business to attend to," he said abruptly one morning, hair unbrushed and free around his shoulders, a hint of growth around his jaw and upper lip, and still in the shirt from the previous week. "I will be gone another day or two."

I heard the clank of metal from the cloth-bound bundle underneath his arm.

He was back in time for Sunday service. The sermon was short, but Zacharias was brighter than normal. He spoke of good times ahead, of not coveting thy neighbour's property. Maude, Claudine, and Ingrid were not there to listen. The message was too late for them anyway. This sermon was for the rest of the congregation. Walter chose to sit away from me across the aisle, his eyes fixed on Master only, his thoughts buried. I wondered about his silence, about the worries he was keeping from me.

"Life will get better," Zacharias said, though I could not see how. The clouds were still above us, and I had heard of another two people arrested in the city for sorcery. Master had not been included in all the interrogations, I heard, such tasks managed by the commissioner. More positions were being filled by new lawmen to collect suspects, and more guards were installed around the city.

At home I asked Master if he would like me to shave him, a task he had always undertaken himself but one I had completed for my husband.

"No, thank you, Frau Jaspers."

He seemed back to normal, as if there were things he knew, better things ahead, secrets. Though he seemed drained, his face gaunt as those returned from battle, there was a spring in his step. It was a mystery where he had been.

I had not seen Margaretha at the church, nor did I spy her in the village in the following days.

When the Master was not home two lawmen arrived.

"Herr Reverend is not here."

"We are not here to speak with him. We wish to speak to you."

The sight of them filled me with dread. Another interview.

They did not ask for an invitation but walked past me to inspect the rooms before returning to the parlour and seating themselves.

"You have a houseboy who lives here. We have come to ask a few questions about him."

"Walter?" I said hesitantly.

"What is his family name?"

"He hasn't got one."

The scribe dipped his quill in ink and then noted this down while the other one conducted the interview.

"What do you mean 'he hasn't got one'?" asked the speaker.

"He was told he was found in a ditch, sir. He was only given a first name by the sisters at a convent who were handed him."

"Have you noticed anything strange about him?"

"Why?"

"It is not your place to ask the questions."

"No, nothing strange," I said.

"We demand your honesty, Frau Jaspers."

They waited and watched me for a short while, for signs of falsity and flaws, but I did not waver from my disguise of calm.

"We have come into some information that is different," continued the lawman. "A letter that was sent anonymously."

"He is a good boy," I said.

"Did he know Herta Jacobs?"

"Yes. Very well."

"Did she have a relationship with Walter?"

"She wished," I said too quickly.

"You need to explain."

"She was here many times trying to gain attention from Walter. Attention that he didn't want."

"Did he tell her that?"

"He tried to."

"Did that make him angry?"

"Sometimes. He was young and gullible, and she sometimes made a fool of him. One time she hid in the barn and frightened him. Sigi was worse. He often made fun of Walter's friend Jon and sometimes punched and kicked Walter just for the fun of it."

"Jon . . . You mean the son of the witch?"

"The son of Zilla Lucke, yes."

"Do you think Walter was angry enough to harm the Jacobs siblings?"

I paused to contemplate my reply.

The scribe stilled his quill, and both men stared expectantly.

"I don't think so," I said.

The scribe bent over his notebook once more, and the interviewer breathed a heavy sigh.

"Is there anything else you might wish to add?" he asked.

"He likes the company of animals."

"How so?" said the lawman, his interest piqued.

"He takes good care of the horses. Walter is good at many tasks. He is never languid."

"Do you favour the boy?"

"He is like a brother, and I know Herr Reverend Engel likes him very well."

The writer and speaker looked at one another briefly before the speaker pursed his lips and stood. The writer closed his book and stood also.

"Thank you, Frau Jaspers. You must not speak of this to anyone. Do you understand? If you gossip about this, you are breaking the law."

I nodded. So many secrets to keep.

When they were gone, I leaned on the back of the door they had exited, fearing the worst.

Another knock at the door the following afternoon and I knew what it was. I knew it wasn't good. From the window I spied the men who stood there, and it seemed an eternity to reach the handle of the door as I gained my composure.

"What are you waiting for?" Master said behind me, and I startled. He had crept down the stairs as quiet as a cat.

I opened the door, and the lawmen pushed their way in.

"Why are you here?" asked Zacharias.

"We have come to take a suspect."

For a moment I feared it was me.

"The boy, Walter, who lives here, he must come with us."

"What has he done?" said Master, blocking them any further.

"He has been accused of sorcery."

"By whom?"

"It doesn't matter. There was a written statement sent, and we have since gleaned more information to confirm. We have come to arrest him."

"Why did I have no word of this?" said Zacharias.

"Our orders are from the commissioner directly. You will have to speak to him."

My master knew there was no point to argue. He knew the men who came. He knew the law.

"I will get him, but you will have to wait here."

I followed Zacharias through to the barn, where Walter was perched on a stool with a chicken under one arm, feeding it by hand. When Master told him that people were here for him, he gently put the fowl down.

"I have not done anything wrong," he said, the last word broken and unfinished.

"Can you think of anything that might have happened recently that has led to this?"

Walter opened his mouth to speak before closing it again.

Master walked outside the barn and looked out across the frozen brook, then up to the sky, and mouthed something I could not read. He dropped his head and his shoulders.

"Come, Walter!" he called as he walked back through the doorway to lead him. "Answer the accusations, and if you are not guilty, nothing will come of it."

At the front door, the men put rope around Walter's wrists and tied them tightly before yanking him forward.

"He is a child," said Zacharias. "You do not need such force."

"You have no say in what we do, and your attendance in this matter is not required."

"I have every say in it. This is my parish. It is up to me to conduct the interrogation of the people you take from here."

"Then you must take it up with the prince-bishop. He has changed some rules. He has brought in new office bearers."

"Can you tell me who has made a complaint against the boy?"

"They have not been named. It came by letter."

The lawmen placed Walter in the back of the cart. I ran towards him, but he had turned his back so I could not see his face, and one of the men put his arm out in front of me so I could not go any further.

"I love you, Walter," I said, but he would not look at me.

Master returned to the house and I followed. From the window in the parlour, I watched the cart disappear along the track and could not contain my tears. Zacharias swilled two glasses of wine, one straight after the other. He poured a third, then sat in the chair by a dwindling fire.

"Do you have any idea who might have written about Walter?" he said, bristling.

"I don't know, sir. Most here don't know their letters and have no skill of pen. I thought his accuser might have been our neighbour, Herr Brühn, but he doesn't know them either."

"Who else do you know who can write?"

"There is Frau Mueller and Herr Kruger," I said. "And Frau Katz," I added lastly.

He sat pondering the names I supplied.

"There is something I have to tell you, sir."

I told him then about the questions I'd been called in for with the prince-bishop. The corners of his mouth twitched almost into a smile. I wondered if it were scorn I saw for a fleeting moment. But of whom?

"I'm very sorry," I said, feeling sickened that I did not tell him earlier when he had talked about trust.

"I understand," he said, his features softening. "You were frightened, and now you have to trust me with everything from this point."

"I'll never not trust you, Zacharias."

It was good to speak aloud his name, which he did not seem to notice.

"I have something to give you," he said. "Wait here!"

He left the room, then returned minutes later.

"Hold out your hand."

I did so and he placed in my palm a shiny red ribbon.

"What is this?"

"Something you can wear in your hair."

He put his hands on my shoulders and turned me around. He removed my cap to release my hair, then drew it into a loose tail and tied it with the ribbon. He turned me back to face him, twisted the tail to fall over the front of my shoulder, and nodded to admire his work.

"I want you to do something for me."

Anything, I thought, *anything at all.*

"I want you to stay indoors and pray for Walter. Pray for your soul, too."

"Of course."

"I have to attend to some very important business tonight, and I may be gone for hours."

After he left, I went up to his room and lay on his bed. I smelled his pillow and stayed there for some time, dreaming of the future. He had left me wanting, as he always did.

I went back downstairs and stoked the fire, then paced around the house. I thought about his words, and the more I revisited them, the more confused I became about their meaning. The sight of him, the closeness, the touch of his hands, had blinded me temporarily from understanding. What was I missing? I pulled the red ribbon from my hair and stared at it. A memory returned of Ilerta in the kitchen.

Returning to my room, I stopped suddenly. On my bed was a doll made of sticks and straw like the ones that had been destroyed, like the one found on Cilla Graf that Master had given me to throw in the fire. I picked up the faceless, unadorned doll and walked towards the fire, then changed my mind and placed it in a pocket.

I pulled around my shawl and headed south to the city. The half-moon shone a light for me that night. People said that a half-moon was good luck. I just had to make certain it was not luck for someone else.

I remembered the words he had said on the way back from the Meyers'.

The Devil hides in plain sight, Katarin.

EXCERPT

The Witch Hunts—Förner

The men I had tasked to follow Zacharias Engel reported of no irregularities, only that he would take long walks in the forest. However, it had been brought to my attention by a lawman that Engel dismissed the Devil's sign on the skin of one accused. It may have been nothing but the poor eyesight of one of my men. But for my work that grew too full of leads in the city, Engel's reported lax interrogation was a matter that was never investigated, our interviews of suspects in recent days too numerous, work shared between us.

One day, I was woken when there were still some hours left before sunrise. The gaoler had sent a messenger to advise that Engel had come to interrogate the boy, Walter, at the prison and that he had specifically requested I not be notified. He clearly underestimated the loyalty of those men beneath me. I stepped quietly towards the door of Walter's cell, and when the guard turned, I put my finger to my lips, the man returning to stare at the wall in front of him. I was curious as to the clandestine reason for this meeting. I suspected that I would learn more if my presence was not known.

"Have you been mistreated?" Engel asked the boy.

"No," said Walter, though he did not strike me as one to complain.

"Here," I heard Engel say, followed by the chewing sounds I assumed were from the boy.

"Walter, you have been accused of a number of things," he said, and I had to strain my ears to hear. "I managed to find out some of them from the guards. In an anonymous letter that I have not yet seen, a witness states that you broke into Margaretha's place; they saw you climbing through a window."

"That is not true!" he said, sounding genuinely astounded.

"It is more serious than that. You have been accused of Herta's and Sigi's deaths."

It was I who had received the letter that implicated Walter. It was I who ordered the lawmen to interview the maidservant about the boy, and later sent them to collect him.

"I had no reason to kill them," he said and began to sob.

"Did she and her brother harm you?"

"Herta didn't harm me, but she annoyed me at times. Her brother harmed a lot of people, not just me . . . But neither deserved to die."

"I believe you are a good boy, Walter; however, I need more of the truth from you. Do you have any idea who might want to harm you?"

He sniffed back his sobs.

"I believe that you know things that you may not have told people. Is this correct? That you are protecting people you love."

There was a pause.

"What is it, Walter? What do you know?"

"I saw something."

"Go on," he said gently.

"Herta was in our kitchen talking to Katarin . . . As she was leaving, Katarin gave her some food from our pantry because Herta's father was away and Sigi had spent the money that he left them on ale.

"Katarin asked me to take some apples to them. I admit," he said, "that I kept two for later. It was wrong, but—"

"Never mind that!"

"I delivered the bag that night to Herta, the last time I saw her alive. The following morning, I found two dead mice in the barn near where I had hidden the apples I was planning to eat that day. One apple had been chewed. I checked the other apple that was still whole, and it had a small hole pierced through the flesh. When I put my nose to it, I smelled something strange."

"Are you saying that there was poison in the apples?"

"I think so."

"Yes or no."

"Yes."

"And do you know who put it there?"

"I believe it was Katarin," he said after a period of silence.

I put my hand to my chin, reliving the times I had spoken to the maidservant. I had seen intelligence behind those green eyes, especially during the interview with the prince-bishop, and wondered now if that were not cunning or something worse.

"Is there a reason she would want to harm them?"

"I heard Herta talking in the kitchen. Katarin and Sigi . . ."

"Katarin and Sigi what?"

"There was something between them."

"You heard this in the conversation?"

"Herta said that she had learned about the pair of them, that she wanted them to marry."

"And is that what Katarin wanted?"

"I don't think so."

"Who do you think sent the letter about you?"

"I believe it was Katarin."

"Isn't it true she cannot write?"

"She can, sir. Katarin was educated at the castle and is clever. She knows words. She likes to pretend she doesn't. She has even read to me from books that were taken from the castle and taught me many words."

I shook my head a little. I heard truth in the boy's words, and for the first time since I had taken this commission I wondered if I were losing my edge. I may well have missed the signs of evil that had been under my nose for some time.

"Will I be home soon, Reverend Engel?"

"I will make certain of it. But you must tell the officials everything you know, exactly how you told me. Walter, I must examine your body. I must see if they will find anything."

"I have no marks but bruises on my shins from carrying heavy pails," said Walter. "There is one more thing . . . Katarin has been following you. I do not know why."

"Thank you, Walter. I am aware of that also . . . Guard! I need some water," Engel called, his voice louder as he had moved nearer the door.

I kept my back flat against the wall in the shadows as the guard walked past me.

"Walter, I want you to do as I ask . . ."

The door clanked shut and I could hear no more.

After weeks of investigations, of working day and night, skin chafed red from the cold, my mind numb with lack of sleep, I returned to my bedchamber. I cannot say why I left the cell without making my presence known, or why I said not a word about the incident to the prince-bishop, who was in the process of writing to Rome of his concerns about the priest's lack of adherence to certain procedures. In that instance I had trusted Engel; perhaps I thought I would hinder whatever plan for justice that would ensue. In any case, when questioned later, the boy told me all that he had told Engel.

Some days later, a letter arrived with accusations of maleficence against Katarin, the details of which I'd heard in the prison cell, and more against her. We sought to bring her in, but she had vanished. With my joints beset with an incurable stiffness, which would shortly confine me to a desk with the tasks of record-keeping and administration only, it is one of my many regrets in life that such a woman had evaded us, that the men I would ultimately send to find her were unsuccessful in her capture.

Walter was released, I saw to it personally. If the truth lay in a person's eyes, I saw only innocence in his, and I never saw him again. As far as I know he never returned to the village, and I can hardly blame him. The taint of such an association with witchcraft was likely to remain.

As for Zacharias Engel, that would be the last business he would conduct here. He died shortly after these events, his body returned to Rome.

CHAPTER
TWENTY-THREE

I knew that Master was going to the prison. I knew his interview with Walter would not be long because it was not sanctioned by the prince-bishop. I waited for him on the ice of the river beneath the bridge, pushed up against a pillar to make myself invisible. Several guards walked across the bridge above me, and one of them coughed, then spat over the side only inches from where I stood. I heard ice pickers on the river and the night sweepers brushing the crusts of dirt and snow, which flew off the bridge around me. After the guards had changed over and there was no more activity, I climbed further up the embankment still hidden by a ledge of stone but with a view of the path that led downward from the fortress.

After roughly an hour, I caught sight of Zacharias. I watched his dark shape, tall and commanding like the Devil himself I imagined, as he strode down the path from the prison cells. The sight of him made me shiver, the secrets he held from everyone that I would hopefully uncover, where he would disappear to in the dead of night. His cloak lifted in the wind behind him like bat wings, and he passed me by so close I could hear his breaths.

I followed him. I had to know for certain that his heart was with me, that his touch before he left was real, and if the doll meant something.

That the red ribbon was not some lure, or a sign, the same ribbon taken from Herta after death.

One time Zacharias stopped and cocked his ear as if he had heard a noise behind him, then adjusted his hat and kept walking. I weaved through the streets before briefly losing sight of him. Had he sensed me? I wondered. A movement to my right and I saw him there in the distance crossing a laneway towards the bridge that led from the city to the villages. I followed again, and he led me where I expected, to Margaretha's house. I saw him enter and close the door behind him.

Through the trees, there was an unusually bright glow from within Maria Unger's house. The shutter that was normally closed at the side of the house where Margaretha's bed was placed was fully open this time. I crept nearer the window with a sense that my worst fears would be revealed.

I peered inside. A fire was blazing in the hearth, and Margaretha wore a nightgown that exposed much of the skin around her neck and shoulders. Zacharias's hands reached behind her, and he placed them on the centre of her back. He leaned down, and she with her back to me tilted her face upward to meet him. She raised her hands to cradle his face. A voice inside me, the jealous one that festered like a sore, told me to look away. But I couldn't. He leaned forward and kissed her with such passion, their bodies pressed tightly together it seemed they were one person. As he gently drew away from her, he slid the garment from her shoulder, the nightgown slipping to the floor to reveal her naked form. At that precise moment he looked over her shoulder towards the window and I ducked below the sill.

It was all I needed to see. Those nights away weren't spent at the castle. He had been keeping Margaretha warm.

My heart was heavy, and I had difficulty breathing. I sat below the window and tears fell down my cheeks and turned to ice. Margaretha had been secretly keeping him from me.

Zacharias left when the air was coldest, just before light touched the day, and I stayed by the side of the building, teeth chattering, ice flakes on my eyelashes as sunlight caressed me with its fingers. It was a sign, I thought. The plan that was forming in my mind must be executed that day else I lose the one I truly loved. Walter I felt was already a great loss, but a necessary one. Zacharias, however, could be saved. I felt inside my pocket. I knew what I must do.

I listened to Margaretha busy at the fire, the smell of oatmeal bubbling and of warming milk. Once I thought her seated, I knocked on the door. She answered in her nightgown and a shawl for modesty.

"What is it that you want this time?" she asked me sharply, a small frown breaking the smoothness of her forehead.

"I need to confess something to you."

"You should save it for Reverend Engel."

"It is something that I can only share with you."

She sighed, squeezed her lips together, and opened the door a little wider for me to enter. I thought of spiders and their prey and knew which one was she.

The curtain had been drawn back, and Maria Unger lay supine, awake, her face twisted towards me.

"Sit down," Margaretha said, indicating the second chair at the table.

I glanced over the room taking note that some of the bottles were missing. The book of herbs was not on the table.

She sat down opposite me and crossed her arms, her expression hostile. I presumed she knew it was me who had denounced her to Zacharias. Her cheeks and neck were reddened, and I tried not to think of the passion that had ignited such.

She sipped from a cup in front of her and did not ask if I required anything.

"Well?"

"I want to say sorry," I said.

She raised one eyebrow.

"I thought you were the witch."

"The witch?" she said.

"The person possessed, who is killing the animals, who has killed small children."

"I thought those persons had been burned already," she said.

"I told the reverend that I thought you were guilty."

"He has cleared me of any wrongdoing," she said defiantly.

"Good. Because I think we can be friends."

"I'm not sure that's going to happen."

"I'm hoping by the end of the conversation you will see things differently."

She was curious then, some of the hostility gone.

"How is Maria?" I asked.

"She is making progress."

"It was not a contagion then?"

"It does not appear that way," she said.

"I miss her," I said, looking fondly at the person in question.

Maria flung her arm out suddenly, groaned, and attempted to raise her head. I was stunned to see signs of recovery. She had been so still before. Margaretha got up to offer soothing words, then covered her with a blanket. Maria grimaced and groaned again, her head rolling side to side. She knew things. She could see what was to come.

"It's all right, Maria," comforted Margaretha. "There is no need to worry."

Margaretha came back to take her seat once the patient was settled, her eyes then closed.

"I am guessing that you want to know if the rumours are true about me," Margaretha said. "It's what you are really here about, isn't it? In part they are, but there are pieces missing from the story you presented to Reverend Engel."

"It wasn't my story," I said. "I was just repeating truthfully what I had heard."

"I did have an affair of the heart with a married man once many years ago when I was just a girl. That much is true. But I would not have done anything to hurt him nor his wife. She had been sick for a while. I tried to tell the nobleman, who wouldn't listen. He was too in love with me to notice."

She cleared her throat, sounding nervous, then took several sips of milk.

"It was a delicate situation. I vowed as soon as the wife had the baby that I would leave. I had already asked him for a reference, and our relationship had stopped prior to her death. It was mutual. The guilt was too much. When she died, he had to blame someone."

"How do I know if you are being truthful?" I asked.

"You don't have to believe me. I don't care if you do."

I bit my top lip while she drank some more.

"Maria Unger could not talk when I stumbled across her for help. I cannot deny that it was opportune. I already understood much about healing. Lately, she has shown improvement. She has found her voice, forming words. I will take her with me when I leave. I know someone in another village who will take good care of her. Some place where she will be safe."

"You are planning to leave?"

"Yes," she said. "This place is becoming dangerous because of people who falsely accuse others."

Maria interrupted us with her rasping sounds of sleep, her chest rising and falling gently.

"You should know," said Margaretha, "that she has uttered your name in moments of lucidity, enough that I have become suspicious. I know that she fears you. Is that why else you came? To tell me why?"

Margaretha wore a smile, smug like someone who was victorious. I was not expecting her to say that. I wondered if she had shared her suspicions with her lover.

"So why are you here?" she asked.

I had been waiting for this moment, to unburden, to display how much I could deceive, how a poor servant girl could go undetected.

"Would you care to hear my story?" I said.

She shrugged, suggesting her indifference, but she would learn my story whether she wanted to or not.

"I was sold to my husband by castle administrators when I was thirteen," I told her. "I had to sleep with a man I despised. A man who was cruel, who had no love for anyone but himself. Who beat me each time I lost a baby, to the point that I enjoyed losing them."

She was examining my resentment, the smile gone. I could see the colour draining from her face, the glow of lovemaking completely gone.

"Then when I finally brought a boy to full term three years ago, he was an abomination. The pity that Maria felt for me made me angry. A purple-faced child, so hideous I couldn't look at it and neither could my husband. He and I had finally agreed on something. That we didn't want it."

Margaretha's mouth was open slightly and she watched my lips move as if she could not quite bring herself to believe it, her hand placed against her temple.

"The ending to this story is not a happy one, as you can imagine. I asked Maria to take the child away. She did so as a favour. She knew I had suffered, and she sent the child out to a family who lived reclusively far away. My husband gave them money, and we both hoped the child would die. My spouse's temper grew worse with time, and one night when he was groping me as I was preparing his supper, I hit him on the head with a pan. Then I hit him again and he fell onto the stone hearth of our fine house. Oh, but it was a fine house in the city. A house that was no longer mine. You see, I needed a son for his estate to pass on to if I were to continue living there.

"If I'd understood better the laws of property, I might have waited for another birth before killing him. When he stopped moving, I went to fetch Maria, who had been a good friend to me. Pity." I looked across at Maria and continued, "She could tell what happened from the wounds to his head. But she knew the abuse I had suffered and did not report me. She gave me a character reference as maidservant for Reverend Stern. It was only recently when she turned on me. The creature I had spewed from my loins had been handed back to her secretly. She called me out late one night. I opened the door and set eyes on that thing born from hatred, now walking and uttering words.

"'Say hello to your mama,' said Maria, and the child, who had obviously been coddled, rushed at me and put his arms around my legs. I could not return the affection and stood there in horror.

"'The couple cannot afford food for themselves let alone for the child in these times,' she continued. 'They have brought him back. You must take care of him now, Katarin. He is your flesh and blood. You must love him and not be ashamed. You must teach him not to be ashamed.'

"I objected. Stern would have not accepted such a child in the house."

"You don't know that for certain," Margaretha said, as if she knew him better than I did.

Her face began to change, scrunched, no longer beautiful as she rubbed the back of her neck in irritation.

I ignored her and continued.

"Maria encouraged me to hold him, though I'd had no desire to do so. The boy regarded me with curiosity and reached out to touch my face. I felt nothing. I took him straight to the forest and killed him. Unfortunately, I was not strong enough to bury him deep enough in the snow." I laughed a little at that point. "Weeks turned into months. I thought I had gotten away with it, but then it was God's wrath that a beast did not find his shallow grave before a hunter."

"It is what Maria was trying to tell me," Margaretha said, and I read fear in the girl's eyes then. She stood up and stepped back and held on to the table to steady herself. She glanced down at the cup on the table, then met my gaze. She could see her death coming.

"The worst killing and the most regrettable was Cilla," I said. "All the children loved me, thought I was pretty. I would bring them food. But she had caught me with Sigi in the church. It was not the first time we'd been together. It was Sigi's idea to take her for a walk in the woods

297

behind the church and lose her and hope she froze, but it was me who convinced her to come. Her mother had told her to never veer from the track, and at first, she did not trust me. She was one of the few who was wary, who had a good instinct for someone so young. I told her that behind the church there was a magic horse in the forest with wings, and I saw wonder in her expression. I had her. I held her hand and she smiled and skipped in anticipation. I had no plans for what we would do when we got there. I didn't like the idea of releasing her. There was a risk she would still find her way back."

Margaretha clutched at her stomach with those same small hands that had cradled my master's face.

"Cilla started crying when she realised there was no horse to see. We didn't get far, and it was getting late. I knew her mother would be worried and come looking for her. We had to act swiftly. She cried louder. I was worried someone would hear. I put my hand around her mouth and covered her nose, and she continued to cry and scream, and she kicked and bit, so I held tighter. Eventually she stopped screaming and fell limp onto the ground. We laid her in a shallow grave. I finished her by using Sigi's knife to slice across her neck to make it look the same as Lottie's murder, should the animals not find her first. Sigi held that over me, but I had that over him as well. We would both be hanged, I told him . . . A dead child anyway would not weigh upon his conscience, and such an act of mine made no difference to his continued pursuit of me. I had certain ambitions to be the wife of a blacksmith, I thought back then, not a servant for Stern. That changed when the Reverend Engel arrived."

I pulled the doll from my pocket and set it on the table between us.

"I assume there is a reason that Zacharias put this on my bed," I said.

"I suspected it was you," she whispered, slurring her words. "You tried to incriminate me with it. You placed it under my mattress when you broke in, except I found it first before the search and gave it to

Zacharias. He suspected it was a ruse to condemn me. You wanted them to think I used sorcery, that I was somehow responsible for the deaths."

She closed her eyes and gently shook her head in disbelief. "And the other children, are any of those kills yours?"

"I can't be blamed for the deaths of the others. Those murderers are still free. I'd had no part in Lottie Pappenheimer's murder, but it was the doll—evidence I had spied with Stern—that gave me the idea to divert people from my doorstep. Kleist was as good as dead anyway. When his guilt and the murders were whispered in the marketplace, I visited Inge to comfort her and planted a copy of the doll to ensure a conviction; and later, one with Cilla.

"It was news to me about the contaminated wheat. I had destroyed Maria's notes and correspondence should there be something in them that implicated me. Unknowingly, I had burned a letter that suggested Kleist was innocent. It seems luck had favoured me.

"But a new problem arose after Cilla. Stern had been walking in the forest behind the church. He had seen me slice the girl's throat. I had to do something about that. I ran through the forest to get home first. I crushed some mandragora and henbane and placed it in the ale in his room. The same poison I had originally harvested one summer when I thought to kill my husband that way. It should have been enough to kill the fattest pig. The same poison I used on Maria, the same I am using on you now."

Margaretha was fading, as I knew she would, swaying and struggling to stay upright, and blinking often to remain focused.

"Did all this give you satisfaction?" she said with a tinge of venom.

She made me think, assess my feelings.

"Yes, it did in a way. I discovered I had power with it. I could alter outcomes. I regret Maria," I said, looking at her. "She had kept a secret and been like a mother to me. For weeks Maria had been asking what I'd done with the boy until one day she could not take my silence anymore. She knew of course that the creature was dead. I told her that I needed time to make amends by doing God's work, that I would eventually hand myself over to officials to determine a punishment. But when she grew impatient, there was no other course to take. Poor Maria. It did not give me joy, but neither was I happy when I learned she was found alive, and then surprised to learn of you."

"And Ursula? Did you have a hand in that, too?"

"We both did. You provided the remedy. I merely told her to take the whole contents, not a few drops. It sent her madder than she was. She did not deserve another child. I did her a favour."

"What dark affliction must you carry in your heart," Margaretha said.

"The same that all of us carry and act on at some point."

"You are wrong!" she said with a wheeze then in her chest. "I suspected it was you who killed Sigi and Herta. You made it look like she had murdered her brother, then took her own life."

"Sigi was a brute and deserved it. All the same we had fun for a while until Zacharias Engel arrived. Then I did not want a brute anymore. It would have been a miserable life in hindsight. He became bold and more aggressive. He would come and visit me in the night, and I would send him away. Then Herta, stupid girl, wanted us to marry. She was going to tell her father about our relationship, and he would undoubtedly have us married in the hope of settling down his son. I would have had no choice in it of course."

"Zacharias Engel would not have married you, if that is what you were thinking, that you were then to be with him!" she spat before losing her balance and tilting sideways, her hand out first to reach the floor to prevent a worse fall.

It cut me, what she said, but it didn't matter. I would win him in the end.

She began to make choking sounds, and I stood above her as she knelt on the ground. Her complete collapse would take mere minutes from the quantity of powder I had dropped in her milk while she had left the table to comfort Maria. This time there would be no mistakes.

An Age of Winters

"People leave me no choice when they take away mine," I said. "I could not let anyone tell me what to do."

She crawled along the floor. She was trying to reach Maria it seemed, only she didn't get far.

"I stole your bottle of poison to link to you and have you imprisoned, if not burned. When that didn't work . . . Well, I'm taking correct measures now. You have to understand that. You will be blamed for everything after your death. I will somehow connect it all, in time."

She coughed again. Red spittle came out of her mouth, and then she collapsed in the middle of the room. She was so small and pretty, her chest heaving from the poison that spiralled through her blood. I had a moment of reflection and regret, as had happened with Maria and Cilla.

"It will be over soon," I said, sounding kindly.

She muttered something, and I leaned down to listen.

When she was still, I threw the doll and Herta's ribbon on top of Margaretha's body. I hoped this would be my final crime. I emptied the jars of healing plant oils from the shelves and splashed them across the sedge-strewn floor. I then dipped a taper into the burning embers and once it sprouted to flame, I put it to the oil and rushes.

The fire took off in different directions. I saw Maria squirm, as thick black smoke stung my eyes. I coughed several times, then rushed to open the door to breathe. Air burst in to fan the flames, and I stood a moment to watch smoke fill the room. Then I ran.

Once home I could see the smoke from Maria's house rise to meet the sunrise that was golden for the first time, in what seemed an age, and released a sigh of relief.

The city was doomed, I knew. The deaths unsolved, suspicion would continue. I would convince Zacharias to leave the village. I could explain Cilla's doll that Margaretha had found in her house, the one I'd hoped would seal her guilt. I would say that she had stolen it from my room when we were out. I would suggest she is a witch. In time he would forget her.

301

I shuddered again, bringing to mind the picture of hellfire in the church, of pitchforks, of copulation with the Devil, and remembered Margaretha's words in those moment before she closed her eyes. *"You took many innocent lives, and your punishment will be hell for eternity."*

I had to assure myself that the Devil looked after his own.

CHAPTER
TWENTY-FOUR

Two days had passed since the fire. I had walked past the house and seen the remains of ash and objects twisted and blackened out of recognition. Zacharias had been solemn since he learned the news, and he had said very little. I imagined that Margaretha had been a passing fancy. In any case His Reverence was not so holy, and I knew his secret.

He held a special mass for Marla and Margaretha. Zacharias had concluded that the fire was likely an accident from a candle, that the two women had been sleeping. Such fires were not uncommon. He spoke about them, about their work, about the village's loss. I examined the faces of the congregation. The women were crying, and it annoyed me that these two could be loved so much. But I did not remain annoyed for long. I stared at the painting of hell that no longer filled me with terror.

Outside the sun was shining, and though sadness hung over the village, people in the market were filled with new hope. The ice was glistening with thaw, the brook and river shades of blue, and men were meeting on the shores to discuss the day like they did in years gone by. Of course, the sun and the warmth didn't mean that the witch hunting was over. There was more to come, which I would learn later, worse than ever, and greater in number. I contributed to the mayhem, to the velocity of the arrests initially, but I just gave the people what they wanted. Justification for their suffering, to punish someone, anyone, for their own miserable lives.

On the night of the service, I cooked a feast that would rival those in the castle, and Master smiled at me when I laid it before him on the supper table. I had done him a favour. He didn't mention the doll. I wondered if he had simply left it there for me to burn, whether Margaretha had actually passed on her suspicions about me, and if she'd been as jealous of me as I was of her. In time I would tell him stories that she had lain with many in the village.

I had always believed that I was an illegitimate daughter of someone eminent, someone highborn. I had always felt superior in intellect to many of my peers and that by some cruel trick I'd been denied my birthright. Maria had told me otherwise, words that stung.

"You were abandoned as a child by your parents to starve," she told me. "It was I who found you wandering, your parents long gone. I couldn't look after you with what I had, so I took you to the kitchens at the castle and they put you to work. You had straw on the floor, food in your belly, and a roof above you. Which was more than many orphans."

I was treated like a slave, then given to Herr Jaspers as part of his absolution by the papacy, I reminded her. His cruelty and deviancy with women were then contained to me. Such activities were no longer sins under an oath of marriage.

Maria Unger's face dropped. I could tell she was regretful about the course my life had taken till then, but it didn't matter. The damage had been done. I told her what had happened to the boy, what I had done to him. I saw the pain of that news in her face.

"Life has not always been kind; even so, that doesn't mean you curse others, that you take away something from them," Maria said.

I sobbed, but it was more from what might happen to me.

I mentioned earlier about loss and grief. I have grieved since for the loss of my babies, but only because I lost the opportunity to control my husband's fortune.

"Child," she said, how she often referred to me. "I kept your secret, but this is too much. I will have to tell officials about this boy of yours. You must tell me what you have done with him, where he is lying. He must be buried properly. He deserves it."

I sobbed harder.

"Wait," I said. "Before you do, give me days, even weeks, and I will turn myself in. I just want time to do good by you, by the village, to somehow make up for my sins. I will then tell you where he is buried."

"How do I know you will not run away?"

"I promise. I will always be loyal to you."

She nodded, then asked me to leave. She didn't want to look at me. The words meant nothing. When I strangled my son, I did not wish to look into his eyes either. Was it because I was worried about what I was going to do? No. I could not look at him because I did not want to be reminded that I could birth something so abhorrent.

⟡

"What will happen to Walter?" I asked Master the morning after the service, when he appeared in lighter spirits.

"Unfortunately, he will have to answer for his sins. He has confessed to the killings of Herta and Sigi. He will likely be executed shortly. The prince-bishop has given the order. It is out of my hands."

I did not feel any joy knowing Walter would have been tortured. Even then he'd not divulged my crime. If only he hadn't told me he knew about the poisoned apples. If only he had kept it to himself. I loved Walter. I still do. He was the only one who never expected anything from me. Who loved me unconditionally. I would go to the execution not to gloat but to pay my respects.

I was glad that it was just us now in the house. I did not mind mucking out the stalls. It was easier with a sun on the horizon.

⟡

That night, when the larks sang to one another and the moonlight shone through the kitchen window, I heard creaks from the staircase. I took the candle to investigate and found Master near the front door. He carried his large bag, stuffed full of items that he'd arrived with, and wore his cloak and hat as if he was going on a long journey, his hair tied back, his holy robe gone.

"You did not tell me you were leaving."

"It will be all right," he said. "I will be back."

He was lying.

"Take me with you!" I said.

He laughed and put down his bag. "I can't. You will be safe here until I return."

"Except you don't plan on returning, do you."

He still thought he carried an advantage.

"Zacharias," I said, "I know your secret."

He leaned against the wall at the base of the stairs. The smile was replaced with a frown.

"And what would that be?" he said in a condescending tone.

"That you can't read or write."

He raised his eyebrows and seemed amused that I knew the truth. "Is that all?"

"That I possess those skills. That I read the letters you received, all the correspondence, that it was I who sent the letter to the castle about Walter."

He tilted his head and narrowed his eyes.

"I know even more about you," I said.

He picked up the bag. "I don't have time for this."

"You aren't Zacharias Engel. Who are you?"

He could not hide his surprise this time.

"Did you think I didn't know you were an imposter?" I said.

The bag went down again.

"The papacy did not send you here. I admit, you fooled me for some time. You seemed to be versed in theology and law. The way you beguiled the parishioners who thought you were holy, as did I. But little things I pieced together. I found no writing in your diary. You sent no correspondence. Your mail would sit unopened, messages unread. But probably the biggest hint was a pair of engraved royal crested goblets I found stuffed beneath your mattress."

"Very well," he said, clapping his hands. "You figured it out."

"How did you get away with it? Did you get help from Margaretha with reading and writing?"

"Yes. From the beginning."

He was very forthright. I was not expecting him to confess to it so readily. I was happy to live with him as Zacharias Engel and forget what came before. And I had been prepared to lower my mask if necessary. That time had come.

"Take me with you, wherever you are going."

"Why?"

"Because I love you."

He blinked a few times.

"Will you say yes?"

He didn't say anything.

"We belong together," I said.

He laughed a little. "You know so little about me, Katarin."

Stepping forward, I reached for his hand to place against my heart.

"We are both pretenders. I believe we are the same."

He pondered things. I could see him thinking of a future.

"And what if I don't agree?"

"Then I will report to the commissioner that you are an imposter."

"And?"

"They will hunt you down."

He lifted one side of his mouth, which made him look cruel, and I admit I was afraid that he was capable of harming me.

"Very well. But hurry, fetch only what you can carry. We must travel far tonight. There will be no rest."

I returned to my room and collected the coins I had hidden. There were few possessions to my name so that they fit in a small cloth sack, and I took Stern's coat near the entrance. After Zacharias had saddled the horse, he threw his bag on top, mounted the horse, then held out his hand and helped me up behind him. I put my arms around his middle as we left, travelling through the forests towards the east until daylight, when we stopped at a village.

He bought me warm mead and a meal.

"What is your real name?" I asked.

"What does it matter?"

"You will always be Zacharias to me."

He seemed distracted yet courteous, and was gentle when he once more lifted me up onto the mare to continue the journey. At one point he placed his hand over mine. I felt myself relax when he touched me, as if all my worries would disappear. We set out again, and I wondered if and when we would be missed. Who would knock at the door of our house? I was pleased to be gone, to leave my misdeeds behind me, to start a new life with the only man I would ever love. I rested my head against his back, and he tied a rope around the both of us so that I would not fall should I become drowsy. We mostly travelled much through forests. He knew the area well. The swaying of the horse put me to sleep for the remainder of the night, until we stopped in front of a small, thatched dwelling.

"Is this your house?" I asked as night was falling.

"No. I found it on the way here. It is where I hoard the items stolen from the castle and from those in the city with too many riches to notice them gone."

Inside, something scurried away to the corners. It was sparsely furnished, with one chair and a table and some straw bedding near the hearth. There were signs he'd spent some time here. On the table were a jug of ale and a loaf of bread.

He put some wood in the hearth. I was exhausted and lay down on the straw. He lay down next to me. His manner was cool, but I believed I could make him love me in time. He had once told me of a place where the sun rests on the water at the end of the day. I'd only ever heard about the deep-blue sea, that rose to great heights in a wind, where large fish leaped into the arms of fishermen.

The following morning, we ate the bread and drank the ale, and he left to find some more for the journey. I saw there were sacks in the corner of the room and investigated. Inside were silver candleholders, gilded plates, gems, and pearls. There was so much wealth he might build his own house and farm, someplace free, where we would live well for the rest of our lives.

I waited several hours for him but did not fret that he wouldn't return. The bags full of riches told me that he would.

He brought us bread and nuts.

"You look tired," he said in the early morning. "You must sleep more. I'll keep watch that you come to no harm."

I fell back asleep, smiling from the comfort he gave me. My dreams were vivid, warm, and colourful, but I woke up suddenly, cold and alone.

The clouds were back, and there was a light fall of snow. Winter was returning, and I would learn that it would once again be fierce. I ached to leave the territories and go to places that did not experience such cold.

I closed my eyes a moment, forgetting where I was and imagining Zacharias's hand over mine, my cheek against his warm chest. But that day I faced a different reality. Zacharias was nowhere to be seen. I stepped outside. There were trees in the distance and snow-covered peaks. We were miles from any town, yet I heard voices coming from behind the house. I walked to investigate, and my dreams fell away.

Margaretha and Walter stood beside Zacharias. My first thought was that Margaretha had come back from the dead. Zacharias did not look like the man in the robe anymore. There was something mischievous about him. His hair was swept back high and he wore a smile that creased his cheeks, which I had never seen him wear. One that said, *Life is good.* I looked about me. I felt exposed, humiliated. I shuddered at their deceit, realising I was outsmarted after all.

"How, you ask?" said Zacharias, grinning cruelly. He walked over, kissed Margaretha for several seconds, then lifted her up and swung her around with one arm around her waist. "Let me introduce my wife, an artist, an actress, a raconteur, a charlatan like me."

Margaretha appeared far from coy.

"I can assume you are neither healer nor midwife."

"On the contrary," she said. "I know much about both, but it is you who are the greater imposter."

Zacharias did not leave me to wonder how long he'd known, how long I'd been the fool.

"I had my suspicions about you after Herta's death, and I began to wonder. Then the doll, Cilla's doll, that I asked you to burn, that you planted under Margaretha's mattress. I knew for certain. Then everything has since been confirmed by Margaretha, after her death."

He winked as he said this, and the pair shared a smile. I felt ill. I didn't want to ask how they got away with everything they did, but they told me anyway.

"Days before he was taken to prison," said Zacharias, "Walter found a bottle of poison in your room and swapped it with crushed grain to make the powder look the same. He knew what you did to Herta and Sigi and what you might do again."

"In a small skin bladder, I had animal blood which I bit down on," said Margaretha. "We use such methods to entertain people in plays."

I remembered Margaretha falling to the floor. I remembered the blood from her mouth.

"You took a risk by having Walter imprisoned," said Zacharias.

It was calculated. He would have sounded even guiltier trying to incriminate me. Everyone knew I was good. Everyone knew he was strange, and I did not believe he would say anything.

"He loved me too much to betray me," I said. "I know him well."

Zacharias laughed.

"Not well enough, it seems."

"Walter . . . I'm sorry."

Walter remained unmoved and clenched his jaw.

"It must be hard for you to see all your work come undone," said the girl who called herself Margaretha. "When you set the place on fire, something I did not foresee, I climbed out through the window with the help of my husband, waiting nearby, though I still bear some scars." She lifted her skirt so I could see the skin inflamed on her thigh where she had been burned. "We tried to save Maria, of course, but could not. The bones that were left, *the reverend*"—she said mockingly with emphasis—"buried as us both. Meanwhile, under interrogation, Walter revealed some truths of his own. Like the fact that you hated me, that you were jealous, and you had planned to be rid of me somehow. That you sacrificed children to the Devil. That you gave a love potion to Walter so he would be loyal to you—"

"I never did that."

They were beating me at my own game.

"Lies have not bothered you before . . . Besides, there is more. We instructed Walter to reveal how you boasted about the killing of Herta and Sigi, and your husband. That you threatened him if he told anyone. Then some truth . . . That the marked child in the forest was yours, and you killed him also. But the final evidence was the best and needed no embellishment. You see, Stern still babbled and did not make much sense; however, my husband understood fully what he was trying to say when he visited him only recently, what haunted the old man at night. The good Reverend Engel had found him being cared for in a monastery. The sisters handed him a drawing Stern had been working on. The likeness to you, of course, was uncanny."

I had found my name scrawled on paper in Stern's coat pocket, probably the last thing he had written—evidence that I destroyed in the hearth.

Zacharias finished the account.

"The image signed by the shaking hand of Stern, with the words 'the Devil,' was submitted to the prince-bishop as further proof just prior to the good Reverend Engel's departure.

"And for a minute, I did think our luck had run its course when you raised suspicions about Margaretha. We decided it would look better to speak up first. An odd-shaped mole on her side may have been her undoing, but she bravely scratched it out with a knife beforehand.

"It is over for you, Katarin. The prince-bishop's men are doubtlessly looking for you now."

"I will return," I said. "I will tell them about you, Zacharias Engel, the charlatan. I will tell them the truth."

"I'm afraid I have some sad news about the Reverend Zacharias Engel. He is dead, and letters have been sent to Rome, his body being transported back there now. You see, the true Engel, a decade older than me, was on the way back to Rome when he fell sick and died. He had sent a letter to the prince-bishop prior, or rather I had through Margaretha, advising that he would be going home to give his report in person to the pope. He wrote that he felt poorly and was disappointed that such an evil had taken control of the village, and that he looked forward to more guidance about the matter once in Rome."

I was confused. I did not yet understand at that point just how cunning Zacharias was.

"On our travels, months earlier, my wife and I encountered the good reverend, alone and travelling in a heavy fall of snow. We only meant to rob him, but he flew at me from his horse and cut me with a knife."

Zacharias, for I know not what else to call him now, pulled open his shirt near the collar, and I saw the small scar. I remembered the blood marks on one of his shirts that I had scrubbed away.

"I pushed the true Zacharias Engel hard, and he fell backward to the ground, then clutched at his heart," the charlatan said. "Regrettably, he died moments later, and we buried his body not far from here. Margaretha, unlike myself, can read, and so we learned about him from his diary, and the letters he carried, and the notes he made inside his books. We opened the letter he was meaning to post to Rome about his journey. I put on his cloak and carried his bag. But my wound turned bad, bringing with it a slight fever. We sought the midwife at night who Margaretha had learned of along the way. When Maria Unger didn't answer the door, we let ourselves in and found her collapsed on the floor. Her name was confirmed in her book of herbs and healing. We tried to help her, but she grew more ill overnight. Margaretha applied ointment and medicines to treat me also, and my fever. While we filled our bellies on Maria's food, we decided on a plan to send the letter back to Rome, delayed of course because of weather, just as Reverend Engel had intended, which would show that he was alive and well." Zacharias reached out to hold Margaretha's hand. "Then my beautiful wife and I parted ways. She to remain in Maria's house and me to ride into the village as Zacharias Engel."

I did not need to ask their reasons. The sacks of spoils revealed as such.

"How else were we to survive the winter?" said Zacharias. "Here was a man of wealth, and even dead he would give me warmth and access to riches that I hoarded like a bear. So I assumed his identity and then in recent days found his body still preserved in the snow. I took it to another village and organised transport back to Rome with his belongings"—he shrugged—"and, well, a little less coin he originally brought with him."

"You are no better than me," I said numbly, my destiny in their hands. "You killed a clergyman then burned Kleist and Zilla!"

"On the contrary, we are nothing alike. I admit I have been in many fights, and I bear scars to show for that, but I only ever killed a man in self-defence," said Zacharias. "You cannot say the same, Katarin. You are a cold-blooded killer. You have stolen the lives of innocent children, of Maria's, whose calling was to help others, who worked for next to nothing but gratitude and donations.

"You fooled many," he continued. "You rescued the boy in the forest, but it was because you wanted to impress me, not out of any goodness."

"You are a woman just as I am," I said, appealing to Margaretha. "You would know that we have to fight for everything. That if we don't, we are nothing, we are used. You would have done the same as me to survive."

"No, I would not," she said coolly. "I am not a perfect person, and yes, I have had to survive, but you . . . You are something different, something dragged from hell."

I started to cry and felt very alone, these strangers around me. In frustration, I rushed at Zacharias with my fists raised, but before I could pound his chest, he grabbed my wrists so tightly the pain brought me to my knees.

He released me roughly and I fell hard to the ground.

"What are you going to do with me?"

"You won't be coming with us," said Zacharias, "if that is what is in your thoughts. We are going where it is warm, where there is beauty and life, and fruit trees that grow on the cliffs overlooking the sea. Back to where I spent my early childhood. And I now have money to buy a house. Something I have wanted my whole life. I was an orphan, too, on the streets, learning the tricks to survive. Begging for food, I travelled north and discovered street artistry, then met Margaretha. That is when my luck changed. I'm returning to where I can use my real name and give my wife everything she has ever wanted, and Walter the freedom to choose his future. With his voice, he could entertain. He should make a great addition to the theatre I plan to open one day."

"Walter," I said, "part of the reason I tried to kill Stern was for you, for how he treated you."

He shook his head. He could see the lie.

"I loved you," I told him. "You have to understand how hard it was for me."

"I saved you from death once," Walter said grimly. "I won't do it again."

The snow on our shoulders grew thicker. There was no point in running. I would die here in the wilderness with nothing.

I leaned over then and retched into the snow.

"I will kill you mercifully, Katarin. Otherwise, they will hunt you down, and if they catch you, they will torture you."

I knelt in the snow, begging Walter to stop them. But he did not speak, and turned his back.

"I will make it quick," said Zacharias. "A knife to the heart."

"You will have to live with this," I said, sobbing. "It is murder."

"It is justice. There will not be a moment of regret, I can assure you."

"Let me into the wilderness, where I might die anyway of cold and hunger."

He stepped forward and drew his dagger. Walter walked away.

I stood up suddenly. I undid the ties of my kirtle and pulled it over my head. Then I tore apart my shift to show my breasts and rounded belly.

Walter turned when he heard Margaretha curse. He stared in disbelief, as did she, while Zacharias's gaze was fixed coldly on my naked body.

"If you kill me, you kill an innocent also."

Zacharias cursed, put his hands atop his head, and walked a few paces away.

"It is Sigi's child."

I had done everything I could to be rid of it. Every herb, every medicine, and the same as Ursula took. But nothing would take this wretched bastard from my body.

Zacharias moved towards me with his dagger, hands clenched, and teeth clamped.

"No," said Margaretha and touched his arm. He looked down at her briefly and stepped back.

"You will give this child no life," said Zacharias. "You will be living day to day, begging on the side of roads—that is, if the lawmen don't find you first. You will be on the run for the rest of your days. You will live like a pauper in permanent exile."

"I will take my chances."

"You will murder again."

I said nothing, for I could not promise otherwise.

Margaretha closed her eyes in dismay, and Walter grimaced with disgust.

"Get out of my sight," said the man I knew as Zacharias Engel, who could no longer bear to look at me.

I dressed as I ran through the snow, tripping on my clothes, and then kept running, afraid they would change their minds, until we were separated by a savage storm. The sun, I was sure, had moved to meet them at the end of their journey. I headed south to avoid an encounter with anyone from the bishopric of Würzburg. Winter had returned, angrier and more menacing than before. The sun had been shining for them, not me.

I never saw them again, but sometimes I picture them together in an image I have created of my own. I see a giant sun glistening on the water, trees with deep-green leaves and plump bright-coloured fruit. I imagine Margaretha in a tunic, her long, thin arms and feet bare, her hair tied back from her long neck, and Walter, sitting on the side of a low wall of rock, sun-kissed face, feet dangling in the water that I'd once heard described. It is not a pleasant image. It is one that follows me everywhere: they are to me ghosts that will haunt me into death.

I saved you once, Walter had said, and I wondered what he'd meant. Then I remembered the deer in the forest when I nearly died. I remember the voice I thought I heard as I lay there preparing to die. It wasn't Margaretha's; it was Walter's. But how? It was magic. I was certain of it. I laughed loudly, the sound bouncing all around me like a coven of cackling witches. Could there have been a witch in our village after all? Could it have been Walter? It is a thought that has stayed with me since and has made me laugh at times, too. My Walter. My sweet Walter. I felt a hole, though fleeting, for the special friend I had lost.

After our parting, I begged along the tracks from people that I passed until I reached the southern territories. One night, when I felt the child coming, I knocked on the door of an elderly couple. I told them my husband had left me and I had nothing. By the fire on a thick rug, I birthed a healthy baby girl. She was swaddled in a grubby blanket. I felt nothing for the child, and I was sick for several days afterwards. The woman treated me until I was well again. The couple had meagre food and means and eventually were compelled to send me away. I carried the baby with me for a time; then, as I neared a village, I left her by the side of a tree.

I stole some clothes and washed in a stream, then pondered my future further south.

I would survive.

EPILOGUE

Doctor Sebastian Spengler, a nobleman, with much wealth and a newly built house nestled in trees on the edge of a river facing west to the sun-filled sky, sat across from his wife of four years, Katarin, and their healthy baby boy, who rested in her lap. She had convinced him to move to Alsace, where she told him she was born. And even though he lost some business, pleasing his wife had been the right decision.

She had turned up on his doorstep seeking employment, as he had earlier suggested. God, he thought, had sent him an angel.

Sebastian was aging, but he was the happiest he had ever been. He had lost his first wife and children to the plague.

Despite the luck of finding a good wife, he had been feeling poorly of late, pains in the stomach, and had decided that he must put in place a bequest that would ensure his wife and son never wanted for anything. He would ensure also that his cousin would not claim his property, and neither would the Church.

"I am seeing the lawyer tomorrow, my dear."

"You shouldn't talk like you are going somewhere," said Katarin. "I'm worried about your health."

He looked sallow and thinner than when she first arrived.

"I will live a time yet, but I have to take care of you both," he said adoringly, tickling the chin of the baby with his short, thick fingers.

Each day when he rolled over to face his pretty wife on the bed beside him, his eyes lit up. He was a lucky man, he thought, to have a comely wife so young, less than half his age, and a healthy baby boy.

"Let me hold our son," he said gently and kissed his wife on the crown of her head.

She passed the child tenderly to her husband, then made to leave to supervise the cook. She wore a dress of yellow Asian silk and a short white ermine cape.

"My love," said Sebastian, "before you go, I must mention that I heard from an acquaintance who has a brother in Würzburg. He learned that the prince-bishop had razed the village of Eisbach to the ground and destroyed the bridge that crossed to it. He wanted to 'scourge the earth of its poison' since over half the villagers had been accused and burned for the crime of witchcraft. It is a terrible situation. I am certain that the executions are unlawful." He tutted. "I do not believe that the alleged demonic possessions applied to those poor women, men, and children burned, but rather to Ehrenberg himself."

"What terrible news!" said Katarin, covering her mouth in a show of horror. "Those poor people!"

"Thank goodness you left that village, else who knows what would have happened to you."

She hung her head, appearing melancholy.

"Don't think too hard about it," he comforted. "Don't take it to heart."

Katarin left the room and stared at the ground a moment. Her lips quivered with the commencement of a smile that was gone before she entered the kitchen to give her orders for the evening meal.

AUTHOR'S NOTE AND ACKNOWLEDGMENTS

Europe's witch trials occurred between 1300 and 1850. From those events recorded, roughly 43,240 women, men, and children from all walks of life were placed on trial and prosecuted, resulting in an approximate 16,333 executions. Germany recorded the highest number with 16,474 tried and 6,887 executed.[1] Outbreaks of disease and changing weather patterns that affected trades and farming led to famines and community unrest as rulers and residents sought to find justification for their dire circumstances. Philipp Adolf von Ehrenberg, an actual figure in history, commenced an intense period of witch hunting in his bishopric of Würzburg that continued after his death.

The Little Ice Age followed a warming period in medieval times, two phases of which extended into the nineteenth century. Climate extremes occurred with colder and longer winters, storms, and short, wet summers, wreaking havoc on farms across northern and central Europe, while similar events happened in other parts of the world. Polar ice caps and glaciers expanded, resulting in the destruction of Alpine villages in France, Switzerland, and elsewhere. Agrarian

---

1   Peter T. Leeson and Jacob W. Russ, "Witch Trials," *Economic Journal* 128, no. 613 (August 2018): 2,078.

practices adapted to these climate changes, such as the Flemish and Dutch cultivation of more crops for human consumption and an increase in the number of livestock that would prevent a famine in harsher times. These particular practices would ultimately be adopted across Europe. The climate extremes were blamed on divine intervention by some in this period of fear and superstition, although studies have concluded that such events relate to volcanism, solar output, and changes in the atmosphere.[2]

In a publication in 1595, Daniel Schaller, pastor of Stendhal in the Prussian Alps, wrote:

> There is no real constant sunshine, neither a steady winter nor summer; the earth's crops and produce do not ripen, are no longer as healthy as they were in bygone years. The fruitfulness of all creatures and of the world as a whole is receding; fields and grounds have tired from bearing fruits and even become impoverished, thereby giving rise to the increase of prices and famine, as is heard in towns and villages from the whining and lamenting among the farmers.[3]

For the story I have used a dash of artistic licence for the length and location of the climate anomaly in the region the book is set; nevertheless, Ehrenberg and the witch hunts are of historical relevance in Germany's history. The character of Frederik Förner is very loosely drawn from ecclesiastic historian Bishop Friedrich Förner, who was

---

2   "Little Ice Age," Britannica. https://www.britannica.com/science/Little-Ice-Age.
3   Rudolf Brázdil, Rüdiger Glaser, and Christian Pfister, "Climatic Variability in Sixteenth-Century Europe and Its Social Dimension," *Climatic Change* 43, no. 1 (1999): 44.

a proponent of witch-hunting in Bamberg and a fierce opponent of Protestantism.

My thanks to Lake Union Publishing; Brilliance Publishing; Danielle, Tegan, Carissa, Karah, and the rest of the editing, proofreading, and production team; and the art, design, and marketing staff; all who continue to exceed my expectations.

ABOUT THE AUTHOR

Photo © 2024 Oscar Liviero

Gemma Liviero is the bestselling author of the historical novels *Half in Shadow*, *In a Field of Blue*, *The Road Beyond Ruin*, *Broken Angels*, and *Pastel Orphans*, which was a finalist in the 2015 Next Generation Indie Book Awards. In addition to writing fiction, Gemma's career includes copywriting, corporate writing, feature articles, editorials, and editing. She holds an advanced diploma of arts (writing) and continues her studies in history and other humanities. Gemma is a wife and the mother of two grown children and lives on the outskirts of Brisbane, Australia. For more information, visit www.gemmaliviero.com.